False Witness

'**The courtroom**
gives Dias – a barrister himself – his best moments,
revelling in the slippery games that pass for British
justice.'
The Guardian

'**The writing**
has a disturbing edge that lifts it above the
conventional.'
The Bookseller

'**A fascinating**
look behind the scenes of a murder trial.'
Manchester Evening News

'**An excellent**
first novel, strong on black humour and courtroom
drama'
Daily Telegraph

'**A chilling**
courtroom drama'
Today

About the author

Before being called to the Bar, Dexter Dias was educated at Sevenoaks School and the University of Durham. He is now a barrister specialising in criminal defence. He practises from a set of chambers specifically created to represent people disadvantaged by poverty and discrimination. He has already written on a variety of legal and political issues, but the real stimulus for writing his first novel, *False Witness*, came when he met Ruth Rendell while he was defending a murder in 1993.

Hodder and Stoughton will publish Dexter Dias's second novel, *Abnormality of Mind*, in 1996.

FALSE WITNESS

Dexter Dias

CORONET BOOKS
Hodder and Stoughton

First published in Great Britain in 1995 by Hodder and
Stoughton
A division of Hodder Headline PLC
First published in paperback in 1995 by Hodder and Stoughton
A Coronet Paperback

ISBN 0 340 63973 3

Typeset by Phoenix Typesetting, Ilkley, West Yorkshire.
Printed and bound in Great Britain by
Cox & Wyman, Reading, Berks.

Hodder and Stoughton
A division of Hodder Headline PLC
338 Euston Road
London NW1 3BH

For my parents
And for Katie

ACKNOWLEDGMENTS

My thanks are due to many people. To Mike for opening my eyes to the possibility of writing fiction. To Teresa for spotting, supporting and advising me. To Carolyn and Kate at Hodders for their editorial and administrative input. And finally to Ruth Rendell, for taking the time to speak to a case-weary barrister and convince him that he *might* be able to do it.

The author also wishes to thank the following who have kindly given permission for the use of copyright materials:

Chatto & Windus for extracts from *The Panther* from *Selected Poems* by Rilke, translated by J B Leisham; Curtis Brown Ltd on behalf of Joanna Richardson for the translation of Baudelaire's poem *The Vampire*. © Joanna Richardson.

PART I

TRIAL

Then the young man asked Him, 'What good thing must I do, that I may have eternal life?'

To this He replied, 'Do not murder, do not commit adultery, do not steal, do not bear false witness.'

Matthew 19:16–18

Chapter 1

'And to the first count, how do you plead? Guilty or not guilty?'

There was silence.

Then again the question. 'On the first count, you are charged with outraging public decency. How do you plead?'

A breath. A pause. And then an answer. 'Guilty.'

I suddenly remembered why I was sitting in the front row of Court 8 at the Old Bailey. I adjusted my horsehair wig and told myself that I had to stop daydreaming while the court was in session.

But I was puzzled by the previous night's dream. For I had again dreamt of Stonebury, where the murder was committed. I had dreamt of the village and of the rain and of a young girl being led quietly to the circle of stones. And I was puzzled by a voice. For I had been asked a single question. It was this: Is a dream something you possess, or is it something that possesses you?

I didn't know the answer back then. If I did, perhaps I would not have sat and listened to the charges being read out, but would have taken off my wig, neatly folded my gown, and would have then disappeared from the court with the minimum of fuss.

The furore caused by the death of Molly Summers has died down. The case came to court over a year ago and I suspect that no one but me really thinks about that trial any more. Yet when I am alone, and especially when I am tired, the memories begin to well. Usually it is the scent of perfume or the texture of muslin that first comes to mind, and then, like an old movie with shadowy figures moving in silence, the story unfolds.

What I do find strange when I look back at it all, is that I could have become so involved. I still return to Stonebury every few months, which must be an admission of some kind. There are certain things that I cannot explain and other things I do not wish to. And when I return and walk around the ancient circle, the place where the broken body was found, I realise that I was partly to blame. I realise that I bore some of the guilt. But I was too weak and the desire was too strong and then, I suppose, there was Justine.

At one time a barrister's life had seemed so straightforward: you're born, you're called to the Bar, you take silk, you die. I imagined that nothing would interrupt my procession from Bar to oblivion except, perhaps, hair-loss, the odd affair, and a couple of hard-earned ulcers. It was safe, if predictable, progress. And then I started dreaming about the stones.

To the press, the case was a sensation. To the law, it was a scandal. But to me, it was simply a journey. It was a journey to the centre of the circle. But this was a circle of my own creation, a place from which even now I find it hard to escape. Even now.

'You plead guilty?' asked Leonard, clerk to Court 8.

He was in a bad mood. But then Leonard, the oldest of the Old Bailey clerks, had been in a bad mood since the 1960s when they abolished capital punishment. He missed the black caps, he once told me. Then there was the 'You will be hung by the neck until you are dead' line. Leonard never understood that, he said. After all, where else could they hang you from? When I once made a suggestion, Leonard didn't speak to me for a year.

The public gallery was full by the time that proceedings began at 10.30 a.m. There was even a long queue outside stretching a fair distance along Old Bailey towards St Paul's. Everybody wanted to see *him*.

And there he was: my client, Richard Kingsley, sitting quietly in the dock oblivious to everything. There was Richard Kingsley, pulp novelist, celebrity and guilty as any one of us can be. He sat hunched up in his wheelchair with a slightly shrivelled arm and waited to be punished.

At least they could not hang him.

'And on the first count,' repeated Leonard, more irritably, flaring his nostrils, 'you plead guilty?'

'Yes,' said Kingsley. 'Guilty.'

Leonard waited for the murmuring in the public gallery to die down. Then he said, 'And on the second count, Richard Kingsley, you are also charged with outraging public decency.'

My tatty wig pricked me when I heard that. My winged collar cut into my throat for I had always thought it a ludicrous charge. Didn't it assume that there was something called the public? And that it had a sense of decency? And that despite all the obscenities that had become part of our lives, it could still be outraged?

Leonard read on. 'And the particulars of the offence are that you committed acts of a lewd and disgusting nature, tending to corrupt the mind of a fourteen-year-old girl in Stonebury.' He clearly enjoyed reading that, and looked around the court at the open mouths in the galleries and the bored faces of the court staff. Then he asked the question. 'Are you guilty or not guilty?'

Kingsley looked at me with his unnaturally white face. I nodded.

'Guilty,' Kingsley said.

It was 10.41 a.m. I had already secured two guilty pleas. It was excellent progress. Because that was the deal. Plead guilty to some of this, not guilty to some of that, and it was all going to be over by lunchtime. The defendant would get a lighter sentence, the police could say they solved some crimes, the court could wheel in the next case and, of course, I would collect the money. Everybody would win.

That first day was, I recall, a bright Monday in December. First thing, at nine o'clock, I had seen Kingsley in the cells below the Old Bailey. He sat in the artificial light and talked about his crimes. He was a phenomenon. Richard Kingsley could discuss the corruption of the young and the abuse of the innocent as though it were a lesson in algebra with certain given axioms and inexorable conclusions.

'You have studied the brief, I suppose?' he said to me, stretching his tiny frame.

'Of course,' I replied.

'So you know what I did to those other girls?'

'What they *say* you did.'

'Ah, yes. I'm presumed innocent, aren't I? I keep forgetting that.' He moved his wheelchair a little closer to me so that he could whisper. 'But what if ... I was not quite innocent? What then? I just wondered, would *your* morals be outraged by my – little games?'

'Isn't that my business?'

'Surely I'm entitled to know the type of man who is defending me? You see, I suspect you aren't sure if I did it.'

'So?'

'So you wonder. Yes, you wonder, don't you, Mr Fawley?'

I considered very carefully how I should answer him and finally decided that I should begin as I intended to carry on. I lied.

'Let me tell you something, Mr Kingsley,' I said. 'I wonder about a great many things. I wonder about the size of my overdraft. I even wonder about the meaning of life. But I can sleep well enough at night without knowing the answer to either.'

It was all lies.

Even before I had been sent the case papers, the dreams had begun. At night, I could not sleep without dreaming about the stones. I used to dread sleeping by myself, because I feared there would be no one to wake me up and then the dream would go on and on.

At first there were just flashes, the hint of a colour, the ghost of a shape, which never lasted more than a few seconds. In fact, I only started to worry when the figures began to emerge. They were wild, truncated: the top of a slim leg, the back of a head, a hand clasping something. And through it all, I never saw a face. There were never any faces.

Initially, I tried to ignore the dreams. There is, after all, a lot of nonsense spoken about them. And then I read an article. I found it in a dog-eared colour supplement while I was waiting for my dentist to bore into my gums. I learnt that Aristotle classified dreams and that Alexander the Great never went into battle without his dream-interpreter. It said that the waking world does not own us completely, that we retreat from it for one-third of our lives, deliberately seeking a place that is quiet and still and dark, and that is the province of dreams.

The worst dream of all, the one I seemed to carry with me, had no images. There was just a dull greyness, like a television screen after the programmes have finished, and emerging from it, almost imperceptibly, was the weeping, a pitiful weeping. Who was it who was crying so inconsolably? Was it someone else? Or was it me?

At 9.32, Kingsley again wheeled himself close to me in the cells.

'Shall I tell you what I'm really guilty of?' he asked.

'Look,' I said, wincing at a loose filling. 'If you want to confess, get yourself a priest. Or do yourself a favour, and sell your story to the tabloids. At least make some money from it. But don't tell me.'

'But you're my lawyer. Don't you need to know the truth?'

'Save it for your memoirs. We're on a tight schedule. The curtain goes up at ten thirty.'

Kingsley became silent and neither of us spoke for a while.

I paced around the small room and Kingsley looked through my papers.

'Listen to me for a moment,' I finally said. 'You just don't understand, do you? We're playing a game and you don't know the rules. That's all it is. I know you haven't done anything like this before.'

'You mean, I haven't been caught before.'

'It's the same thing.'

'Is it?'

'Well, legally ... look, I'd better explain.' The light flickered slightly but did not go out. 'When you go through the doors of the court, you go through – well, you sort of go through the looking-glass. And the truth doesn't count. You see, us lawyers need the truth as much as doctors need vaccines. A little is fine. Too much and we go out of business.'

'So what *do* you want to know?' Kingsley asked.

'Nothing,' I said. 'Or as near to nothing as your conscience will allow.'

'Not a particularly moral stance, Mr—'

'You should read your Bible.'

'My what?'

'Your Bible, Mr Kingsley. You know, that all-time bestseller.'

'That nobody reads. Except, of course,' Kingsley said, somewhat enigmatically, 'in prison.'

'How do you mean?'

'Well, the Bible's the one thing more widely available in prison than drugs. Everyone's offered a free copy.'

'I didn't know the Gideons did prison visits,' I said.

'Not the Gideons, the government. A particularly cruel form of mental torture. No doubt devised by some junior minister whilst being whipped into a lather by his rent-boy.'

'No doubt,' I replied.

'The perks of high office, I suppose,' Kingsley said, sighing. 'Still, most people take up the offer.'

'Why?'

'Comes in handy when the loo-roll runs out.'

'Well, did you ever take a peek at the Book of Ecclesiastes?'
I asked. 'I mean, before you ran out of Andrex?'

'Ecclesiastes?'

'You know, "The more we know, the more we suffer," and
all that. You must be familiar with the quote. "The more we
know, the more—"'

'A cynics' charter?'

'In the finest traditions of the Bar. You see, the less you tell
me, Mr Kingsley, the better it gets.'

Richard Kingsley seemed delighted with my answer, but
I wasn't sure why. Did he think he had found a kindred
spirit? Or did he sense my apprehension? Did he smell it
and conclude instantly that I was weak and was someone to
be used?

'I'm very glad I instructed you, Mr Fawley,' he said.

'Why's that?'

'Because unlike those hypocrites who pretend to have
morals, you're proud to have none. Call me old-fashioned,
but I like that in a man.'

'Was that a compliment?' I asked.

'More of a diagnosis,' he said. 'Besides, there's something
else.'

'What?'

'I know you won't judge me.'

'And how do you know that?'

'Because you're too busy judging yourself,' Kingsley said.
'You know, I think we shall get along famously.'

And we did. By 10.03, the crumpled little man had decided
not to contest any of the sex offences. Guilt and innocence?
They simply did not come into it.

In those days, I think I could claim to be the most indifferent,
cynical and lazy excuse of a man who ever dared to toss on
a barrister's wig. I suppose I could spout all that *Rumpole of
the Bailey* stuff about how brilliant a barrister I was. But I
wasn't.

Tom Fawley got by. Just.

I could pretend that I never lost a case like those sharp lawyers in American films. But that wasn't true either. Like a pretty average gambler, I lost and won in about equal measure. The result of a case had little to do with me. It seemed to be more affected by the composition of the jury, the mood of the judge, and the defendant's horoscope. I always used to read those.

And another thing: I hated the Old Bailey. For most criminal lawyers, a trial at the Bailey was the pinnacle of their profession, the height of their ambitions. I detested the place. To me, the building always seemed full of headless corpses, severed limbs and bloodstains. It was the closest thing in the law to an abattoir. If ghosts existed, they would make a point of haunting such a place.

As the morning wore on, Leonard read out yet another charge in Court 8. There was uproar when he mentioned that the corrupted girl was eleven years old.

'You're evil,' shouted one woman.

'Animal,' shouted another.

Kingsley was also called a piece of scum which he ostensibly was not, and a monster which he possibly was. In fact, we were treated to all the usual platitudes as the public pretended to be outraged. But I suspected that they enjoyed the spectacle. After all, it was free.

Through the turmoil, Kingsley sat impassively, as if the abuse was aimed at someone else. When I looked at him, he even tried to smile, but his eyes were as dead as ever. I glanced at the jury box and was relieved that it was empty, that I'd got a deal, that there was to be no trial, that I wouldn't have to pretend Kingsley was innocent. I was relieved that I wouldn't have to live the lie.

And that, I suppose, was my trade. I had spent my fifteen years at the Bar living out other people's lies and I was tired. So by the age of thirty-nine, my eyesight was failing, my waistline was expanding and strange things had begun to sprout from my nostrils. There I was on the apprehensive side of forty, waiting for my libido to abscond and my hair to fall out.

When Kingsley finally pleaded guilty to all the sexual offences, Leonard sat down and shuffled his papers frantically. I knew what he was looking for. It was the Bill of Murder. And I thought, even if Kingsley was convicted, what difference would it make? For in my experience, the criminal law was the art of trying to prevent crime, while finding it everywhere, judging it incorrectly, and punishing the wrong people in the most inappropriate ways.

But it was a living. All those fancy words, the ones with the capital letters, like Justice and Mercy, just made me feel like vomiting into my wig box. Lawyers saw the other side. We did society's dirty work. The criminal courts were its moral dustbins. We cleaned up the mess and they didn't even give us gloves.

Silence had again settled over Court 8 at the Old Bailey. As Leonard stood up holding the murder indictment, I could see the liver-spots on the back of his hands. His age was really beginning to show, and I wondered how many more murders he would see, and whether any of them would be as appalling as this one. The document shook between his fingers as he began to read aloud.

It was then that Richard Kingsley was accused of murdering Mary – also known as Molly – Summers.

Chapter 2

Everyone was on edge. How would he plead?

However, I did not so much as blink twice when Kingsley entered a plea of not guilty to murder. That was the plan. As I surveyed the astonished faces in court, with their mouths opening and shutting, I hoped that Kingsley would remember the second part of the plea, the difficult part, the part without which there would have been no deal.

Just before I left the cells at 10.17, Kingsley had almost seemed relieved that there was to be no trial. He sat in his wheelchair and talked it through.

'So what *do* you want me to say when we go up to court?' he asked.

'Look,' I told him, 'all you have to remember is to add, *But guilty of manslaughter*. That's all. The Crown will accept that you ... that you did it by way of diminished responsibility.'

I was very pleased, it was easy money. In seventy-seven minutes, I had persuaded one person to take the blame for killing someone else. Not a bad morning's work. 'I can't believe it,' I said.

'What? That I murdered Molly Summers?'

'No. That the prosecution agreed the deal. It's too good to be true.'

'What I don't understand,' said Kingsley, 'is if they accept I wasn't *really* responsible, then who was?'

'What do you mean?'

'Well, who or what made me do it?'

'Oh, don't worry about that,' I said. 'Leave that to the philosophers and the tabloids. They'll sort it out. Articles will be written about you, Mr Kingsley. Tory backbenchers will rue the fact that you still have possession of your testicles. Your sexual thrillers will sell out. Look at it as a bit of cheap publicity with rent-free accommodation thrown in.'

Kingsley's eyes caught a spark of light from the corridor outside the cells. 'What if ... well, what if I didn't *really* kill her?'

'With great respect, Mr Kingsley,' I began. 'That's all very interesting, I'm sure. But the court will sit in about ten minutes.' I was excessively polite to him, but then I always was polite when I was trying to persuade a client of mine to plead guilty. 'I mean, what defence could you run?'

'Defence?'

'Yes. Sorry to be all technical. But when people plead not guilty, they normally run a defence. It usually helps.'

'Well,' Kingsley said, 'how about ... alibi?'

'Do you have an alibi witness?'

'I could have.'

'What does that mean?' I asked.

Kingsley was silent.

'Well, who would it be?' I continued.

'Do I have to give a name?' Kingsley asked.

'We've got to give the prosecution advance notice of any alibi evidence. If you're going to call your witness to testify, I have to know everything. His name, his address, his inside leg measurement, which side he dresses on – everything. So tell me, who is he?'

'Philip Templeman.'

'A friend of yours?'

'Not really.'

'So what do you know about him, Mr Kingsley?'

'About the same as I know about you.' The little man crouched in his seat and stared straight at me.

'How do you know you can trust him?'

16

'How do I know I can trust you, Mr Fawley?'

'Look. This is a matter of the utmost gravity. If we put Mr—'

'Templeman.'

'If we put him on a notice of alibi, the police will be entitled to interview him.'

'They would have to find him first.'

'So where does he live?'

'I can't really say.'

'What does he do?'

'Nothing, really.'

'Is he of good character?'

'As far as I know,' Kingsley said.

'At least that's something.'

'But then I was of good character before I was caught.' Kingsley smiled, but only a little.

'Do you think he will tell the truth?'

'Do you think I will, Mr Fawley?'

'I hate to be rude,' I said. 'But it does all seem rather far-fetched. We might as well say you were water-skiing with Lord Lucan in the Gobi Desert. It's about as believable.'

'I can't water-ski,' Kingsley said, shuffling in his wheelchair.

I realised how insensitive I had been. 'Look,' I said, 'why pin your hopes on this Templeman?'

'It's not him I'm pinning my hopes upon.'

'Then who?'

'You, Mr Fawley. I'm pinning my hopes upon you,' Kingsley said, undeterred. 'You see, what if I didn't murder Molly Summers at the stone circle?' he said.

I could see that this would be a complication, and I had to quash any delusions of real innocence immediately. 'You never said you did murder her.'

'Quite.'

'But you never said you didn't either.'

That seemed to silence him for a short while. I spent the time describing in detail the horrors of a trial: the public demanding blood, the sleazy reporters, the court artists who would portray him with demonic features and bad skin, then there were the cold stares of the jury and that dreadful moment when the verdict was announced.

I wasn't sure whether he was really listening, but when I had finished, his mood had changed. When I started to explain the benefits of a guilty plea yet again, Kingsley suddenly stopped me. And he agreed to plead guilty to manslaughter.

So when we finally went upstairs, I sat in the front row of Court 8 and waited for the defendant to fulfil his part of the bargain. I even turned towards the dock and started to mouth, 'But guilty of manslaughter.'

Kingsley looked away.

'Perhaps you might like to take some instructions from your client, Mr Fawley.' Of course, there exists a state of limbo between the Bar and oblivion called being a judge. The nearest incumbent rattled his chains, not even attempting to hide his displeasure. But I knew Mr Justice Manly very well.

Ignatius Manly was one of the first black men elevated to the High Court Bench. He was not a bad judge, which is not to say he was a good judge – which of them were, when you were defending a hopeless case? But he was fair. Black folks know a thing or two about justice, he once told me, slipping as he occasionally did into a mid-Atlantic vernacular. Yes, we know about justice because we've had none for five hundred years.

After Manly had spoken to me, I adopted that half-crouched scuttling position barristers rather shamelessly assume when the judge is in court. Manly sat at the front, high above me. As I got up, the prosecution team sat to my right. The defendant was detained at the rear of the court. It all appeared faintly ridiculous to me. We were in the new part of the Old Bailey and the courtroom was full of stripped wood and spongy seats. It looked rather like the departure lounge of a tacky provincial airport.

On the way to the dock, I passed Justine Wright.

'Shall I cancel the Savoy, Tom?' she whispered. 'The table's booked for twelve thirty.'

Suddenly, I was behind schedule.

Justine Wright was on the other side of the legal divide. As prosecuting junior, she was separated from me by a Chinese wall. But given a little *foie gras* and a lot of vintage Burgundy, I hoped that such walls – and who knew what other barriers? – might come tumbling down. Lunch at the Savoy with Justine was one of the fringe benefits of a guilty plea. Of course, I hadn't told Kingsley this. He would be dining at Her Majesty's pleasure and then slopping out.

I reached the dock, which was like a wooden play-pen at the very back of the court. Varnished wood came up to chest level and there was a gate-like opening guarded by a dock officer.

'What are you doing?' I asked.

'Nothing much.'

'So there's no problem?'

'There's no problem,' Kingsley said. 'Well, not for me. You see, I'm going to fight the case. I hope that's not going to be too inconvenient for you, Mr Fawley.'

Chapter 3

Kingsley sat in the dock and played with an ancient ring on his shrivelled right hand, while the whole court waited for me to resolve the situation.

'We had a deal,' I said.

'You had a deal,' he replied.

'Yes. I had a deal, Mr Kingsley. It's the best deal *I'm* going to get.'

'Really?'

'Yes, really. Funny thing is, it's not me who will get a life sentence for murder. It's you.'

'I think I had noticed that.'

'Well, have you also noticed those rows of good citizens with saliva dribbling from their jowls?' I pointed a little histrionically to the public gallery, but Kingsley ignored me.

'You see, Mr Fawley, I've decided: I don't do deals.'

'Well, you better start.' By now my voice had risen to an indecorous, that is, audible level.

'Is there a problem?' Ignatius Manly's rich baritone boomed across the court; it bristled with impatience, and I could feel an attack of the vernacular coming on.

'There isn't a problem, M'Lord. But—'

'But what?'

'But I'd like a little more time.'

'And I'd like to win friends and influence people, but I've got a court to run.' Manly threw down his pencil, a favourite judicial trick. 'Now is your client pleading guilty or not guilty?'

'I . . . I don't know.'

'No,' he said. 'Why should you know? You're only his barrister.'

'Yes, M'Lord.'

'You know, Mr Fawley, in my day at the Bar, a barrister used to take the trouble to find out whether his client was pleading guilty or not guilty to murder. We had a word for it. It was called being a professional.'

This public humiliation riled me and I attempted to fight back. 'I *have* been trying to get instructions, M'Lord. But I haven't had much luck.'

'Well, you better get some.'

'Luck or instructions, M'Lord?'

'Both,' he shouted. 'Now get on with it.'

I turned to Kingsley and tried to adopt my most professional tone. 'If you fight the murder, you're bound to be convicted.'

'How do you know?' he asked.

'Trust me.'

'Can you think of any good reason why I should?'

I could not. So I decided to try another line of attack. 'Plead to manslaughter and you'll only get ten years. With time off for remand and remission, you'll be out in six.'

'That's easy for you to say. But can you imagine what a six-year sentence means?'

'Mr Kingsley,' I said, straightening my back and trying to look down imperiously, 'I've been married for seven years. This is the best deal you're going to get.'

'Six years is a long time.'

'Life, they tell me, is a little longer,' I said. 'Look, if you convince some dotty bishop you've found religion, they might let you out even sooner than six.'

'No deals.'

'They might even campaign for your release. You might become a miscarriage of justice.'

'No deals,' he said in such a way that I knew it was the end of the discussion, for his eyes rolled over and even seemed white, like those of a shark when it has made its kill. And I imagined Kingsley among the stones, and a knife was in his hand, and the hand was no longer shrivelled, but healthy and slender, like a woman's, and there was no discussion as he went about his – little games.

When I returned to my position in counsel's row, my junior, Emma Sharpe, had drawn a gallows and a noose in her notebook with a question mark against it. But I wasn't in a playful mood as I knew the judge was waiting.

I needed to compose myself. The glass of water rattled against my teeth as I took a sip. I was wearing my midnight blue suit which was double-breasted, naturally, a battered pair of brogues, scuffed at the toes, black stuff gown, and a wig – ashen grey, filthy, and held together with pins. I was the picture of the thoroughly modern barrister. I was going to trial on a murder and didn't have a prayer.

'The plea of not guilty stands, M'Lord,' I said.

For a moment Mr Justice Manly was lost for words which, on the whole, was a welcome state of being for a hostile judge. He whispered something to Leonard. Leonard sulked. But then Leonard always sulked when he saw a black man as opposed to a black cap on the Bench.

Two dozen people were brought into court. They had an almost comical variety of tired faces, trash novels and rolled-up newspapers. They looked bored and annoyed, as if they were waiting for a charter flight to Torremolinos and had been delayed yet again.

Leonard shuffled the cards and selected twelve of this jury panel at random. They were strangers to each other, strangers to the law – they didn't even know what the case was about. And I knew nothing about them. The law specifically prevents two classes of person from being on a jury: criminals and lawyers. Apart from that, they could be virtually anybody. And they were to decide whether Richard Kingsley murdered Molly Summers.

I wished it was a Friday. Friday at the Old Bailey: fish

served in the Bar Mess and a diet of rape and buggery pleas downstairs. Friday was a day of reckoning. Not too many people pretended they were innocent on a Friday. But there we were in Court 8 on a bright Monday morning. Start of the week, start of the trials, high-water mark of the hopeless defence, and despite all my efforts, Kingsley's case was to be no different.

As each of the jurors was sworn, I hurriedly drafted a notice of alibi, including the name Philip Templeman. When I had given it to the prosecution team, the trial began.

Chapter 4

'Members of the jury,' said Aubrey Davenport QC, the prosecution leader, 'the evidence that Richard Kingsley murdered Molly Summers is overwhelming. But' – here Davenport glanced at the judge – 'but Mr Kingsley has pleaded not guilty.'

Like many large men, Davenport had a slightly high-pitched voice, as though a tape of his speech was being played back at the wrong speed. He was eighteen stones, pigeon-toed and had a revolting moustache, all of which made me suspicious of him. He whistled Puccini arias at the Old Bailey urinals, always ate red meat, never drank white wine, and salivated at the sight of female jurors. He was mediocre at speeches, passable in cross-examination, yet prided himself on his eloquence, which was his incorrect diagnosis of a chronic bout of verbal flatulence.

But the most disgusting thing about Aubrey Davenport, and it was a truly disgusting thing amid stiff competition, was his special knack for inserting his fat tongue into women's ears in the backs of taxis. What astonished me was that surprisingly few complained, and when they did, it was more an objection to his rough bristle on their earlobes rather than to the insertion of the offending organ in the first place.

At the front of Court 8, Davenport licked his lips and said, 'So to this, the most serious of charges, the defendant has pleaded not guilty. That is his right. But after you've heard all the evidence, if you're sure he killed this sixteen-year-old girl in cold blood, you will convict him of murder. And that, ladies and gentlemen, is your right.'

Mr Justice Manly scowled, not at Kingsley but at me, his eyes brooded and I imagined his lips whispering unknown indignities to come. He scribbled something down in his red, leather-bound notebook.

Earlier, Manly had invited all counsel into his private chambers. It was an invitation that could not be refused. He asked me if I could indicate which issues were likely to arise, which was coded language for: What on earth is your defence? I told him that I didn't know and then looked around the room, trying to avoid his eyes.

Manly's chambers were little different to those of the other Old Bailey judges. The room was full of dark wood, sombre leather and the mauled bones of defence counsel who had said the wrong thing. But above his desk, Manly had a rather badly painted watercolour. It was of a Caribbean beach with gaily painted fishing boats and the sun breaking through on to distant mountains. I had always liked it.

Judges' chambers are that part of the law the public is not allowed to see. They are half private club, half trading room. The commodities are familiar enough: crime and punishment, probation and prison. But it was the secrecy that used to make me feel guilty, the skulking around behind closed doors. It was as if I had entered into an alliance against my client, as if he was being auctioned and no bid would be too low. And I felt that another kind of judge, who was even more formidable than Ignatius Manly, had entered a mark against my name in a book that was even darker than his.

After Davenport had been speaking for fifteen minutes, two things had begun to happen. His elephantine frame began to break out in sweat, and the jury started to glaze over. They sat there bemused, somewhat embarrassed to be in the spotlight, trying desperately not to fidget or yawn. No one volunteers for such a job. The electoral roll spins and there they are: dragged, if not kicking and screaming, then with a certain reluctance from their sitting rooms, betting shops, public houses and dole offices.

When I started at the Bar, I was told to look at the jury carefully. Work out who they were, how they would vote, what made them tick. Get to know your jury. Who were the movers and who were the muppets? I soon discovered that it was a futile exercise. I had little idea about the people I knew well and, at times, even less about myself. So what was the point?

The more trials I did, the more frightened I became of the jury. They smiled at my jokes, they nodded during my cross-examinations, they took notes during my speeches, and then they convicted my clients. And every time I felt a personal insult, a sense of rejection.

Davenport stood facing the jury unashamedly adjusting the rolls of flesh that convened around his midriff. He said, 'There are a couple of questions you will want answered, members of the jury. Firstly, you may ask, where is Stonebury? Well, it is set in a valley surrounded by the gentle hills of the Devon and Dorset borders.'

There seemed to be no hint of recognition on the faces of the jurors. That, at least, was a good sign.

But Davenport continued, 'More importantly, what was so different about Molly Summers? Well, nothing really. For years she'd been in care, moved from foster home to foster home. It's right to say that she ran away occasionally. That she didn't settle. And she finally ended up in a residential home in Stonebury. The home is called the West Albion. You might hear a little about it during the course of the trial.'

A little, I thought. Why only a little? Surely the home was at the centre of this? My musings were interrupted by Davenport's change of tone.

He paused, looked at the jury and dropped his voice. 'West Albion is the type of centre that is run by local authorities when there are children with certain ... difficulties. Perhaps the defence will make much of this. I don't know. The problems these girls might have had does not, cannot excuse violence towards them. Keep your eyes on the ball, members of the jury. Why – that is the real question – why would anyone want to murder Molly Summers? This young girl ... poor, lonely ... and in eyes of the law, innocent ... this truly innocent girl—'

I got to my feet. 'M'Lord, I hesitate to object.'

'Well, hesitate a little longer,' said Manly. There were a few sniggers around the court.

'But, really. M'friend knows perfectly well that it is highly undesirable for prosecuting counsel to use such emotive language.'

Davenport turned on me. 'Is my friend suggesting that innocence is an emotive word?'

'The prosecution is not supposed to excite prejudice against a defendant.'

'I was not.'

'What were you doing?' I asked.

'Exciting sympathy for the girl.'

'The dead girl,' I said, and as soon as I had, I knew it was a mistake. There was no sound in court, but I could feel my heart pounding as all eyes fixed upon me. I felt as though the blood was draining from my legs and I sat down.

'Ladies and gentlemen,' said Manly, turning to the jury and ignoring us. He folded his hands and closed his eyes as if he were about to pray. At that moment Ignatius Manly made Job himself look like a man who would fly off the handle at the merest slight. It was another of Manly's ploys. 'Members of the jury,' he said, 'you will not decide this case on the interventions and histrionics of counsel. No, you will decide this case on the evidence. Are you going to mention the evidence at any stage today, Mr Davenport?'

'M'Lord, yes,' he replied. Davenport took a sip of water and brushed a couple of stray droplets from his moustache, which seemed to curl around his top lip and sneak into his mouth. 'When you hear the evidence, ladies and gentlemen, you will ask yourselves: What possible defence can Richard Kingsley have?'

I turned to Emma who was writing all this down. 'That's a question I keep asking myself,' I said. But she ignored me.

I was hoping that Emma would respond. Few people can realise just how tedious advocates find the speeches of other advocates. Especially if they waffle on like Aubrey Davenport.

One of the best ways to relieve the monotony is to chat to your colleagues around you. It is surprising how little the jury can hear. And one of the primary arts of defence is the whispered aside. A groan, a cough, a *sotto voce* mutter can do wonders to put off your opponent. After all, nine-tenths of defence work is an exercise in sabotage. But Davenport, with his mind-numbing oratory, was messing it up all on his own.

Soon Davenport described the layout of the village. He spoke of Stonebury in almost reverential terms, characterising it as the epitome of a rural world that was vanishing. The sort of place where you'd half expect the Mayor of Casterbridge to bump into the cast of the *Archers* and have a chummy discussion about the price of turnips.

The ancient part of the village was entirely surrounded by the stones. There were three concentric circles of diminishing sizes – outer, middle and inner – culminating in a group of bluestone blocks known collectively as the Sepulchre. The other stones were made from granite. In local lore, they were called Sarsens.

The village had approximately three hundred residents. The surrounding farmland, where two thousand or more people lived, also came under the official title of the Parish of Stonebury and extended for about five miles to all points of the compass. I knew that the estate of His Honour Judge Wright, Justine's deceased father, lay somewhere nearby. He had once been the presiding judge in the area.

Davenport continued, 'Molly Summer's body was found the next morning. At the place of execution. She still lay within the inner circle at Stonebury. The area is partially paved to make it accessible throughout the year. There were few obvious clues but blood covered the Sepulchre. And, of course, there was the semi-naked body.'

I noticed a couple of the seedier members of the press take this down. No doubt it would feature in some tabloid report between the bare breasts and the bingo.

Davenport was beginning to get into his stride and soon came to a topic that continued to puzzle me. 'How then were the police pointed in the direction of Richard Kingsley?' he said. 'Shortly before the body was found, there was an anonymous phone call to Stonebury police station. I cannot tell you the content of the call. The informant never came forward, but the police immediately went to the Manor, Mr Kingsley's residence in the village.'

I had seen bundles of photographs of Kingsley's Stonebury home. It was dimly lit by narrow, Gothic windows and was filled with strange tapestries and statues. In the hallway, where most of us would have coat-hooks, Kingsley had a row of African masks with hollow eyes. Of all the people I had ever met, only Richard Kingsley could have lived in such a place.

'When the police first searched the Manor, nothing was found,' said Davenport. 'No doubt Mr Kingsley breathed a huge sigh of relief. But the refuse-collectors were late that day, a twist of fate, perhaps? For in the dustbin, something was found. You can see it here.'

With that Davenport brandished something metallic at the jury and said, 'Here, members of the jury, is the murder weapon.'

Chapter 5

The knife was bigger than the photographs had suggested and I had never seen its like. It was curved, almost crescent-shaped, like a five-day-old moon. It was heavy and sparkling and sharp.

Davenport waved the knife at the jury as if it were a feather duster and he was brushing some cobwebs away from their eyes. 'You will hear from a forensic scientist who will give expert evidence that this knife' – he held it up to the level of his eyes – 'matches precisely the dimensions of the instrument that punctured the body of the sixteen-year-old girl.' He looked at the jury with great deliberation. 'Punctured her body *forty-three* times.'

He thudded the knife on the bench next to him and it made a dull, dead sound. There was complete silence in court, and I had to admit it was a dramatic moment. As counsel for the defence, you never know where to look at such times.

I looked at the jury and it was a mistake.

A woman in her thirties, wearing a floral print dress, struggled to fight back the tears. A man in a tweed suit jotted something or other down. A few jurors turned and looked at Kingsley, and this time he did look away.

But there was a young woman who wore jeans and a baggy blue sweat-shirt. She had the same blonde hair and grey eyes as Justine. But while Justine ignored me, the juror did not. She just stared and stared at me. I knew that look, I often saw it in my dreams: How could you, it said, how could you defend *him*?

31

And then you feel like an accomplice, as though you took part in the crime, and you want to say, yes, I'm guilty as well, but what can I do? These are the dark moments of the job; such moments are the sowers of doubt, the heralds of failure.

'God, I wish we could reply to this rubbish right now,' said Emma. She was not intimidated; Emma Sharpe was remarkably resilient.

'And what would we say?' I replied. What, after all, could we have said? That our client needed to have sex with young girls, but didn't kill this one? And all the time I knew that Davenport was saving the best part for last.

'But trials are not about science,' he said. 'They are about people. In this case the prosecution will call eye-witnesses to the crime. They will testify that they saw Richard Kingsley at the scene of the murder. They, too, are young girls. Young girls, you may feel, of considerable courage.'

'Looks like they've persuaded the orphans to blab,' said Emma. No doubt she regarded it as an interesting development and would be fascinated to see how I dealt with them, an upward blip on her learning curve. I dreaded it.

There had been considerable doubt as to whether these eye-witnesses would testify. They had refused to say a word in the magistrates court committal, but if they came up to proof, they would destroy the last vestiges of a defence.

Davenport continued, 'There's only one person in this court who really knows if Mr Kingsley is guilty, and that is Richard Kingsley himself. So what does he say? When interviewed with his solicitor he made no comment, as he was entitled to do.'

'What's he on about?' asked Emma.

'So where was Richard Kingsley on the night of the murder?' said Davenport. 'Two police officers arrested him when the knife was found.'

I looked at Justine Wright and she looked away.

'One will testify,' said Davenport, 'that Kingsley confessed to being at the murder.'

The jury was amazed, there were murmurs in the public gallery, Kingsley shouted, 'No, no', and Manly demanded silence. I turned to Justine.

'I told you to stop Davenport mentioning the confessions,' I said in a voice that the jury could not hear. The plan was to get the confessions excluded on a legal technicality.

'I'm sorry, Tom,' she said, all doe-eyed. 'I forgot.'

'Don't try that "I forgot" stunt with me again, Justine.'

'What do you mean?' She feigned innocence, but knew I was referring to the last time we were in court together. It was a murder. We were co-defending but our client was convicted.

'You *know* what happened,' I said. Our client had committed suicide in prison.

'Want to rake up the past, Thomas?' She went on the attack. 'Of course your hands are spotless.'

'I didn't say that.'

'What are you saying then?'

'It wasn't my . . .'

Emma watched this bemused as Davenport continued to drone on. One or two jurors watched us but wouldn't have been able to hear what we were saying.

'It wasn't my—'

'Spit it out, Tom,' Justine said defiantly. 'It wasn't your what? Why don't you say it, Tom? It wasn't your what?'

'I'm not blaming you.'

'Back off then.'

'Look, Justine—'

'I have to say, Mr Fawley' – she moved very close to me, and I could feel her moist breath on my neck – 'you really know how to woo a woman.'

Justine could always tie me up in knots; it was one of the things, in a perverse way, that attracted me to her. She exposed my sense of uncertainty, hypocrisy even, about my job, my marriage, about myself. She brought it out into the open with her piercing words, and made me face it. She managed to make my longing for infidelity feel – almost honourable. And for her part, she despised and yet enjoyed my weakness. Spineless, she called me once.

It was years before the trial. There was a party in Justine's chambers. It was to celebrate Ignatius Manly taking silk. Justine did her pupillage, her apprenticeship, with Manly and Davenport. But her place was guaranteed: the chambers had once belonged to Justine's father.

She was very drunk. I had been waiting to make a move on her despite the fact she was my wife's best friend. I saw the party as an ideal opportunity.

She allowed me to touch her hair. And when I did, her perfume wafted into my face. She put her hand in the back of my belt and drew me to her body. I could just feel the points of her breasts against my chest as she ran her fingers over my buttocks. I needed to kiss her but as my mouth touched hers, she pulled away. Justine said she was already seeing someone. She said it was Manly. Rather foolishly, prompted by the cheap German wine, I asked what Manly had that I did not.

'He's got backbone,' she said. I remember she looked at me with contempt. She put a slender finger to my lips as though she was about to reveal the mysteries of the universe. She added, 'I quite like that in a lover.'

She left me sipping my plastic cup of Liebfraumilch.

'So what is Richard Kingsley's defence?' asked Davenport, his voice now thinner and higher with the strain. 'Through his lawyers, he has served a notice of alibi. This states that at the time of the murder he was not at the stone circle but was with someone called...' Davenport leaned over towards me and whispered, 'I can't read your writing, Fawley.'

'It says Templeman,' I said. 'Philip—'

'With someone called Philip Templeman,' Davenport announced in an ominous fashion to the jury. 'The defence will say that Mr Kingsley was with this man. We say this is a lie. For who is this man? Is he flesh and blood? Or is he another of Richard Kingsley's fictional creations?'

Davenport glanced at me. And I was grateful that I was not required to give answers to these questions immediately.

'When you have heard the evidence,' Davenport continued, 'you will have no doubt that Richard Kingsley was at the scene in his wheelchair. But that is not the end of the matter. The notice of alibi was only served this morning.'

Davenport paused and left the words hanging in the air for the jury to consider. I looked at Justine, but she very pointedly turned away.

'Why?' Davenport asked. 'Why the delay in serving a notice that is required by law? Does the alibi represent the truth? Or is it just the latest instalment of Mr Kingsley's glittering literary career?'

There was a creak at the back of the court as the defendant wheeled himself a little nearer to the front of the dock.

Davenport, seeing the opportunity, improvised. 'So the defence comes to this,' he said, 'mistaken identity. You've identified the wrong wheelchair. It's preposterous, is it not?'

The Fleet Street hacks enjoyed that but the jury did not smile – they never smile on the first day of a murder.

Davenport then raised his voice, which trembled slightly. 'Whoever is guilty in this case, never forget one thing. Molly Summers is innocent. Innocent in law and innocent in life. Your verdict will not bring her back. But if Richard Kingsley murdered her, he must be convicted by you and punished by law. It is all we can do.'

When he had finished, there was silence in court. As Davenport sat down, Emma tugged at my gown. 'I've got to tell you something, Tom.'

But I wasn't interested. I stared at the young juror and she stared at me.

Emma pulled at my gown again. 'Tom, it's important.'

As I looked at the juror's eyes, I wondered whether she would ever realise how similar they were to the grey eyes of the murdered girl.

Chapter 6

Through clouds of stale smoke and the pleasant haze of a five-year-old Meursault, I saw Justine and Davenport enter the wine bar. It was inevitable. Everyone came to Johnson's after a day in the legal salt-mines. It was the communal jacuzzi of the criminal Bar. No one really remembered if it was ever officially called Johnson's. New owners came and went, the name on the sign outside changed. One year it said Smithfields, the next it said Taylors. Very often we didn't know what its proper name was. But we just called it Johnson's, as we always had. It was the only place to be seen. Above the door, there was even a quote from old Dr Johnson himself:

Sir, I have found you an argument,
but I am not obliged to find you an understanding.

When I saw the prosecution team, I was in a quiet corner with Emma Sharpe. There was a general mood of despondency around the wine bar that well matched my own.

'What's everyone else got to be so glum about?' I asked her.

'Crime figures are out.'

'Bad?'

'Awful,' she said.

'Up by much?'

'Five per cent down.'

'I can't believe it,' I said. 'Now even crime's in recession.'

'Look at them all,' Emma replied, pointing at the dark-suited hordes of criminal practitioners, 'crying into their South African Chardonnay.'

I knew that some legal hacks were reputed to follow the rape and robbery statistics with the same fervour that shareholders follow the fluctuations of the stock market. Any fall was unexpected. For Crime PLC had a stock that seemed to have increased ever since Eve pinched an apple and Cain took a bit of a dislike to his brother.

'I mean,' Emma continued, 'what are the poor loves going to do?'

'How do you mean?'

'Well, think of all those private school fees to pay. Think of all the Tuscan villas to maintain. And what happens? Their ungrateful clients decide to go straight. It really is too criminal.'

I couldn't share Emma's frivolity. In my mind, I kept seeing the strange shape of the knife and I wondered what could motivate someone to puncture a young body forty-three times. Emma continued to outline the impact of the falling crime rate on the Bar. When she saw that I was not listening, she stopped.

'Tom, what's the matter?'

I did not answer.

'This media circus has really freaked you, hasn't it?' she said.

'What did you want to tell me? You said in court—'

'Tom, what has happened to you?'

'I thought everyone knew. Worst kept secret at the Bar.'

'God, they really got to you. Didn't they, Tom?'

'I don't want to hear this speech again.'

'Well, you're going to hear it. Again and—'

'What? From you? What have you defended? A punch-up in Romford and a couple of naff burglaries?'

'I've defended in drugs trials.'

'Trendy friends of yours. Pushing cannabis at student raves. Well, that's really the big time, Emma.'

By the time I had said that, my voice was hard and the words were pointed. I knew they cut into Emma and she said nothing for a while as she slowly sipped her wine.

'I wanted to be your pupil,' she finally said. 'You know, everyone said it was a mistake, that you were – well, sliding. But I knew, Tom.' She looked at me and her eyes were wide. 'I knew.'

I sank into my seat as she spoke about a barrister I hardly recognised.

'All of us were reluctant to have a man defending Sarah Morrow. I mean, the campaign was run by pretty strict feminists and all that, but you had a reputation of being a fighter and that's what we needed.'

It was a big issue for the women's movement. Sarah Morrow lived in the general Stonebury area. She had killed her husband after years of abuse and wanted to say that over a period of time she was provoked into the stabbing. It wasn't a defence known to law, but we fought it.

Court 8 seemed a lot bigger in those days. I suppose I was just not used to it back then. I had tried really hard to forget the case.

'I never saw such ... well, I guess, such passion in a courtroom,' said Emma. She was sitting beside me gabbling her words. 'You tore the policemen to shreds, you destroyed those shrinks; you couldn't have done any more—'

'I could have won,' I said.

'Sarah knew the risks.'

'Did she?'

Emma didn't seem to hear that or didn't want to hear it. 'The law doesn't like women standing up for themselves. It was always going to be tough. The point is you fought it.'

'And lost.'

'But we can win Kingsley's case,' she said.

39

'You just don't get it, do you? People get hurt.'

'That's life, Tom.'

'No, Emma. That's the law. And one day pretty soon you're going to learn the cost of defeat.'

Again we were silent. Eventually, I was fortified by the workings of the Provençal sun, and broached what I knew to be a sensitive question. 'What is it with you and Justine?'

'With me and Miss Whiter-than-White?'

'Yes, you and Justine.'

'Too pure to get her hands dirty defending the bad guys?'

'She *used* to defend.'

'Exactly,' said Emma. 'Pass me the wine.'

When I had poured out a little more Burgundy, I said, 'Justine's just doing a job, you know.'

Emma laughed at that. 'It's not a job to her,' she said.

'What is it then?'

'Really want to know?' I looked at her impatiently and she continued. 'I know this is going to sound weird' – she looked around to see there was no one near – 'but it's like ... it's like some sort of mission to her.'

'What nonsense,' I said.

'You haven't twigged, have you?'

'What?'

Emma took a large gulp of wine and then spoke very fast. 'She thinks she's the Angel of sodding Vengeance.' Before I could protest she added, 'And let me tell you something else' – again she looked round – 'she's going to make Kingsley pay for Molly Summers.' She wolfed down the rest of the glass and slammed it on the table. She was a little manic which was rare to see.

'Does Justine know Kingsley or something?' I asked. 'I mean, isn't there a professional conflict?'

'I don't think so. Stonebury's small, but people tend to keep to themselves. Or so Sarah Morrow told us during the campaign. Apparently, no one really knew Kingsley – except, of course, the Stonebury Girl Guides. Still, the locals hate him now. That's why it's been moved to the Bailey. Local prejudice and all that.'

We sat in silence for a while trying to think of things to say. Generally I trusted Emma's instincts, but I thought she was wrong about Justine. Justine had become rather depressed after Sarah Morrow's suicide. The gloom would not lift. Depression became illness and Justine left the Bar for two years. When she returned, she gave up defending.

'Another bottle?' I said.

'Look, I like partying. But not during a trial. We've got a murder tomorrow. Or have you forgotten your appointment with Mr Justice Manly?'

'Half a bottle?'

'Work, Tom.'

'A glass?'

'All right then, you old soak. But we've got to discuss the case.'

Emma took out a bundle of photographs. They were of the dead body. I knew the prosecution would introduce them the next day.

'So,' she said, 'what are we going to do about these, Tom?'

'Nothing.'

'Brilliant. Tom, you're just so full of enthusiasm for this case. I mean, can't we object or something? They're so prejudicial.'

'The jury has a right to see—'

'What? A pre-pubescent girl mutilated on a stone with a muslin dress over her head?'

'She was sixteen, Emma.'

'I know, but have you noticed how all those Stonebury women look the same?'

'No,' I replied.

'Well, take Sarah Morrow. She was the same. Thin as a rake and no breasts. I mean, haven't these people heard of puberty? They're just like the landscape around there.'

'Why?'

'Even the hills are flat. And all the women have got that same countryside sort of look.'

'What do you mean?'

'You know, like Twiggy on horseback. Inbreeding, perhaps?'

'No,' I said. 'Too little pollution and too many turnips. Can't be healthy.'

'Talking of vegetable matter,' Emma replied, 'have you seen? Davenport is over there with—'

'No.'

'Liar,' she said. 'Are you going to get some more wine or what?'

In those days, of course, that was precisely the type of question that I found far easier to answer.

Pushing through the crush in Johnson's was a delicate art-form, one they should have taught in Bar school. There were so many legal toes to avoid treading upon, so many professional backs to scratch. I pushed past barristers deploring the vices of alcohol, past others propounding the virtues of oral sex.

There was dark wood everywhere and some prints from *Vanity Fair*. The rest of the wall-space was taken up with mirrors. The clientele was predominantly legal and male. The bar staff was female. The air buzzed with extraordinary forensic triumph and tragic, but courageous, defeat. No one believed what anyone else said, but that didn't matter. The telling was all.

As I approached the bar, I saw Justine. She very pointedly ignored me, still smarting, no doubt, from our confrontation in court. She talked to the officer in charge of the case, Inspector Stanley Payne. Next to them, Davenport was puffing at his cheap cigarette between telling everybody about his brilliant opening speech and lining up a young pupil for the taxi ride home.

Justine looked so small compared to Davenport. I suppose the effect was exaggerated because she still had girlishly blonde hair. She looked younger than her thirty-five years.

I remembered what Emma had said about Molly Summers, and I suppose Justine also had that same Stonebury look. She was very slender. I could never work out whether that meant that she was fragile or resilient. Was she more like a piece of cane or a dry twig? If I pressed her, would she bend or would she break?

I returned to Emma with another full bottle and she didn't seem to remember the terms of our compromise. She finished jotting down some notes for the next day, and put them in her wicker bag.

'Who was to blame?' she asked me without blinking.

'I don't understand.'

'Rubbish. Who was to blame, Tom?'

'To blame for what?'

'For Sarah Morrow's case. Five years ago.'

'Look, Emma. I don't think I can—'

'Oh, do cut the Sir Galahad routine, Tom.' She paused so that I looked directly at her. 'Now, you and Justine. Who was to blame?'

'If we're going to discuss this, I want my lawyer present,' I said.

'You have got your lawyer present,' Emma replied. 'Who was to blame?'

'I don't understand you lot. It was your women's group that instructed Justine as junior counsel. Or have you forgotten that little detail?'

'It wasn't *my* group. I had no say in it.'

'Well, the sisters then. Collectively. They must have wanted Justine to defend.'

'I think it came from the family. Sarah Morrow once went to the same school as Justine or something.'

I then remembered being told something similar a few years previously. 'So it was the Stonebury connection?' I asked.

'I suppose so,' Emma replied. 'Anyway, the point is Justine simply didn't have her heart in it. Didn't care. Only in it for the publicity.' Emma sipped some more wine. 'Justine's a bit like ... well, rather like one of those birds. You know, the ones that go after shiny objects.'

'Jays? Or magpies?'

'I'm not a bloody ornithologist, Tom. The point is, they're just attracted to the glitter.'

'Perhaps she was misunderstood.'

'And perhaps you just wanted to get into her knickers.' We both knew that was a cheap shot. 'You're so pathetically weak with women. A toss of the hair, quick whiff of perfume and you're putty, Tom.'

She emptied her glass. 'God, this wine is rough,' she said and tried to smile, but it was not very convincing. 'You see, Tom, I sometimes worry about you.'

'About what?'

'About ... well, about your disgusting little soul. Christ, now I'm sounding like your priest.'

'I haven't got one.'

'Perhaps you should.' She picked up her bag and brushed herself down. 'I'm just worried about what you're doing to yourself. Justine Wright is trouble, Tom.'

'Emma,' I said, 'let me just say—'

But she put her finger to my lips a little like Justine had done at Manly's party years ago. For the first time in her life, Emma Sharpe pressed her cheek against mine. She immediately recoiled in embarrassment, not wanting me to take it the wrong way. But I could not, not with Emma.

'Want to know the truth?' she asked as I nodded. 'I'm a little frightened about what we might find in this case, Tom. I don't give a damn about Richard Kingsley; as far as I'm concerned, he can burn in hell for ever. He's pure evil.'

'To you, he's evil,' I said. 'To me, he's just another client suffering from a dodgy alibi and an acute lack of innocence.'

'That's what you always do,' Emma said. 'Try to joke it away.'

'Well, innocence is a much overrated commodity. Don't you think?'

Emma paused but did not smile. 'You see, Tom, no matter what you might say, there's something at the heart of all this. Something rotten. You know, a bit terrible. I'm not sure what it is, but I think you might just stumble your way into it.'

She started to walk away, but stopped after a couple of paces and added, 'That's why I'm worried about you, Tom.'

Chapter 7

The bedroom at home was as cold as ever. Penny, my wife, insisted on sleeping with the window ajar whatever the season. There was a slender shaft of moonlight on the bed and I could see her baggy white tee-shirt – she never wore negligées or anything like that. Too prissy, she used to say.

And then I felt a movement somewhere below my belt-line. In Kingsley's novels, such a scene would result in the hero's 'manhood' becoming engorged and throbbing. But the only thing that throbbed was my forehead. And all that I felt further down was a faint tingling. I knew that it would happen. It occurred disconcertingly often in those days. I got drunk and wanted to make love. The irony was that I probably couldn't, but that wasn't the point.

Surveying the target area, I tried to decide upon my best strategy. Penny always complained that my hands were cold when I came to bed after her. That was Step One: I put my cupped hands to my mouth and blew into them several times. Penny stirred and rolled on to her back, while I began to undress, balancing precariously on the bottom of the bed.

'Tom, is that you?' she asked. I just told her to go back to sleep. Penny reached out with one arm, but I was too far away. When the hand fell limply back to the sheets, I put my head next to her on the pillow. Penny smelt of sleep.

'What time is it?' she asked.

I did not answer. That would have been certain disaster. Instead I moved closer and tried to kiss her forehead. Penny rapidly pulled away.

'You've been drinking,' she said.

I had made a huge mistake. Usually I would brush my teeth and gargle with that sickly tasting mouthwash, but she could smell alcohol and my task had become doubly difficult. As I crawled under the duvet, I thought that there was still hope. It required tact, timing and just a little luck. I giggled foolishly.

Her body was curled tightly and she started as if shocked when I moved against her. There were obviously parts of my anatomy that I couldn't warm up – the pulsing blood inside didn't seem to reach the outer skin.

'Pen,' I whispered.

There was no response.

'Pen, are you asleep?'

It was, of course, a ridiculous question. She mumbled something.

'Penny,' I started to stroke her hair. Mousey, she called it and seemed to wash it less and less as she grew older and it grew darker. My fingers got caught in the knots.

'What are you doing?' she asked.

She knew. We'd been through the routine on so many occasions. I felt humiliated. Although I believed that a husband has no right to expect anything from his wife, deep down I still felt ludicrous having to plot and scheme just to sleep with Penny. The longer we were together, the more difficult it became to make love.

'I'm asleep,' she said.

'Penny,' I whispered. It was my last chance. I slowly moved my hand across her body and started to caress her left breast. That was Step Two. Slowly the nipple grew harder.

'What are you doing?' she said.

'That's obvious isn't it?'

'Well, don't,' she snapped with a crashing finality.

The bedside light went on and Penny looked at the clock. She stared at me but said nothing. As I tried to keep my eyes fixed on the ceiling, I could feel her feet passing against mine.

'Thought so,' she said.

'What?'

'You want to screw. You're so bloody predictable. Lights off, socks on. *So* romantic.'

I knew it annoyed her, but my toes got cold when the window was open. There was no point replying – all was lost.

'Been boozing, have you?'

'No,' I said.

'Don't lie. You stink of alcohol. It's revolting.' Then there was a much gentler inflection in her voice. 'Darling, come here.'

Dutifully, I rolled over. She ran her small fingers smoothly down my stomach, past my thighs. I ached for her and was melting. I thrust myself towards her palm but she withdrew it swiftly. Suddenly there was broken ice in her voice.

'If you must accost women in their sleep,' she said, yawning, 'if you must pester women, be decent enough to have a proper erection, Thomas.'

She used my full name. That was a bad sign. Thomas meant I was in trouble. Thomas meant no groping, no fondling, no sex and no breakfast. It meant I'd cut your dick off with my nail-scissors if it wasn't so pathetically small. I hated it when she used to call me Thomas.

The light went off.

I couldn't stand it. I had no place in that house, in that bed. My bathrobe was still damp from the morning – nothing dried properly in those Arctic conditions. I flung it on and rushed towards the door.

'Justine called round,' said Penny. 'She left a note in your study.'

'What about?'

'Well, I didn't read it. I'm not going to read a *billet-doux* between you and your—'

'She's not my—'

'Of course she's not,' Penny said. 'Justine's just up to her old tricks again. That's all.'

'What old tricks?' I asked.

'Oh, leaving things in strange men's studies.'

'What on earth does that mean, Pen?'

'Look, ask Justine about ... Alex,' she said.

'Who?'

Penny did not reply but pulled the duvet over her head and curled up.

When I crept along the landing, I had a desperate urge to look in on Ginny, my daughter. Her door was shut and I couldn't bring myself to open it in case it woke her. So I edged my way down the stairs, feeling terribly alone.

I had a little gas heater in my study. When I was forced to work through the night, getting up a brief, it was a source of comfort. Penny forbade the central heating's use during the night. I tried to light a match but my hand was shaking too much. The matchbox fell to the floor, matches were everywhere.

On the desk were various piles of case papers. Emma had photocopied the entire Kingsley brief so that I could work on it at home – not that I was bothered. There was a crisp white envelope tucked in the Kingsley depositions. I understood immediately what it was. I picked up a broken match and used it to prise open the rear of the note.

Justine's writing was deliberate, full of ornate letters, with deep strokes almost tearing through the paper.

> Dear Tom,
>
> Sorry to miss you. I've jotted down the name of a witness we do not intend to use. The police don't want to disclose it (for some reason). I think you should have it – in fairness. It might help.
>
> Love, Justine

Love, she wrote. She had never written that before. I'd known Justine Wright for many years. From the moment I met her at one of Penny's old schoolchums evenings, she invaded an untroubled corner of my imagination. I didn't resist. Did she really write Love Justine?

As I stared at the stacks of dog-eared papers and the unlit gas heater, my bedroom seemed very distant. I sat in my armchair with a damp bathrobe draped around me – wondering.

Chapter 8

It was the second day of the trial and I was late.

For that night I had slept little but had dreamt a lot. And what I had dreamt was this: there was a great field. And in the field were numerous stones. But these stones were not scattered. They were arranged in three circles. And I thought: Why three? Three for luck, perhaps? But good luck or bad luck? And luck for whom?

For some reason, I imagined myself walking around the circles, noticing a debris of acorns and straw. But I awoke with a start and realised that I would be late. And is this not the way of things? No sooner had I crawled out of my Fred Flintstone boxer shorts than I forgot about such insubstantial matters and worried instead about the very terrestrial terrors of being late in the court of Mr Justice Ignatius Manly.

When I reached the security doors at the Old Bailey, I remembered that crusty old sages in the robing room used to say that the great defence barrister, Edward Marshall Hall, used to keep the court waiting deliberately. He would stalk outside courtroom with his cushion. He suffered from piles, which along with thinning hair and an overblown sense of one's own importance, was an occupational hazard. There Marshall Hall would remain until the tension became unbearable. Then the doors would be flung open and he would march into court with a triumphant swirl of his gown.

When I arrived at Court 8, I peeped my head through the double doors. I was in trouble – the court was in session.

I delicately shut the door and scampered along the corridor. Every step echoed around the halls. I sneaked past statues of great legal reformers, solemn paintings of judges as my temples pounded and my tongue felt like sandpaper. What I wouldn't have given to be back in bed. For ten minutes tucked up in my duck-feather duvet, I would gladly have sold that small knot of indigestion which I sometimes mistook for my soul. I needed to hide.

I tried to recall the excuses I'd given Manly in the past when I'd been late, but couldn't remember. I had a versatile repertoire: car broken into and brief stolen, burst water-pipe, daughter taken sick. I used to be particularly ashamed of the last one – but it worked. It was too risky, I decided. There was only one solution: I had to think of something new.

Suddenly I came across a funny little man with a sheepish expression.

'Are you involved in the trial in Court 8?' he asked.

'Why?' I replied. 'Are you a witness in the case?'

The man laughed.

'Prosecution or defence?' I asked.

'That depends,' he said.

'On what?'

'On which way you look at it.'

Then I had an idea. 'You're not Philip Templeman, are you?'

Again, the man laughed. 'No,' he said. 'I'm not Philip Templeman. Can you tell me where the public gallery is?'

'The queue is outside,' I said. 'Anyway, only barristers and witnesses actually giving evidence are allowed inside the building. I don't know how you got past security, but – never mind. You better hurry.'

But it was me who did the hurrying as I headed towards the staircase. I wasn't sure what to do and then it came to me. For there is, I suppose, a certain low cunning in a drunk. And by climbing the stairs, I reached the small library attached to the Bar Mess at the very top of the building. From there I was able to buzz down to the reception on the internal telephone.

'This is leading counsel for the defence in Court 8,' I said, trying to speak as impressively as I could. 'Tell the court clerk to give a message to Miss Emma Sharpe of counsel. I am digging out some important legal authorities. For some reason – it really is most annoying – the wretched clock has stopped. Ask Miss Sharpe to hold the fort until I arrive.' The receptionist's scribblings finally caught up with my lies. 'Immediately,' I said. Then as an afterthought, 'And send someone to mend the clock.'

I put the phone down and exhaled with relief. There was a rickety armchair in the corner of the library. Its dark tan leather peeled off it like dried skin and when I clambered on to it, it was easy to pull out the electrical wires behind the clock and move the hands back to 10.20. I can't remember whether I spared a thought for Emma, who I had condemned to endure Davenport's heavy-handed oratory, as I headed to the Bar Mess for a coffee.

'Where on earth have you been?' demanded Emma.

The court had risen for five minutes and I took the opportunity to sneak in.

'Researching the law,' I said.

Emma looked at me with a mixture of incredulity and irritation. 'You haven't looked up the law since your Bar exams – and I'm not sure you looked at it then. Where were you?'

'All rise,' bellowed Norman, the usher. He loved that moment. Norman prided himself on having the loudest voice at the Bailey and in the days of Dick Whittington and public floggings he would have been the town crier or the person who counted out the strokes of the lash.

There was a rustling of winter coats and heavy suits as everyone got to their feet. Manly strode in with two Aldermen from the City of London, who sometimes accompanied an Old Bailey judge into court. I rather think Ignatius Manly enjoyed having all those white folks bowing to him.

Manly took his place on the Bench directly behind Leonard, the clerk. Then the judge spotted me. I'd taken the precaution of carrying as many legal tomes as I could manage, and bowed deeply towards him.

'Why were you late, Tom?' Emma was not satisfied.

'Considering the brief,' I said. Her expression was unchanged, so I added, 'Well, sleeping on it actually.'

Norman called for silence in court, looked pointedly at me, and began to swear in the first witness. Once she had sworn to tell the whole truth and nothing but, Norman snatched back the Bible. It was one of his favourite props; when juries went out he loved reading from the Book of Revelations. He turned to Judge Manly, bowed to an almost indecent degree, and returned to his crossword.

Standing alone in the witness box, like a miserable stick planted in a large plant-pot, the girl surveyed the ceiling of the court. Something caught her attention and she tilted her almost shaven head backwards at an acute angle. She wore black denim jeans and a black woollen shawl. Protruding through a crinkled white tee-shirt were two slender arms, gripping the rail of the witness box. She had a dried spot of blood on her left nostril where a nose-ring had once hung and looked so much like a member of the Manson family that you would have expected to see 'helter-skelter' tattooed across her forehead. But there was something strangely gentle about this teenager with the alabaster features, something vulnerable, and I imagined that an unkind wind wafting through Court 8 would blow her clean away.

Due to the sensitive nature of the trial and the allegations of under-age sex, we were not allowed to know the true identities of the girls. This one was called AA. They were each allocated a pair of letters like an exhibit and, in a sense, they did become just another piece of common property to be inspected. It worried me. But that was the way it was.

'You reside at the address given to the court?' asked Davenport. His folded pink hands again rested on his stomach.

The girl had spotted something in the far corner and cocked her head slightly like a bedraggled sparrow. Davenport gave the scruffy note containing her address to Norman who thrust it rudely at the witness.

'Is that your address?' asked Davenport.

She fingered the frayed edges of the paper.

'Did you tell the police your address?' he asked.

The girl nodded.

I could see that the jury was captivated: no one doodled, no one yawned, no one dozed. There is nothing like a human being on display in the witness box, being prodded and poked, to bring a criminal trial shuddering to life. Live flesh, that's what it was all about, live flesh.

Davenport asked, 'Did you know Mary Summers?' He tried his obsequious best to be charming, but failed.

'Who?' asked the girl.

'Also known as Molly Summers?'

'Who?'

'Molly.' Davenport put on his bedtime story voice. 'Did you know Molly?'

The girl gazed up at the ceiling again and said rather carelessly. 'I know lots of Mollys.'

'But we're only interested in one, you see. Molly Summers. Did you know her?'

'Can't remember,' she said without looking down.

'Is there something of interest on the ceiling?' asked Davenport.

She didn't answer.

Emma leant over to me and showed me the back page of her notebook. There she had jotted, in large letters, 'Going Bent??'

I shrugged. It was too early to tell if someone had got to this witness. She didn't testify in the preliminary hearing in the magistrates court, so had never given her story in court.

'Have you ever met Richard Kingsley?' asked Davenport. His hands were still folded but clenched slightly.

'Can't remember,' said the girl.

The judge immediately asked, 'What page, Mr Davenport?' He wanted to know where he could find her statement in the papers.

'Third NFE page thirteen, M'Lord,' Davenport told him.

The girl's full statement was served upon the defence as a Notice of Further Evidence. Kingsley assured us she wouldn't testify.

'Do you know whether Molly Summers is dead?' asked Davenport.

'Well, I ain't seen her around.'

'Where were you the night Molly Summers died?' Davenport was sweating now and began to speak more quickly.

The girl's mouth opened. 'I ... You sees ...' She hesitated and looked from Davenport to the ceiling. 'I ... I can't remember,' she said.

'Do you know Richard Kingsley?' asked Davenport.

The girl ignored him.

'Well, *do* you?' He slammed down the glass. 'Do you?' he shouted.

The wretched girl turned her back on Kingsley and the court and faced the judge. From my seat I could see her arms trembling.

'You don't know what it's like,' she cried. 'You just don't.' She sniffed a couple of times deeply and wiped her nose.

I noticed Ignatius Manly inspecting her very carefully. Then, in an extremely calm voice, without taking his eyes from the girl, he said, 'Perhaps you might like to retire for five minutes, members of the jury.'

Norman led the reluctant jurors out of court. When the thick wooden door slammed, Manly began to speak softly.

'Now listen, young lady,' he said. 'If you refuse to answer I will have to consider that a contempt.'

She pulled the black shawl around her shaking body.

'A contempt of *my* court,' said Manly. 'I can and probably will send you to prison. Do we understand each other?'

The girl stood there shivering.

'Will you answer the questions?' asked Manly as gently as he could.

How tiny she seemed to me standing there in the witness box.

'I can't,' she finally wailed. I still could not see her face properly as she sobbed and sobbed. Her fragile body convulsed as she pitifully cried. 'Oh, I *can't*.' The black shawl slid down her back.

Manly wrote something in his notebook, looked at the girl, rubbed it out, and wrote at much greater length. When he had finished, he slowly put down his pencil but did not look back at the girl.

'Take her down,' he said without a trace of emotion.

Richard Kingsley smiled a little as the star prosecution witness was led to the Old Bailey cells.

Chapter 9

Pathologists are curious creatures. They saunter into court with just the hint of death in their briefcases and make the dissection of a human body sound little more than the carving of the Sunday joint. I was deeply suspicious of them.

Harry Molesey, however, had given evidence in many of my cases. He was a squat little man, very nearly round in shape. You could barely see his feet move as he bowled his way out of the mortuary and into court. His spectacles were huge, each lens like a glass ashtray, and he always wore the same tatty brown suit fraying at the cuffs. There were jet black tufts on his head which were almost furry, and if he ever washed his hair properly, you would really wonder what sort of things might have come tumbling out.

Harry Molesey encountered death every day, it sent a good stream of interesting work his way, and over the years, I imagine, they had grown rather fond of one another.

'Can we have your qualifications please?' asked Davenport.

The jury had been brought back. They were clearly bemused. Nothing had been said about the missing girl. When Manly ordered the prosecution to proceed, I agreed to have Molesey's evidence out of turn. Harry had an appointment with a dismembered corpse at a quarter past two.

'I am a doctor of medicine. A doctor of pathology.' Molesey looked around the court squinting. He always seemed embarrassed about his achievements. 'And ... umm ... I'm a Fellow

of the Royal College of Pathologists.' He blurted out the last
few words hoping, no doubt, no one would notice.

'Where do you work?' asked Davenport.

'I am attached to the Home Office Forensic Science Laboratory. I am also consultant to the Devon and Dorset police,
and have twenty-four years' experience as a pathologist.'

'Did you conduct a post-mortem on the deceased Molly
Summers?'

Molesey did not answer. He picked up his scruffy tan
briefcase and rested it on the edge of the witness box. The
locks made an oddly hollow sound as they clicked open.
Harry's head momentarily disappeared while he rummaged
inside the bag, then he surfaced clutching an untidy pile of
yellowing notes.

'I was requested by Her Majesty's Coroner to conduct a
post-mortem on one Mary Summers.'

Davenport asked, 'Are these photographs of the deceased?'

He handed a thick green bundle to Norman, who appeared
annoyed at having to leave his Quick Crossword. Molesey
grabbed the bundle with a little dark paw, held the first
photograph right up to his lenses, squinted, moved the
photograph around his face in a small semicircle and sighed.

'Yes,' he said when he finally lowered the photographs.
'This is the deceased.'

'Shall we call that Exhibit One?' asked Manly.

Davenport bowed. 'I'm grateful, M'Lord.'

The judge asked to see the bundle and inspected every
photograph impassively. He asked, 'There are bundles for the
jury, Mr Davenport?'

'M'Lord, yes.'

'Mr Fawley?' asked Manly.

This was the moment I dreaded. There was nothing like
the jury seeing photographs of the body for themselves. In the
bundles, there were pictures of Molly Summers lying twisted
in the stone circle like a broken doll. There were others from
the mortuary, photographs of the young girl on the slab, partly

covered with a green sheet, photographs taken from every conceivable angle. The camera could not pry too closely, there was no part of her that was not violated. Davenport, despite Justine's protests, had actually agreed to remove the most disturbing shots, so the jury were not going to be shown Molly Summers's eyes reflecting the grey sky above Stonebury.

But. from the moment I first saw the bundle, I could not forget any of it, and I constantly saw the girl's dead eyes in my sleep. I had seen them again the previous night after Emma had produced the photographs in Johnson's.

'Do you object, Mr Fawley?' asked Manly.

'No,' I said.

Davenport smiled. 'We'll come to the photographs in a minute, members of the jury. So perhaps you'll be good enough not to look at them just at the moment.'

The jury dutifully obeyed.

'Now Mr – I'm sorry – Doctor Molesey,' he said, 'did you in fact conduct the post-mortem?'

The pathologist reached for his mess of notes, shuffled them about, dropped the bottom sheet, caught it in mid-air and said in his peculiar high-pitched voice, 'Yes.'

'Can you tell us, Doctor – how many wounds did you find?' Davenport was constantly flicking through the thick bundle. It was an old prosecutor's ruse to increase the sense of mystery for the expectant jury.

'I counted, let me see,' said Molesey, quite neutrally, 'yes, I counted ... forty-three.'

There was an ominous murmur from the jury box. I didn't dare look up.

'But it is a little difficult to be precise,' said Molesey.

'Difficult?' asked Davenport feigning surprise. He knew exactly what the problem was: it was spelt out in great detail in the forensic report. 'How can it be *difficult*, Doctor?'

'Some of the wounds are multiple-entry and some of the wounds are so close together that it is difficult to say whether they are truly distinct.'

Davenport turned to the jury. They had got the point. He turned back to Molesey and took him through some of the tedious details about dates, times, places and exhibit numbers. He also revealed how one of the wounds was cut out of the body and sent to the freezer section of the Home Office laboratory.

One of the advantages of defending is that you sit closest to the jury. But it can also be a terrible strain. As Davenport and Molesey crawled through the formalities, I noticed the female juror. Her eyes flitted around the court waiting for an opportunity. She deftly moved the bundle below the front of the jury box and looked. Her expression did not change, but the colour drained from her cheeks. She neatly put the photographs back and folded her arms tightly. Our eyes met. She knew I had seen her.

Davenport was slowly working his way through the wounds, milking the moments for all he could. Eventually he scratched the most pendulous of his chins and pretended to search for an appropriate word.

'Would you describe this attack as ... as frenzied?' he asked.

Molesey put his round nose in the air, as if he were sniffing out a scent. He used his right middle finger to push back his glasses.

'That is a subjective word,' he said. 'It is an opinion. Opinions can be wrong. The facts are never wrong. I prefer those. The fact is I counted forty-three wounds.'

Harry Molesey was completely straight: he had no interest in innocence or guilt. His life was corpses and, as he once told me behind the old Hammersmith Coroners Court, there is a slab awaiting us all.

But Davenport was not satisfied with the doctor's professional caution.

'Let's consider the organs then,' he said excitedly, straining at the leash. 'The liver?'

'Punctured,' said Molesey.

'The kidneys?'

'Punctured.'

'The heart?'

'Well—'

'The heart, Doctor?'

'Punctured.'

'How many times?'

Molesey fingered his notes with his chubby little hands. 'Three times,' he said.

'And let me ask you this, Doctor,' Davenport raised his voice. 'Were there any wounds on the hands?'

'No,' said Molesey immediately.

I knew this was coming. This was the strangest thing of all.

'And using your twenty-four years' experience as a pathologist,' said Davenport, 'that is indicative of what?' Then he added, 'In your professional *opinion*?'

'In my opinion, as you have asked for it,' said Molesey. He hesitated.

The jury were on the edges of their seats; three of them had pencils poised. One of the women covered her eyes.

'In my opinion,' said Harry Molesey quietly, 'Molly Summers did not fight back.'

'What?' demanded Davenport.

There were gasps of astonishment in the public gallery.

'Forty-three wounds and she did not fight back?' said Davenport.

The pathologist did not answer. He realised, as did we all, that it was a comment and not a question.

'She didn't fight back – at all?' asked Davenport again.

'At all,' said Molesey.

All around me people were furiously scribbling this down. Emma marked the passage with a yellow highlighter, then decided it deserved pink as well. Justine glanced at me and her face was completely white.

'Doctor, can we deal with the murder weapon?' Davenport brandished the knife found at Kingsley's home.

I was about to object. I was going to say that the Crown was assuming that which it seeks to prove, or something equally lawyerly. But as I got to my feet, I saw Leonard, the clerk, whispering to Manly.

'I see,' muttered the judge.

When Leonard sat down, he grinned at me knowingly, revealing his tartar-stained teeth. It had to be bad news.

'What's up?' asked Emma, sharpening a blue pencil.

I looked down at her helplessly.

'Gentlemen,' said Manly with a sad resignation in his voice. 'There has been a development.'

The judge closed his eyes, highlighting his long, curly eyelashes, then began to massage his eyeballs with his thumbs. I could hardly breathe.

'Gentlemen,' said Manly, 'the previous witness has decided to give evidence.'

The pathologist was asked to withdraw and the girl was brought in. She looked different.

Chapter 10

'You see, all I want you to do is to tell the truth,' said
Davenport.

The girl eyed him suspiciously. She was clearly a stranger
to human affection.

'Do you understand what I've said?' asked Davenport with
a foolish smile.

It was her face that had changed. For the features had
suddenly aged as though the fret of two weary decades had
been visited upon her in one morning.

'Did you speak to Molly Summers on the night of her
death?' asked Davenport. He must have known that he had
just one more opportunity with this witness and he was
a soggy bag of nerves: every pore of his body seemed to
perspire, his hands shook, even his moustache appeared to
wilt. I did notice however that for some reason he skated over
any facts about the home. Was it incompetence or was there
another explanation?

'Did you see Molly the night,' he said, wiping away some
sweat, 'the night she died?'

The girl began to drum her fingers on the rim of the witness
box and in the silence of the courtroom, I could hear every
finger land.

'So did you see her?' asked Davenport.

Without looking up, the girl nodded slowly.

Aubrey Davenport was elated. 'I'm sorry, madam – er, miss,

but for the court record, you see. Can you say yes or no? We can't hear a nod.'

It appeared to require much effort for the girl to raise her eyeballs from the bags under her eyes, and when she did, her gaze pierced Davenport's bulk as a scalpel would cut through lard.

'Yes, I see her,' she whispered.

Leading counsel for the prosecution spent the next five minutes trying to establish the whys and whens, failing miserably to do anything other than provoke an occasional sniff from the girl and a sigh of despair from Justine.

I noticed for the first time the tattoo on the back of the girl's hand.

After a few more abortive questions, Davenport's resolve had disappeared and he was about to sit down when Justine prodded him with her gold-plated fountain pen.

Davenport duly tossed out a forlorn query, his face buried in his notebook. 'Did you go to the stone circle?'

The witness put one hand on top of the other, then she swapped them around. I noticed that in doing so she concealed the tattoo.

'I was at the stones,' she said. There was a curious expression at the corners of her mouth. It could have been a smile. 'I like them stones,' she added.

Davenport dropped the counsel's notebook from his right hand, knocking over a glass of water which Justine urgently mopped up. Here was Davenport's opportunity. 'Did you see anything unusual at the stones?'

'How you means unusual?'

'Well, out of the ordinary?'

No response.

'Abnormal?'

Still silence.

'Exceptional? Memorable? Bizarre? Um … peculiar?' Davenport ran out of adjectives.

The girl began to drum the rim of the witness box again,

but more slowly, and I could see that she had virtually no fingernails, and the tips of her fingers were sore, and the areas of flesh underneath the little pieces of bitten nail were bloodshot.

Davenport was exasperated and took a stride along counsel's row towards her. 'Was anyone sitting down?'

'I must *object*,' I shouted, surprising myself with the vehemence of my words, but this was a scandalous question. 'M'Lord, this is the worst type of leading question.'

Davenport ignored me, edged a little closer to the girl, trying to hold her in his stare. 'Is that what you saw?' he asked.

'M'Lord, really,' I protested.

'Is that it?' said Davenport.

'Mr Davenport,' said Manly, 'I forbid you—'

'Tell us,' pleaded Davenport.

'Sit *down*.' Manly was furious. 'You will sit down *now*.'

Aubrey Davenport slumped to his seat with a desperate sigh.

Manly turned to me and in a calmer voice said, 'I understand that you have an objection, Mr Fawley.'

'M'Lord, yes,' I said, pulling my gown over my shoulders. 'Mr Davenport is well aware of the rules against leading questions. I only ask that—' I couldn't finish. I was interrupted by a tremulous voice from the witness box.

'I didn't sees it at first,' said the girl. 'But after I was sure.'

I was astonished and felt Davenport pouncing to his feet at my side. Even Norman looked up from his crossword.

'What did you say?' asked Davenport.

'I didn't sees it at first.'

'You've already told us that. What didn't you sees – I mean, see – at first?'

'That thing.'

'What thing?'

'The what-you-call-it.'

'I don't know,' said Davenport. He was admirably patient here. 'You will have to tell us what *you* call it.'

The girl sniffed so deeply that I felt sure that her lungs would explode. She wiped her nose twice with the back of her hand. She said, 'The wheelchair.'

At this, there was urgent mumbling in the public gallery, notes scrawled down in the well of the court; my heart pounded twice before deciding to sink. The only two calm people present were Davenport and the defendant, Richard Kingsley.

Davenport took his time. He must have sensed victory. 'And can you tell us who was in the wheelchair?' he asked.

The girl looked at her feet and I noticed a chaotic pattern faintly visible in her tightly cropped hair.

'It's terribly important, you know,' said Davenport.

The girl eventually looked at Kingsley, but only for a moment, for he stared back with eyes that were now unwavering, blackish and defiant.

'Who was in it?' asked Davenport softly.

The witness looked to the judge and then back to Kingsley.

'Who?' whispered Davenport more softly.

The girl twisted towards Ignatius Manly and opened her eyes plaintively. Her narrow back was now to Kingsley and she breathed deeply with her little shoulders heaving.

Manly avoided eye contact. 'I'm afraid you must answer,' he said.

'But I's said enough,' she said and the anguish in her voice pierced my heart.

'You must answer,' said Manly.

'Why?' she cried.

'Who was in the wheelchair?' asked Davenport. 'Who?'

'You must answer,' said Manly.

'No,' cried the girl. 'No more. Please, no more.'

'Are you frightened?' asked Davenport. 'Of someone in this court?'

While she looked at her feet, the girl's head moved up and down.

Chapter 11

'We're not going to push her,' said Davenport as he puffed away greedily at one of his toxic little cigarettes below a 'No Smoking' sign in the corridor outside Court 8.

Manly had adjourned for five minutes. I wanted to talk to Justine, who stood by Davenport's side. I wanted to invite her out to an Italian restaurant. But my mind was awash with images of the frightened girl: the tattoo, the hair, the coarsely bitten fingernails.

'Fawley, did you hear what I said?' Davenport said. 'We're leaving her evidence there.'

'Just too dangerous,' added a precise voice to my right. 'Too distressing.'

'You do know Doctor Stone?' asked Davenport.

'Er – yes,' I replied.

'Jenny's advising us on what you might call the "psychiatric" aspects of this case.' With that, prosecuting counsel blew a poisonous cloud in my direction.

I had first met Doctor Jennifer Stone about three years earlier when she was prison shrink at Wormwood Scrubs. She sectioned off a client of mine who fervently believed that he was the lost son of God. But in fact he was just a bit bonkers. I imagine that in her time Jenny Stone has seen more messiahs than all the Old Testament prophets combined.

'How's life at the Scrubs?' I tried not to inhale Davenport's smoke.

'I'm at Holloway now,' she snapped. She was one of the

cold, distant people you meet now and then who seem to breeze in from Siberia with a heavy dose of flu and a bad toothache. Her nondescript hair was tightly pinned back, her jacket buttoned right up to the neck, and her mouth was thin and mean. 'I have advised the prosecution not to press her,' she said. 'The damage could be permanent.' She ran a hand across her forehead, daring a single strand to be out of place. None had such courage.

Then Stone and Davenport put their heads together and whispered among themselves. The rotund silk licked his lips. I noticed how dangerously close his tongue was to the psychiatrist's unpierced earlobes. I used it as an opportunity to speak to Justine.

'You don't agree with their decision?' I asked Justine.

'If Kingsley gets away with this one, who will be next?'

'I can't say that I've thought about it,' I replied.

'Well, you should, Tom. You should think about it really hard. But you're a barrister. A professional. Abuse happens to other people's daughters, not your own.'

I did not reply. I allowed a few seconds to pass for the tension to subside. It did not seem the time to invite her out for some pasta.

'So how are you?' I asked, unable to think of anything more profound.

'Just fine, Tom. How's your wife?'

I pretended not to notice the question. 'Thanks for your note,' I said.

'Not here,' Justine whispered, looking around quickly.

'Why not?'

'Not here, Tom. Can't we change the subject?' Justine asked.

I saw that Davenport and Doctor Stone had finished their conversation. As they approached, I asked Justine, 'Who is Alex?'

Justine seemed furious. 'Did Penny tell you?'

'No, she just told me to ask you. So?'

72

'So it's none of your business,' Justine snapped as she stormed back into court.

'Try not to upset my junior, there's a good chap,' Davenport said, putting his arm around my shoulder. He gazed at me through a cancerous fog. 'We won't ask the girl to name your punter. Got the other filly up our sleeve. She'll do the job – after a spot of lunch.' He tried to smile, but conceit took over. 'Just thought you should know.' He left me coughing smoke from my throat.

Doctor Stone and I found ourselves alone together. It was a little embarrassing. As professionals in the same sort of game, we should have had much to discuss. But I could not think of a single thing to say.

Finally, she could suppress her thoughts no longer. 'Whatever happened to that funny little man?'

'Which one?' I asked.

'The one you represented.'

'I'm afraid I've got a lot of those.'

'You know the one. Got a message from—' she pointed to the heavens.

'Oh, you mean Ezekiel.'

'Ezekiel Smith, wasn't it? You know, about as charming as an enema.'

His real name was Edward or Ernest, but he was a bit of a religious freak. I became suspicious when Jenny Stone showed an interest in this client of mine. In fact, ex-client was more accurate. He sacked me. I was briefed to represent him on a nasty affray in Essex, when he got a message. A message from God. 'Sack your barrister and have faith in the Lord.' It had been revealed to Ezekiel that he should defend himself. God told him he was sure to be saved. God, it seems, lied.

'He got two years,' I said. 'What's it to you?'

'When he sacked you, I had to see if he was sane.'

'And?'

'And I thought he was. Came in front of Judge Manly. He said Ezekiel couldn't be completely mad if he sacked Tom Fawley.'

'How very touching.'

'Listen,' she said, tightly folding her arms, 'you're not going to traumatise that girl, are you?'

'Why ever do you say that?'

'Because I know your reputation. When you get blood in your nostrils, you're like a dog after a rabbit.'

'I'm after bigger game, Doctor Stone.'

'You know, I've always wondered about you.'

'What?'

'Whether you could possibly be as neurotic as you seem. I'd love to examine you. You see, I'm doing a paper on anal fixation and the criminal Bar and—'

Just then, Norman announced that we all had two minutes to resume our seats.

I headed towards Court 8. 'Fascinating as it has been, Doctor Stone, I'm afraid my bottom is required in court.'

'Don't traumatise that girl,' she ordered.

'I'll do my best.'

'That is precisely what I'm afraid of.'

When she had joined the rest of the prosecution team in court, I realised that all around me were groups in animated discussion, arguing about Kingsley's prospects, debating how I would attack the girl in cross-examination.

People think that you plan such things months in advance. Often that is not true. You've read the papers, you know the facts, but you haven't a clue where to begin. At such times, I wished I worked in a bank, or had become an accountant, or even wrote tales of titillation like Kingsley. I used to wish I was anything but counsel for the defence. You feel all eyes upon you – waiting.

There was only one thing to do. I headed for the toilet.

I was sure that the police had convinced the second girl to

testify and that she was bound to be a far stronger witness, prepared, no doubt, to name Kingsley. But when I reached the lavatory doors, there was a violent tug at my gown and a jab to the kidneys with a well-practised elbow.

'You've got to do it.' I recognised Emma's voice without turning around. 'I know what you're thinking, Tom. But you've got to do it.'

My head was beginning to ache. 'Give me a break,' I said.

'Do you want to win this case? Or are you going to throw in the towel?' Emma adopted one of her attitudes which seemed to say, Listen – this is your conscience speaking. 'There is no option. You've got to do it, Tom.'

One of the newspaper reporters pushed past us with a bladder full of extra-strong lager. For a second I glimpsed the sanctuary of the cubicle doors, and could hear Davenport whistling *Nessun Dorma*.

'Tom,' shouted Emma, firmly blocking my way and prodding me in the solar plexus.

'Look, there is no way in heaven or earth that I'm going to cross-examine that girl,' I said. 'And I don't care how many times you violate my body.' I could see Emma fuming silently, so I added feebly, 'Anyway, the girl hasn't actually named anyone yet.'

'Bullshit.'

I knew Emma was right. She grabbed the corner of my gown and led me along the corridor, past astonished onlookers, and into the conference room near to the court.

I groped for the light switch.

'Leave it off,' she said.

'Emma, let me explain why—'

'Just listen,' she said. 'The girl's scared out of her wits. Right? But she's mentioned the wheelchair. The police have the knife and they've got Kingsley's confession. We can't get round it. You've simply got to destroy her, Tom. The jury's ready to lynch Kingsley.'

'Well, you tell me then. You're so full of bright ideas. What do I say? Sorry, love. You're mistaken. You didn't see your friend brutally hacked to death.'

'Don't be ridiculous,' she said.

My temples throbbed.

'There's only one thing for it,' she decided, after pondering a while. 'Put in her form.'

I could hardly speak. The jury had a lot of sympathy for the ordeal the girl had been put through; harassing her about her previous convictions would make matters worse.

'You've got to dent her credibility,' said Emma.

'The jury will think I'm picking on her.'

'Her record is our best weapon.'

'It's sheer lunacy.'

'Got a better idea?'

'Yes,' I said. 'Plead guilty.'

'No chance. It's too late now. The Crown won't buy manslaughter. Not now. Why should they? They can get Kingsley on the lot.'

She was right.

'All we can do, Tom, is to go on the attack. What was it you once told me? Attack being the best form of—'

'It'll add five years to the sentence.' I knew Manly would take it into account when recommending the minimum term of detention.

'It might get Kingsley off.'

'Do you *really* believe that?' I asked.

Emma paused. Her silhouette seemed hardly to move but her words were highly charged. 'Look. I really believe we've got to do what we can. If you leave it, Tom, he'll definitely go down. We've got to try.'

I wondered just how far I could push the girl.

Chapter 12

The court bristled with excitement. The jurors sat in their box muttering in pairs. The shorthand writer was wrapped in debate with Leonard, the clerk. Only Norman seemed unmoved. He sucked on a clear plastic biro, toying with the anagram at thirteen down.

Emma barred my route to counsel's row. She had a puzzled expression upon her face. 'Kingsley wants a word,' she said, gesturing towards the dock.

One of the dock officers opened the door. The other continued to examine page three of the *Sun* and pretended not to listen as I entered the dock. Kingsley beckoned me closer still. How low he seemed, slouched in his chair, his right hand clawing at the wheel. His breath was unusually cold on my neck.

'Tear her throat out,' he whispered. His mouth was smiling but his eyes did not move.

I had less success than Davenport. The girl did not answer my questions and I could establish virtually nothing about her friends or her links with Stonebury. Whenever she was cornered, she feigned confusion.

'You say you saw a wheelchair?' The girl stared back at me with narrowing green eyes. I took that as a 'yes'.

She fidgeted a little, her hands at her sides.

'Well, what sort of wheelchair was it?'

Again, she didn't answer.

'What sort?'

'The sort what's got wheels,' she said.

Two of the tabloid hacks to my right sniggered audibly and scribbled away. The exchange would make good copy – maybe even the basis for a cartoon.

'I'm suggesting you're wrong about what you saw.'

'I know what I sees.'

'Don't you mean, you *think* you know?'

I could hear disapproving tuts from the jury box. The witness was baffled and turned to the judge. It was far from my most elegant question.

'What are you driving at, Mr Fawley?' asked Manly. He tapped his red pencil impatiently.

I looked at him and then at the girl and I knew I had to press on. 'Does Your Lordship have a copy of the 609?'

Emma pulled at my gown. 'Leave it, Tom. Let's forget it. You'll wind up the jury.'

I chose to ignore her. It was too late.

Justine handed a pair of stapled white sheets to Norman. He passed them to Leonard who handed them to the judge.

Manly frowned profoundly.

'Are you an honest person?' I asked the girl.

'Mr Fawley, I have to warn you,' scowled Manly. The jury was intrigued. 'You understand the consequences of such a question?'

I understood the consequences of very little that I did in those days, but this was a legal matter. 'I understand perfectly, M'Lord.'

'Well, you have been warned,' he said.

'So it appears,' I replied, knowing that Manly was threatening to allow the prosecution to cross-examine Kingsley about his convictions.

Emma tugged somewhat harder. 'Can't you leave it, Tom?'

'Did you hear my question?' I said to the girl. 'Are you an honest person?'

The witness sniffed a little artificially and spotted a reply. 'Honest like how?'

'Either you are honest or dishonest, aren't you?'

'Honest then.'

That was the reply I wanted. An elderly juror wearing a scarf from Fortnum and Mason smiled at the girl.

I asked, 'And when you shoplifted a skirt from M and S, was that honest or dishonest?'

She did not reply. The juror still smiled at her, though not quite as much. I could see what she was thinking – I would have probably thought the same – spot of youthful crime, nothing too bad, what was the harm?

I continued, 'And when you committed burglary were you honest then, too?'

The girl liked this even less. 'Yeah, but I never stole nothin',' she said.

'Remind us. Where were you caught?'

'I never nicked nothin'.'

'Where were you caught?'

'Er ... can't remember. Too long ago.'

'Let's see if I can jog your memory.'

'Well you can't.'

'Let's try, shall we?' I looked quite deliberately at the elderly juror. 'Didn't you burgle an old people's home?'

'I denied it.'

'But you were convicted. You don't disagree with that?'

The girl was clearly annoyed. So, too, was the elderly juror, but I felt that her anger was no longer directed at me.

'Do you have any other convictions?'

'Can't remember.'

'Well, is that because you have too many convictions or too little memory?' That was one of my favourite lines.

'You tell me.'

'What were you doing in January last year?'

'I can't think that far back.'

The atmosphere was beginning to change in court, shifting slowly, almost imperceptibly, like the sands along a beach.

I paused until the girl was forced to look at me. 'Weren't you in Stonebury on the night of 10th January?'

'Dunno.' She gave a careless wave of her hand.

'Well, I do. You visited some friends of yours.'

'They were still in the home.'

'Oh, yes,' I said. 'The home. West Albion. Do you smoke?'

Manly, who had been watching this exchange with mounting irritation, asked, 'What possible relevance can that have, Mr Fawley?'

'I'll let the witness answer that,' I replied impertinently, 'if Your Lordship pleases.'

He huffed, but let me continue.

'So do you smoke?'

'No.'

'Where did you get the matches then?'

The girl was beside herself. 'I never dun that. I never dun it.'

'Done what? Perhaps you'd care to tell us – if you can remember that far back.'

'What they said was lies,' she protested.

'You were convicted of setting fire to the home. Was that another mistake?'

'I was innocent.'

'But you confessed to the police.'

'They fitted me up.'

'And you pleaded guilty?'

'My brief made me do that.'

'Well, you must be the unluckiest young lady in the West Country.'

'Mr Fawley,' said Manly, 'please don't comment.'

'Poor you,' I continued. 'You were caught with some matches when you don't even smoke, the police say you confessed when you didn't say a word? You were forced to plead guilty when you really were innocent? Come, come. That's not the truth.'

'I hated that home. Molly did, too,' blurted out the girl. 'They used to make us—'

'I'm not concerned with that,' I tried to interrupt.

'They beat us and put us in—'

'Please. We're not interested.'

'They put us in that room,' she cried. She turned to the judge. 'Don't let them put me back in the Hole. I'll tell you what you want.'

I had to try to stem the flow of such damaging information. I appealed to Manly.

'I'm afraid you rather opened the door of the West Albion, Mr Fawley.' The judge clearly enjoyed my discomfort.

Emma had her arms tightly folded and looked at the floor. No notes, no help, just stern disapproval. I could now see why no one wanted to grapple with the issue of the home. It cut both ways and was extremely dangerous.

'Let me move on to ... another topic,' I said. No one was fooled – I couldn't even fool myself. I was losing the battle.

'Mr Fawley, have you finished with this witness?' Manly wanted to press on. 'Or do you want to know anything else about her childhood?' He flourished his pencil in a taunting fashion.

At first I did not realise what I had found. My hands nervously fingered the papers in front of me, and I toyed with a sheet somewhere near the top. It was crisply folded and quite neatly typed.

Manly asked Davenport if he wished to re-examine. Davenport declined.

'You're free to leave, young lady,' said Manly.

Doctor Jennifer Stone tightened her belt and started to usher the young girl from the court with that cold compassion that used to be shown by workhouse governesses. Norman rose reluctantly and looked at Davenport to see who the next witness would be. Davenport conferred with Justine and they agreed on the second girl, the other 'filly' as he had called her. And all the time I was looking at the sheet of paper and thinking, what can it mean? I had not read the whole brief properly as Emma had urged me to do. So when I looked at the sheet, I could not truly say whether the note had been there all the time or whether it was new.

The Past is a River of Many Streams

The court door was opened and the first girl slipped out. Jenny Stone cast a venomous glance in my direction, tightened her belt still further, and also departed.

When I looked back at Kingsley, I realised that I was still on my feet. He seemed – as did everyone – miles and miles away from me. A vast distance below me, Emma refused to look up.

There comes a time in any trial when all is at stake. The balance is perfect. At such times, do you have a choice? Or is it all ordained? I instinctively felt that the note had a bearing on the truth of the case. But if I had been asked at that precise moment what that was, I could not have said.

'M'Lord,' I said, 'I have not finished my cross-examination of the last witness.'

Emma was speechless. She gawped at me, her mouth wide enough to accommodate a sheaf of her notes.

'Do I understand that you want the young lady recalled?' The colour seeped out of Manly's face. 'Do you object, Mr Davenport?'

The prosecutor saluted his good fortune, smirked and shook his head. The girl was hauled back, her screams of protest pouring into the well of the court and then rushing round and round. When I saw her, she was disorientated, her head flicked from one corner of the ceiling to the other.

Jennifer Stone glared at me, no doubt trying to think of an appropriate psychiatric disorder for my behaviour.

The sheet of paper in my hand was not the product of a word processor. It had been typed on an old-fashioned typewriter. The underside was bumpy. The content was meaningless.

I read the note again.

The Past is a River of Many Streams

One night I had heard similar things. At least, I thought I had.

Chapter 13

The first thing I ever learnt about advocacy was from the novel, *To Kill a Mockingbird*. A lawyer in the Deep South was defending a black man on a rape charge. The attorney's child said, 'Never ask a question unless you know the answer.' It is sound advice, but there are two exceptions. Ask what you like if you want to know the truth. And ask about anything if you don't really care.

As I looked at the girl trembling again in the witness box, it became very clear to me that I didn't give a damn.

'You know exactly what happened,' I said to her.

She did not answer me. Her nail-bitten fingers danced along the witness box.

'Don't you?' I said under my breath so she could barely hear. It forced her to look up and strain to hear. 'Don't you?' I shouted.

My right hand moved up the edge of the sheet. 'Look at this,' I said as she stared back at me defiantly. 'If you wouldn't mind.'

Norman petulantly stamped across the court to deliver the sheet so noisily that I was able to ask Emma where the note came from. She didn't know. I half looked at Kingsley when I heard the rustle of paper in the witness box. He lightly fingered his neck.

'Now, tell us,' I said. 'What does it mean?'

The girl dropped her head vacantly, like a fast-wilting bloom. She waved the note and turned it over and over.

'Well, what does it mean?'

Emma hissed urgently to me. 'Tom, just leave it. Leave it there.'

'Have you got something to hide?'

The girl became whiter. The spot of blood on her nose stood out strangely.

'I'm going to ask you for one last—'

Manly intervened. 'Can you read? Young lady, are you able to read?'

She shook her head.

Manly turned sharply towards Norman. 'Give me that,' he growled. The judge read the note and jotted something down. 'Do I understand you want to put *this* to the witness, Mr Fawley?'

'No,' whispered Emma.

'Yes, M'Lord,' I said.

'Very well.' Manly turned towards the box. 'Young lady, I'm going to read this note to you, do you understand?'

She seemed completely empty.

Manly cleared his throat and then did so again. He held the sheet of paper in front of his face and read slowly and clearly.

'The past is a river—' He broke off and looked at the witness. She was gazing at the ceiling, her eyes quite pale. He continued, 'A river of many streams ... do you recognise that?'

She said nothing. Her mouth was open, and I could see that half her teeth were rotten little stubs. But still she said nothing.

Manly put down the paper and addressed me. 'I really think that is as far as we can go.'

I was about to agree with the judge when the girl began to speak, and her voice was different, somehow older.

'When I met Molly we went to the woods,' she said. The strip lighting played on her horizontal face. 'I says to Moll, we're sure to get caught. I'd never done it ... not like that before.'

I didn't know whether to get to my feet. Emma decided the issue by holding me down firmly by the wrist.

'It's so cold,' said the girl, reaching for the shawl that was no longer there. She wrapped her frail arms desperately around her chest. 'The grass was so wet. There was twigs and acorns. On the ground, like. But Molly says, I will if you will.' She looked at the judge and her eyes bulged with fear. 'It was *her* idea. I swears it. She told me to do it.'

I could contain myself no longer. 'She told you to do what?' Emma still held my sleeve so my shoulders sloped ludicrously.

'She told me to take—'

'Yes?'

'To take off our – well, you knows.'

I thought I did, and at that moment I imagined that I could actually feel the strange texture of muslin. 'Was it just the two of you?' I asked.

'At first it was.'

'And then?'

'Then there was more.'

And now I knew I must press on. 'Who else was there?'

'Jesus, Tom,' called up Emma.

I repeated more slowly, 'Who else was there?'

The girl looked at the public gallery.

'Who?' I asked.

'I'm a good girl. I never meant no harm to no one.' She wiped her nose violently. 'They said they'd pay us if we did it.'

'Who else was there?' I asked.

'When I met Molly, we went to the woods and—'

'Who else?'

'They didn't give us no money. They's just took Molly.'

The strip light above her flickered and one bulb fizzled out.

I said, 'We must know – who else was there?' I blinked hard and wondered whether what I saw was a trick of the light.

The noise the girl made started as a word and ended in the type of howl you hear when you want to wake up but cannot. 'No ... No-ooh,' she screamed again and again.

There was now blood seeping from one of her nostrils.

'*Lies*,' shouted Kingsley from the bowels of the court. 'Lies, it's all lies.'

The girl was convulsing and that momentarily checked the sound. As Jenny Stone approached her, she lashed out again and again as though a bird of prey were swooping from the ceiling and tearing at her face.

'No, Molly,' screamed the girl. 'Don't do it to me, Moll.'

The lights were flickering more violently now.

'Please, Molly. Leave me alone.' She tried to shield her face and then she imagined she was attacked from another direction.

The faltering light in court was in perfect contrast to the steady darkness that emanated from the wretched girl.

Chapter 14

Manly summoned us all to his room. It was now approaching the end of the afternoon. When we finally settled down, there was an awkward silence. Emma sat next to me, Justine was behind Davenport, and the judge rocked back and forth in his red leather chair.

'What news of the girl, Mr Davenport?' he asked, rummaging around in his desk, trying not to seem overly concerned.

The shorthand writer began to type away.

Davenport replied, 'It's too early to say, Judge. The bleeding has stopped. The prognosis is good.'

I gazed at the well-worn carpet which was deep scarlet and only reminded me of one thing. I waited to be blamed.

'Please feel free to smoke, gentlemen,' said Manly. 'That includes you, Miss Wright,' he said to Justine.

Davenport vainly searched for a packet in his amorphous rolls of flab and accepted a suspiciously small cigar from Justine.

'Ashtray?' Manly slid a foil dish across the desk in Davenport's direction. 'You're ready to go ahead with the other girl, I suppose?'

'Well, now you mention it, Judge—'

'Problem?'

'Not exactly what I would call a problem,' said Davenport. 'Then what would you call it? She is willing to testify?'

Davenport took a little time, scratched one of his chins

and chose his words with care. 'I have not been told any different.'

'Good,' said Manly. 'We'll crack on then.'

'I wonder if—' Davenport said. 'You see, she seems to have ... well, sort of disappeared.'

Manly stopped rocking. 'Well, you'll just have to sort of find her.'

Manly watched Davenport's head wobble, and turned to the stenographer who was still trying to catch up. 'Perhaps you'd like to leave us,' he said.

Without an official record, I knew there would be some straight talking. It was by no means unusual for reluctant witnesses to remove themselves from court and go to ground for the duration of a trial. The real question was, why had it happened here? But before I could think it through, Manly had begun to speak. He had already started to slip into his drawl.

'What sort of case have you got here, Aubrey? One witness disappears and little Miss Muffett starts talking in tongues?'

'I admit, Judge, there have been some ... problems. But we—'

'Cut the bull, Aubrey. We're in the bloody twilight zone.'

Davenport stubbed out his cigar, spreading cakes of ash all over the judge's desk-top. He blushed as he frantically tried to scoop it up.

'Forget about that,' said Manly. 'Tell me, where is your case?'

Davenport's left eye sneaked towards Justine. She whispered something to him which I could not hear.

'We've still got the confession,' he said. 'And then—'

'It's in breach of virtually every provision of the interview rules. No doubt Mr Fawley specifically went to the library to arm himself with a wealth of authorities to demonstrate that. Is that right, Tom?'

I peered at Manly and thought that perhaps my flight to the library was not in vain.

'If,' continued Manly, 'the defence applies to exclude the confession, I shall find such an argument hard to resist.'

Davenport was always a little slow under pressure. 'You'll throw it out?'

'No, Aubrey. I'll toss off my wig and gown and do a tap-dance routine on the Bench. Of course I'll throw it out,' Manly said, rapping his knuckles on the desk.

Justine prodded Davenport, her svelte fingers disappearing into his mounds of flesh.

He said, 'We've also got ... er ... the knife.'

'No,' replied Manly, clearly irritable now, 'you've got *a* knife. And it's probably the wrong knife. I understand it's got no forensic link to the defendant. Correct, Tom?'

I kept gazing at Manly and tried to effect a smile.

He said, 'I want all you learned people here half an hour early tomorrow.'

We dutifully agreed and began shuffling out of the door. Manly again began to rock in his chair.

'Oh, Aubrey,' he said in a sing-song voice, 'no witness, no case.'

'I'm sorry, Judge?'

'Now don't go dumb on me, Aubrey.' Ignatius Manly gazed longingly at the fishing boats in the painting above his head. And I thought I noticed a certain sadness in his eyes, as though that was the place he really longed to be. But he continued, 'No witness, no case. Savvy?'

Probably for the first time in his obtuse legal career, Aubrey Davenport savvied.

Chapter 15

That evening, I sat alone in a window seat in Johnson's near to the quote of the old doctor. I thought about the girl who had disappeared but did not understand. What could she be afraid of? I stared out of the window and into the darkness and imagined I heard a wailing in the distance. Then with flashing lights an ambulance swept past.

The voice that intruded upon these thoughts was like a clenched fist. 'What you need is a dram of malt. And gimme none of that Irish muck.'

Jamie Armstrong delighted in exaggerating his gentle Borders brogue when he was drunk. He used then to pretend that he was Glaswegian, but he could never really do the accent. He raised his voice and moved very close to my face. Jamie had a habit of doing that, especially when he was inebriated. I could smell the whisky on his breath, which was sweet.

'Listen, Jamie. I've got to go.'

'You still got half a bottle.'

'Like a glass?' I asked. It was a silly question. In his day, Jamie was the best advocate I had seen. A natural. But it all went wrong. Too much whisky, too little work, and before any of us knew it, Jamie was an outcast. He was an object of ridicule, untouchable, unclean, screaming his head off in the legal wilderness outside the Temple like a lost prophet.

'You know, you shouldn't drink on your own, Tommie,' he said mockingly.

After the Sarah Morrow suicide, I affected an interest in wines and started to go to tastings in the City. Usually I went alone. I would have gone with Justine, but by then she was ill. I never spat out the wine. I never knew how and, anyway, I didn't want to learn. Soon I quite enjoyed drinking alone. I deceived myself into thinking that it showed character, proved my independence, and all the time I knew I needed it more and more.

Jamie didn't bother to get a clean glass from the bar. He picked up an abandoned champagne flute from the next table and poured the dregs on to the floor. After he had vaguely attempted to wipe off the lipstick around the rim, he helped himself to my white Burgundy.

'Cheers,' I said.

'Up yours.' He didn't even bother to look at me. He gulped down the wine, wincing all the while, coughed once and said, 'Right. Now for some real booze.'

'I can't,' I told him. 'I was late for Manly's court this morning. So I can't get drunk again.'

'You're already drunk, Tommie. Pass the bottle.' He again wolfed down the wine in one mouthful. 'You've forgotten Armstrong's First Law,' he said.

In fact, I hadn't forgotten it. Every alcohol-induced piece of philosophising that emerged from Jamie's lips became Armstrong's First Law. There were hundreds of them.

'Remind me,' I said.

'To cross-examine is to examine crossly.'

'Crossly?'

'With a hangover.'

'Why?' I asked.

'Makes you aggressive. Short. To the point. And you can't have dinky little butterflies when your head's splitting apart.'

That was the winning argument. Pretty soon, we stood in the entrance and tried to hail a cab.

I looked up at the sign above the door. 'What do you think old Samuel Johnson meant?' I asked Jamie, pointing at the quote.

'It's obvious,' he replied.

'Not to me. I'll find you an argument but not an understanding? What was he trying to—'

'Look, some bugger gets in trouble. We defend him. But we don't need to like the bugger.'

'I still don't—'

'Get them out of the dock, Tommie. But don't jump into bed with 'em after.'

I tried to hail another taxi to take us to Soho, but Jamie pulled my arm down. We both fell into a lamppost. Jamie was a big man, much taller than me. So when he grabbed me by my lapels, he practically lifted me off my feet.

'I've got a wee place for you t'see,' he said as he led me back through the night towards the Old Bailey.

We headed towards the river, which flowed silently and was little more than a dark cord through the centre of the city. Then after we had walked through the back streets of Blackfriars, we entered a cobbled alley.

'There she is,' said Jamie. 'You beauty.' He smiled as if he was intensely proud of what he saw.

There was a building with empty warehouses on each side. Above the door was a neon sign which didn't work. Through the gloom I could just make out the words, Il Paradiso.

'Has the best malt whisky south of Berwick,' boasted Jamie.

It was extremely odd. I had lived almost forty years in London, had worked for fifteen years in that small part of the city and I had never been down that road. In fact, it was somewhere between Back Bridge Street and Butter Lane, but you would never have known it existed.

'Where are we going?' I asked.

Jamie looked up and down the alley suspiciously. 'Beyond your wildest dreams,' he said.

* * *

93

'Used to be a wine bar during the eighties,' said Jamie as he led me down some spiral steps made of cast iron. 'Full of obnoxious yuppies. Served fancy Italian wines.'

Probably designer-label Super-Tuscans, I thought. I had come to learn a little about wines.

'Went bust, thank Christ,' he said.

'Why are we here?' I asked.

'Best malt—'

'Yes, I know. South of Berwick.'

'And I regard it as my sacred duty to complete your education, young Thomas.'

'Bit late tonight, Jamie?' said the barman. He was red-faced, had a shock of ginger hair and rejoiced in the name of Donald. A couple of his front teeth were missing, which made it sound as if he were whistling the words without a tune.

'Damn work,' said Jamie, at which the barman laughed.

'Two fingers or three?' asked Donald. He held up a dark green bottle of malt whisky.

'Better make it four,' said Jamie.

'Bad day?' asked Donald.

'Bloody awful,' Jamie replied.

I had been standing rather foolishly at Jamie's side, but when he had ordered the drinks, he led me to a table in the corner of the dark room.

Jamie put his hand on my arm and I could see the dirt under his nails. He said, 'This, my dear Thomas, is to the Bailey what Sodom was to Gomorrah.'

I tried to gauge the atmosphere of the place. But there was none. It was a void: dark emptiness and incessant heat. The tables wobbled, the jukebox was broken, and the glasses were dirty.

'Of course, this place doesn't exist,' he said.

'I need your help, Jamie.' I was worried about what to do if the second girl reappeared overnight.

'Doesn't exist officially.' Jamie ignored me and continued sipping his malt while staring straight ahead. 'Got raided last year. Some hot-shot young broom in the City of London police. Donald just laughed when he saw the warrant – ex-Drugs Squad is Donald – and pointed downstairs. Flying Squad boys were furious. Ruined their poker game. Sent the City plods packing, shiny uniforms and all.'

'Will you help me?' I asked.

'On this dog's-dinner of a murder you're doing?'

'I don't know what to do if they drag the key witness to court. I'm a bit lost.'

'First principles, Tommy.'

'The alibi?'

He made an enormous, disapproving grunt. 'No, first principles,' he said and looked at me with profound disappointment and his eyes seemed to say, Did I teach you nothing? After another sip, he asked, 'Who really knows if Kingsley did it?'

'Local police?'

'Yokels and sheep-shaggers. They know bugger all.'

'The Crown Prosecution Service?'

'Jesus,' he said, waiting for the whisky to bite. 'You, Tommy. You're the one. You tell me. Did he do it?'

'I don't know.'

'Bull.'

'I really don't.'

'But what do you *think*?'

It was the first time I had really faced up to it. 'I think ... I think he did it.' When I glanced at Jamie, his eyes were red and his hands shook. 'But I'm not sure.'

'There you are,' he said. 'There's your doubt. The only man who knows – really knows – if the punter is guilty, is his lawyer. And you don't know. Armstrong's First Law: If you can't be sure, how can the jury? Hammer away at the standard of proof.'

'You make it sound so easy.'

'It is easy. It's the drinking that's the hard part.'

I paused. As Jamie cleaned his fingernails with the end of a beermat, I swallowed a large mouthful of whisky.

'Look,' said Jamie. 'The prosecution case is white and the defence case is black, all right? And the truth, Tommy, the truth – thank Christ – gets lost in the grey fog between. I know, it's a crap system. But it's the only one we've got.'

After that neither of us much wanted to talk. I tried not to look at him as he guzzled his whisky. For I feared that I was becoming more like Jamie Armstrong. And I wondered whether in years to come I would bring a younger man to that place and would tell him how it was with a bottle of malt.

Then I heard a clipped voice, bristling with irony. 'Well, if it isn't Tweedledum and Tweedledee,' it said.

When I screwed up my eyes, I could just make out the features of Inspector Stanley Payne. He was the officer charged with putting Kingsley behind bars for life.

'I never thought you had it in you, Mr Fawley,' he said. I nodded in his direction, feeling terribly embarrassed, like a child caught red-handed pinching the custard creams. 'Of course,' said Payne, 'it's nice to see you in here again, Mr Armstrong.'

Jamie looked up at him with contempt. 'Why don't you crawl off and catch some real criminals?'

'Oh, but we've got one already, Mr Armstrong. Haven't you heard? Oh, yes. We got ourselves a real bad 'un this time, haven't we, Mr Fawley?'

I didn't reply.

'Things look a little grim for poor old Kingsley,' Payne said, 'now that we've found the second girl.'

I didn't know what to say.

Payne carefully took off his long leather gloves, pulling at one finger at a time. He was a very pale man, viperous almost. The veins stuck out on his neck as he spoke and his skin had a strangely luminous quality.

'What's the defence then, Mr Fawley? Wheelchair was punctured, was it?'

'Don't speak to him,' said Jamie.

By then, however, I was lost somewhere between inebriation and unconsciousness. 'Alibi,' I said.

Payne was delighted. 'Come, come, sir,' he said. 'A man of your' – he looked me up and down and smiled when he saw the wet yellow stain on my shirt and the drunkenness in my eyes – 'a man of your calibre can do better than that.'

'I'm warning you, Payne,' said Jamie. I was frightened of Jamie when he was like that.

'Alibi,' I repeated. 'Philip Templeman. Our alibi.'

'But you can't run alibi, Mr Fawley.'

'Some ... some law against it?' Jamie was rapidly losing both his temper and his power of speech.

Payne tutted to himself. He held his leather gloves in his left hand and stroked them as if he were holding a small kitten.

As Payne hovered in front of me, I asked, 'What's wrong with alibi?' I could make out his face and little else now.

'You got no witness,' he said. 'Gone. Flown the nest. Scarpered.' Then he added in a melodic voice, 'They seek him here, they seek him there, those bobbies seek Templeman everywhere.'

He repeated this refrain twice as his voice slowly receded into the bar. Just before he vanished, he turned and said, 'You see, no one can find your witness and we've suddenly found ours. Strange how things work out. See you in court, sir.'

Jamie and I again sat in silence.

I finally said, 'I don't want this case.'

'What you want,' said Jamie, 'is a swift nightcap. Set you up for tomorrow.'

Chapter 16

As I fought through the crowds at Blackfriars Station on the third day of the trial, I had a bitter taste, like burnt almonds, in my mouth. I hadn't slept well that night. Nor had I expected to. I dreamt that I was falling and falling, but never reached the ground.

Throughout the tube journey I had short stabs of pain behind my eyes. Lurking somewhere just below the surface was something I didn't want to know.

Once I arrived at the Old Bailey, I barged to the front of the queue patiently waiting to enter. A girl in a faded denim jacket protested. It was the young juror.

'Get to the back,' shouted one of the security guards.

'I'm counsel,' I said as arrogantly as I could.

''Fraid everyone's got to be ticked off.' The guard wore his peaked cap at an irritating angle. 'Guvnor's orders.'

'Listen,' I panted. 'I'm late.'

'More than me job's worth.'

'Judge Manly's waiting and—'

'Orders is . . .' He paused and looked at me, digested my words and blushed suddenly. 'You had better go through, sir.'

I didn't bother to robe but dashed straight to Court 8, slipping on the newly polished stone steps. What excuse would I use? I pushed past a solicitor's clerk reading a copy of *Viz*. Suicide at South Kensington? Oh, M'Lord, you wouldn't believe the chaos. I turned the corner past the lifts and was astonished to see a quiet crowd milling outside Court 8. Davenport had his grubby hands on Justine's shoulders, and she didn't seem to mind.

Emma rushed over to me as I put down my briefcase. I said, 'You wouldn't believe the mess at South Ken. Some idiot only goes and jumps under the—'

'Shut up, Tom.' There was sadness in her voice.

'Was Payne lying then?' I asked. 'Have they not found the second girl?'

It didn't seem as if Emma was listening. The shorthand writer staggered out of court supported by Norman who was buckling under the strain. He had his newspaper tucked under his armpit and his much-chewed biro tucked behind his ear. He hadn't started the crossword – something was seriously wrong.

'What's wrong, Emma?' I asked again.

She did not reply.

'What is it, Emma? No witness?'

Her bottom lip quivered slightly. 'No judge,' she said. 'No judge.'

Hilary Hardcastle wore her familiar judicial frown in Court 4 as she muttered something to Leonard. Years before, Leonard had come south at the same time as Hardcastle when she descended from the legal wastelands north of Stockport to dispense justice to us soft southerners. Leonard said that Hardcastle's greatest regret was that she was elevated to the Bench after the abolition of the death penalty. Naturally, Leonard approved.

'Has the jury been brought in and discharged?' asked Hardcastle. That was the usual procedure after the death of the trial judge.

'Yes, M'Lady,' said Davenport. 'Mr Justice Gritt did that when Mr Fawley *finally* arrived.'

'Oh, none of this "M'Lady" palaver, Mr Davenport.' Hilary Hardcastle prided herself on being the salt of the earth, the people's judge, a grammar school in Blackburn and Manchester University, straight-talking, full of bluff northern common sense. 'No,' she said, making her magnanimous concession to the march of democracy, 'just call me "Your Honour" – that will do.'

'Indeed.' Davenport bowed obsequiously.

'So what remains?' she asked.

I got to my feet. It was now approaching lunchtime and the trial was in tatters. 'There still remains the question of bail, Your Honour.'

Hardcastle fixed me with her reptilian eyes. If Hieronymous Bosch had turned his talents to gargoyles, Hilary Hardcastle would have been one of his most treasured creations.

'I wasn't addressing you,' she lashed. 'What about the question of bail, Mr Davenport? The Crown objects ... I assume?'

Hardcastle's court was in that ancient part of the Old Bailey. The courtroom was cramped and uncomfortable, full of dark wood and unnerving memories. It was the set you saw in every Agatha Christie court scene; at any moment you expected Charles Laughton to lurch across the room.

'Mr Davenport?' repeated Hardcastle. 'Where I come from, it is a common courtesy when people are addressing you to—'

'I suppose things have – altered somewhat,' he said. 'And ... taking into account the recent developments—'

'Oh, for goodness sake. Do you oppose bail or not?'

'Possibly,' said Davenport who was all at sea without Justine to prompt him. She was still outside.

The judge huffed mightily and moved her wig towards the space where her eyebrows should have been. 'What do you say, Mr Fawley?' She always pronounced my name, Folly. I never really decided whether it was deliberate or not.

'In my submission, the defendant should be admitted to bail pending the retrial.'

'And when is the retrial to be?'

'In two weeks,' I said. 'Or so the list office says.'

Hilary was unimpressed. 'Hasn't Kingsley been convicted of a number of sexual offences?'

'He pleaded guilty,' I said.

'Perpetrated on young girls?'

'He's spent a year in custody.'

'And he still faces murder?'

'The evidence is weak.'

'And he's confessed?'

'He is presumed innocent, Your Honour.' I tried once more. If Kingsley was granted bail, he might have absconded before the retrial and I would be free of the case. 'This prosecution is very dubious.'

'So is your submission, Mr Folly.' Hardcastle's tongue was her sword and she ensured it did not rust. She lacked the art of conversation but, sadly, not the power of speech.

'My client is a man of good character,' I said.

'*Previous* good character,' she snapped back. Her eyes flared, the lids palpitated.

I was angry at myself for giving her such an easy opportunity to score.

'Bail is refused,' she said.

'But I haven't finished—'

'Yes, you have,' she said with her wig overhanging her face like a jagged rock.

I braced myself for a final assault. 'One witness disappeared yesterday—'

'Sit down, Mr Folly.'

'The other has lost her—'

'You have been warned.'

'The forensics are inconclusive.'

'Bail is *refused*,' she said. There was now little forehead between her wig and her eyes.

Emma got up beside me. 'Your Honour, we are all a little upset.'

'I'm sure we all admired Mr Justice Manly,' the judge said. But Leonard once told me over a pint of northern bitter that

Hardcastle resented a black man, such as Ignatius Manly, being elevated to the High Court Bench ahead of her. His death would do nothing but advance her ambitions. 'Yes, Miss Sharpe, we all admired Judge Manly,' she continued. 'But common decency does not fly out of the window at times such as these.'

'No, Your Honour,' said Emma, trying to elbow me into my seat.

'Thank you, Miss Sharpe.' Hardcastle blinked several times. Her wispy eyelashes were almost invisible. 'Bail is refused.'

From the corner of my eye, I could see Justine talking to Inspector Payne by the back door. 'I wish to be heard,' I said.

'But I do not wish to listen.' Hardcastle enjoyed that.

'This is outrageous,' I said, waving one of Emma's pens melodramatically.

'Not another word from you, Mr Folly.'

'It is disgraceful.'

'Sit down.'

'I haven't had the opportunity to—'

'This is your last warning.'

'I have a right—'

'You'll have the right to be represented by counsel before the conduct committee, if you continue.'

'But I—'

'And stop pointing that pen at me.'

'But *you*,' I said, aiming the nib somewhere between her dilating pupils, 'but you haven't had the courtesy to listen to all my arguments.'

Hardcastle raised her nose and peered down at me coldly. 'You will be reported,' she said.

'I've been in far higher courts than this and my conduct has never been criticised,' I replied.

'Perhaps you weren't impertinent there,' Hardcastle said.

'Perhaps I had no need to be.'

Justine had by then come back into court with Payne. She conferred with Davenport, her eyes red and puffy. He stumbled to his feet holding something that was obscured by his gown.

'Your Honour,' he said, 'this was found in the defendant's cell while he was up here in court.' Davenport passed me a scrunched-up piece of paper with uneven, intense handwriting upon it. He said, 'The words exactly ... duplicate matters that the unfortunate girl was cross-examined upon. Something about the past being a river of many streams.'

'The past being *what*?' Hardcastle did not follow.

But I knew it was the end. Kingsley must have put the typed version of the note in my papers when I had visited him in the cells on the first day.

Davenport continued, 'And this document caused the witness to, as Mr Fawley put it, to lose her ...' His voice trailed off but he had said enough.

Hardcastle licked her colourless lips with a grainy red tongue. 'Bail is refused.'

I sat down wearily and thought of how the sun shone so gently on the mountains in Ignatius Manly's painting.

Chapter 17

That evening, friends and colleagues gathered in the old chambers of Ignatius Manly. Most of the Old Bailey judges were there. Hilary Hardcastle was conspicuously absent.

Swarms of dark-suited barristers stood around the reception and administrative areas on the ground floor. They told their favourite Ignatius Manly stories, each vying with the other to claim the most humiliating put-down suffered at the hands of the judge.

I stood at the back, trying to recall a few lines from Tennyson. Finally, I remembered them: 'For my purpose holds, to sail beyond the sunset and the baths of all the western stars until I die.'

I could not remember the rest of the poem. For in my mind, I saw Mr Justice Manly sitting in one of the gaily painted fishing boats from his painting. And there was Ignatius, tacking serenely towards his Caribbean isle. Then I realised: no one had explained how the 'accident' – as they called it – had really occurred. It was said that he was found at the bottom of the stairs. But how did he get there?

To me it had sounded a little too much like suicide to let the matter rest. But no one would talk, especially not to me. The problem was that judges never died, they merely passed away to that great Appeal Court in the sky. Plaques were put up, scholarships were founded, but no one would ever discuss what really happened. And to suggest suicide? Just the mention of the 's' word would be sufficient to stamp an indelible blight against your name in some dank cavern within the bowels of the Lord Chancellor's Department.

The Liebfraumilch that was served was much the same as it was all those years ago at the party when Manly took silk. But I could barely drink it. I had become a snob.

I stood alone, thinking a little and sulking a lot. I tried to take in the scene. A set of barristers' chambers in the Temple. That miracle of legal London. A dozen rooms, two dozen egos, and the constant cry of, When will I get paid for that buggery in Luton? The rooms were full of old briefs, pink ribbon and disintegrating wigs that smelt like badgers. Was this what I had worked for? Was this what I had aspired to? Suddenly, Manly's Caribbean isle seemed immensely attractive.

After a couple of embarrassing hours, Emma sidled up to me with a bottle of wine. 'Where's your cup, Tom?'

'Lost my thirst,' I said.

'Come on. One for the road and I'll drive you home.'

'You know, Emma, I think I've had it with this game.'

'You're just a bit squiffy,' she said, giving me her plastic cup. The wine was syrupy with warm pieces of cork bobbing in it.

'No, really. I'm sick of it all. The lies, the deceit. The hypocrisy of it all.'

'Don't go all maudlin on me, you old goat.' She put down the suspiciously blue bottle. 'You see, Tom. Some people choose to be barristers. And some people are chosen.' She held my forearm gingerly. Her eyes were clear and I knew she was right. 'And you've been chosen.'

'Don't you ever want to do anything else?' I asked.

We both noticed Hilary Hardcastle making a dramatic late entrance on a pair of dangerously high heels.

'You may have to,' said Emma. 'Unless you apologise to Hilary.'

'She can screw herself.' This was something upon which I had no intention of compromising.

Emma tried to change the subject. 'We never tracked down Kingsley's alibi, after all. I suppose we didn't need him.'

'We might for the retrial. Look, Emma. I can't face talking about the case just now.'

'Then what do you want to talk about?' she asked.

'Where's Justine?'

'I think she went upstairs.'

I gave the cup back to Emma and headed for the barristers' rooms on the upper floors.

Until my seventeenth year I was more interested in cricket and stamp collecting than in those strange creatures called girls. The reason was simple. I went to a Catholic boys' school and was taught a very strange creed. I now know it was all rubbish. But what was a teenage boy with a bad attack of puberty and the Book of Revelations supposed to do?

Mary, I was told, was a virgin. Mary Magdalene was a whore. Some women, it was implied, fell from the former state to the latter, leading unsuspecting boys into temptation as they went. God was white, male and had a son called Jesus who was only technically a Jew until he had the sense to become a Christian like the rest of us. Everybody – with the exception of the Pope and, possibly, Mother Teresa – sinned. But Catholics were the only people with sufficient guts to go to confession and admit it.

Good things in life included incense, celibacy and, if this was impossible, the rhythm method of contraception. Bad things included missing Mass on Sundays, masturbation and the kind of smutty humour practised by Benny Hill. For years, I tried to work out the link between these last three items.

Despite this somewhat unpromising start, something finally clicked. It was in my final year before university. I took a walk to the public library. It was a ramshackle building full of pensioners and tramps, and always smelt of Vapo-rub. When I thought that no one was looking, I took out a book. It was called *The Interpretation of Dreams*.

I had not the slightest interest in the subject, but secreted at the end of the leather volume with the crumbling spine was *On Sexuality* by Sigmund Freud. I read it again and again. Soon there was nothing I did not know about foot fetishes, castration complexes and a rather confused Greek chap called Oedipus.

In the school lunch-hours, I held surgeries in the bicycle sheds and diagnosed my friends as perverts and freaks. Some of these youthful predictions have been subsequently borne out by history. Penny would have been amused if she was told all of this. She always claimed that I didn't find her clitoris for more than a year.

It was, then, with this background that I knocked on the impressive oak door of Justine's second-floor room. My palms sweated and I mentally flicked through the pages of Freud's book, trying to understand my intense feeling of guilt, trying to put out of my mind images of the Madonna, the Magdalene and Benny Hill.

There was no reply from inside Justine's room.

I turned the handle. The door creaked as it opened. The room was in darkness. But sitting on the Regency desk by the French windows, silhouetted by the lights from Temple Hall, was a lonely figure carelessly swinging her feet. She looked so small and vulnerable, I barely dared to speak.

'Is that you, Aubrey?' she said, still looking out of the window.

'It's Tom.'

'Oh.' Justine seemed disappointed. 'Well, thank you for coming.'

Silently I stepped two paces across the deep pile carpet. 'You all right?' By now I was almost at her back. Her blonde hair seemed silver and her shoulders alight.

'He was like a father to me,' she said.

It was the old lie. She must have forgotten what she had told me all those years ago in that very room. The oak door creaked eerily again and closed itself.

'Must get the clerks to oil it,' she continued.

'I don't know if this is the right time,' I said, 'but what really happened to Ignatius? I heard some rubbish about him falling—'

'Down the stairs?' Justine said.

'Did you hear that, too? Come on, Justine. You must know what the truth really . . .'

Justine put her head in her hands.

Then I realised how tactless I had been. I said, 'I am very—'

'Shh.' Her eyes were moist but not particularly so. 'I spent my first day in pupillage here at this desk. It was originally my father's. But when he . . . well, Ignatius took it over. I had a chair at the end.'

'You rarely talk about your father.'

'You rarely talk about your wife.'

'True.'

'You see, Tom, there are some things that are better left unsaid.'

I tried to think of something to change the subject. But my imagination had been flooded with cheap German hock. So I merely asked Justine, 'What sort of pupil master was Ignatius?'

She paused to consider. 'Interested,' she said and looked up at me childishly, biting her bottom lip. 'How's things with Penny?'

'You mean the wife I rarely talk about?'

'How are things?' Justine insisted.

'The usual,' I said.

'That bad?'

'Worse.'

Through my white cotton court shirt I could feel that Justine's hands were warm and damp, like mine, but her fingers were accurate and did not fumble with the buttons.

'Tom, what's *this*,' she said teasingly. She sent shivers through my body. 'Why, Mr Fawley, you've grown a spine.'

'Justine, you know I've always—'

'I loved how you stood up to that old witch, Hardcastle.'

And now I could feel her fingers moving lower, more slowly.

'Do you think Kingsley did it?' she asked.

I was finding it difficult to concentrate. 'Possibly,' I said.

Her feet were no longer swinging. 'Has he told you what he did ... to those other girls?'

By now she had undone my belt. 'Yes,' I breathed.

'And do you think about it?'

I stared at the velvet curtains, which were slightly parted. I ached very badly. 'Justine, please.'

'Do you dream about it, Tom?' Her fingers moved very slowly and rhythmically over me. 'Do you?'

At that moment I couldn't speak.

'And do you dream of me?' she asked.

I nodded and noticed she had taken off her shirt and wore nothing underneath. Her breasts were hardly developed and she did look young. And I remembered again what Emma had said about Molly Summers and the Stonebury look.

As she moved her head closer to me, I felt her moist breath on my stomach, and again I imagined I could feel the texture of a muslin gown, and then the moistness moved lower, and although I looked at the stained-glass windows of the Great Hall in the Temple, I only saw the ancient circle at Stonebury, and when her lips finally arrived, I only saw one thing, and was sick to my very soul, for I saw the face of the murdered girl, Molly Summers.

PART II

LONDON

His gaze, going past those bars, has got so misted
with tiredness, it can take in nothing more.
He feels as though a thousand bars existed,
and no more world beyond them than before.

The Panther
Rilke

Chapter 18

There were to be two weeks until the retrial. In the interim, Kingsley had been transferred to the hospital wing of HMP Battersea. This was supposedly due to an unspecified illness which seemed, to me, to have no physical manifestations whatsoever. Yet I sometimes perceived a kind of sickness, a disease that buzzed around his head like a swarm of wasps.

I followed a prison officer, his peaked cap low over his eyes, through the corridors with camp beds on both sides. They would have been called wards, except for the newly painted bars on the windows.

The trial had been aborted two days earlier. Benjamin Goldman, Kingsley's solicitor, had arranged a conference at Battersea. The firm of Goldman, Goldman and Goldman were Kingsley's libel lawyers, instructed to scrutinise his populist works of sleaze and sexuality. He kept his lawyers busy. So busy, obviously, that Benjamin Goldman had not managed to attend the prison.

The jailer and I pushed our way through thick sheets of translucent plastic which hung from the ceiling in place of doors. The dark stone floors had been scrubbed with disinfectant but there was a lingering smell of the sick.

'Why, Mr Fawley.' The voice to my right was mocking. 'How nice of you to spare me your time.'

There was Kingsley. Alone. Wheeling himself through the prison completely unattended.

'Surprised?' he asked. 'They allow me a free run of the

place – more or less. Doctors say it's good for me. "Get a little exercise, Mr Kingsley." They call me that, you know.' He began to yawn meekly. 'But I do get so tired. No one really worries about little old me,' said Kingsley. 'I can hardly jump over the wall. Can I?'

'Any problems from the other inmates?' I was worried that Kingsley wasn't segregated off on Rule 43 – the block for sexual offenders. But he preferred the freedom of the hospital wing.

'Oh, Charlie,' said Kingsley to a young doctor with an ankle-length white coat. 'Has my television been fixed yet? The picture keeps rolling so annoyingly.'

'I'm sorry, Mr Kingsley. I'll get it sorted out.'

'You're so kind,' he said as the doctor started to leave. 'But you *did* say you'd do it yesterday. You did say that, didn't you, Charlie?'

The youth flushed the colour of a young claret. He scribbled something down on his mortar board and almost bowed as he moved away.

'The staff are so good to me here,' said Kingsley.

'And the prisoners?' I asked.

'Either incapable or incontinent.'

'But they haven't caused you any problems?' I asked.

'No, I haven't been accidentally lowered on to the hot-plate, Mr Fawley.' Kingsley looked round at me. His eyes darkened. 'Are you disappointed?'

'I've done a written analysis of the evidence in the case,' I told him. In fact, Emma had done it. 'Perhaps you'd like to glance at it?'

As we approached his cell, there was a line of five or six beds on the right-hand side. Two of the men were strapped down. The first tossed his head from side to side in silent anguish, while the second smiled.

Kingsley looked across to the second strapped-down man. 'Morning, Legat.'

The man was muscular, his skin weather-beaten, almost

sepia, as if he had been tied to one of the stones at Stonebury and exposed to the elements. He strained at the straps but could only let out a low grunt.

Kingsley's cell reminded me of a tutor's study in one of the older Oxford colleges. There were books and piles of manuscripts carelessly strewn over the floor. I saw two Dostoevsky novels, a critique of Roman law, and various books on the occult. There was a colour television in the corner and next to the barred window was a plastic bottle of mineral water that had been cut in half and contained some wilting flowers, their blooms shrivelled as they stood in water the colour of urine.

I picked up one of the occult novels by someone called Dyson and read the first page.

'"My Friends, the Age of Innocents is one that never was. For who amongste us was not borne in a State of Sinne? And which of this Parishe does not but reach the Grave in precisely the same Fashione?"'

I looked at Kingsley. 'You don't read this rubbish, do you?'

'No,' said Kingsley. 'I don't really read it. Lately, I prefer to read the newspapers, actually.'

I saw copies of *The Times* and The *Telegraph* by his bed. 'And what about your writing? Haven't lost your muse, have you?'

'No, Mr Fawley. I've lost my freedom. It's surprising what incarceration does to dry the juices.'

There was a gust of air that was sickly and warm and turned over my stomach.

'You know, at Newgate Prison they used to have a windmill,' he said. He lay flat on his back and seemed about twelve years old in his blue striped pyjamas. As he stared at the wall behind his head, the pupils virtually disappeared from the eye sockets. 'I'm sure the windmill did a better job than this useless air-conditioning.'

'No doubt you're right,' I said, trying not to look at him.

I glanced at Emma's jottings. 'It seems to me that we will have to get a statement from your alibi—'

'Philip Templeman?'

'Unless you've got another,' I said.

'Why do we need a statement?'

'Calling a witness without a statement is a little like playing Russian roulette. It's suicide. Didn't Dostoevsky write a story about that?' I asked.

'It was Tolstoy, in fact,' Kingsley said, as if he were giving me a tutorial in nineteenth-century Russian fiction. 'A lawyer: rich, successful ... suicidal. Because—'

'Because what?'

'Because he was committing adultery, Mr Fawley. Not that lawyers do that kind of thing nowadays. Are you...'

'What?'

'Are you going to try to persuade me to plead guilty?'

'No,' I said. However, it was at the back of my mind.

'One last attempt, perhaps?'

'I forgot my thumb-screws.'

'No, no, no.' He hurriedly pulled himself upright using the leather straps hanging above his bed. 'Thumb-screws were for extracting confessions.'

'I'm sorry, I forgot—'

'Never mind,' he said.

'I forgot that you've already confessed.'

'Ah,' said Kingsley, exaggerating the sound. 'You like playing games, Mr Fawley?'

'And you don't?'

'I only enjoy those I will win.'

'By fair means or—'

'Does it matter?' he asked.

'Sometimes,' I replied.

The light appeared to be fading from the room and Kingsley was getting excited, coming to life, always rubbing his hands eagerly.

'*Peine forte et dure*—' he said.

'I'm sorry?'

'Oh, surely you're familiar – pressing to death? A delight from the reign of Edward I.'

'I still don't—'

'To force a man to plead guilty.' He rubbed his hands more quickly now as if the chill had suddenly sharpened. 'I'm taken to a low dungeon, laid upon my back, token cloth around the loins – maybe they would dispense with that in my case? – and then I'm loaded with weights. A slow and rather painful death.' His eyes left the wall and pointed towards me. 'Of course, take away my television and I'll tell you what you want to hear.'

I couldn't even manage a grin.

'Why are you so keen I plead guilty?' he asked.

'It's in your interests.'

'Or in yours, perhaps?' Kingsley's eyes moved slowly over my face. 'Of course, Sarah Morrow didn't plead guilty when you represented her. And look what happened to her.'

I did not know how to reply.

'Such a tragic death,' Kingsley said. 'There seem to be so many in Stonebury. Now why do you suppose that is?'

Chapter 19

'What do you know about the Sarah Morrow case?' I asked Kingsley.

'Stonebury is a small place, Mr Fawley. Five years in an old village passes in a blink of an eye. It's because of that case that I insisted on instructing you.'

'But she killed herself.'

'Yes, but you fought it. And her case was more ... hopeless than mine. You look tired, Mr Fawley. Haven't been sleeping well?'

'I'll survive.' In truth, the dreams were becoming more vivid and I felt a kind of need to have them, almost an addiction. I had noticed in the mirror that my face had become washed out. I had developed that pallor that people get when they spend too long in front of a computer screen. Only the images in my mind were in black and white. And I felt that with the dark rings under my eyes and the paleness of my skin, I was becoming more and more like one of the figures I saw at night.

'Do you still want to know?' Kingsley said.

'What?'

'What I know about the stone circle.'

I felt like saying, There's little point. I've seen so much of it in my dreams, all you could do would be to provide a few faces. But that's not our job, it's the prosecution's. It sounded foolish, so instead I told him, 'I have a saying. Never listen to clients before the trial and never believe them after.'

He was clearly interested and held a finger to his narrow mouth pondering the proposition. 'I can see the wisdom of the first part, but I don't understand—'

'If they're convicted, they tell you they're innocent. And if they're acquitted they tell you—'

'That they did it?'

'Precisely,' I said.

'And what about me? What will I be telling you after the trial?'

'That you're grateful – for my sterling efforts in your defence.'

'Not a bad reply,' said Kingsley.

An orderly knocked at the door and was summonsed in. He was a huge pink man with a tiny head.

'Your tea,' he said timidly.

'Don't be frightened, Billy. This is my barrister, Mr Thomas Fawley.'

Unlike Kingsley, the big man wore a prisoner's uniform. He didn't know what to say.

'Put the tray down, Billy.' Kingsley touched the movable table at the bed. When the man had lowered the tea and had begun to back out of the room, Kingsley continued, 'Oh, Billy. Tell Charles – I mean, Doctor Fogarty – to attend to my television ... if he would be so good.'

Uttering some kind of compliant groan, the orderly slid the door shut.

'One of our prize specimens,' said Kingsley. 'Wonderful with tea-trays but lethal with little girls. Shall I be mother?'

I deliberately looked at my watch. 'Don't know if I've got time.'

'But we haven't discussed my defence,' Kingsley said, pretending to be hurt.

'Well, perhaps, just a little—'

'Don't worry, Mr Fawley,' he said, gaily dipping the camomile sachets, 'gone are the days of bromide in the tea. They have a rather quaint name for it – the prisoners.'

He spoke as though he were not one of them. 'Liquid cosh, they call it. I quite like that.'

Finally he tossed a steaming tea-bag into a red plastic bin at the end of the bed, and started on the second cup. 'I didn't do what they say, you know.' He lifted the sachet out of the water. 'A little longer perhaps?'

'No. That's fine,' I said.

'You don't believe me, do you?'

'What?'

'You don't really believe I'm innocent?'

'Not my job.'

'Come, come, Mr Fawley. That might do for your shoplifters and burglars. But I'm up for murder. How can I trust you, if you don't have faith in me?'

'Faith?'

'Yes, faith. I suspect that faith is not one of your strong points, Mr Fawley.'

'Well, I believe that a benevolent God would have given us a break between acne and hair-loss, if that's what you mean.'

Kingsley eyed me coldly. 'You don't trust me, do you?'

'You lied to me about that note in court.'

'*Did* I?' he asked, pushing the cup towards me.

'That was foolish,' I said. 'They'll get the handwritten note examined. You know, the one Payne found in your cell.'

'The one Payne said he found. Anyway, I would rather like a graphologist to see it.' He was smiling, his mouth full of corners and angles.

'Did you slip the other note – the typed copy – into my brief?'

'Why would I do a thing like that?'

'If you lie to me, if you change your story, I could be professionally compromised.'

'But I never—'

'Don't push it, Mr Kingsley.' We had entered dangerous waters. These were the treacherous seas of legal ethics and morality. I said, 'I had a friend once. Lizzie. Heartthrob of

123

the boys at college. Wanted to be a nurse. I saw her one Christmas. I asked, How's nursing? She said, Tom, I never want to see another penis as long as I live. They'd placed her on the geriatric ward, you see. She was put off for life.'

'So?' Kingsley hadn't followed the story.

'So that's what the criminal Bar's like. Cures a bad dose of moral curiosity. The truth is, Mr Kingsley, I don't need to know if you killed that poor girl.' And then I lied and said, 'I don't even care.'

The door suddenly slid open. There was a gargantuan ward sister, her forearms as monstrous as those of any prison officer I had ever seen. The uniform she wore had a large brown stain by her midriff.

'Two minutes,' she roared.

'But, Sister, my barrister and I were—'

'Two minutes, I told you.'

I immediately put my notes into the briefcase at my feet. When she slammed the door even the flowers in the urinous water seemed to wilt a little more.

'I'll tell you what I know,' said Kingsley.

'Not interested,' I said.

'Then I'll tell it to the court.' He tried to haul himself higher. 'I really will – and where will that leave you?'

'One minute,' screamed the sister through the door.

Kingsley's eyes flitted nervously from me to the door and back again. '"The first of punishments", Mr Fawley.'

I knew the quote from Juvenal, but didn't rise to Kingsley's bait.

'"The first of punishments",' he repeated, reaching a withered arm towards me. '"No guilty man is acquitted – if judged by himself."'

I stared directly at his quickly moving eyes.

'How about you?' he said.

'Why don't you sack me?'

'What are you guilty of? Or are you too ashamed? Is that it? Those desires. Sometimes they hurt, don't they, Mr Fawley?'

I took three steps to the corner of Kingsley's bed. I was now within touching distance. 'You know all about those Russians and Romans, but you know nothing about yourself. Do you know what you are, Mr Kingsley?' I didn't wait for an answer. 'You're a sordid little pervert who's going to prison for life.'

I turned sharply on my heels and slammed the door.

From behind me, his words seemed to crawl through the cracks in the door-frame. 'Such passion. Can't wait for your closing speech,' he said.

And as I walked swiftly down the corridor and passed Legat, who was still strapped to the bed, I heard Kingsley call out something that sounded like, 'Keep riding the Stang.'

Legat smiled grotesquely.

'Keep riding the Stang, Mr Fawley.' Richard Kingsley's voice had all but disappeared. 'Keep riding the Stang. Keep riding the Stang.'

Chapter 20

'I don't see why we couldn't go to the Savoy,' I said, looking around the post-theatre crowd in the restaurant later that evening.

Justine did not answer immediately. She took a long draw on her slim cigar and mouthed the smoke from cheek to cheek, all the time knowing that I was bound to find this mildly provocative, despite my aversion to smoking.

'Because,' she said, finally billowing out the orange smoke.

'Because what?'

'Just because.' She was being evasive, irritating and very Justine.

My encounter with Kingsley had left me both ravenous and confused, although not necessarily in that order.

She continued, 'How was your . . . beef—'

'*Bistecca Fiorentina*,' I said.

'I don't know how you can eat it so rare. It was barely cooked. There was blood everywhere.'

'We booked a table at the Savoy at the beginning of the trial, so what's all the fuss?'

'That was different,' she said.

'Why?'

'Because we had nothing to hide.'

'So?'

'So now we do.'

What did that mean? I hoped it was the possibility of sex that night, but when I looked at her, she looked away and increased my longing. I had phoned Justine the day after Manly's memorial. The day after she had whispered strange things in my ears and torn my court shirt and scratched my back; Penny, of course, hadn't noticed. When I tried to phone her, she had hung up. The next day I rang her in chambers. She had to speak to me. Finally, I compelled her to meet me.

She insisted that we met in an inconspicuous restaurant, she said that the eyes of the Bar were on us, she said there were no promises.

So we settled on an anonymous Tuscan place off St Martin's Lane. It was called Il Gallo Nero. It was not so much a restaurant as a place to be humiliated by waiters with fake accents, where food was overpriced and undercooked, where there were more wines from Canberra than Chianti. But with Justine opposite me, it seemed perfect.

'Do you want to get the bill?' I asked, finishing off the bottle of Chateau Bondi Beach.

'Steady on,' Justine replied. 'I haven't ordered a – what's it called?'

'Tiramisu.'

I have always been clumsy and awkward with women; either dithering embarrassingly or diving in recklessly. Justine must have sensed my insecurity and deftly fingered the back of my hand.

'I'm not going anywhere, Tom.'

'I just thought we could—'

'Yes?' She feigned innocence. A winsome smile, a toss of the hair.

'I mean ... Penny's home. Ginny's not well, you see. And well, that hotel—'

'The Strand Palace?'

'Yes, that one. It's just round the corner.'

Suddenly Justine's eyes were a forest of colour. She held her left hand out, palm upwards. 'That's fifty quid, mate. Up front. Hundred without yer boots on.'

'Justine, I only thought—'

'That's the point. You didn't think. Not of me. What do you take me for?'

The waiter arrived. '*Signori?* For the desserts?'

'A cheap whore?' said Justine.

I tried to retrieve the situation. 'A tiramisu for the—'

'Just the bill,' she snapped.

The waiter was confused. He had served me several times before when I was with Penny.

'Can you order a taxi?' I asked. 'For Chiswick.'

'*Si, signor.*'

'And do you have any *vin santo?*' I did not know why I asked this.

'Yes, er ... *si*,' he said.

'*Allora due, per favore,*' I said.

He looked at me somewhat quizzically. When I held up two fingers, he gave a shallow bow.

Justine had been watching a little bemused. 'What are you plotting, Tom?'

'You'll see.'

'It sounds terribly naughty.' Suddenly she was playful again. I could have screamed. 'Friends?' she said.

'I suppose it was rather insensitive of me.'

'Penny was my best friend, you know. Well, out of the girls at school. None of them really liked me. I don't find this easy, Tom.'

I tried to take the initiative by offering a sacrifice. 'Perhaps we should ... forget it,' I said, trying to look casually at the Renaissance reproductions on the wall behind her.

'Don't be an idiot all your life, Tom,' is all she replied.

Ten minutes later, Justine twisted another smouldering stub around the ashtray savagely. 'So how was the conference with Kingsley?'

'Different.'

'Quite a ... character, I bet.' She enunciated the syllables of 'character' with excessive care.

'He is, if you go in for that sort of thing.'

'Interesting?'

'Dangerous.'

'Have you got a chance of winning?'

'You tell me,' I said.

The waiter finally returned with two small, heavily cut glasses, newly polished and filled to the very brim with a rich straw-coloured liquid smelling of the Tuscan hills.

'This is delicious,' said Justine. 'What on earth is it?'

'*Vin santo*,' I replied. 'Holy wine. Makes you tell the truth.' I sipped a little and looked at Justine. 'Well?'

She did not reply.

'Perhaps it's best we don't talk about it,' I said. I tried to summon the waiter over, but when I caught his eye, she began to speak.

'I would say your chances are pretty good. Our witnesses are silly little girls and the forensics are a bit suspect.'

'What about the confession?'

'Are you defending him or am I?' I didn't answer this and she continued, 'I know ... I know Aubrey is a little worried.'

'About what?'

She put a finger to her moistened lips. 'Ever look up that witness?'

'Which one?'

She lowered her head and whispered, '*That* one.'

'Why the secrecy?' I didn't imagine that a restaurant full of bit-players would be interested in the case of the Queen against Richard Kingsley.

'I still haven't told Aubrey I disclosed her details to the defence.'

'To the *defence*?'

'Well, to you then,' she said.

I took another sip of *vin santo* and wondered whether her betrayal was a first tentative flirtation, a kind of foreplay. I said, 'Goldman tells me he got some High Street solicitors in the West Country to act as his agents. But—'

'But what?'

'But they couldn't find the witness. She's some kind of hermit or hermitess or whatever you call them. Of course,' I said, wondering how far I could push my luck, 'of course, you've seen—'

'Her statement? So what if I have, Tom?'

'So you could tell me whether it's worth busting our butts to find her.'

'I can't help you on that.'

'Won't, you mean.'

'Listen. I gave you her name because I didn't think Davenport was complying with his duties of disclosure. Not playing fair. That's all. You'll get nothing more from me.'

'Is it worth seeing her?'

'Were you listening?'

I tried to imagine Justine's room in chambers, the Regency desk, her silver hair and the softness of her whispers. 'Come on, Justine.'

She blinked twice very softly and bit her bottom lip like she did *that* time. 'I gave her details to you, didn't I?'

The waiter interrupted and announced my taxi which, much to his annoyance, I told him to send away.

'I never thought Italian food amounted to much,' said Justine.

'This is authentic,' I replied.

'We'll have to come again.'

'So there'll be a next time?'

'Maybe.' She lit up again. 'Any problems with the trial bundles or the unused material?'

'No. You – and I mean you and not Davenport – have been very good.' Minute beads of sweat had broken out on my forehead and my eyes were beginning to haze over. 'By the way, what does your graphologist say?'

'What graphologist?'

'About Kingsley's handwriting?' I said. Then seeing that

Justine did not reply, I added, 'You know, the note Payne found.'

'Well, we haven't actually instructed—'

This I could not believe. 'You are joking?'

'Aubrey thinks ... well, you're not disputing that Kingsley wrote that note, are you?'

'Kingsley is.'

'But Payne found it in Kingsley's cell, Tom. Be realistic.'

I still felt uneasy about the origin of the two notes. If Kingsley did not put the first in my brief, then how did the typed note get there? As for the second, I wondered whether we could argue that Payne's search of the cell was illegal? But the truth was that everything pointed to Richard Kingsley as the author. I said, 'Kingsley insists we test the handwritten one.'

'Your funeral,' Justine replied and immediately realised what she had said. Her eyelids flickered a little. 'Poor Ignatius,' she whispered, her eyes becoming two sad pools.

The robing rooms of London were awash with theories of how a High Court judge was found at the bottom of his stairs with his neck broken. I wanted to press Justine, but this was not the right time. 'You couldn't help our graphologist see the original, could you?' I asked.

'Sure.'

'You know how difficult it is. No one knows where exhibits are pending a retrial.'

'I'll get on to that little toad, Payne,' said Justine.

'So you don't like him either?'

'Watch him, Tom.'

'Why?'

'You'll have to work that out,' she said. Justine looked at me and there was something in her eyes that thrilled me and made my heart pound painfully. 'Can you stay over?' she asked.

'Not again.'

'Why not?'

'I've run out of excuses,' I said.

'What? After one night's fornication?' She used rather a biblical word which reminded me of sermons and pulpits and priests and incense. She said, 'What did you tell Penny last time?'

'Said I got legless at Manly's bun-fight and slept on Nick Mellor's leather sofa in chambers.'

'Penny believed that?'

'Think she was relieved I didn't come home drunk.' I knew I should have said, Come home drunk *again*. But I was unsure how much Justine knew about my drinking.

'Why don't you come down to my place?' she asked.

'Your country mansion?'

'I'd hardly call it that, Tom. I've just had new central heating installed at the cottage.'

'I heard that your father owned an obscenely large residence near Stonebury.'

'He did.'

'So why can't we stay there?' I asked.

'We just can't. I haven't stayed there since my father—'

Justine broke off and seemed upset. Again I had pressed the wrong buttons. I decided to try to lighten the conversation.

'I *am* grateful for your kind invitation to join the great and the good among the turnip fields,' I told her. 'But I'm afraid I object to the life of the landed gentry. On moral grounds.'

Justine looked at me coldly. 'And how about adultery? Do you object to that, Tom? On moral grounds?'

I did not reply.

'So what did Penny say?' she continued. 'When you finally told—'

'You're not serious?' It had actually flashed across my mind in a moment of guilty weakness. But what would confessing have achieved? It could only have hurt Penny and got me into trouble, although I was not certain which of these two considerations was the most important. So I said, 'I'm not going to tell her.'

'Don't be ridiculous, Tom.' Justine's face crinkled and she

133

appeared very old. A line, like an old scar, ran from her right eye to the corner of her frowning mouth.

'It'll devastate her,' I said.

'What if she finds out?'

'No, really. She'll go absolutely—'

'Penny's my friend. We don't have secrets. Never have.'

'For Christ's sake, Justine. You don't know what you're saying.'

'You've got to tell her.' She put her lighter into an unimaginably expensive handbag. 'You've got to tell her, Tom,' she said as the orange cloud of smoke began to clear. 'Or I will.'

Chapter 21

Justine and I left the restaurant together, but soon I was alone and in a taxi racing through Westminster. Big Ben struck once rather dolefully. I was not sure what time it was, but it was late.

Penny would be hurt either way, whether I told her or Justine did. If I confessed, I would gain a little credit from Penny and I might impress Justine. But that was too easy. Life was not that simple. I wondered whether Justine could be bluffing. Maybe she was trying to provoke me into action? Maybe I could fake her out? But there was that look in her eye. The same look as when she talked about potting some particularly vile criminal, the look she had when she talked about Kingsley. She was not bluffing – I had to confess.

Once home, I did not sneak up the stairs. If Penny woke up, I intended to have it out there and then. It was the honourable thing to do. I almost felt righteous.

The bedroom door was slightly ajar. Along the corridor, I could hear Ginny tossing fitfully in her sleep and coughing, coughing so painfully. My daughter was clearly unwell and I had been guzzling antipodean plonk with my mistress.

I took a tentative step into the bedroom. The floorboard groaned. Standing there, I could see that Penny had thrown off the duvet and was lying completely naked in a foetal position. An icy blast of wind struck my left cheek, which was still blushing with the wine. The window was wide open and the glass rattled in the frame.

Penny did not move but said, 'Where have you been?'

'Out.'

'Really?'

Another rush of wind. I could feel my resolve shrivelling. 'Yes, really.'

'Anywhere in particular?'

'No. Nowhere in particular.'

'You've been out with Justine, haven't you?'

This was the moment. How to broach the subject? Did I start gently and start discussing our problems? Or was it better to tell her directly: The truth is, Justine and I are having an affair.

'Have you been out with Justine?' she repeated. 'Tell me.'

'No,' I said. No? I felt thoroughly ashamed. How could I have said no?

'Tom, I just want the truth. Have you been out with Justine?'

Fortunately, I had another chance, it was not too late. I took a deep breath. 'No,' I said more firmly.

Penny sprang upright and threw the pillow at me. 'Liar,' she screamed. 'I can smell her, you liar.' She was not crying. It would somehow have been easier if she were. 'Are you having an—'

'I don't know.' I had retreated into my corner of the room and squatted on my pile of dirty laundry. 'Really, I don't.'

'It doesn't surprise me. If a woman is after you, you're an erection waiting to happen. You're *so* pathetic.'

The last word was particularly hurtful but deserved. I simply waited for Penny to continue.

'I hope you're more adventurous with your mistress than you are with me.'

'What do you mean?'

'Well, you only know two positions. Eyes open and eyes closed. It's hardly the *Kama Sutra*, is it, Tom? Still, it had to happen really.' She drew two blue knees up to her chin, her head seeming to bounce on them as she talked. 'You didn't have a prayer.'

'How did you know?' Like so many of my less successful crooks, I was more interested in how I was caught than in the terrible consequences that follow discovery.

'The cigar smell for a start,' she said. 'And I thought, Why would he lie about seeing Justine?'

'Pretty impressive.'

'Thanks.'

And suddenly we were being almost civil. 'I'm sorry,' I said.

'I know,' she replied.

I slowly started undressing, neatly placing my suit on thick wooden hangers; my normal practice was to fling it over the back of the chair. Penny drew the duvet up to her knees. I could only see her head, one side of which was lit by the moon.

'You'd better come to bed, I suppose,' she said.

Penny did not move as she began to speak, staring, always staring, through the gaping window as the winter air seeped into the room. 'There was a man – well, he was no more than a boy really – caused a bit of a scandal at school. Alex ... Chapple, I think it was. We all fancied him, I suppose. But he only had eyes for one person.'

'Justine?' I asked.

'Who else? He used to teach us – English, I think. Introduced us to John Donne and Marvell and all the Romantics. He got the job because he knew Justine's father, or something like that. No one really knew.'

'And what was Justine's father like?' I asked.

'Well, she seemed to ...'

'Love him?'

'Worship him.'

'That's not really what I asked, Pen. What I meant was—'

'Put it this way,' she said, 'what's anyone like who sends single mothers to prison for shoplifting?'

'Doing his job?'

'And loving every second of it, Tom.'

I was still confused. What was the relevance of all this? Penny seemed to be building slowly, convincing herself before she shared these memories with me.

'Tom,' she said, 'this ... this thing between you and Justine' – she tugged a little at the duvet and a jet of icy air sped up my back, setting me on edge – 'is it just a passing thing? An infatuation?'

'Penny, I swear ... if I knew, I'd—'

'You see, Alex was—'

'Alex?' I asked, and then I remembered the earlier part of our conversation. 'Oh, *Alex.*'

'He was the teacher. Good title for it. I suppose young girls can be tutored in all sorts of things. Alex ... oh, was it Chapple?'

'Is it important?'

'No,' Penny said.

'I asked Justine about him but she just told me to mind my own business.'

'What a surprise,' Penny said. 'You see, Alex *seemed* shy, innocent, supposedly unavailable. Of course, absolutely irresistible to a classful of girls. But it was all hushed up.'

I was no longer listening very carefully, for I wanted to tell her what I had decided, what was bound to hurt. 'I'll have to go to the West Country for a couple of days,' I said. 'For the case.'

'You'll miss your daughter's birthday.'

'I'll be back by then.'

'Yes, it was Chapple,' she said confidently. 'That was his name.'

Outside, the moonlight flickered as a cloud scudded across the garden trees, cloaking their upper branches in purple, then grey.

'Justine was found in his study,' Penny said in a matter-of-fact way.

'Is that what you meant? Her old tricks? Leaving—'

'Leaving things in men's studies?' Penny paused. 'I suppose she left—'

'Her clothes?'

'Her cherry.'

'That's terrible,' I said.

'Oh, don't be such a prude. Everyone has to lose it sometime. It's just...'

'Just what?'

'Just in *those* circumstances,' Penny said.

'The study?'

'Don't be silly, Tom. There's nothing wrong with being bonked on a desk-top. We should try it sometime – except your desk is always full of your bloody murder briefs.'

'Then what was so awful?' I asked.

'That night,' Penny said, her voice suddenly very distant. 'It was...'

'Yes?'

'It was the night Justine's father died.' Before I could say anything at all, Penny continued, 'Chapple was sent away, naturally. I'm not sure what happened after that. He disappeared. Some people say he stayed in the area but I never saw him again.'

I turned round to face her and noticed that the downy hair on her nape was standing on end. 'Penny, did you hear me? I might have to go—'

'If you go,' she said, 'we won't be here when you return.'

Chapter 22

'Your client,' said Judge Hardcastle, 'demonstrates a refreshing amount of realism.' She fixed me with one of her eyes.

I was seated in Hilary Hardcastle's chambers behind Court 4 with my prosecutor for the day, Rupert Livingstone. I was representing Emmanuel 'Whitey' Innocent. Whitey was a drugs dealer. He was also a grass. A good grass. A supergrass.

True informers are born and not made. For some people feel the desire to betray as others feel the need to tend to the sick, or to teach children or to sit in dark confessionals and listen to the sins of others. But unlike doctors and teachers and priests, informers held a special fascination for me, as I was always intrigued to see what would drive a man to betrayal. It was, very often, surprisingly little.

'Perhaps you might like to read this, Judge,' I said to her as I passed over a sealed envelope.

'Any objection, Mr Livingstone?' she asked.

He grunted reluctantly.

I did not know the exact contents of the letter. What I did know was that it was from Chief Superintendent William Heggarty of the Flying Squad, and was a curriculum vitae of my client's informing activities. As the judge slowly read the handwritten note, I gazed around her chambers. They could not have been further removed from those of Ignatius Manly. Hardcastle had prints of the guillotine, the gallows tree at Tyburn with gibbeted highwaymen hanging from chains, and a graphic portrayal of the crushing of the Peterloo Riot with ranks of uniformed troopers attacking an unarmed crowd.

'These matters are always sensitive,' she finally said. 'I suppose we must fight crime by any means necessary.' She looked at the two barristers before her and said, 'Do I take it that Mr ... is it, Innocent?'

'It is,' I said.

'Is he pleading guilty?'

'Yes, Judge,' I said. 'I'm afraid he doesn't live up to his name very often.'

On that day, even the obvious comment met with the approval of La Hardcastle. 'He does have an extraordinary name,' she said.

'He does,' is all I replied.

In fact, Whitey was born in Trinidad but had lived most of his adult life in that netherworld between Lewisham and Catford. He never gave the police his correct address. Although ethnically Afro-Caribbean, he was an albino. The tight curls on his head were snowy white and dusty from some skin complaint, his eyes were never more than half open, which is to say that they were invariably half shut, and he was caused terrible pain by sunlight, shingles and telling the truth. Whitey was a pupil of the Judas Iscariot school of trust and loyalty.

'I suppose,' continued Hardcastle, 'I shall have to give him a very substantial reduction in his sentence, for his ... assistance.'

Livingstone groaned again and looked at his impeccably manicured nails. He didn't want to offer Whitey a deal, but he had it forced upon him by the CPS, who in turn got the word from the Flying Squad.

'May I ask how important an informant Mr Innocent is?' asked Hardcastle.

Rupert Livingstone, former young conservative and now a prematurely old and irritable one, consulted his brief. 'I understand he has provided Flying Squad with some intelligence about certain Jamaican armed robbers.'

Whitey had grassed up the Yardie Blaggers, to use Jamie

Armstrong's parlance. That was a dangerous business and I felt it right that the judge understood the risks involved in such treachery.

'I understand, Judge,' I said, 'that my client has provided more quality information than the next half-dozen informants put together. And' – I paused to try to reinforce the point – 'and two of those gentlemen have recently been exposed.'

'Oh dear,' said Hardcastle.

'And they were both murdered,' I added.

'Really?'

'Quite brutally, I understand.'

'I see,' said the judge.

Central Drugs Squad, who had arrested Whitey for dealing heroin, were also unhappy. They had to accept a plea to supply of a little cannabis when the word came down from Flying Squad. Five years' imprisonment had suddenly become nine months, and with remission and remand time it was practically a walk-out.

Emmanuel Innocent had to be given his thirty pieces of silver.

As I put my wig back on, and headed for the corridor leading to the court, Hardcastle stopped me.

'Good news and bad news, Mr Fawley,' she said.

'For who, Judge?'

She ignored my comment. 'Bad news is that my buggery has been taken out of my list for the next sitting. To give the defendant a chance to think. I hope someone will knock some common sense into his head. I can't stand sodomites.'

I looked at Hilary Hardcastle perching on a frugal chair, no cushions, no padding, when a shaft of light momentarily crept through the clouds that had laid siege to St Paul's. She looked like a chameleon on a stone.

'And what is the good news?' I asked.

She turned her head a little towards the light and licked her lips quickly. 'And the good news, Mr Fawley, is that I'm available to do the Kingsley murder.'

Rupert Livingstone's mood improved for the first time that day. As we shut Hardcastle into her lair, he gave me his most patrician of smiles.

'Another one for death row,' he said, running a manicured hand through his hair.

Livingstone was obviously going through his Oscar Wilde period of fey, disaffected youth. Except Rupert Livingstone was no longer young, and was not disaffected but faintly disgusting. I tried to decide whether to answer him or to jab my biro under his fingernails. But instead, as usual, I did nothing.

The jailer closed the huge outer door to the Old Bailey cells behind me. He puffed at an ornamental ebony pipe carved into the shape of a shrunken head.

''Fraid we're absolutely chocka today,' he said. 'Peak season, Mr Fawley. Can't put you in one of the luxury suites.'

It was his only joke, his whole repertoire. He was at the reception desk of a luxury hotel on the Costa del Crime, no doubt somewhere near Torremolinos, the cells were suites, the prisoners were guests, and their lawyers were visitors.

'You'll have to take suite number six. No sea view, sadly.' A ribbon of black smoke curled towards the ceiling. 'Mr Innocent will be with you presently.'

I was led to a dark square-shaped room. A loudly buzzing strip light flickered. The room had graffiti daubed on the walls and there was an enduring smell of stale human sweat.

When the half-glass door opened, Whitey Innocent slid in. The bulb finally went out and the dimness was only relieved by the yellow light from the corridor.

'Shall I call someone?' I said, pointing at the light.

'Better like this,' said Whitey. 'My eyes, Mr Thomas.' He always called me that. 'Worse all the time.'

A lily white hand started to gesture towards the top of his head, but fell limply. His pale face was only interrupted by a browning set of upper teeth which protruded so completely that you could never see whether he had a lower set to match. Below the lids were two slits. These were his eyes. He had the overall appearance of an old dog on its last legs. A dog that had grown so accustomed to sniffing out his way that he no longer needed his sight.

'Me eyes are no good,' he said, 'but I see many things.'

'Cut the mystic routine, Whitey. I've heard it all before.'

'You done good up there, Mr Thomas.' He finally sat down. 'Please,' he said, pointing towards a small table.

'I prefer to stand. You know, it had nothing to do with me.'

'Me Obeah man say it come out right.'

'You're not still paying that crook?'

Whitey scratched his snowy scalp with a long dirty thumbnail. We had had arguments about this before. Whitey subscribed to a creed somewhere between voodooism and the Freemasons. He paid his Obeah man, his kind of priest, sums of money. Sometimes Whitey paid him thousands of pounds to pray for him, to write out magical chants and even to attend court in a crisis.

'You pay insurance?' asked Whitey.

'Yes, but I pay Legal and General, not some old geezer who bets it on the dogs at Walthamstow.'

'It was a result,' he said.

'It was a fix,' I replied. 'So, got any plans when you get out? I hope you're not thinking of going straight?'

Whitey did not smile. 'I prefer it inside. You safe there. Mr Thomas, there's some bad shit going down.'

It is at such times that alarm bells should ring for any prudent lawyer. It is during such conversations that you can compromise your next case and hear things you shouldn't. So I just said, 'I don't want to know.'

'Really bad shit, Mr Thomas.'

'It's nothing to do with me, Whitey.'

'Mmm,' he said and scratched the table annoyingly with his dirty thumbnail.

People who are about to be carted off to prison can be desperate for advice, for hope on appeal or simply desperate for a little human company. They will engage you in all sorts of spurious conversations. They will pretend they know terrible secrets about the police, the witnesses, even the judge. But what they really crave is a last moment's attention, someone to take them seriously before the prison gate finally shuts.

I waited for Whitey to explain himself, but he just muttered *sotto voce* and dropped his eyelids still further. 'Now don't go all mysterious on me,' I said.

Although I tried to laugh it off, I was beginning to be worried, because Emmanuel Innocent did not fit into the above categories. He had spent more of his adult life behind bars than walking the back streets of Lewisham. Prison was bad for his drugs business but good for contacts. For a grass, prison was not an occupational hazard, it was part of the occupation.

'Why you think I get pulled?' he finally said.

'Could it be, Whitey because you were dealing heroin which, they tell me, is a little against the laws of the land?'

'Me been dealing heroin some years. Why me get pulled *now*?'

'Because you were caught?' I was getting a little tired of the game.

'You see but you do not see,' he said. 'New Babylon in town.' Whitey still used the old slang occasionally. I had never quite understood why some West Indians called the police 'Babylon'. Jamie said it was something to do with slavery.

'This Babylon, he real serious,' said Whitey. 'Come from Bradford or Bristol or some West Country shit like that.' Being one of the London posse, that part of England beyond the M25 was a mystery to Whitey. 'But me is Heggarty's man. He scratch my back and I—'

'Grass up Yardies?' I said. 'Dangerous game, Whitey.'

'Only game me know. So this blood-clot detective come see me with this other man.'

'Who was the other person? Police?'

146

'Nah,' said Whitey.

'How do you know?' I asked.

'Me can smell your Babylon. This other man just there. He was real short, but he was the guv'nor. No doubt.'

'Fascinating as all this is, Whitey, can you get to the point? Your carriage to Battersea nick's waiting.'

Then Whitey put on a strange accent, 'This detective tell me, "I need some dirt on that brief o' yours." So I says, Mr Thomas, I tells him, "Get out-a me face," and he says, "I'll cause you so much pain, you won't have a face when I finish with you." And I become scared.' Whitey did look up here and his face was even paler. 'He get them Drugs Squad to nick me. You see what me has to deal with, Mr Thomas?'

'Frankly, I don't.'

'Mr Thomas, you're not listening. This Babylon he want the dirt—'

'So?'

'On me brief—'

'Yes?'

'On *you*. He say, "Just in case..."'

There was a cursory knock on the glass and the jailer, still puffing away, put his face round the door.

'Van for Battersea's waiting. Let's be having you,' he said.

'What did you say?' I asked.

'I said the Battersea van is leaving and—'

'Not you.' I grabbed Whitey's hunched shoulder. '*You*.'

He turned slowly, stood on tiptoes and whispered in my ear, his eyes narrow but somehow bright. 'You in serious shit, Mr Thomas.'

'What did that mean "Just in case"? Just in case of what?'

Whitey was walking along the corridor and didn't appear to hear me. 'Real serious,' he muttered as he was led to the prison van. '*Real* serious.'

Chapter 23

When I left the Old Bailey, I decided to walk along the Embankment to the Temple. I wondered whether Whitey's thinly veiled warning was a pretext to force me to visit him in Battersea. To bring him cigarettes or perhaps to run some messages on his behalf. On the other hand, he had practically served his sentence while remanded in custody. So what motive did he have to lie?

I was daydreaming as I walked and imagined another conference with him, and when it ended Whitey was let out and, to my horror, I was taken to the prison van.

The Thames sulked under a heavy blanket of fog, the boats on the river were shadows, and the colourless people were little more than slowly moving apparitions. I could not bear going back to chambers and pretending to be friendly, I couldn't face going home and confronting my wife. A flat barge hooted in the distance, the sound echoing again and again under the Waterloo arches. I traced the river as the banks disappeared westwards, and wondered how near to Stonebury it flowed. For an instant, I felt myself drawn upriver as the tide receded to the west.

When I got to the door of 3 Dickens Court, I saw my name on the board outside, along with the other thirty-odd barristers who constituted my chambers. Getting your name on the door, that was the thing. It used to seem so important. Every year nearly one thousand law students, among the best in the land, frantically searched, chased and begged for the, perhaps, two hundred spaces on the door. And that day, as I saw my name-plate, the black letters fraying away, the background paint yellowing, I just thought: What was the point?

When I phoned Justine's chambers and was told she would be going to the Bar dinner that night, I wandered the empty streets for hours, waiting for darkness, waiting to see Justine, while the fog seemed to seep in through my ears, creating a dark haze behind my eyes.

The Bar Mess dinner is a sumptuous meal followed by soporific speeches, anodyne debates or mock trials. It is a key event in the professional calendar. I rarely attended, but that night was different. Driven by a raging desire to see Justine and a determination to avoid Penny, I found myself in the rococo banqueting hall of the old London Bridge Railway Hotel. There was no one there apart from sixty barristers and a solitary judge, the special guest speaker, eager to enrich our lives with firebrand wit.

Hilary Hardcastle was already on her feet, a few minutely scribbled notes in hand, addressing her captive audience. Her strange head scanned the room in precise jerks.

Justine and Davenport flanked Hardcastle on High Table. Davenport was the Mess Leader and Justine was his guest. When I saw her sitting there, I wished I had not arrived late, as I desperately wanted to tell her how I felt, to be forward, to articulate my desires for once. That was the plan. But I had no opportunity. The dubious reward of my tardiness was to be sat on a table by the door with Mess Junior, Rupert Livingstone.

Now that speeches had begun, it was Livingstone's solemn task to guard the oak-panelled doors and prevent the entry of 'strangers'. For this dangerous mission, he had been armed with a jeroboam of vintage claret.

Hilary Hardcastle was reaching the heart of her speech. 'In my day, the Junior Bar was seen and not heard.' There were a few port-induced guffaws from the constellation of silks.

'We knew our place in those days. Maybe, gentlemen' – she ignored the scattering of 'lady' barristers – 'Maybe, gentlemen, it is a sign of the times. Everyone wants his say. I am led to believe this is what they call democracy.'

At this, laughter. I did not really see why.

Hardcastle took a sip of port; her lips became momentarily ruby. 'I see barristers in court talking about the truth. About justice. They'll be talking about the American way next.'

Livingstone was sitting behind me. He leant forward and whispered, 'She's a tartar, don't you think?'

'I can think of other words for it,' I replied. Then I remembered those strange words that Kingsley had called after me in the prison. I turned to Livingstone. 'Rupert, old chap,' I said, speaking the only language he understood. 'You appear to be a chap who knows everything about everything.'

'Well, yes,' he said smugly. 'There is that.'

'Does riding the Stang mean anything to you?'

'Don't be an ignorant pleb all your life, Fawley,' he said.

'So what is it?'

'It's a form of punishment.'

'What sort?'

'Oh, do shut up, Fawley. Hilary's reaching her climax.'

This was a phenomenon that even I had a vague interest in seeing.

The diminutive judge looked hard at my corner of the room. 'You see, gentlemen, cases are taking too long. Every Tom, Dick and Harry is asking questions.' I could have sworn she stressed the 'Tom'. 'Too many of you are fighting hopeless cases, running dishonest defences.'

Her little eyes didn't move from my end of the table. Hardcastle was becoming more and more fervent as if she were an evangelical preacher. Only that with one heretical exception called Fawley, she was preaching to the converted.

'The code of conduct permits you to give strong advice about pleading guilty. My strong advice to you is don't shirk from that duty.'

Hardcastle's voice rose. It cracked, spat, and pestered. 'Gentlemen, you are not concerned with real guilt and innocence. That is the province of the Church – and of God.'

Justine stared up at Hardcastle, her delicate chin cupped in the same delicate hands that had moved so expertly through my shirt.

'The system of criminal justice is a huge...' Hardcastle frantically searched for the words and after looking down at her plate she said, 'The system is a huge slaughter-house. A right ruddy meat factory. And more meat is being fed in every day. Most of it fouled, some of it rotting, all sorts of muck.' She took a final sip of port; her tongue, as red as a rhododendron, lapped the corners of her mouth. 'So don't clog up the system, gentlemen. It will create an awful stink.'

Then there was a cacophony of applause and cheers from around the room; mirth and merriment lubricated by old tawny and a feeling that we were all in on the secret.

I could stomach no more. I couldn't wait for Justine – this was her world, not mine.

As I reached the door, Livingstone barred my way. 'Can't leave, Fawley. Against the rules.' He preened his flaxen locks.

'Let me out,' I said.

Around me I heard barristers thumping the table and crying out, 'Forfeit, forfeit.' The penalty was supposed to be half a pint of claret.

'You've got to pay a forfeit,' said Livingstone, lapping up the attention and inspecting his manicured nails.

I took the chance to push him aside and slip through the door. He staggered down the dimly lit corridor after me.

'You're not one of us, Fawley,' he shouted. 'You never will be.'

As I was about to leave the hotel, I noticed a pay-phone in the foyer and decided to ring home for messages. When I put in the first coin, I heard Penny's voice. It was the answerphone. She had recorded our message.

'We can't answer your call right now. Please leave us your name and number and we'll get right back to you.'

I felt strange. For the first time in my marriage, it sounded odd to hear Penny say *we*. How long, I wondered, would it remain so? I triggered the messages. The first was from some anonymous bureaucrat from the Bar Council about Hardcastle's complaint. It was official.

Emma's voice was next, bright as ever. 'Hi, Tom. I know this sounds crazy, but I need you to meet me at a rave tonight. I've got some info' about the case. The club's called Stairway to Heaven. Sounds awful, doesn't it? It's on Old Camberwell Road. There's someone you should meet.' Then her voice changed slightly. 'Hi, Penny. Hope you don't mind me borrowing your husband for a while. Don't worry, I'll get him home soon.'

Before I had a proper opportunity to digest Emma's bizarre request, one of my clerks, Steve, spoke.

'Good evening, Mr Fawley. Just to tell you you're doing paperwork tomorrow.' This was a clerk's euphemism for: You're unemployed. No one wants you to work for them. 'You've got two urgent messages, Mr Fawley. Mr Goldman wants to speak to you about the Kingsley murder. And you've got a message from – who wrote this? – sorry, can't read the writing, must be the temp.'

I could hear Steve conferring with Rose, the other clerk. There was a rustling of paper. Steve finally said, 'I think it says "Real Lives". Isn't that some television programme, Mr Fawley? You could be famous. "*Real Lives*. Personal ... personality? Tomorrow." Sheer gobbledegook. I don't know.'

It made sense of a sort to me. Perhaps I wanted it to. Who were they profiling? Kingsley, Davenport, Manly? A conceited little voice somewhere behind my left ear whispered, Tom, wouldn't it be nice if ...

'It's signed,' said Steve. 'I can't read – I'll kill that temp.'

Again there was Rose's voice in the background.

'It's signed, "Love Milly". That's it,' said Steve.

The money ran out again. What was Rose saying? I knew no one called Milly. We sometimes get journalists and reporters ringing us up for a story. But why me? Who was Milly?

I had one coin left and used it to replay the message. I put a finger to my other ear to eliminate the bustle from the increasingly crowded foyer. This time I tried to concentrate on Rose.

As Steve said, *Real Lives*, I could faintly hear Rose say, '"Read *Times*". I think it says *The Times*, Steve.' And then she said quite banally, 'No, Steve. It's signed ... doesn't it say ... "Love Molly"?'

Chapter 24

By the time my taxi reached Camberwell, I realised how tired I was. I found the nightclub in an alley, strewn with litter and unseen fighting cats screaming at each other in the fog.

There was no one on the door. In fact, there was no door, just a bleak void with well-worn stone steps disappearing quickly underground. I could already hear the thud-thud of the bass.

I felt ridiculous. There I was, almost forty, dressed in a double-breasted suit going to an illicit rave in south London. No doubt I looked like a pimp. I certainly felt like one.

It was black inside. The music was so loud that you imagined you would never hear again. Drips of hot sweat flew off young bodies gyrating in the darkness. And suddenly a little light. A stroboscope and a glimpse of a hundred grotesquely moving silhouettes, heavy limbs swimming through treacle. I took off my jacket and loosened my tie.

'What *do* you look like.' Even through the infernal din, I recognised Emma's voice. She was wearing a very baggy tee-shirt, button-up jeans and what my daughter would call a 'kicking' pair of trainers. 'You could have changed, Tom,' she said.

'Came straight from the Bar Mess.'

'You never went to – never mind.' The strobe stopped and a brilliant yellow light filled the area, revealing that we were in a fecund cellar crisscrossed with arches. Emma surveyed my face and said, 'What *has* happened to you? My God, you look like you've seen a—'

'Don't joke,' I said.

'Whatever is the matter?'

Did I tell her? If Steve *had* got it right, how foolish I would have looked babbling on about a message from a dead girl.

'I'll tell you about it sometime,' I shouted.

Emma nodded her head rapidly, but I wasn't sure she heard what I said. She grabbed my arm and started to lead me towards the throbbing mass. All at once the room was filled with a spectral mist which billowed from strategically placed ducts in the wall.

I dug my heels in and said, 'Who do you want me to meet?'

'Can't see him now. He's ... sort of busy.'

'Emma, I've come all this way—'

'See them?' She pointed to two rather clumsy women standing by the next arch. Each held a full bottle of pilsner.

'Friends of yours?' I asked.

Emma shook her head and waited for an especially jarring synthetic sound to ebb back into the general din. 'They're plod,' she said.

'Are you sure?' They didn't look like the WPCs I'd cross-examined.

'Definitely.'

'How can you tell?'

'White shoes, handbags. Look like they're going to a disco in Dagenham.'

On closer inspection they did look unnecessarily 'tarted up', as they used to say in pre-feminist days. Each had an elaborate hair-do and wore thick red lipstick. In contrast, it was difficult to distinguish the male tee-shirt and jeans on the dance-floor from the female of the species.

Emma chuckled, clearly enjoying her detective work. 'And,' she added, 'they've been nursing those drinks all night.'

'What are they doing?'

'Drugs,' is all she said. 'That's why you can't meet Danny.'

'Who the hell is—'

'You'll see.'

'You've not dragged me all the way here to meet a pusher. I thought it was a friend of yours.'

'It is a friend of mine.' Emma jigged around unconsciously to the infectious rhythm to which, it appeared, only I was immune. 'I met him during Bar finals. Cambridge man.'

'Well...' I said. I was about to say, That's all right then. What had the Bar done to me?

'Failed the exams. Became a New Age traveller.'

'A Stonehenge hippy, you mean.'

'A New Age traveller,' Emma insisted. 'Now he organises raves and—'

'And?' I looked straight into her dilating pupils.

'So he deals a little. Nothing heavy.'

'Jesus.'

'Oh, chill out, Tom. Don't be such an insufferable prude.'

'Hadn't you better warn your friend?'

'He's street, Tom. He can handle the busys.'

It was clear to me that this New Age traveller had some decidedly Old Age vices, but I didn't say that to Emma. The strobe came on again and her jigging seemed almost comical.

'I'll be back in a sec,' she said.

I didn't want to be left alone, the darkness of the cellar, the noise, even the dancers left me unaccountably helpless. 'Where are you going?'

'Got to see a man about a dog.' She undid my tie and disappeared into the lavatory.

I retreated into a deserted corner garnished with trampled cans of Lucozade and chewing-gum wrappers. Very soon I was approached by a man wearing a psychedelic track-suit and a string vest. His muscular black torso glistened with oil.

'You Mr Thomas,' he said.

It was not a question.

'I'm sorry, but do I know you?'

'Nah,' he said, still chewing something. He had perfect teeth and hundreds of them, unblemished save for two golden caps over the middle top. 'But I know you.'

'Well, that's all right then.' I knew it was a dumb thing to say.

He smiled and put his arms against the wall, placing me between them. I had an oiled bicep in each ear, which was a novel experience.

'I'm a friend of Whitey. Sees you in court.' The bright yellow light flashed on him, igniting the glitter in his short dreadlocks. 'See, me need some help and Whitey say how's you a good man.'

'What sort of help?'

'Me in trouble. Them blood-clot magistrates say if I don't pay them fines, I go's inside.'

'Have they ordered a means enquiry?' I felt slightly ludicrous discussing the finer points of sentencing procedure while sandwiched between a set of rippling muscles in a Camberwell cavern.

He told me that the court had not ordered a means enquiry and I said that he was 'laughing' then.

But he did not laugh.

'Whitey say how's you a *good* man,' he repeated, still chewing.

And yet again I remembered that in the criminal law there was no such thing as a free lunch. Life was cheap, freedom even cheaper, and many of our constitutional rights practically worthless. But nothing was free. There was always a price. Had Whitey tried to set me up with his coded warnings? Did he think I was such a soft touch? This, presumably, was the pay-off.

I was furious. 'You tell Whitey Innocent ... you can tell him to stick his good-for-nothing backside—'

Before my tirade had reached its crescendo the arms had disappeared and I was no longer trapped. The man had gone. I looked around me somewhat bemused and noticed in front of me, balanced precariously on their stilettos, the policewomen.

'Has he got any gear?' asked the first. Then she remembered her briefing. 'Only I'm looking for a fix ... like.'

It was hardly the most subtle piece of covert policing.

'Yeah,' said the other, playing with her perm. 'Me, too. Looking to score ... like.'

I tried to look ignorant and stupid, which was not too much of an effort that night. Behind the officers, I could see Emma furtively beckoning me towards her. She stood in the men's lavatory.

'Do step into my office, Mr Fawley.' The lanky man next to Emma was dangerously thin. He stood outside a row of cubicles and in an inch of suspicious water on the toilet floor.

There was a row of sinks filled with a soap solution, all of them dripping on to the tiles. A soggy roll of toilet paper covered a pile of something or other. Syringes everywhere but very few needles.

'Emma told me about your problem,' he said. His right arm was heavily scarred, the veins almost black.

I looked swiftly at Emma and wondered how much she knew. I said, 'What problem might that be?'

'Stonebury,' he said.

'Is that a problem?'

Emma tiptoed through a pool of stagnant water. 'Come on, Tom. Danny's only trying to help. He thinks he's solved the puzzle.'

'What puzzle?'

'The note in your brief,' she said.

I turned to the youth. 'Who put it there then?'

'Dunno,' he said.

'Brilliant,' I snapped. 'How could I ever have doubted you.' I began to walk out of the lavatory.

'But I do know what it's about,' said the man.

'Danny read Anglo-Saxon, Norse and Celtic studies at Cambridge,' said Emma.

'I'm very pleased for him,' I said.

A shadow appeared in the doorway.

'Hey, I'm a busy man.' Danny's accent dropped a couple of income groups. 'I'll check you later, star.'

'Sweet,' said the vanishing shadow.

The base started up again and this time the very tiles seemed to rattle.

'*Magistri sapientiae*,' said Danny, picking up a syringe and examining its contents. 'The most just of men. Elders who oversaw the sacrifice. Find out who they were.'

'You *see*,' said Emma, doe-eyed. 'I told Danny about the weird language in the note, about the murder and about the stones and ... well, Danny thinks it all fits together.'

'Yeah. *Falce aurea*, the golden sickle. A sacrificial knife. Was there straw, too?'

That struck a chord. I seemed to remember something about straw. Then I remembered the dream I had had on the first night of the trial. How did he know?

'A river of many streams?' He swaggered as arrogantly as his emaciated frame would allow, splashing towards the urinals. 'Blake's *Jerusalem*.'

'Rubbish.' I scowled, glad to contradict him.

I knew the poem tolerably well: some chariots of fire, a land that was green and pretty pleasant, even the odd satanic mill, but definitely no rivers.

The shadow again appeared at the doorway. 'You better chip, spar.'

In confusion, I looked to Emma.

She translated. 'I think we ought to leave.'

Danny tossed the syringe expertly out of the window, removed three silver-foil balls from his mouth and tried to flush them.

'So what's this about?' I asked.

He had waded his way to the door. 'The real clue is from the Greek.'

'What is?'

'The real clue. *Drus.*'

'Did you say Bruce? Who the hell is—'

'No, *drus*,' he said, spelling it out. 'D-R-U-S. *Drus*. From the Greek.'

I grabbed his baggy white tee-shirt and could have sworn that the pattern on it was little different from the pattern shaved into the witness's head at the Old Bailey. Then Danny's tee-shirt was tugged from the other side of the doorway.

'I'm Woman Detective Constable Leslie Roach. I am arresting you on suspicion of allowing these premises to be used for the supply of controlled drugs.'

Danny tried to look amazed, but failed.

'You have the right to remain silent,' she began to caution him. I was quite excited, never having seen a live arrest. 'But anything you say—'

'I know that crap,' said Danny.

The two women escorted him through a funnel of jeering ravers towards the staircase.

As he reached the second step, he turned and shouted, 'Children.' The jeering subsided. The ravers did appear young to me but this seemed rather patronising. 'Children,' he shouted with a broken voice. 'Children of Albion.'

Was this a reference to the home in Stonebury? And if so, then why? What was the connection between Kingsley, the contents of the notes and West Albion? However, the two policewomen had no such problems. They merely looked at each other, shrugged, tucked their white handbags under their unshaved armpits and pushed the man up the stairway.

'Danny thinks there may be some kind of cult involved,' Emma said.

'There is,' I replied. 'The cult of the personality. His personality. A thoroughly pretentious one.'

'He was just trying to help, Tom.'

'No, Emma. He was trying to sell drugs. I wonder what the

Greek is for five years in the slammer?' Although I tried to joke it off, a seed had been planted. The seemingly disparate pieces in the jigsaw might, after all, be connected. But what was the picture?

Chapter 25

The next morning was bright, with a crisp sun skimming off the Thames in an almost blinding way. The Middle Temple lawns were opal in colour as I walked slowly towards chambers. No court work, but I still had plenty to do.

I had been gazing at the river from my third-floor room for about twenty minutes, when the phone rang. Steve, my clerk, put through a call. The voice at the other end was round and soft, like a cheese that had been left out all night.

'This is Dove,' it said.

'Is it?'

'Yes, Dove. Gerald Dove. 'Bout that report. Much as we thought.'

'Really?' Had I missed something? What report? I tried to bluff it out and said more emphatically, 'Oh, *really*.'

'So that's 'bout it,' he said. 'Guess you won't be needing me after all.'

'No, I don't suppose we will.'

'Right then, goodbye.'

'Oh, just one thing, Mr Dove.'

'Fire away.'

'What on earth are you talking about?'

I heard him tapping the phone at the other end. 'Sorry, thought you said, What on earth—'

'Yes, I did.'

Another tap of the receiver. 'Didn't Miss Sharpe tell you then?'

'Tell me what?'

''Bout me seeing the stuff.'

'The stuff?'

'The handwritten note Inspector Payne found in your punter's cell.' It started to make sense. 'Do you want the good news or the bad news?'

How I hated that game. 'Go on,' I said.

'Good news is, my conclusions are ... well, pretty conclusive.'

'And?'

'And the bad news is, your man wrote the note.'

Why then did Kingsley want a graphologist to check the handwriting? It was sheer lunacy. I consoled myself that one of the benefits of defending is that you are not obliged to disclose unhelpful expert reports to the prosecution. But the police would know that a graphologist had inspected the note from Kingsley's cell, and it would be obvious why we didn't dare call any evidence.

'Can you be sure?' I asked rather optimistically. 'I mean how certain can you be that Kingsley wrote it?'

'Never can be certain. Not in our game. You see, nothing is certain. But to use a technical term – it's as near as dammit.' He sniggered at his *bon mot*. All experts had one so-called joke, except the short-sighted heart-throb of the mortuary slab, Harry Molesey. 'You see, Mr Fawley, graphology isn't an exact science.'

'Well, what is it – exactly?'

'An opinion. But an expert one.'

'And what's yours?'

'That Richard Kingsley wrote that note.'

The line crackled and I muttered under my breath, 'Bloody idiot.'

More vigorous banging of the receiver. 'What did you say?'

'No. Not you. Kingsley. Mr Dove, is it ... possible, just possible, someone else wrote the note, I mean impersonating Kingsley's hand?'

'Anything's possible, Mr Fawley.'

An opening? Microscopic, but perhaps it would provide a little room for manoeuvre? 'Well, how possible is this?'

'Let me put it this way. Physicists say that in theory an elephant can hang off a cliff with its trunk holding on to a daisy. That's technically possible.'

'I see.'

'And if I had the choice?' he continued.

'Yes?'

'I'd back Nelly the elephant against your client every time.'

'Thank you, Mr Dove. We won't need to trouble you at trial.'

When he hung up, I buzzed the clerk's room. 'Steve, ring Goldman and Goldman.' I was in no mood to mention the third Goldman. 'I need a con at Battersea prison this afternoon in the case of Kingsley.'

Steve was as clueless in life as he was in the law, but he had learnt the first rule of administration: Procrastinate at all costs. 'Bit short notice to arrange a prison con, Mr Fawley. You sure?'

'No, I'm not sure,' I said. 'But I'm as near as dammit.'

I suppose I used to take a certain contrary pleasure in describing myself as the most ignorant excuse of a man to toss on a barrister's wig. It did earn me what Emma called 'street cred' with some of my clients. But, at times, it could be a nuisance. This was one of those times. If a little learning is a dangerous thing, none at all could be a decided disadvantage.

I had no idea whether Danny, Man of the Streets – and the urinals – was talking complete drivel. He did know about the straw, but perhaps Emma told him that. So where did that leave me? A police informer trying to squeeze me for money and a message from a dead girl. And all this on legal aid. I needed a coffee.

There was a little Italian cafeteria on the Embankment which, the sign above the door boasted, made the best cappuccino from here to Milan. The sandwich-maker was, in fact, Sicilian. Vinny had chestnut-coloured skin and a neatly trimmed moustache.

He always asked about my cases. Vinny couldn't understand the fuss. If they were innocent, they would be acquitted. If they were guilty, they would go to prison – unless they had enough money and sense to bribe the judge and jury. The law was just another business like making salami sandwiches.

'What's wrong?' Vinny asked as I pushed my way past a tramp in the doorway who was looking at a copy of the *Financial Times*. 'You look like shit.'

'A cappuccino, Vinny.'

'I got some lovely Danish.'

'They look stale. No, Vinny, coffee's fine.'

'What's a matter?' he asked.

'I don't know.'

And it was true. It was not just the case or Penny or Justine. It was something more. It was me – I just couldn't seem to be around people. I annoyed them, they annoyed me, I annoyed myself – constantly. Nothing seemed to make much sense, but I could vaguely discern a force, or maybe it was a presence, just out of my grasp.

Vinny handed me a white plastic cup with bubbles frothing under the lid, which reminded me of the sinks in the nightclub. My stomach turned – I needed some solids.

'Give me a Danish, then,' I said.

But Vinny had spotted a temp from the management consultants across the road and preened his moustache with a white plastic fork before handing over the pastry.

The tramp had retired to a wooden bench just beyond the side gates to the Temple. As I passed him, he spouted out in a most perfunctory way his standard request. 'Got fifty pence for a cup of tea, guv?'

'Tea's only thirty pence,' I replied.

He neatly folded the newspaper. 'Well, that's inflation for you. Those interest rates, they're a killer, ain't they?' He scoured the share prices with the thoroughness of someone who had nothing to do for the rest of the day.

I handed him a coin and gestured towards the newspaper. 'Do you mind?' I asked.

He gave it to me and proceeded to inspect my coin as though it were a forgery. He bit it. 'Can't be too careful,' he said. 'Lot of sly ones around. Don't know who you can trust.'

I turned to the television listings and there it was:

'9.30 p.m. *Real Lives*. Tonight no-nonsense judge, Hilary Hardcastle, addresses the European Society of Christian Lawyers on how English judges strive to protect the rights of the innocent.'

But who, I thought, would protect the innocent from Hilary Hardcastle? It seemed, then, that my clerk Rose had probably got it wrong. The message must have been *Real Lives* and not, Read *Times*. Did that mean that Rose had also got the name wrong? Did the message read Love Milly? Thinking again about it, as I chomped my way through the stale Danish pastry, it could not have been from Molly. Could it?

Chapter 26

As I sat in Temple library later that day, surrounded by the brooding portraits of illustrious judges, I glanced through a book that made fascinating, if gruesome, reading. I had remembered what Rupert Livingstone had said about punishment, and decided to do some investigating.

The pages of the book were full of the instruments of mutilation and punishment: whipping-posts, pillories, gibbets, racks, whirligigs, branding irons and stocks. Chapter Eleven: the Brank – a metal cage for the head, used for gagging a brawling woman. I tried not to speculate whether Hilary Hardcastle's head would have fitted into the cage in the picture.

The book was called *Punishments of Yore* and had been written by some particularly ghoulish court clerk in Rochdale at the turn of the century. What, I wondered, prompts a man to write a book about scalding, burning, torture and transportation?

I flicked through chapters on executions and witchcraft, on church sanctuary and the laws of the Saxons, when I found what I was looking for.

'The Stang. An ancient custom of ridicule.'

I tried to remember the precise context in which Kingsley had shouted out those strange words, but could only resurrect the dismal vision of Legat strapped to the bed.

'An effigy of the offender is mounted on a pole – a Stang – and taken around the town amid boisterous abuse.'

It seemed incongruous to have so banal a punishment in amongst that catalogue of ordeals. What game was Kingsley playing? I tried to remember his cell with its television and the putrid flowers, his manuscripts and the doctors running around him; I tried to picture Kingsley but now not only his eyes, but the very face itself was white and soulless and—

'The Stang (the offence). Inflicted upon a husband who had been unfaithful to his wife.'

It must have been Kingsley's twisted idea of a joke. He had to demonstrate his acumen, his learning; he could not just ... then I had a thought, and it was this: How did Kingsley *know*?

I tossed down the book, causing the cover to fall off in a small puff of dust, and I rushed to the telephone outside the Common Room. I phoned the clerks.

'Steve, what are the visiting hours at Battersea?'

'I'm sorry,' he said. 'I already told you, Mr Fawley. Couldn't get you a con.'

'What are the visiting hours at Battersea, Steve?'

'Starts two thirty. But I—'

'Ring the prison. Tell them I shall be there at two o'clock.'

'They won't like it,' he said defensively.

'They're not meant to keep people out. They're meant to keep people in, for Christ's sake.' I hung up on him which is something I had never done before.

My chest was tight, my fists clenched. I knew I ought to think clearly, but was sure I could not. How could Kingsley know? I had told no one except Penny. Justine wanted to keep it quiet. Perhaps we had been seen? Maybe by one of the officers in the case? I sat in one of the rusty armchairs in the Common Room and waited for two o'clock.

The Common Room itself was an indulgently comfortable area. On the tables in front of the armchairs were chess sets and unfinished games of backgammon. The furnishings were soft, faded and the walls were covered with the finest literature and poetry. It was a place frequented by law students in awkwardly fitting suits pretending to be barristers, and barristers drinking warm beer and eating peanuts trying to relive their student days.

I tried to close my eyes and rest. My sleep was becoming more and more troubled. But when I shut my eyelids, the images that flashed before me were far worse than my racing thoughts. Yet again I saw Stonebury. But now I was closer and stood at the outer circle. I could not keep still and suddenly found myself with an anthology of poetry.

The poem on page ninety-three was familiar: *those* feet taking a walk in ancient times, green mountains, but – as I suspected – nothing about rivers and streams. Four verses in outdated typescript. But there was a footnote for the penultimate line; it concerned the word Jerusalem.

'Lines from (Preface to) *Book of Milton*. Known commonly as "Jerusalem". Not to be confused with the long prophetic poem, *Jerusalem*.'

There were *two* Jerusalems.

Then the sweet odour of twelve-year-old whisky was unmistakable. Jamie's gait was almost steady as he walked through the door, but his cupped right hand shook just a little. Insert a small glass and no one would have noticed the withdrawals. He looked as rough as I felt. Was this how I was beginning to appear to people?

'Come to brush up your iambic pentameters?' I said.

'Early bath,' he replied and sat down heavily opposite me.

'Client didn't turn up?'

'Oh, he turned up all right, the little tea-leaf. So did his mother. Said I was drunk. Can you believe the effrontery. It's an—'

'It's an outrage, Jamie. That's what it is.'

'Anyway,' he said, smoothing out a newspaper on his lap, 'he can get his beloved mother to defend him.' He looked at me, pleading with the wide eyes of a child who knows he has been

171

caught. 'I swear, Tommy. This morning ... I never touched a drop.'

'I know,' I said. It was probably true. But I also knew that he did not need to. The recognised boundaries between morning and night had long since lost their clarity in Jamie Armstrong's hazy world.

He said, 'I see that old bat Hardcastle is out pontificating again.'

'Nine thirty tonight, isn't it?' I said. 'Too close to the watershed for my liking.'

'No,' he said. 'She's droning on at six.' He handed me the paper open on the Court Circular page. Visits by dukes and duchesses, the closing of factories, the opening of job centres. Halfway down the page was this entry: 'Lecture. European Society of Christian Lawyers. Hardcastle J. 6 p.m. Friends Meeting House.'

'She is on the box later as well,' I said. They must have planned to tape her speech, considering it far too risky to unleash the firebrand wit live to the nation.

While Jamie looked forlornly at the locked bar, I surveyed the page. It was an odd mixture. Births and Deaths, Flatshares and Funeral Arrangements. The In Memoriam section was the saddest. It was headed 'Private'.

| JD | Always yours. | RL |
| LC | Never forgotten. | DC |

Who was supposed to read these? I almost felt as if I was intruding as I scanned through these messages of private grief. As I handed the newspaper back to Jamie, I noticed the next entry.

Who's met or seen red?   M

Then I saw the dedication. It was to TF. Then I realised that the newspaper, of course, was *The Times*.

TF   Who's met or seen red?   M

172

Chapter 27

I found a bookshop on a south-facing corner of Fleet Street, not far from the round church of St Mary's in the Temple. In the eleventh century bands of crusaders set off to wrest the Holy Land from the 'infidel'. By 1118, one band had assumed the name of Knights of the Temple and they built a round church which still stands. Of course, I could never hope to match their grandeur. But I, too, had a private search for Jerusalem. Not so much a quest as a grubbing around in the undergrowth trying to sniff out the truth.

I imagined that a Greek dictionary would be rather intimidating for someone whose grasp of antiquity was limited to a couple of years of Latin, *Up Pompeii* and Frankie Howerd in a toga. But once in the bookshop, I used an index of Greek letters to translate *drus* into the funny symbols that Aristotle once used. I vaguely knew that our letter D was delta in Greek. The rest came quickly. Soon, I found the place.

'*Drus*, oak tree.'

So now I knew. *Drus* was Greek for oak tree. What is more, I knew that oak tree in Greek was *drus*. But how did that help? In my experience, oaks were about as English – and about as banal – as bangers and mash. They hardly resonated with mythical significance. Perhaps I was missing the point?

I was more optimistic about William Blake. In a far corner was a shelf full of black-spined paperbacks claiming to be classics. I tilted my head to that ridiculous angle people adopt in bookshops, and scanned the Bs.

Bacon, Balzac, Baudelaire, Beauvoir (de), more Balzac (why did he write so many novels?), Beckett, Bible (The), Blake.

There were two books. The first was called *Songs of Innocence and Experience*. Hurriedly flicking through it, I was intrigued, if slightly repelled, by the poems, which were surrounded by gaudy pictures. I had never seen such images.

Flaxen-haired children in nauseatingly coloured smocks walked through strange woods with lambs at their feet and serpents in the trees. And the words were even more fantastic: tiger spelt Tyger, invisible worms flying through the night, poison trees, a little girl lost, beds of crimson joy.

The second book was instantly more promising. *The Marriage of Heaven and Hell*. That was something I could relate to, and inevitably thought of Penny.

I was getting nowhere. Where was *Jerusalem*? However, there were no more books by Blake so I tried the *New Companion to English Literature*.

J: Jabberwock, Jane Eyre, Jekyll and Mr Hyde (The Strange Case of Dr), Jeronimo, Jerusalem.

Something, somewhere clicked.

'*Jerusalem: the Emanation of the Giant Albion.* A long prophetic poem by Blake.'

Giant *Albion*. What was it Danny shouted as he was led away in handcuffs? Why did that word keep coming up? Who or what was Albion?

There was a growing queue at the till, which was out of order. A secretary, purchasing her weekly Mills and Boon, waited for her change from a young assistant. He had clearly been brought up on credit cards and calculators and struggled with the sums. Glancing at my watch, I saw it was nearly twelve o'clock.

I pushed to the front of the queue. 'Where can I buy this?' I asked pointing to the entry in the *New Companion*.

'What?' said the assistant.

'*Jerusalem.*'

'You can't.'

'Why not?'

'Not in print.'

'Why not?'

'Ask the publishers, mate.'

'Well, I'm asking you.' My patience was waning. 'And don't call me mate.'

'Move on,' said the youth. 'People are waiting.'

'Where can I find a copy of it then ... to read?'

'Dunno.'

'Well, can't you find out for me ... mate?'

The assistant seemed about to mouth some sort of obscenity when the manager emerged from a trap door, somewhere behind the till. He was tall, thin and aesthetic-looking, wearing John Lennon glasses and a herringbone waistcoat.

He took off his glasses, cleaned them and then looked at me solemnly. 'You want the Tate,' he said.

On arriving at Pimlico tube station, I passed through a strange hinterland of seedy guest-houses and sophisticated mews before reaching the Tate Gallery. On the cascade of stone steps outside the museum was the usual scattering of the youth of Europe, browsing through *Rough Guides* and listening to their Walkmans. The gallery's collection was blessed with an embarrassment of artistic riches. But there was only one thing I wanted to see.

As I approached the rooms that housed the permanent Blake collection, my steps started to echo in the empty rooms and the light seemed to fade. Surrounding me, strewn across the walls, were images of strange gods, corruption and decay. There was a painting of a man standing before a fiery chariot. He was naked and his head was bowed by the brilliant light emanating from a wrathful figure with a shock of white hair and a fearsome nose.

'God judging Adam.'

It was a woman's voice. I used to hate people speaking to me in public. For me, galleries were little different to churches: places for silence and for some sort of reflection – whatever you could manage. And for those reasons I had long before abandoned going to either.

'Don't like it, do you?' she said.

I still hadn't taken my eyes from the frightening colours of the painting.

The voice was small, but hectic, all over the place like a buzzing fly. 'I suppose I quite like the horses,' she said. 'They are horses, you know – two of them, you can just see the hind legs of the second. See?' A delicate arm covered in brushed denim and smelling somehow of adhesives, hovered near the canvas. 'People used to think those lines came from this painting. You know, "Bring me my bow of burning gold" – all that chariots of fire stuff. But it's really nothing to do with it at all; shame really; still, it's interesting. Well, if you're interested in that sort of thing – of course, I am. But then I would be ... oops. Here I go. Gabbling on. Better dash. Work to do and—'

'Don't go,' I said.

She was small, as fragile as one of the children in the poetry book, but her hair was not flaxen. It was tied behind her small head. She constantly bobbed up and down on the balls of her feet, trying to hide her lack of height, but she was not the sort of person to wear heels. She had thick glasses that reflected the yellow and red streaks from the melting sun in the painting.

She continued, 'Sorry to butt in. We don't get many people down this end really. Everyone goes to the Turner. You know, tour parties: Blake? Who the — is William Blake? Which way to the Turner, they ask? Still, their loss is ... sorry, there I go again.'

'No, please. I don't mind.'

'It's just ... I hardly speak to anyone all day. Then when I see someone: bang. Away I go.'

'Do you work here?'

'Sort of. I'm doing some research on old W.B. Oh, it's too tedious. I won't bore you with – actually, it's called: "Blake

– mystic or madman". That's the trend nowadays. Snappy titles for your thesis. User-friendly.'

'I need some help.' Before us Adam still cowered.

'Help? Really?' She tried to hide her excitement, failed, moved her head towards me. The flanks of the horses appeared in her right-hand lens.

'Yes. Some help with Blake,' I said.

She threw both denim sleeves towards the ceiling. 'Oh, thank you, God. Thank you.' Then she looked at the fearsome visage of judgment. 'This way,' she said, leading me into a shadowy corner with all the fanaticism of a train-spotter at Clapham Junction.

'Should be a doddle.' She seemed pretty confident after I explained what I was looking for. Not everything. Just what was safe, and sane, to relate. 'We've got colour copies of all one hundred plates of the book of *Jerusalem*. My name's Anna, by the way. Where do you want to start?'

As we wandered along rows of dimly lit reproductions, the girl chattered away at a thousand words a minute. She told me about the Romantics and opium and hallucinations; about giant fleas and about God, but not in that order.

'I think this is what you want.' Before me was a plate with minutely printed writing. Intense writing, the writing of a man with something to say. '*Felix culpa*, really. Well, Blake's version.'

'Felix who?'

She was obviously tempted to laugh, but flicked a non-existent speck away from her glasses and bobbed once again. 'The *felix culpa* myth. From Eve to Mary. Women's guilt and all that. You know, the dark ages, pre-bra burning and Germaine Greer. Lead us not into temptation, unless you happen to be a woman, and then we'll bite the apple and blame you. Very right on – I don't think.'

Eventually we got to Plate Number 61. Her crooked little fingers ran under a passage no different from any other. 'Then Mary burst forth...'

'Rather an ugly image,' she said, as she continued reading. '"She flowed like a river of many streams."'

I read it out loud. Then again. Louder. 'What does it mean?'

She looked at me and ran her fingers through her hair. 'I could be really snotty and say, Well, what does anything mean? But to tell the truth, I'm not sure. You won't tell anyone, will you?'

'No, of course – but Mary as in?'

'Mary as in Mary. You know, Hail Mary full of— the Mother of God.'

Then I realised and I remembered the charge: Richard Kingsley, you are charged with murder and the particulars of the offence are that you murdered Mary – *also known as* Molly – Summers.

The woman said, 'I'm sorry I can't be of more assistance. I'm more of an academic, I suppose. Sorry.'

'There's no need to apologise,' I said.

'Why not?'

'Because of this.' I pointed to another of the plates. And there, in a heavily slanted Gothic script was a fragment of a sentence that I could barely read.

All things begin and end in ... Albion's rocky shore.

'Where is Albion?' I asked.

'Where or what,' she replied.

'How do you mean?'

'Well, Albion was the ancient Celtic name for Britain. But for Blake, Albion was a kind of mythical giant. The source, the seed, the father of all things. I hope that's not too esoteric?'

I did not reply.

'I'm getting more esoteric all the time,' she said. 'You see, doing a thesis is like having a pet. You grow more and more like it. At night I have these weird— you know, like Blake did. I suppose I'm very much like old Willy. Except I can't paint. Mind you, some would say he couldn't either. Paint, I mean—'

'What's that?' I asked.

Behind her, rising from her shoulders, was an image of fallen angels and showers of blood and threatening skies and – most vividly of all – circles of stones. I felt a strange sense of *déjà vu*. It was as though someone had taken a photograph of one of my dreams and coloured it with oil paints.

She put on an academic voice. 'Much debated that one. It's the final plate. A sort of culmination of the book of *Jerusalem*. It's thought the figure on the left is—'

'What are *those*?' I pointed to something strange at the foot of the stones. 'Are they clouds? Why are they on the ground?'

'They're not clouds. They're trees.'

'Trees? What sort of trees?'

'Oh, I don't know ... oh, yes – one school of thought says they're ... oaks.'

'Did you say oaks?'

'Yes, oaks. Oaks, you know, as in oak trees. As in, from little acorns do large oaks—'

Again I remembered what I had imagined on the first night of the trial. Walking over wet grass, scattered with acorns, which must have come from oak trees. But what had oak trees to do with the murder of Molly Summers?

Finally, I said, 'And oaks as in *drus*?'

'Ah,' she said. 'So you can read Greek?'

'No, I can't,' I replied. 'But I know a man who can.'

Chapter 28

I was let into the prison immediately, and not long after two o'clock I was walking past the strapped and contorted figure of Legat.

When I entered Richard Kingsley's cell, he was not in bed. His wheelchair faced the high barred window in the way that a spring bloom arches towards the sun. All I could see of him was a cruelly hunched back and a tangle of hair as he craned his neck towards the warmth. But you knew that the soil was infertile and this plant could never fully develop.

He did not turn round. 'I was just thinking that there were one or two points of detail I should like your advice upon. Fine-tuning, nothing more—'

'Who told you?' I snarled.

His pale head slowly rotated past an immobile shoulder. 'I'm sorry?'

'Who told you, Kingsley?'

'Forgive me. I thought it was a convention of sorts to be courteous to one's client.'

'Who told you?'

'This is a novel approach. What is this? Method advocacy?' He wheeled himself towards me.

'Who told you?'

'You did.'

'*What?*' I had not expected that answer.

'You did, Mr Fawley. I wonder, could you just?' He pointed

181

towards a pristine white cushion for his back, which I automatically handed him. 'They want to keep me strapped up. Rigid. Straighten the spine. But one must pamper oneself – at least, sometimes. Now, where are we? Oh, yes. It was easy really. I do hope you're not as obvious with the secrets of my defence.'

'This is all bullshit.' I towered way above him.

'It's the way you looked at her.'

'And how was that?'

'Hungrily.' He licked his lips. 'Also you had made some sort of assignation with her—'

'You heard that?'

'—once you thought you'd forced me to plead guilty. The Savoy, wasn't it?'

I sat down on the bed.

He said, 'I can't fault your taste.'

'Justine Wright?'

'No, the Savoy. An excellent selection of clarets. Though their older Burgundies are a little overpriced, don't you think?'

'What are you after, Kingsley?'

'After?'

'What are you up to?'

'Am I to understand that I'm being cross-examined now? This might be fun.'

I paced around the bed, and took a deep breath. 'We got the forensic report on that handwriting.'

'Of course, it was mine,' he said nonchalantly.

'You mean you already—'

'If someone is trying to set me up, of course they will do a good job.'

'Or if you're guilty as sin and desperate to wriggle your way out, then you'll try anything.'

'Well, yes,' he said. 'That is equally consistent with the facts.' He rolled in the direction of a square table with a small bunch of white orchids, their petals beginning to shrivel at the edges.

When he came to a halt, I said, 'I think you'd better stop messing us around.'

'And I think we should get the knife tested.'

'You are joking?'

'I never joke, Mr Fawley. Not when my future is at stake. There are, I presume, independent fingerprint experts available to the defence?'

'It's a waste of time.'

'But are there such experts?'

In fact, I had frequently used Geoffrey Snyde, editor of an excruciatingly tedious journal called *Fingerprint Quarterly*. Snyde was one of the leaders in the field but I wasn't about to tell Kingsley that. 'They haven't said it was your fingerprints on the knife.'

'Nor have they excluded me.'

'True.'

'How many of those ... ridge characteristics, is it? ... do you need?' he asked, meaning the bumps and furrows that make anyone's fingerprints unique.

'They have to find sixteen points that are identical,' I said.

'Well, I want an expert's opinion, to see if my prints match those on the knife *in any way*.'

I told him that I would think about it, but refused to make any promises.

'There's something else I want to discuss,' he said.

At that moment the ominous shadow of the ward sister appeared at the door and seemed to fill the room. Kingsley put a right index finger to his lips and almost magically the room was in silence.

Having his chamber-pot removed in the presence of a visitor was an indignity Richard Kingsley felt so acutely that it actually made him wince.

It is a source of constant astonishment to me how nurses in a hospital can brandish a container swirling with human waste with complete indifference. But the sister left in a very matter-of-fact way and told Kingsley that although the pot wasn't as full as the previous day, she had 'better empty it all the same'.

After that Kingsley did not appear quite so confident.

'Mr Fawley, I was wondering how I should ... well, how would you advise me to behave in court?'

Clients often ask this. It is important. A few stage directions can give a performance a spurious credibility.

I told him, 'Treat it like church. Dress in black, sit in silence – and pray.'

'Quite so. But pray to whom?' A half-smile surfaced on his otherwise expressionless face. 'Do you think I killed that girl?'

'If you want to know, the truth is, I don't know what to think.'

'And you don't want to know?'

'I didn't say that.'

'You did before. You see, Mr Fawley, there is something I should tell you.'

He stared at me intensely with his head cocked to the left. This is how he would plead to the jury for his freedom. If, that is, I allowed him anywhere near the witness box.

'Perhaps I'm a little fussy,' he said, 'but sixteen is a little too old for my tastes.'

'Well, that's a cast-iron defence. I didn't kill Molly Summers, members of the jury, because I only have sex with under-age girls.'

'Is that what I said?'

'It's what the prosecution will say.' The reptilian features of Hilary Hardcastle flashed through my mind. 'Or the judge.'

'You still don't understand my sexuality.'

I remembered the sign above the door in Johnson's. 'Look, I'll find you an argument in court, but I'm not obliged to find you an understanding out of it.'

'And what does that mean, Mr Fawley?'

'It means that I haven't really thought about you.'

'No.' He wheeled a little closer to me as I sat on the bed.

'No, you don't want to understand me. You find my sexuality revolting.'

'I have no opinion.'

Kingsley adopted a solemn voice, as though he was reciting a psalm from the Bible. '"Henceforth,"' he said, seeming to quote from somewhere, '"I shall do all I can to outrage the laws of both nature and religion."'

'Well, Mr Kingsley. At least you're consistent,' I said. 'Is it a quote from one of your books?'

'Not mine.'

'Then whose?'

'The Marquis de Sade's.'

'You're quoting a dead Frenchman to me?' I said.

Kingsley ignored my flippancy and said, 'Have you read *One Hundred and Twenty Days of Sodom*?'

'Not recently, Mr Kingsley.' A smile flickered across my face, I was not sure why. 'I've read *A Hundred Years of Solitude*. I suppose it's the next best thing.'

'It is a joke to you. You think once somebody has lost the ability to walk, he should lose other ... urges as well.'

'Does it really matter?'

'There are some things so powerful, Mr Fawley, that nothing will, nothing can contain them.'

This was not a conversation I wished to have.

Kingsley continued, 'You look at me and you think, Well I might play around a bit and cheat on my wife, but I'm not like Kingsley. Heaven forbid. Touching little girls. Little girls like my daughter.'

'You're a sick man.'

'But you've noticed how she sometimes flirts with you when Mummy's not home and how she's beginning to fill her school blouse.'

I did not answer.

He looked at the orchids with their falling petals. 'We shouldn't feel guilty,' he said. 'There's too much guilt in the world. I mean, do you blame a wasp for stinging?'

185

Kingsley had a rather attractive voice which is something I kept forgetting. And I imagined him whispering with those sophisticated tones into the small ears of a fourteen-year-old girl.

'Our minds, Mr Fawley, are like very sensitive receivers. And just because you don't tune into a certain frequency, it doesn't mean it's not there. It is. It's all there. Everything you've ever wanted. Everything you've been denied. All of it. Just waiting.'

'Is that the Marquis de Sade, too?'

'No, that's me. They didn't have radio transmitters in pre-Revolutionary France. Or didn't anyone tell you?'

'I just thought—'

'There's no need for you to think, Mr Fawley. No need at all.' Kingsley's eyes changed from their usual dismal hue to a yellowy white. 'You see, Mr Fawley, like me or loathe me, I'm just a product of our society.'

'In the same way that sludge is a product of pig farming?'

'No, like adultery is the product of marriage.'

I had again made the mistake of trying to compete with Kingsley. I was stung and I was angry. 'Whether or not you killed Molly Summers,' I snapped, 'you're part of this, Kingsley. Now the jury might convict you or the jury might acquit you. I don't know and frankly, I don't care. But what I do know is that unless you level with me, the truth will come out about that girl ... and if you mess me about, I'll be the one who makes sure that happens. During your trial.'

'Don't make trouble for yourself,' Kingsley said.

'Are you threatening me?'

'Warning you.'

'From what?'

'From yourself.'

I laughed at that, but did not much feel like laughing. 'I can do anything that I want to in this case. You're locked up with the bed-pans and the nurse from hell, remember? So how can you stop me?'

'I don't need to.'

'Meaning?'

'Meaning, I don't need to stop you, Mr Fawley. There are plenty of other people who will gladly prevent you from meddling around in Stonebury.'

I stood up and moved towards the door. 'What will I find when I go there?'

'I warn you not to go,' he replied.

'Will I find Philip Templeman? Is that what you're worried about? What's his connection to this case, Kingsley? Does he know of your other – indiscretions? Is that it?'

'Take my advice. Don't go to Stonebury.'

'Why? What have you got to hide?'

'I don't have the monopoly of skeletons in the village.'

'And what does that mean?'

'I think our little chat is at an end,' Kingsley said.

'And, of course, you know absolutely nothing about *The Times*.'

'Goodbye, Mr Fawley.'

'Or Whitey Innocent? Who just happens to be in the same nick.'

'Nurse,' he called.

'And what about William sodding Blake?'

'*Nurse*,' he shouted. In the ward outside, I could hear Legat's crazed voice echoing the call.

The sister arrived with her sleeves rolled up like a bricklayer.

'Mr Fawley would like to leave,' said Kingsley. 'Please show him the way out.'

'You've dug your own grave, Kingsley,' I said as the sister laid her calloused hands on my shoulders.

'And you want to look in it?' he said.

'I'll find what there is to find in Stonebury.'

'You just don't understand, do you?'

'Understand what?'

'That when you look into the abyss, Mr Fawley—'

187

'Into the *what*?'

'—the abyss looks into you. It's Nietzsche,' Kingsley said. 'A dead German.'

Legat broke into insane laughter as the cell door was shut.

Chapter 29

A question criminal barristers often ask themselves is: How would I cope if it were me in the dock? Thanks to the petty-mindedness of Judge Hilary Hardcastle, my stubborn refusal to apologise, and the bureaucracy of the Bar, I was about to find out. That day.

When I had left Kingsley the previous afternoon, I took a cab to Soho and wandered through the slumbering 'streets until dark. I debated whether I should abscond and fail to appear before the professional conduct tribunal. But I had never broken the law, never really defied authority, never done anything I should not. So at 2.15 precisely on a Friday afternoon in December, I entered the Grand Parliament Rooms, the Temple's inner sanctum, to hear the proceedings in the case against one Thomas Fawley.

'Are you ready to enter a plea?' the chairman of the conduct tribunal asked. It was usually presided upon by a High Court judge. The fates were clearly conspiring against me – I had drawn Mr Justice Gritt, trial judge at the Sarah Morrow trial. The one member of the judiciary to detest me more than Hilary Hardcastle.

'I'm ready, M'Lord,' I replied. Then I denied the charge of conduct unbecoming the profession of barrister.

The conventional wisdom when hauled up in front of the hastily convened inquisition is to get an establishment silk to represent you, to grovel profusely, and to try to get away with a stiff ticking-off.

'Do you wish us to wait for your counsel, Mr Fawley?' Gritt asked.

'No, M'Lord.'

I had chosen to represent myself. I had no intention of grovelling and fully expected to be disbarred, though only for a relatively short period. I intended to look upon it as a well-deserved break.

Gritt was delighted at the prospect of having me attempt to defend myself, no doubt remembering the adage that someone who represents himself has a fool for a client.

The tables and chairs of the room had been arranged for what looked like a prayer meeting. There was, of course, no dock. But nor, I feared, any pretence that I was innocent until proved guilty.

Everyone was in dark suits. Gritt was flanked by two senior barristers known as Benchers and a Lay Assessor. This interested member of the public was Major General Arthur Ponsonby, veteran, it was rumoured, of various firing squads in the war, a man for whom insubordination ranked with high treason and homosexuality in the forces.

'Do you wish to open the case, Mr Livingstone?' asked Gritt.

Prosecuting me was the man who, on our last meeting at the Bar Mess, I had technically assaulted. If I were seriously contesting the absurd allegations, I would have objected to Rupert Livingstone for no other reason than denying him the pleasure of casting the first stone.

As Livingstone got to his feet, he whispered to me, 'Why don't you surrender now? You haven't got a hope, Fawley.'

'How do you know?' I hissed back.

'I know everything about everything, remember?' He stood up tall and effected his most obsequious voice. 'May it please the court, this case is very straightforward. It is alleged Mr Fawley was intolerably rude' – he stressed the word intolerably – 'to a judge sitting in open court at the Old Bailey. And it is your task, once you have heard all the evidence to decide whether he is not guilty or—'

'Yes, yes, whether he is guilty,' said Gritt. 'We know our task. Get on with it. Not much evidence is there?' He looked at his pocket watch. 'Only I've got another appointment. An *important* one.'

'There is only one witness, M'Lord.'

'Well call him.'

'Her,' said Livingstone. Then rather solemnly he announced, 'Call Hilary Hardcastle.'

When the diminutive judge scuttled into the room, in the same ill-fitting suit and dangerously high heels that she wore to Manly's wake, my heart sank.

The usher picked up the Bible and was about to offer it to Hardcastle when Gritt threw down his pen.

'My sister judge does *not* need to take the oath.' By some ancient convention judges were deemed incapable of uttering anything but the truth.

Livingstone then began to lead Hardcastle through her evidence as to how she was forced to take over the Kingsley trial at short notice after the 'tragic' death of her Brother Judge Manly.

'Mr Fawley lost his rag completely,' she said. 'I've never seen the like in all my years on the Northern Circuit or sitting in London.'

'What in fact did he say?' Livingstone had resolved to go for an early kill.

'When I refused his client bail—'

Gritt intervened. 'The murderer?'

I got to my feet. 'The man accused of murder ... M'Lord.'

'Sit down,' shouted Gritt.

'You see,' said Hardcastle with a well-practised sigh of judicial exasperation.

Livingstone paused a moment to ensure that all the members of the tribunal had grasped the point. They had. Then he repeated, but this time more slowly, 'What in fact did he say?'

'He said, "This is outrageous."' Hardcastle looked at Gritt

and pretended to be on the verge of bursting into tears.

'He said *that*?' Gritt was fuming.

'In open court,' Hardcastle added.

'And did he say anything else?' asked Livingstone.

'He said, "This is disgraceful. I haven't had an opportunity."
He also babbled on about his rights.'

'His *what*?' asked the major general.

'His rights.' Hardcastle's voice was barely more than a
whisper.

The old soldier shook his head incredulously, ruing the day
conscription was abolished, the proles were given the vote and
capital punishment was removed from the statute book.

Livingstone had finished. He told Hardcastle to wait where
she was. 'There *may* be some more questions.'

Gritt looked at me, defying a repeat performance of such
colossal insubordination.

'No questions, thank you,' I said. I did not even get up.

'Nothing?' asked Gritt.

'No, thank you.'

'At all?'

'At all,' I said.

'Not even ... not even – an apology?'

'No questions, thank you,' I repeated as politely as possible.
I even managed to effect a little smile which sent Gritt
spiralling into an unspoken rage.

Livingstone bowed as low as decency would allow. 'That,
M'Lord, is the case against Mr Fawley.'

Gritt muttered to his colleagues and then he addressed me.
'I presume you wish to call evidence, Mr Fawley?'

'No, thank you,' I said.

'No evidence?'

'No.'

'Not even ... with a view to mitigation?'

'I haven't been found guilty yet,' I said, and as soon as I
said it, I knew it would add a couple of months to the ban.
Agriculturists have striven with great ingenuity for decades

to cultivate tomatoes as red in hue as the shade Mr Justice Gritt's face then became. Just when I thought his anger had reached its height, the door opened.

It was Justine.

'M'Lord,' she said. 'I know this is a little unusual, but may I be heard? As an *amicus*?'

'As a what?' barked the major general.

'As a friend,' said Gritt. 'Of the court.'

'Isn't this very irregular?' The soldier was itching to get the rifles loaded.

Justine moved a couple of paces forward, and although she did not look at me, she looked stunning. 'I was there,' she said. 'I fear there has been some terrible mistake. It's my fault entirely.'

Gritt was astonished. '*Your* fault?'

Justine explained patiently. 'A handwritten note was found in the cell of Mr Fawley's client.'

'Found by whom?' Gritt demanded.

'By the officer in the case, Inspector Payne.'

'Obviously a most diligent policeman,' said Gritt.

'I didn't show the note to Mr Fawley in time. That's why he said: "This is outrageous." I suppose it was ... an outrage, I mean. He should have seen it first. And that's why he said, "I haven't had an opportunity." You see, I hadn't given him one. He did have a *right* to see it.'

'Is this true?' Gritt looked at me.

I said nothing.

'I'm very sorry,' said Justine. 'But it was all rather chaotic.'

Gritt was confused now. 'Do you wish to add anything, Mr Fawley?'

I shook my head.

The tribunal muttered amongst itself and then decided that it wished to retire before delivering verdict. As they left, Justine joined me at the opposite end of the room. She lightly touched my hand.

*   *   *

'It is always with a sad heart,' Mr Justice Gritt proclaimed, the stench of his briar pipe filling the room, 'that this committee hears allegations of misconduct concerning members of this honourable profession. But we are entrusted with the duty to protect the good name of the Bar. We have heard from Miss Justine Wright. And, of course, we accept her evidence. She does justice, if we may say so, to an honourable family name.'

'Fan of yours?' I whispered to Justine.

'No, my father's fag at school,' she replied. 'Useless fag, excellent crumpet-rack.'

'Miss Wright,' Gritt continued, 'gave evidence to the effect that in the aftermath of the death of our Brother Manly, chaos and confusion reigned in court. That may be so. But this does not excuse Mr Fawley's behaviour. Not at all. Not for an instant. Accordingly, we find this matter proved.'

Livingstone gloated unbearably and ran his fingers through his hair.

'Stand up,' Gritt said to me. 'You will be barred from practising as a barrister for six months.'

Justine gasped below me.

'But solely because of the evidence of Miss Wright – and for no other reason – we are prepared to suspend the disqualification.'

The major general grumbled audibly. Clearly he was out-voted. The firing squad would have to be stood down. The smile also vanished from Livingstone's face.

'You might know everything about everything,' I whispered to Livingstone. 'But you really understand bugger all.'

Gritt raised his voice and pointed the end of his pen at me. 'But I warn you, Mr Fawley. One more petulant or intemperate outburst from you in court and the ban will be enforced ... with full severity. These proceedings are closed.'

It was a spineless compromise. If they had any guts, they would have thrown me out. Just then, that was my most ardent wish.

Chapter 30

Having finished early, we went to the pre-theatre sitting at Il Gallo Nero. Justine wanted to celebrate my salvation from what to her was the unimaginable horror of having to earn an honest crust without a tatty pile of horsehair on one's head. And whilst I could not help but be touched by Justine's gaiety, I sat there among the piles of lightly oiled *fettucini* realising it was merely a stay of execution. There was little more than a week until the retrial. And that was to be presided over by Hilary Hardcastle.

My car was parked in a side street off Long Acre. In general, I frowned upon drink-driving. But that night the old boundaries began to disappear. I felt a strange sense of release, a certain light-headedness, in the way your head spins when you give blood. It was as if I had been mysteriously transported to the margin of things. I saw myself and I was on the outside, like someone half watching a down-market soap opera, when you want to know what happens next – but not very much.

We walked out of the restaurant, past an abandoned cinema with tattered posters of Visconti's *Ossessione*, past old bookshops and modern boutiques. When Justine thrust me against a wall.

'Let's fool around,' she said.

'What, here?'

'Why not?'

I objected to kissing in public. I could not imagine that

the unedifying spectacle of my tongue wriggling in another person's throat could be of the slightest interest to the man on the Clapham omnibus. However, that night I kissed Justine.

We walked up towards Covent Garden passing droves of painted young people in leather and chains. In the distance was a high-pitched wailing.

'Will you come with me?' asked Justine.

'Where?'

'You know.'

And, of course, I did. 'Penny has sort of thrown down the gauntlet,' I said.

'So you told her?'

I was far too inebriated to articulate the niceties, if that is the word, of our impending break-up. So, as the wailing grew louder, I merely said, 'Something like that. She said she would leave me. If I ... you know, with you.'

Justine looked at me desperately. 'It's your call, Tom. There's still over a week till the retrial.'

'Look, don't tempt me,' I said.

'Why not? That's what I'm here for.'

'I'd love to get away from London and the Bar and ... well, everything—'

'You don't need to explain,' she said. 'I understand. These things happen. Penny's a big girl.'

'But Ginny isn't,' I said. I had hoped that the last vestiges of my former loyalties would have vanished with my disappearing sobriety. But it was not as easy as that. I suppose it was something that I had always known. 'There was a time, Justine, when I knew what I wanted. But nothing seems that simple any more.'

'Why not?'

'Well, we hear so many lies in our job. I sometimes wonder if they're ... well, sort of contagious. I know this sounds stupid, but I sometimes wonder whether I'll ever hear the truth again.'

Justine burst out laughing as we neared the side street. 'Just relax, Tom,' she said. 'Don't take everything *so* seriously.'

'All right then,' I replied. 'Are you telling me that you know what you want?'

'Yes.'

'Well, what?'

'You want me to tell you now?'

'Right now, Justine.'

'Well, right now, Mr Fawley,' she whispered, all the time drawing me closer, 'right now I—'

'Yes?'

'I want to fuck your brains out.'

We finally entered the side street. There was complete chaos. Lights were flashing on my car, the side window was smashed, the alarm was screaming. Justine and I ran to the passenger door, but the radio had not been stolen and nothing was missing.

'Someone must have caught him in the act,' she said.

In the alcoholic haze that had descended around me, it all seemed rather amusing. When Justine suggested we should find a policeman, I found the prospect irresistibly funny and couldn't stop laughing.

Suddenly a car came round the corner and accelerated towards us. It was a Sierra and in the half-light was just a blur. I noticed a bag of powder on the front seat of my car. It was wrapped in see-through cellophane and the granular contents were clearly visible.

'Don't touch it,' shouted Justine.

The Sierra got closer. It was fifty yards away and started to brake loudly. I reached, or rather fumbled, towards the package, the contents of which were rather like a couple of pounds of refined brown sugar.

'Leave it, Tom,' Justine again shouted.

The Sierra drew alongside us. One door opened.

'Run,' shouted Justine.

But before we could move, the car sped off again, the tyres screeching, and the smell of burnt rubber filled the air. I

197

followed its course and could just make out the two uniforms that had entered the side street.

Justine grabbed me roughly by the arms. 'Tom, just keep quiet,' she said as I giggled childishly. She tightened her grip painfully. 'Are you listening? Just shut up. Understand?'

When the officers arrived, Justine stood in front of me.

'You the driver, madam?' the first asked. He looked over Justine's shoulder. 'Or is he?'

'I am,' she replied.

'Break in?'

'No real harm done,' said Justine. 'They didn't get the stereo. Broken window. Nothing serious.'

'See anyone?'

'No,' she said.

'Better report it ... for insurance purposes.'

'Thanks anyway.' Justine half waved as they continued on their beat.

I leant on the car bonnet, my legs beginning to give way. 'They ... they trashed my car.'

'Shut up, Tom. For God's sake.'

'Why should I? You told me not to take it all so seriously.' And I began to laugh. 'They trashed my—'

'Know what that is?' Justine pointed to the transparent package, and held my head in its direction.

I shrugged inanely as I tried to focus on the granular substance.

'That's Brown,' she said.

'Brown?'

'Brown.' She opened the passenger door and pushed me in. 'Where are your keys?'

'But you're not insured,' I feebly protested as I handed over the fob. 'Brown?'

'Jesus, Tom. How many drugs trials have you done? It's heroin, you idiot. About five years' worth,' Justine said. 'That's how they package it.'

'I've defended in crack and coc, and speed and grass,' I said. 'But I've never really *seen* heroin.'

'Well, you have now.' Justine turned on the engine and drove towards Chiswick.

It was 4 a.m. I was soaking in cold sweat and vivid images buzzed around my pillow. I saw myself in a strange room. There was a window that was tall and narrow that gave on to a circle of stones. And there I was rolling in the wet sheets of a four-poster bed. Around me, millimetres from my face, were endless mosquito nets, and although I tore at them, and ripped them with both my hands, they became tighter and tighter. I was increasingly frantic for I knew, and this was all I could be certain of, I knew that the mosquitoes were on the inside.

Penny had gone. I didn't know where. She had taken our daughter.

I got up and looked out into the garden. Every shadow on the lawn appeared to be someone stalking up to the house. I convinced myself that every indistinct shape in the room was another package of heroin.

I was frightened and I was alone. Justine told me before she got a cab home that the case would not go away. It was a little like the heroin that we had tried to flush down the loo. For a while it would disappear, only to surface again later in a slightly different form.

Whoever planted the heroin knew where I was. I realised on that night that I could not evade the truth. And rather than let it come and find me in the week or so until the retrial, I made a decision. As I shivered in the moonlight, I remembered a line from the Blake reproductions in the Tate:

All things begin and end in Albion's rocky shore.

I realised at that moment that there was only one place I could go.

PART III

STONEBURY

Your sons and daughters shall prophesise,
your old men shall dream dreams,
your young men shall see visions.

Book of Joel 2:28

Chapter 31

The Molly Summers trial eventually came to an end about a year ago. But I still return to the village every three months. I do not really understand why. No one likes me here, not after all that has happened. But I feel as though I am sweating out a virus and I must keep returning until the fever finally disappears.

I always make a point of going to the very centre of the circles. And sometimes, when my spirits are low, or when my last wisdom tooth begins to ache, I see myself on another kind of circle. I imagine myself on a type of large wheel, where the past is not behind me nor the future ahead. For when I close my eyes, the faces and events of the Summers case swirl around my head and again I see the first trip I made to Stonebury. I see the village and I see the stones and – most of all – I see Justine.

Two days after we found the heroin, we went to Justine's cottage near Stonebury. We drove all the way through Dorset and arrived on the Devon borders on a Sunday night. To me, it seemed like hours from London. It was certainly a strange journey. As the hours advanced, I somehow felt that time was moving in the opposite direction: from present to past, from history to prehistory. And I felt that we were not just driving towards the end of the country, where this island dips its foot into the Atlantic. I felt as though we were driving into the centre of things. But if I had been asked, I could not have said what a single one of those things was.

Of course, being the profound cynic that I then professed to be, I attributed these odd sensations to the carrot and turnip soup that Justine and I had wolfed down in a pub along the way. We got on well. And by the time we had arrived, Justine had persuaded me to stay a whole week before returning to London for the retrial. The case was not scheduled to start until the Monday of the following week. For the first time, we could be together.

The time flew past. The sex was fantastic.

Justine and I contrived to spend the best part of two days in bed. We walked around the cottage with only the duvet draped around us. We built log fires and took the phone off the hook. However, Justine did not always manage to come. I explained this by a defect in my technique from too much kneeling in confession and also by the fact that we were in Stonebury. As a result, I tried to postpone my orgasm as long as possible using the well-worn stratagem of thinking alternately of the greatest goals of Peter Osgood and the Archbishop of Canterbury.

From the windows of the cottage you could just see a part of the main house. It was separated from the somewhat modest cottage grounds by a high fence. There was no entrance that could be seen. Once or twice, in a post-coital glow, I tried to ask Justine about it. But she either pretended to be asleep, massaged my belly-button into oblivion or rolled over and sat astride me and then I forgot about everything else.

Finally, on the third day, we rose from the sheets. I had agreed to join the local hunt. Although I hadn't ridden for years, I had once been reasonably proficient, motivated largely by an abject fear of falling off, and a desire not to land in the horseshit.

Justine's cottage lay three miles outside Stonebury so we left for the hunt early in the morning. Somewhere in the distance I could hear the ravenous yelping of unfed dogs. The smell of warm leather surrounded me and I could faintly detect Justine's perfume.

'It's just not fair,' she said, continuing to trot slightly ahead of me.

'What isn't?'

'What people think of hunting. Simply unfair.'

'Yes,' I said. 'How *can* they think it's just the idle rich hunting defenceless animals with a pack of bloodthirsty hounds? What an outrage.'

At the right moment, the barking grew louder. 'You peasant,' she said.

Since I had been in Stonebury, I had thought of nothing else but Justine. When I awoke in the morning, she was the first thing I saw, all day I was with her and at night I could feel her warmth. It was as though nothing else in Stonebury existed except – and this was the interesting thing – except for those unpredictable hours of sleep.

I still had the dreams and they must have kept Justine awake most of the night, for each day she was increasingly tired, although she never blamed me. To me, it had almost become a sickness. For it was something I longed for. I desired to be there, near to the stones, and I wished to see. Yet I was repulsed by the images that flashed across my imagination.

Perhaps Kingsley was correct: nothing was forbidden, everything was there, just waiting. Our minds, he had said, were like sensitive receivers. And here I was in Stonebury. In some ways I had tuned into the end of the dial. And beside me was Justine.

The clatter of our horses' hooves bounced down the country lane. We were not far from the arranged meeting place.

'I don't know what all the fuss is about,' said Justine. 'I mean, it's our land.'

'Yes,' I said. 'But it's not your fox. I think that might be the point.'

'You don't have to do this, Tom.'

'I want to ... I think.' What I really wanted was to be near Justine and I knew I would have to try to understand her world.

Justine had the full kit: cream-coloured breeches, scarlet coat, long leather boots. It was oddly provocative, like a taste of the other side. She had lent me her father's old tweed jacket, a Ratcatcher she had called it. Her horse was speckled white and had a shaggy mane; sitting on her mount, floating above the frozen winter ground, Justine was completely at home, at ease, in a way she never could have been in London.

'You know,' she said, 'it's not so bad down here.'

'Who said it was?'

'You're London, Tom. Always will be. Town. There are some things you'll never understand about the country. You think it's all cattle rustling and incest down here.' She looked at me and she had a gleam in her eye. 'Well, mainly it is. Couple more fences and we're there.'

The howling of the dogs became more desperate, and a frightening edge appeared in their barking. But my horse did not flinch. And nor, of course, did Justine.

When we arrived at the Meet, the field of hunters was everything I expected and worse. Overweight landowners and retired colonels cavorted on uncomplaining horses. They greedily drank their stirrup-cups while below them, standing around their horses like Nubian slaves, were the hunt followers, impoverished local lads, heads bowed, hanging around for orders.

Justine's voice rose above the babble of appalling accents. 'Good morning, Master,' she said.

Then a familiar voice. 'Ah, Fawley. Glad to see you're game for some real sport.'

I recognised the revolting moustache.

'Didn't I tell you?' said Justine. 'Aubrey is Master of the Hunt.'

Davenport's horse was monumentally large, the type you would imagine hauling a brewer's dray. It waddled towards me as Davenport pointed to the sea of dogs. 'Look at my beauties.'

'If you're in at the kill, Aubrey can blood you,' Justine told me.

'Do you *actually* have to kill it?' I asked. 'I mean, can't you just chase it a bit and then bugger off home for some South African sherry?'

'We've got to keep the hounds in blood,' said Davenport. 'Charley won't mind. Good sport is Charley.'

'Charley?'

'The fox,' explained Justine.

I said, 'What if it escapes?'

'Gone to ground?' Davenport kicked his nag a couple of times but it refused to move. 'Well, he is a wise old bird is Charley. But there's no chance of that.'

'How do you know?'

'Stoppers sorted the earths first light.'

'Can't you speak English, Davenport?'

Justine again intervened. 'The men blocked the fox-holes with thorns. The fox hasn't got a prayer.'

'Call this sport?' I said, hanging off the saddle. 'Well, it's not. It's murder.'

'Grow up, Tom.' Justine was clearly annoyed.

'At least give it an even chance to escape. It's so unfair.'

'So's life, Fawley.' Davenport wrestled his beast around. 'Better dash. See you at the death.'

Suddenly the hounds were off across the meadows and there was undiluted excitement. Someone had picked up a scent.

We moved past a copse of barren trees which Justine told me they called Nethersmere Woods. There were wilting branches and roots that reached out of the ground like dead men's hands. Then I heard a cacophony of noise: the beating of drums, the blowing of whistles, and many sirens.

I was behind Justine and could see nothing when she cried out.

'What is it?' I asked.

'Anti's.'

'What?'

'Hunt sabs.'

The noise was like a Schoenberg symphony played at the wrong speed, not that I could usually tell the difference. Then there was a chorus of virulent abuse.

'Bastards ... murderers ... rich scum.'

There were forty or fifty saboteurs, wearing the same green wax jackets the huntsmen would sport in town. Their eyes were full of hatred. One of them, a lanky boy with two pony-tails and a CND badge, tried to pull me off.

'Use your whip,' shouted Justine.

'Are you *mad*?' I replied. I managed to free my leg from his grasp, but lost a stirrup.

Ahead of me was a girl. She had a stereo, like a ghetto-blaster, churning out a tape of the hounds in full cry.

'What do I do?' I called to Justine who was now riding beside me.

'Just keep going.'

Our horses got closer and closer to the girl, but she did not move. I pulled the reins to the left, tugged them to the right, but the wretched horse headed straight for the girl.

'Get out of the way,' I shouted.

'Killers,' she replied.

Our horses were virtually on top of her.

'For God's sake,' I shouted.

She turned up her stereo. 'Murderers.'

'Get out—'

The sound of the baying hounds filled every crevice of my head. The horse bolted to the right and into the woods, where claw-like branches tore through my jacket and pulled at my hair. Further and further the horse charged, leaving the field way behind.

I had lost Justine and what was more, I thought I recognised the girl.

Chapter 32

There were no leaves on the branches, but the light had never-
theless disappeared, losing its way somewhere up amongst
the tree-tops. Behind me, wafting on the still air, was the
sound of the field: the dogs, the horses, no longer menacing,
but constantly fading as I went deeper into the wood.

The glancing shadows of the trees caused me to think back
over the previous weeks, much in the way that a hypnotist's
watch conjures up the memory. There I was in Stonebury,
where it had all happened, where Molly Summers had been
killed. I remembered my conversation with Kingsley in the
prison and how he talked quietly about molestation. Why did
he go so far with Molly Summers? Was physical gratification,
for once, not enough? Did he need something more? Something
better? Did he need some blood?

Soon I came to a clearing in the wood where the tree-line
curved down towards a brook. As I emerged from the shade
the air grew warmer. The frost began to melt and sparkled in
the rough pasture. This was a place of calm.

The horse, however, was on edge.

Near to the fence that ran from the trees to the water was a
stirring, a noise and a movement, almost too delicate to discern
with the eye, but there none the less. The horse refused to
advance, and scuffed a front leg in the long grass. Just then
my attention was drawn to the edge of the woods a furlong
away.

'That you, Fawley?' shouted Davenport.

I did not answer.

'You're going the wrong way, man,' he said. 'We lost the damn thing. Doubled back on its tracks.'

My horse started to inch its way towards the place.

'Hurry up, Fawley. We haven't got all day.'

'With you in a second,' I said.

'You're going the wrong way, man.'

Then I saw it. Sitting between the fence and the stream, where the long grass actually smelt green, looking directly at me, tongue panting, was the fox. I wondered whether the disappearing witness was a little like that animal. Perhaps she had not really gone to ground? Perhaps she was waiting somewhere, waiting to be found?

Davenport drew closer. He was only a hundred yards away. 'Ground too cold to hold a scent. We'll never find it,' he said.

The animal looked at me with vacant yellow eyes. What was I to do? Davenport was very near.

I said, 'I think I've seen it, Aubrey.'

He let out some kind of obnoxious hurrah.

'Where is it, man?'

'There,' I said, pointing behind him back into Nethersmere Woods. 'Deep in there. You better hurry.'

Davenport heaved his horse about and the dogs rushed off towards the trees with their tails pointing in the air. Barking filled the air with saliva and hunger, and the fox began to move – almost casually – through the fence. The wiring was razor-sharp, and its hide was ripped. But it did not make a sound. I turned my horse away from the fox and joined Davenport by some bushes.

'Come on, Aubrey,' I said. 'I'll show you where Charley's hiding.'

'Wise old bird is Charley,' he replied.

Davenport said something else, but I did not hear. I kept wondering whether Molly Summers had screamed, and if she did, why no one had heard. Some nights I imagined the sound, and how it would feel to scream like that, and I would always

212

wake up, never sure whether the screams were the girl's or mine.

As we trotted back towards the start, Davenport bored me with his hunting stories much as he used to bore unsuspecting young women in the Old Bailey Mess with his overblown tales of forensic triumph. It was, however, pleasant enough to pass through the gentle Devon hills for twenty minutes.

By the end of the hunt, the numbers were much depleted. Boys tried to shove reluctant horses into boxes. Everyone was set on a prompt departure before the saboteurs regrouped.

Justine rushed towards me. 'Are you all right, Tom?'

'Doddle,' I said. 'Not so sure about Trigger.' I pointed to the horse who seemed to be flagging. 'She looked after me.'

'It's a he, didn't you notice the—'

'Oh, yes. He's hung like a donkey.'

'Anyway,' said Justine, 'he's not called Trigger.'

'What's his name, then?'

'It doesn't matter.'

'What's his name, Justine?'

'Nigel,' she said. 'But officially, he's—'

'Well, that's just brilliant.'

'Tom, what's the matter?'

'Oh, nothing. I mean, I've been attacked by hippies, I galloped over a girl and for the last twenty minutes I've been trotting behind Davenport's bottom on a horse called Nigel. Apart from that, Justine, everything's hunky dory.'

Justine did not answer.

'Still,' I added, 'shame about Charley.'

We both walked into the middle of a group of riders who were again drinking.

'That depends on your point of view,' said Justine.

'Well, there's always another day.'

'Do shut up,' she said and kissed me roughly in front of the amused crowd, holding my face between her hands.

'Better luck next time,' I said.

'There won't be a next time.' Her fingers came slowly away from my face and I could feel the warm stickiness of quickly drying blood. 'There isn't a next time,' she repeated. 'Not for Charley.'

I had saved the wrong fox.

Chapter 33

The cottage was everything you would expect: coarse stone walls, thick rugs, brass ornaments and a raging open fire. In fact, the only thing I did not anticipate was that I would still be there, and would be happy, and would be with Justine.

When I turned to look at Justine, intensely studying her murder brief in front of the fire, I couldn't help thinking of my wife. Penny was not at home when I had secretly rung that afternoon. I wasn't sure how Justine would react, so I sneaked a call when she had a nap after the hunt. Nor had Penny left any message on the answerphone. I was being punished. I suspected that Penny had gone to her parents, but I didn't dare ring her there. I would just have to wait.

'You were very close to your father?' I asked Justine. I decided to put away my papers. It was nothing particularly important, just another long memorandum from Kingsley drawing up battle plans.

'I never looked at it like that,' Justine said. 'I never knew anything else.' At this, she walked to the back window which was bowed with the weight of years. She looked towards the fence and the main house. 'I could never have lived up there after he ... passed on. Still, I had no choice. It would have been just too expensive to keep up for a teenager with a couple of trust funds.'

I tried to understand yet could not help but see the house as a sort of shrine to her father. It towered over the cottage and dominated the horizon.

'I was just wondering,' I said. 'Was it that … you know, maybe he hadn't quite kept up the mortgage repayments?'

'Maybe it's none of your business,' she snapped, 'and maybe you shouldn't speak ill of the dead.'

'So it's not been repossessed?'

'No, Tom. It's not repossessed.'

'So why don't you live there?'

'Because I don't.'

I could sense that things were becoming decidedly frosty. So I attempted to change the subject. 'What about your mother?'

'She died.'

As usual, I had just made matters worse.

'But I never knew her,' Justine continued.

'When did it happen?'

'When I was born.' Justine was wearing a baggy Argyle sweater and hugged herself tightly. 'I suppose I should feel guilty about it in some sort of way. But I don't. How can I? Never knew her, you see.'

'I guess it made the bond between you and your father all the stronger?'

'Poor Daddy. People say he was devastated. Apparently his hair lost all its colour, turned white. I used to tease him about it something rotten.'

'How do you mean?'

'Well, I used to tell him, All you need to do is grow a beard and you'd look like God. Of course, he never remarried. Lived alone except for Annie, who looked after the house. But even she left. His only companion was his work. I suppose he was married to that.'

'And you never married?'

'What's the point? I always lose them in the end.'

'Them?'

'My men. You'll be no different.' Justine turned and gazed at me over her left shoulder, pleading with me to disagree. 'I'm right, aren't I, Tom?'

'Let's not get into this.'

'How was Penny, by the way?'

'Penny?'

'Don't treat me like an idiot.'

I tried to bluff it out. 'What do you mean?'

'I wasn't asleep this afternoon, you know. I can't seem to sleep,' she said. 'You wouldn't sneak around unless you were calling Penny.'

'She wasn't there. I don't know where she is. Quite frankly, I don't care.'

'Don't be ridiculous. Penny's a wonderful person. Better than you deserve,' said Justine. She walked to the hearth and tossed on two logs. The sap sizzled as the flames lapped the bark. 'Are you going to tell me what's going on?'

'In what way?'

'In a couple of kilos of heroin sort of way,' she said. 'You said we'd discuss it later.' She looked at her watch pointedly. 'Well, it's later.'

'I hardly know where to begin. Really I—'

'He used to say that. Daddy, I mean. Whenever I asked him about the cases he was trying, "I hardly know where to begin, Angel." He used to call me that. He was a fair judge. Old school, but fair. He cared – well, about his work, anyway.'

'Justine, I was told by a source – a most unreliable one, admittedly – that I was in some kind of danger.'

'Who told you?'

'It doesn't matter.'

'And are you?'

'What?'

'In danger.'

'What does it look like?'

She paused and breathed in deeply as she prodded the fire. 'But *why*, Tom?'

'If I knew, I'd—'

'We could, I suppose, go to the police.' Justine said this only half-heartedly as she knew my views.

'And betray the habit of a legal lifetime? Besides, I think they're behind it somehow.'

'Then that leaves—'

'You and me. That's all there's left.'

Justine said, 'You make it sound quite an adventure.'

'Not really. But are you sure you want to be part of it?'

'Quite sure.'

'Beyond doubt?'

'Beyond a shadow of a doubt. Besides—'

'What?' I asked.

'I think we were made for each other.'

'Why do you say that?'

'Because, Tom, there are two types of people in this world. Those who are fucked up and those who don't yet know they're fucked up. And between us—'

'Yes?'

'We've got the complete set.'

As she knelt facing the fire, I moved quickly behind her and held on to the warmth of her jumper and smelt the back of her neck. In such moments you feel strong. For a while you lose your fear, but the magic is tempered because, above all, you know that such moments cannot last.

We had made love. For the first time with Justine it was a gentle experience and I felt very close to her. We lay on our backs, with our pulses still racing, and I ran my fingers over her body. I tried to feel all the contours, to see what I was contending with. Her frame had that Stonebury frailness, like Sarah Morrow, like Molly Summers. But I sensed that Justine had a vulnerability that was more than purely physical.

Then she began to speak. 'Did you enjoy the hunt, Tom? Only you haven't said.'

'It's one way to spend a wet Wednesday . . .'

'There's no need to lie, Tom. Not tonight. Just for tonight, let's tell the truth.'

218

I rolled over and looked at her. 'All right then, I thought it was barbaric.'

'I just knew it.'

'How *could* you, Justine?'

'It's a question of what you're used to. It's just part of life.'

Although I disagreed, I didn't want to argue. 'I saw someone,' I said. 'Well, I thought I saw someone I might have known.'

'What? Down here?'

I moved closer to her and she covered me with the duvet. 'Yes. One of the ... protesters.'

'Oh, the crusties. They all look the same. Generations of in-breeding deep in the forest.'

'You are a frightful snob, Justine.'

'They hate us, you know. Well, they hate me. Hated Daddy before. There's probably not a family in the forest we haven't prosecuted or tried. I cut my teeth down here. Before I got a London practice. That's why I joined Ignatius's chambers. Good links with the western circuit.'

'Rubbish,' I said. 'You joined because your father used to be head of chambers.'

'Well, there was that too.'

'Let's tell the truth, shall we? Just for tonight.'

Justine did not seem to relish being reminded of her own words. She rolled over abruptly and clung to the edge of the bed.

That was my moment. 'You still haven't told me how Ignatius died.'

'What do you know?'

'That he was found at the bottom of the stairs.'

'They presumed it was a heart attack.'

'But the front door was open,' I said. 'And his neck was broken.'

'He was working too hard.'

'I was told nothing was stolen and there was no struggle.'

I had obtained these details from Jamie. Armstrong's First Law, he told me. Always find out how a High Court judge snuffs it.

'Ignatius was always very good to me. I suppose because of my father.'

'How do you mean?'

'Well, Daddy gave him a chance. In those days, if a black man walked into chambers, they'd call him the defendant or call the police. But Daddy saw his potential and gave him a chance.' Her voice softened. 'I remember when I first met Ignatius.'

'Justine, there's something I should tell you.'

'He was very dashing, you know.'

I could easily have led her by the nose into yet more deceit, but I didn't want any secrets to stand between us. So I said, 'You told me about Ignatius.'

'How do you mean?'

'When you were very drunk at that party. When he was made silk. All those years ago.'

She was silent.

I said, 'I know *just* how close you were.'

'Then you should know how painful it is for me to talk about it.' There was acid in her breath and she tugged the duvet angrily.

'Sorry. Just thought I'd tell you.'

There was a little pause as we both reassessed the situation and calculated how far we could go.

'Ignatius wasn't the first, you know,' Justine told me.

'Look. You don't have to—'

'No. I want to. The truth? Just for tonight.'

'Let's go to sleep.'

'No, Tom. You're going to listen and then you'll know everything.' Justine sat up against the pine headboard and tucked the edge of the quilt under her chin. 'I wasn't interested at first. I mean, a trainee teacher, what could be a bigger turn-off? But he cared about the things that mattered, poetry and stuff. I always thought he fancied Penny. Funny that. Did she ever tell you what *really* happened?'

The painful scene from our Chiswick bedroom flickered before me. Penny and I talking for hours, trying to talk it through, baring everything, trying to salvage something from our marriage – and failing. So when Justine asked me again whether Penny had mentioned the scandal about the teacher, I took the only option I knew, the only option I had ever taken.

'Penny never told me much,' I said. 'What happened?'

From that moment I suppose I must have known, deep down, though I would never have dared to admit it at the time, I knew that my relationship with Justine was equally fated, as would be any relationships after that, until I exhausted the very limited supply of females foolish enough to put up with me.

Then Justine said, 'He used to give me books to read. Anthologies of poetry, that sort of thing. Dryden, Auden, Sylvia Plath. My mind was a whirl.'

'How long was he at the school?' I asked. I could vaguely see the outline of Justine's face but not the expression. Her voice, however, was far from doleful.

'He wasn't there long. That was the point. By the middle of the summer term I realised that he would leave at the end of the year – and that I'd never see him again.'

'You could have written.'

'I couldn't bear to think that far ahead. You know what teenage crushes are like.'

I agreed. But in reality I had little idea about young love. I had discovered sex before romance and it was the type of sex found in the moth-eaten pages of a psychology book about fetishes and phobias.

Justine was not really listening to me and continued. 'One day Alex – that was his name. Did I ever say?'

'No, but Penny might have mentioned it. Wasn't his surname Chapple or something?'

'It's not important, Tom. The point is ... well, one morning, it was beautiful and sunny, I remember, Alex asked me into his study. He said he had a poem he wanted me to read. I forget what it was called.'

'Who was it by?'

'William Blake, I think.'

'Jesus,' I said, 'don't you lot know of any other creative artists?'

'What do you mean?'

'Haven't you heard of Johnny Keats or Percy Shelley?'

'Pardon?'

'It doesn't matter, Justine.' I was not in the mood to try to explain my visit to the Tate.

'Well, Alex,' Justine continued, 'read a couple of verses. I can't really remember how it went.'

This did not ring true, for Justine spoke with a vividness as though she had relived that scene once a day, every day in the intervening twenty years.

'It was one of the most beautiful things I'd ever heard,' she said. 'But there was one line, something about youth and maiden bright, naked in the sunny beams' delight. Or something like that. It just seemed to match the weather and . . . everything.'

She paused as if the words clicked into place and I remembered the painting in the Tate Gallery, with Adam standing before his father in heaven. And God sat in a fiery chariot with a shock of white hair and the naked man bowed in repentance before it.

When Justine began to speak, her voice seemed to have a distant echo. '"Children of the future age, Reading this indignant page, Know that in a former time, Love! sweet love! was thought a crime." At first it made me . . . well, almost cry. Stupid, isn't it? Blubbing over a poem. But I realised that Alex would leave me and then I'd be alone.'

Alone. I wondered whether this was an indirect reference to her father's death. I wanted to give her a chance to tell the whole truth. So I asked her, 'What about your father?'

'He was always busy with his rapes. I couldn't bear it. And the poem, I know it sounds dumb now, but I felt Alex had written it – for me.'

'There's nothing dumb about that.'

'Actually,' she said, 'it was called "A Little Girl Lost". It was how I felt, Tom.'

At that moment there was a rush through the trees, a moaning among the upper branches that fell gently into the bedroom.

'Alex kept reading the poem to me. Something about the maiden losing her fear. I giggled the first time he got to that bit. By the second or third time I was in a sort of daze. "There in rising day, On the grass they play. Parents were afar, Strangers came not near, And the maiden soon lost her fear." It was all a bit much – well, for a lonely teenage girl. I was very flattered and hardly noticed ... him.' She paused and tried to control her breathing. 'He had soft hands, you see. Hardly touching me. It just seemed right. Natural. Like it was part of the poem. And before I knew it, I was...'

'Yes?'

She giggled uneasily. 'Well, starkers. I looked into his eyes, but they had changed. They were different, somehow frightening. And I screamed. Someone, I forget who, came rushing in—'

'Penny?'

'Possibly,' Justine said. 'Well, that was it.'

'What happened to him?'

'No one wanted a scandal. So nothing really happened. He was sent away. Life went on. I hardly ever think about it now.'

'Why didn't you tell me about it before?' I asked.

'It just never came up. What was I supposed to have said? Oh, Tom, did I tell you? I was bonked by my teacher over the *Oxford Book of English Verse*, Quiller-Couch edition. Who's your next witness, by the way? You see, it's just never come up, Tom.'

'Justine,' I replied, 'why are you telling me all this now?' When she did not answer, I added, 'Justine, what has this to do ... well, with me?'

'It's just that I'm—' She appeared to struggle to find the right word. 'Well, I'm just bad luck.'

'I'll take my chances,' I said.

Justine kissed me as a child kisses its father and I could taste little salty droplets running slowly down her cheeks. And I began to see that her thin, scarcely developed body was just a reflection of a childhood that had been starved of proper affection.

Then I heard the wind rising and falling outside. Soon the bedstead was creaking. And then I was both ashamed and unaccountably excited to be making love to this lost creature, and I thought of Richard Kingsley and his crimes, and I wondered whether I was really very different to him after all.

Chapter 34

At the hunt, we had arranged to meet Davenport for a lunchtime drink the next day. We waited in a pub on the outskirts of Stonebury near to the Devon county border. But Davenport did not appear. Justine entered one of her darker moods as she contemplated a suitable punishment. I sat next to her at a table in the corner of the bar drinking both the gin and tonics that we had ordered. The room was dark even though it was barely past midday. An open fire provided some flickering light.

Justine asked, 'What do you want to do today?'

'Well, I haven't seen any turnips yet.'

'No, seriously. What do you want to do?'

'What I most want to do in the whole world,' I replied. 'Which is nothing.'

'I always admired your energy, Tom.'

'I mean, why do people always have to do *something*. I'm sick and tired of it. I just want to be left alone,' I said. And then seeing a scowl beginning to contort her face, I added, 'Well, with you as well, of course.'

Justine was wearing an immaculate white blouse made of Italian silk, a neatly fitting skirt and black stockings peppered with little cats. Her blonde hair was pulled back from her face and was in a single pony-tail, her make-up was perfect, her fragrance refined. I had forgotten to shave.

'So you don't want to see that witness?' she said.

'Which witness?' I wasn't really listening. I thought about

what I had dreamt the night before. For the first time I dreamt that I was within the circle of stones. The blocks of stone seemed to crowd in on me. Figures were becoming more distinct, like the images on a photograph when the developer is applied.

'You know the woman I'm talking about,' Justine said.

'Oh, the hermit. Well, she isn't a witness. Not really. You just gave me her details.'

'She lives round here,' Justine said. 'Used to come into the pub to buy a bucket of the local brew.'

'What's that?'

'It's a rough type of the mead wine. They call it Red-eye or something. Poisonous stuff.'

'Right. I'll have a double,' I said.

'We could skip the drinks and try to find that woman.'

'Why bother? Kingsley's going down.'

'You've got to put up a fight, Tom.'

'For him?' I replied.

'No. Not for Kingsley.' She put her hand on my fingers. 'For yourself.' She looked at the empty glasses. 'Look, I know it's none of my business—'

'How very perceptive of you.'

'I couldn't help noticing.' She lowered her voice. 'You know, the drink. I'm a little worried. Should I be?'

'You're certainly right about one thing.'

'Am I?'

'Yes,' I said and lowered my voice. 'It's none of your business.' I rather childishly turned the glass upside down to demonstrate its emptiness. 'Besides, a man needs a hobby and the only poor defenceless animal it'll kill is me.'

'All right. Subject closed.' She took her hand away and folded her arms. 'So what are we going to do?'

'I might just take a wander round,' I said.

'You won't find him, the police—'

'Him? I didn't mention a him.'

Justine looked quickly away. She played with the grip that

secured her hair. Then she said, 'The police have looked every-where for Templeman. He's not even on the electoral roll.'

'Doesn't that worry you?' I asked.

'Why should it? He's supposed to be your witness.'

'Look, I know you don't need to be able to vote for the Blood Sports and Monarchy Party to be an alibi witness, but—'

'Have you finished?' Justine said, looking back at me. When I did not respond, she added, 'So what are we going to do, Tom?'

'Actually,' I said, 'I would like to go up to the residential home. You know, West Albion. It's about time that I saw it.'

'You've already seen it,' Justine replied.

'No, I mean the place Molly Summers—'

'You've already seen it,' Justine insisted.

'Where?' I asked, and then I began to understand. 'The main house? Why didn't you tell me?'

'Why didn't you ask?'

'Well, I did try, Justine. But every time I did, you climbed on top and rode me like a wild stallion.'

'Don't flatter yourself,' she said. 'Anyway, I can't remember you complaining.'

'That's not the point.'

'Then what is?'

'How it comes to pass that the Wright country residence has more destitute children than the orphanage in *Oliver*. That might be the point, Justine.'

An uneasy silence followed and we sat a table's width apart managing not to look at each other. I felt better, safer, back on familiar ground. I had burst the bubble of unreal contentment before – as it must – it burst of its own accord. I knew I had climbed back aboard that old favourite, the well-worn cycle of crisis and calm, the peaks and troughs that propel a relationship and that make domestic bliss almost bearable.

Finally, Justine said, 'It was in his will. Well, the codicil to the will.'

'What was?'

'The bequest of the house to the local authority.'

'But why, Justine?'

'He always was charitable. He granted them a very generous lease.'

'I've heard of charity beginning at home, but this is ridiculous. You see, some people just give fifty pence to Oxfam and wear a red nose for Comic Relief. I mean, where were you supposed to live?'

'I had the cottage,' Justine said. 'And the rents from the lease went into a trust fund for me.'

'But why on earth did he do it?'

'Why not?'

'I don't know, Justine. Because it's not a particularly normal thing to do.'

'Know your problem, Tom?'

'Which one in particular?'

'The one which prevents you seeing the good in what people do. You see, Tom, you defend so many evil people that you just think that goodness is laughable. Somehow weak. Well, it's not. But that's not something that people like you and Richard Kingsley will ever understand.'

I cannot remember how many glasses of the thick mead I drank after that. But it was sufficient to make my vision as cloudy as the liquid. When I was drunk enough, I cursed Hilary Hardcastle and I cursed Richard Kingsley. I tried to forget about Whitey Innocent and the London Bar. For once I was going to do something for myself – and that was nothing.

After an hour, Justine said that we could walk the few miles back to her cottage. And if we got tired or bored, she said, we could phone for a cab from the village.

Stonebury was not particularly different to how I imagined it. What really struck me was the silence. You couldn't hear the sounds a town-dweller immediately associates with a pastoral scene: no bleating of sheep, no tractors, no carts running down cobbled streets. Not even the birds sang. It felt like you were entering a closely confined vacuum, something had been preserved there, but no one – I imagined – could tell you what.

There was a little parish church on the far side of the village, outside the circle of stones which completely surrounded the houses. When we reached the corner of the graveyard, with its fluttering angels of marble and overgrown tombstones, Justine stopped abruptly.

'Better get a cab,' she said.

'I'm all right, really.' I tried to put on a brave face. In truth, I was rather ashamed of my behaviour in the pub. 'We haven't far to go, have we?'

'That's not the point,' she said.

A small group of people were coming out of the church. No one was smiling.

'I just don't believe it,' said Justine.

'Who are they?'

'Just keep your head down and keep walking.' She put her coat collar up and cast down her eyes. 'Just keep walking,' Justine ordered.

From the corner of my eye, I noticed the odd handshake and several sympathetic embraces.

'Justine,' I said, 'do you think it could be—'

'Shut up, will you?' She tightened her belt.

Before we got much further, a woman spoke and her voice quivered in the winter's air. 'You have no right,' she said. 'How dare you.'

Justine grabbed my arm and tried to usher me around the group.

The woman was covered in black lace. 'You shouldn't have brought *him*,' she said, meaning me. 'You ... whore.'

'Now hold on,' I said.

'Leave it, Tom.' Justine kept pushing me on.

'You have no right,' said the woman.

'Look, madam.' I straightened my back and probably

sounded patronising. 'This is a public right of way. We have every right—'

'Don't, Tom,' said Justine. 'They all know who you are.'

The woman shouted again, 'How can you be here? Not today. She was so young ... and now—'

The still air was jolted by the ringing of the church bell. Justine put her hand in the small of my back and drove me forward. We virtually ran past the far corner of the graveyard. The mead swilled around my stomach like one of those wave machines in a theme park.

'You have no right,' cried the woman. 'Not today.'

But we were fifty yards clear. We rushed through winding lanes, with high hedges on both sides, obscuring everything apart from a miserable patch of dark sky above. I developed a stitch. And when it felt as though a black crow was pecking at my abdomen, I had to stop.

'Tom,' gasped Justine. 'Let me explain.'

My stomach heaved mightily. 'I think I know.'

'You *do*?'

'It's almost exactly a year since the Summers murder, isn't it?' I said.

'So?'

'So this is some sort of memorial.'

Justine looked at me incredulously. 'That was a funeral, you idiot.'

'A what? Do people usually get buried on a Thursday?'

'Kingsley's going to walk,' said Justine. 'That was our last real hope.'

I put my hand to my mouth as the pain from my stitch was overwhelmed by another urge.

'The disappearing witness was in the coffin,' Justine said. 'She overdosed.'

'On what?'

'Oh, don't be so obtuse.'

'On *what*, Justine?'

'On heroin, of course.'

230

'Who was she?'

Justine did not reply.

'What was her name, Justine?'

'Diane.'

'Diane what?' When she was silent, I grabbed her sleeve and I repeated, 'Diane what?'

'Diane Morrow.'

'She's never the daughter of—'

'What do you think, Tom?' Justine said.

But I did not reply and I did not really think of Sarah Morrow, for then I was mightily sick.

Chapter 35

It was my fifth day in Stonebury. A fever struck Justine in the early hours and moved through her body quietly. She did not complain. It was as if it were something she expected, something she felt she deserved.

So when I left her after breakfast, she was quite weak, but was too vain to let me see her discomfort. I had obviously wanted to ask her about Diane Morrow, but it would all have to wait until she recovered. So, with some reluctance, I agreed to go out on my own. But I also realised that I could use the trip to make some illicit calls home.

Justine's Land-Rover was easy to drive and could cope with the terrain better than my car. It towered over the other vehicles on the road, and I felt as if I was seated on an eighteen-hand horse. Why is it, I thought, that the upper class insist on travelling with their rears six feet in the air?

The phone box was on the London Road, a half-mile outside the village. I called home. There was no reply. Next I tried chambers. After being put on hold once, and being cut off twice, Steve told me that my retrial had definitely been fixed in front of Hilary Hardcastle, that Kingsley wanted another conference, that Jamie Armstrong rang (garbled message and gratuitous abuse), and that yesterday there was a call on behalf of someone called Molly.

The message was simply, 'Ibid'. The insane logic was beginning to bite. Obviously, I had to buy *The Times*.

I had spotted the local store when we entered the village from the pub side. It was as far away from the church as any building could be in a smallish hamlet. It had reassuringly vulgar tabloids in the window and was doing a special offer on instant coffee.

On entering the shop, there was a stack of unwanted *Guardians* and a few *Daily Sports*.

'Can I help you?' the man asked.

'I must have *The Times*,' I said. 'Nothing else will do.'

'We don't have it, sir.' The shopkeeper's tone was as gentle as his face. He was a little man, slightly balding and had what you might call a pot-belly.

'Do you know where I can buy one?'

'No, sir.' He smiled apologetically. 'But you can have mine.'

'Yours?'

'Well, I am doing the crossword. Twelve down was very naughty. But if you don't mind the scribblings of a shopkeeper, you can have mine.' He had one hand on his stomach and rubbed it as he talked as if he were coaxing the words out.

'You are a godsend,' I told him.

'No, sir. Just a poor man trying to make an honest living.' He handed me the paper and I found the place almost immediately. The message was equally obtuse.

Roses down the mere.

When he noticed that the paper was open at the Births and Deaths, he said, 'If I am not being too presumptuous, do you have good news or—'

'Can't say really. What do you make of this?' I asked, showing him the message from Molly in the newspaper.

'Any more clues?'

'Clues? There was another message, if that's what you mean.'

He nodded slowly. When I opened my wallet and took out the torn scrap of paper from the previous edition of *The Times*, and placed it next to the more recent message, the man put his finger in his mouth, then scratched his chin, frowned, moved the scraps of paper around, looked at me and smiled. He wrote out the two messages next to each other on the back of a 'Historic views of Stonebury' postcard.

Who's met or seen red?
Roses down the mere.

'Easy,' he said, rubbing his stomach. 'Very very easy. Oh, yes. Very easy indeed.'

She was called Vera Cavely. She was the witness the prosecution tried to bury. For all the obvious reasons, I had thought that she might have lived in some deep mysterious cavern, full of stalagmites and cave paintings. But she did not. She lived in a car.

The old Singer Gazelle had probably not moved in twenty years. The metallic black had degenerated into an all-pervasive rust. Hanging from the front and rear windscreens were neat little curtains with red checks that even managed to match the vehicle's rusting chassis. All the side windows had bin-liners sellotaped to the inside. There were three wheels and a tidy pile of bricks where the fourth should have been. Two of the tyres were flat, the third had been slashed. Painted on the bonnet in a childish scrawl were the words: Silence. Someone lives here.

The car was in the middle of Nethersmere Woods, and as the shopkeeper had reliably told me, Nethersmere Woods was an anagram of both the messages I had been sent.

When I arrived, there seemed to be no one inside the car, or rather, no one I could hear. So I waited, sitting on a little rocky outcrop a few feet from the exhaust, the seat of my jeans becoming damp due to the abundance of moss. Here was a restful corner of the woods, where you might believe that the totality of man's endeavours amounted to nothing more than a rusting car.

I must have momentarily fallen asleep, for I did not fully hear the question the first time it was asked and did not really understand it when it was repeated.

'Have you come about the carburettor?'

I rubbed my eyes and tried to focus on the questioner and could not believe what I saw.

'About time too,' she said. 'Still, I suppose you'll tell me it's not your fault. No time for excuses. Just pop it in, will you? It's a long drive to Dakar.'

'I'm sorry?' I said. However, I was not at all clear what I should have been sorry about.

'You're sorry?' The woman turned towards one of the rocks. 'He's sorry? Hear that? He's sorry, thank you very much, and I've got a race to win. Huh.'

If someone had told me that such a creature existed, I should not have believed it. She was about four foot nine, wore toeless leather sandals, had a dark overcoat that was covered with grass and foliage that I swore was alive, and sitting on her head was a Second World War motorcycle helmet with pilot's goggles. In each of her claw-like hands she carried a plastic bag tied with string and bursting with – something. Vera Cavely walked towards me as though her legs were wooden below the knees, which they very probably were.

'Where *is* my carburettor?' she asked with increasing annoyance.

'I'm afraid I haven't got it.'

'Well, you'll have to jolly well go and jolly well fetch it.'

'Actually, I just wanted a word with you.'

She looked at the piece of rock I had been sitting upon. 'Did you hear that? He wants to have a word with me. Charming. Well, I jolly well want to have a word with you – and that word is *carburettor*.'

With this she kicked the rear bumper of the car and the boot sprang open. Smoke came from the area of the exhaust which confused me as the engine was not running. On closer inspection, I noticed a pile of smouldering bones that had once belonged to a small, indescribable animal. There was also a bucket full of a thick liquid.

'Miss Cavely,' I began.

'Don't you "Miss Cavely" me. Just fetch my...' Suddenly there was a vacant expression and she dropped the plastic bags. 'Just fetch my...'

'Your carburettor?'

'Oh, you've got it? Splendid. Pop it in. Do you know the way to Paris?'

'Paris?'

'That's where the rally begins.'

'Rally?'

'Paris–Dakar, of course.' Then she said to the rocky outcrop, 'Can't let them get a head-start, can we, Sunny? Oh, no. Paris here we come.'

Now I knew why the prosecution chose not to use Vera Cavely as a witness against Kingsley. She was two sandwiches short of a picnic. But she did make a statement which they had not disclosed. So what did she know? And why did the messages point to her?

'Miss Cavely, I'm the lawyer representing Richard Kingsley. You do know Mr—'

'He's "Miss Cavely-ing" me again, Sunny.'

'I understand you made a statement.'

'Want another?'

'I just want—'

'Cost you a carburettor. Only last time they promised to fix my car and look at it. So what do you want me to say?'

Then I realised that Vera Cavely must be a red herring. Some over-zealous local policeman had obviously filled out a deposition and got her to sign it – probably so they could object to Kingsley's bail or ask for a further remand into police custody.

I was about to leave and asked, 'So you know nothing about the death of Molly—'

'You know what the three little thingees said?'

'Remind me.'

'See no evil, hear no evil, speak no—'

'Yes, I understand,' I said. 'I shan't need to trouble you further.' I had a twenty-minute walk to where I parked Justine's car on the edge of the woods. 'Good luck with the rally,' I said.

'Luck? Who needs luck when you can drive like a demon, eh, Summers? Do you want some Red-eye?'

That brought me to a halt. 'What did you say—'

'Red-eye. I've got a bucket here.'

'Miss Cavely ... Vera, why did you say Summers?'

She opened the front door of the car and something, a wood-pigeon, perhaps, flew out. She did not flinch.

I said, 'Why did you mention—'

'Oh, Sunny?' She looked at me with complete exasperation. 'Well, who on earth did you think I was talking to?'

I shrugged foolishly.

She began to pull handfuls of damp moss away from the cracks in the rocky outcrop. 'Oh, you *do* get so dirty. Really.'

Very soon I could see that the stone I had sat upon was roughly hewn, something like a primitive gravestone. There was a simple inscription: *He was Summers.*

Chapter 36

The rest of my conversation with Vera Cavely, although inter-spersed with talk of pit-stops, double declutching and desert tracks, provided an inkling as to where the truth may have been found about Molly Summers. I would have to visit the church of St Stephen and the Martyrs. How easy was it, I wondered, to inspect a parish register?

As I walked back to the car, the woods seemed different to me. Around every other tree trunk I could see that quirky little rally-driver, with her pilot's goggles and open-toe sandals, itching to scream away from the green light, but not having moved so much as an inch in twenty years.

By the time I reached the clearing where I thought I had left the car, it was obvious that I had forgotten the way out of the woods. Although I could see the car, I felt that I could more easily find my way to Dakar than to the Wright Estate.

Then I spotted a man marching through the woods, stick in hand, retriever at his heels. I was debating whether to ask him for directions when I saw someone else walking quickly away from the car. His head was down and the collar of his green cotton jacket was up. He had a purposeful gait.

'Excuse me,' I said. 'I wonder whether you could—' He just kept walking. 'Could you just slow down a minute?' His pace did not change. 'I'm looking for the main road.'

He glanced in my direction with a curiously sheepish expression.

I tried to touch his arm gently but he quickened his step.

'Sorry, have I offended you in some way?' I got no answer. 'What's the matter?' A suspicious stare. 'Do you know the Wrights' place?'

He broke into a run. Something was wrong. He seemed vaguely familiar.

I said, 'Just wait, will you?' But he did not listen to me, and went off with little startled strides. I followed him instinctively as he darted in and out of the trees, unconcerned about the sharp branches.

'Please stop,' I said. Why wouldn't he reply?

As I drew alongside him and tried to hold his arm, he pulled up and struck out at me. His swing was pathetic, much as mine would have been, but I ducked and grasped his midriff. We lost our balance and fell to the floor with me on top. I twisted my ankle but continued to lie on him.

'Who are you?' I asked. 'I've seen you before, haven't I?'

Again, no answer. And I couldn't remember exactly where I'd seen him.

'Why did you run?'

He turned his head sharply to the left, into the mud, and kept his mouth tightly shut.

'What were you up to at the car?' It was hardly my most inspired cross-examination.

He tried to shrug me off, but the sheer weight of my body kept him pinned firmly in the mud. I could feel my ankle swelling but tried to ignore the pain.

'Listen,' I said, 'I'll let you up if you don't try anything. Agreed?'

He nodded.

But as soon as I released his arms he hurled a flurry of punches towards me. Most of them missed. Those that did connect were little more than slaps. I grabbed his throat – and squeezed. It felt good. What a sight we must have been: two frightened men struggling in the undergrowth with hideously contorted faces and bulging eyes.

With my free hand I reached into his jacket and pulled out

240

his wallet, still holding his throat. His face did not go blue, as I expected, but purplish. I tipped the wallet's contents into the mud and leaves. The muscles on his snowy neck stood out but I did not let go.

In the heap of notes and coins were two credit card receipts. One of them was soaked and illegible. I could just make out the name on the other.

'The "P" stands for Philip, doesn't it?' I said. It had suddenly become all too obvious. 'I can now see how you got past security on the second day of the trial. Tell them you were a defence witness, did you?'

He lashed his head from side to side, in the way the insane Legat had done in the prison hospital, and I could feel the muscles in his neck rippling as he struggled for air.

'Philip Templeman,' I said. 'I'd given up on Kingsley's alibi.'

I levered myself off him. But he continued to lie there, his feeble body caked in mud. He did not even rub his bruised neck.

'What do you know about the death of Diane Morrow?' I asked. 'Why is it that the girls around here keep dying?' When he did not answer, I added, 'I suppose you knew it was Justine Wright's car, did you?'

He was silent and looked at me fearfully.

I said, 'Did Kingsley tell you to tamper with the brakes or something? Look, why did you deny that your name was Templeman when we met in the corridor at the Old Bailey?'

There was reddening on his neck as he coughed repeatedly. But still he would not answer.

'Don't mess with me,' I said. 'Or with Justine. Or ... or I'll kill you.' I knew it sounded trite, but it was all I could think of. Then I added, 'Still, can't talk. Barristers aren't supposed to speak to alibi witnesses. Not sure if there's a rule against kicking the shit out of them, though.'

He closed his eyes and seemed to sink deeper into the mud as I hobbled to the car.

The museum was situated within the inner circle. As soon as you entered the bleak, dark hall, amongst the collection of plates and pots and axes and arrows, was a skeleton. It was small with a full set of teeth and a distended head. It was a child.

What struck me immediately as I stood over it was how similar the collection of little ribs and vertebrae was to the smouldering pile of animal bones under Vera Cavely's old Singer Gazelle.

'I see you've met Freddy.'

'Freddy?' I said.

'Well,' said the man, 'could be Freda, of course. Bit sad, really. Four thousand years and we can't tell if the poor bugger is a lad or a lass.' The man pulled the peak of his official cap a little lower. 'Mind you, these days youngsters all look the same, don't they? Long hair, earrings, banging on about free love.'

'I think you're thinking of the sixties.'

'Maybe you're right,' he said. He was bluff, burly and not particularly user-friendly. 'Still, thousands of the little monsters traipse through here come summer. And as for the festival? Think you were in a gypsy camp.'

'I put my money on the till,' I said. 'Sixty pence, isn't it?'

'Very honest of you. You'd be surprised how dishonest some folk are.'

'I'm sure I wouldn't.'

'No?'

'I'm ... a lawyer.'

'Ah,' he said. 'You lot wrote the book.'

It seemed faintly ridiculous talking about contemporary mores over the bones of a neolithic infant.

'Buried at the bottom of a ditch,' said the man. 'Facing the sun. See the position? Meant to be asleep. Quick kip, bit of sunshine and eternal life. Shame it didn't work. Poor little bugger. Mind, we don't get much sunshine down this way.'

I couldn't help thinking how peaceful the skeleton looked compared to the contorted photographs of Molly Summers.

'We'd have to close down during the off-season,' said the man, 'if it weren't for *that* fella.' He pointed his nose across the village.

'Which fellow?'

'The writer fella what murdered that lass.'

'You mean Kingsley?'

'Him what writes them dirty books.'

'Can we have a chat about that?' I asked.

'What? About pornography?'

'No. About Kingsley.'

'Sorry, I'm on duty. You know, I don't understand why he doesn't write sommat about Stonebury. I mean, this place makes Salem appear a desirable place to live.'

'Just a quick chat?'

'You can hire me for a tour if you like.'

'A tour?'

'Of the stones,' he said. 'I'm the official guide.'

As the man started to put the lights off in the museum, I asked him, 'Don't you like living in Stonebury?'

'It's not that,' he said. 'Put it this way, apart from me and this little bugger, have you met anyone in Stonebury who is actually sane?'

He bent down and whispered to the skeleton, 'Daddy's got to go out, Freddy. But he'll be back soon.'

Then the man led me to the stones.

Chapter 37

When you got up close to them, it was their very size, the over-awing bulk of the stones that was surprising. They were once natural boulders which had been chosen by unknown prehistoric visionaries and dragged for miles across the Devon hills. None of the stones was shaped or carved by man in any way. But if you looked at them for long enough, if your thoughts wandered across their shadowy surface, each stone had a face with a pair of eyes, a sardonic grin and a character that was unique.

'But why?' I asked, as he walked and I hobbled past a block called the Holestone. 'I mean, what was the point of it all?' The guide had told me that it would have taken five hundred men and oxen to drag just that monstrous rock into position.

'What's the point of anything?' he said, looking through a hole in the rock six feet from the ground. 'You see this stone? People say that it turns on its axis at midnight, but I've never seen it.'

'Why create a circle?' I insisted.

'Probably seemed a good idea at the time. Give them something to do. Now if some of our young layabouts were made to—'

'Who actually owns the stones?' I wanted to cut short his tirade on the maladies of youth.

'Own 'em, you say?'

'Yes. Who do they belong to?'

'Oh, no one owns them. Mind you,' he said, adjusting the peak of his cap knowingly, 'the stones themselves have been known to possess the odd person.'

The frost had not completely lifted and the stones sparkled. The village slumbered within the circles, and there was not a sound except for the crunch of our footsteps on the crisp grass.

'And why a circle?' I asked. 'I mean, why not a stone square or a stone triangle?'

'Now, that's an easy one. Your average circle, right, has no beginning and no end.' He looked at me for confirmation and I nodded, my grasp of geometry extending at least that far. 'Well, these stones are like the beginning and the end. Alpha and omega. Birth and death, that sort of thing.'

All things begin and end in Albion's rocky shore.

'And where is Albion?' I asked, for I felt sure he should know.

'Here,' he said. 'Where the children still worship.'

'Why did you say that?'

He looked at the circles and said, '"These hills and valleys are accursed witnesses of sin ... I therefore condense them into solid rocks."'

'Don't tell me,' I said, 'William Blake.'

'You a bit of an expert?'

'No, just an ordinary barrister defending the case from hell. So what's the official peaked-cap line on Albion?'

'You what?'

'Well, is Albion Celtic Britain or Blake's great Earth Daddy?'

The man looked at me with a degree of suspicion. 'There is another explanation.'

'Such as?'

'Albia was the eldest daughter of the King of Syria.'

'Did you say—'

'I know it sounds a little far-fetched,' he said.

'Believe me, compared to the defence I'm running, it sounds positively mundane. So when was all this?'

'In ancient times.'

'When else,' I said.

'All fifty daughters were forced to be married on the same day. They didn't want it. Who would? I mean, how many crap speeches can you stomach? So on their wedding night, instead of consummating their nuptials, they . . .'

'Yes?'

'Chopped all their husbands' goolies off.'

'That seems a tad excessive,' I said.

'Oh, those were excessive times.'

'You're not kidding. Hadn't these people heard of marriage guidance?'

The man continued, 'Well, as a punishment, he cast them adrift in a ship—'

'He?'

'The King.'

'Of Siam?'

'Of Syria.'

'Oh, yes,' I said. 'The King of Syria. I forgot.'

'Well, finally, they—'

'The daughters?' I asked.

'Exactly. You're getting the hang of this. Finally, the daughters reached this western isle. Albia. Albion. Here.'

'Fascinating,' I said.

'It all started with . . . well, with them daughters. All the trouble started with the daughters, you see—'

'Is that why the home is called West Albion?'

The man did not reply. He was hardly able to contain his excitement as we arrived at a stone which was inclined to an improbable angle. It seemed as if the slightest breath would have been too much and if I had dared to exhale, the rock would have tumbled into the ditch it had overhung for all those millennia. But I did not breathe and it did not move.

'This is the Surgeon Stone.' The man ran his fingers in one of the crevices. 'When they excavated the site in the First

247

World War, they found a man buried at the foot of the stone. From the coins scattered around him they dated him to the Middle Ages.'

'But why Surgeon?'

'Buried with his knives, weren't he?'

'For operating?'

'No. Blood-letting.'

'Blood-what?'

'In those days blood-letting was quite common. Especially for the monks that used to be round here.'

'I'm sorry,' I said. 'I just don't understand.'

He moved very close to me, glanced around quickly and whispered, 'For *libidinous* purposes.' He caressed the stone in the way you might a purring cat. 'You see, them priests tried to be holy, but had – well, impure thoughts what with the pretty local lasses. They thought it was a madness. So to let the madness out, they had to be cut.'

'Hence the surgeon?'

'And the knives.'

'But why was he buried here?'

'They reckons he was killed. By the locals. You see the Church wanted the circles broken up. Pagan religions and all that. And the villagers thought if they could, well, compromise the monks, make them impure, they wouldn't destroy the stones.' The man looked at me. 'Didn't work, of course. The Church just sent another surgeon.'

'How many stones were destroyed?'

'Enough. But the village got its revenge.'

For a moment, he basked in the undimmed glory of a distant generation. Then he continued, 'The two biggest stones were the Male and Female Sarsens. One was very tall and thin, the other smooth and round.'

'Hardly very subtle imagery.'

'You can still see the female.' With that he pointed to a mound, rather like a huge upturned saucer by a cluster of leafless trees. 'She was on the opposite side of the circle to

248

the male. You see, prior to breeding, males and females were kept separate.'

I immediately recognised this as one of the founding principles of my secondary school.

'When the male was broken up,' the man said, 'the villagers hid pieces in their barns. Years later when they built the new chapel at St Stephen's, they secretly used bits of that.'

'You don't mean—'

'Yes. The whole baptismal font in fact.'

'Is made from—'

'A neolithic phallus.'

We had arrived by the Female Sarsen. A type of brilliant green lichen grew over it, darkened, only slightly, by the shadows of the nearby trees.

'Isn't that blasphemous or something?' I asked.

'Religions come and go, but the stones are always here. Them stones has seen more religions than you or I 'ave had ... I mean, Protestants, Catholics, Romans, Druids, Pagans, Beakers—'

'Did you say Druids?'

'At one time this used to be a Druid temple, what with the stones and the oak trees.'

'Oaks?'

Another knot untangled.

The man pointed at the copse of lifeless trunks standing silhouetted against the winter sun. 'Reckon that's where the name is from.'

'Stonebury?'

'No,' he said. 'Druid. You see them Druids used to worship the oak and *drus* stands for oak in some fancy foreign lingo ... I don't know, Latin or—'

'Greek perhaps?' I said.

'Yeah, that might be it.'

'Yes,' I said. 'That might well be it.'

And I thought: *Drus*, oak, Druid, temple, stones, cult, ritual, death, murder, Molly Summers ... Kingsley?

Chapter 38

When I returned from the stones, Justine was still asleep. I sat up late waiting for her, all the time trying to make sense of what I had discovered that day. Again, I had wanted to speak to her about Diane Morrow's suicide. But when I eventually crawled into bed, Justine did not stir. And yet when I awoke later in the night from a vivid nightmare, I could hear her in the lounge listening to Schubert's *Der Tod und das Mädchen*.

The next morning was my sixth in Stonebury. It was a Saturday. Again I found Justine in bed. So this was the pattern. She would sleep all day, and I would dream all night, and we would barely exchange a word. Initially, I was worried. But soon it seemed natural, as if it were the true rhythm of Stonebury, as natural as the movement of the oak trees above the Sarsens. I had dreamt that I was at the Holestone, near the entrance to the circle. I forced my fingers through the oval-shaped hole as the stone spun around and around. And I was frightened.

When I awoke, the swelling in my ankle had gone down. I discerned that during the night, Justine had scribbled something on a torn scrap of paper. It merely said, St Stephen's. I decided to explore Stonebury further.

The village church lay about a half mile beyond the outer circle in a south-easterly direction, something like two miles from the estate. It had a solid tower. It was covered in the same slime that infested the ancient Sarsens. And it was called St Stephen and the Martyrs.

Surrounding the church, in a perfect circle, were the grounds which included the graveyard. They were lush green. Yet beyond the ramshackle boundary walls were vast fields of mud. Whether these fields had been left fallow deliberately or whether nothing would grow there, I simply could not tell. But to the west, as far as the eye could reach, were huge muddy stretches of brown, like the beaches of a forgotten sea which had been constantly in retreat.

Graveyards had always been among my favourite places, a place where earthly pretensions were exposed with every grave passed. At St Stephen's there was a surprisingly varied collection of headstones. A few were simple crosses. Others were more austere, square tablets of stone, no doubt like those brought down from the Mountain, with little odes to the frailty of man.

In an almost empty corner, there was a roughly cut slab, tilting forward like an old man who had fallen asleep in front of the fire. Opposite it was a newly dug mound of earth. There were two wreaths. One of them had a card which, much to my shame, I read.

In memory of Diane
Daughter of Sarah.

Not even a gravestone, nothing permanent to mark the loss of the young life. These things take time. The grave must settle. The worms must do their work. But I wondered if, by then, anyone would care or remember.

Near to the wooden porch was a stone seat which protruded awkwardly from the church walls. It had weathered badly and the strange figures carved into the legs had become unrecognisable as anything that had ever lived. There was a plaque above the chair. It said: Sanctuary Seat of Stonebury.

The slime and the sludge had covered the rest of the writing and the back of my sleeve was thoroughly soiled before the next line became legible.

Sanctuary is mentioned in the Laws of the Saxons.

Where had I seen church sanctuary mentioned before? Then I remembered. In Temple library. When I discovered what Kingsley meant by the Stang. I rubbed the plaque and continued to read.

Sanctuary applied to every church in the country,
If a man took the church's sanctuary, his life was safe.
But he remained a prisoner within the precincts
of the church condemned to a life of penance
until he received the King's pardon (which was rare).

The seat itself was uneven and not particularly large. The back of the seat was in fact the church wall, carved with the legend:

That the slayer might flee hither
And that he might live.
Deuteronomy IV, 41–42

The church bell rang a couple of times and a group of thin crows flew off from the top of the tower and headed towards Nethersmere Woods.

All at once, the skies parted. It was not so much rain as a heavy sheet of water falling vertically from heaven to earth. Flowers that were propped against gravestones by the bereaved were washed out of their holders, and the trees began to bow with the weight of the deluge. I had no umbrella.

The church was not as dark inside as you would have expected. At the front, on either side of the altar, were flickering rows of white candles. There was the smell of incense and newly polished wood.

Then a small woman got up off her knees and approached me.

'Oh, I'm sorry,' I said. 'Did I disturb your praying?'

'Praying? Ha. Praying that the bloody rain will stop, if that's what you mean.' She was just under five feet tall and had her dark matted hair tied at the back of her head. 'S'pose you've come for the Book then?' she said.

'Well, not really.' Then I thought better of my answer, fearing she would send me out into the rain again. 'What time do you close?' I asked.

'Close? Our church never closes. God doesn't clock off at the end of the day, you know. The Book's over here. Come on.'

She waddled off towards the front of the church, with me in her wake guiltily dripping on the shining floor.

'I'll give you twenty minutes. No longer.'

'For what?' I said.

'Well, don't ask me, for heaven's sake.' With that she inspected the dismal trail of muddy puddles, followed it to my soaking boots, tutted, and said, 'You've never messed up my clean floor.'

'I am sorry.'

'Right. You got ten minutes,' she said and stormed off in the general direction of an effigy of St Stephen, which clearly needed a good dusting.

The Stonebury Parish Register was a substantial tome, full of elaborately etched Gothic script. It lay open on a rickety wooden reading-stand, lit only by the glimmer of a dozen candle-flames. The last entry was that of a burial.

Buried. 11th December. Diane Morrow.

During the trial, we were not allowed to know the true identity of the disappearing witness due to the sensitivity of the case. But now I knew. Diane Morrow. A dead daughter of a dead mother. One witness fewer for Richard Kingsley to worry about. What would she have been able to say about the death of Molly Summers? Perhaps only Kingsley would ever really know.

Thumbing frantically through the large leaves of parchment, I eventually arrived at the entries for one year earlier. I was quite pleased to have found it so quickly.

Buried. 11th December. Mary (aka Molly) Summers.

So I was right. It was one year since the burial of the murdered girl. I had only five minutes left. Perhaps there was more to find.

The register was full of deaths, marriages and baptisms, an inky history of these secret people. The woman knelt by the baptismal font, rubbing it vigorously. Did she know, I wondered, what it was made of? She glowered at me after a few seconds and scrubbed away at my damp stains, all the time muttering to herself.

Three minutes left.

I could work out the year of Molly Summer's birth from Davenport's speech. As I turned forward, there was no sign of her baptism in the following year. Nor the next. What age are people usually baptised? As babies, perhaps? Supposedly unburdened by anything but original—

For who amongste us was not borne in a State of Sinne? And which of this Parishe does not but reach the Grave in precisely the same Fashione?

There were only two minutes left, but I could not help remembering what I had read in the Dyson novel in Kingsley's cell.

The woman put away her rusting metal pail and wiped her hands. She ran her finger along the top of an effigy and seemed pleased that St Stephen was not dusty.

Perhaps, I thought, Molly wasn't baptised in that church. Perhaps she wasn't baptised at all. I turned the pages two at a time. The woman's waddling steps sounded closer and closer up the aisle.

One minute.

Of course, Molly Summers went into care. Maybe that explained it? How many children in care were baptised? I didn't know. Another page, three years on. Burial, burial, marriage, burial.

The woman tugged at my sleeve. 'Time's up.'

Baptised. Mary (alias Molly) Summers.

Daughter Of Summers And A Marie Blacke.

'You've got to go,' said the woman. She wiped her nose with the back of her left hand roughly.

'Just another two minutes.'

'Not another two seconds.'

'Please.'

'You come in here, stamping mud about the place.'

'I said I was sorry.'

'Who do you think's going to clean up after you?'

The accurate answer was: Well, I thought you'd do it, that seems to be your job. However, I did not relish being anointed by a bucket of dirty water. So I said, 'I just need to look up one more thing.'

I wasn't sure what that was. It was a device to buy more time. But I had a gut feeling that there was more information between those dusty covers. Perhaps it was the odd coincidence of seeing something to do with my two Stonebury cases. Or perhaps I was remembering something from the dreams. But I sensed that there had to be more.

'I've got to put the Book away now,' she said.

'Can't I look while I . . . wait for confession?'

'*You* want to *confess*?' she said, laughing.

I had not been to confession in – I couldn't really say, perhaps more than twenty years. 'Yes,' I said. 'I haven't been to confession since October.' That was true, but I didn't say October of which year.

'We're Church of England,' she said. 'We don't need to confess.'

'Don't you sin?'

'Of course we do. Protestants sin with the best of them. Only we don't see the point of telling some boozy old priest in a frock. Now what did you want to look up?'

My mind went blank. But as I gazed at the baptismal font again, it came to me.

All things begin and end in Albion's rocky shore.

'I'm trying to discover when someone was born,' I said, thinking that perhaps everyone had got Molly Summers's age wrong. 'You know, when they *begin* their life.'

'I do know what birth means.' The woman went up to the rows of candles and between huge gusts of breath said, 'But I'm afraid that you simply can't look up the birth.' Another puff. 'Not here, you can't.'

'But I thought you said—'

'All records of birth are kept in London.'

I closed the church door behind me and began to walk in the rain towards the London Road, all the time trying to remember Emma's home telephone number. When I thought about it, we had been told very little about Molly Summers. I needed to know more.

The wind blew through the oak trees along the road. I stopped momentarily to listen to the sound. But it was not the wind but my imagination that I heard. For again I heard the sounds from my recurring dream, the distant strains of a woman weeping. And instead of a blank television screen, I saw the haze of my confusion. And I sensed that it was more important to make a call than to confess.

Chapter 39

Emma answered the telephone immediately. 'I have been going out of my mind,' she said. She was particularly angry as I hadn't told her I was leaving London with Justine. There was still much preparation for trial to do.

'Emma, I need a favour.'

'No, Tom. I'm not going to make the peace with Penny. I have just about had it with—'

'It's not that.'

'What then?'

'I need you to do some investigating.'

Her voice expressed her disbelief. 'Investigating? There's a huge bundle of further evidence. Now, *Inspector Payne*. He's been doing some investigating. The solicitors are going up the wall, Kingsley wants another conference and all I can tell them is my leader's disappeared.'

'Doesn't sound too good, does it?' I said.

'I'm trying to hold the fort here and you've been ... where exactly have you been?'

'Down the yellow brick road, Emma. Where do you think? I've been in Stonebury, of course.'

'And what *have* you been doing?'

'Fox-hunting, going to funerals, poisoning myself with Red-eye. You know, the usual sort of rustic things.'

'Tom, be serious. Goldman and Goldman say that Philip Templeman has vanished.'

'No, he hasn't,' I replied.

'Then where is he?'

'I left him in a puddle of mud in Nethersmere Woods.'

'What?' Emma cried.

'Well, we had a bit of a ... well, fight.'

'Jesus, Tom. Most barristers value their defence witnesses. You just beat them up.'

Then the pips went. 'I haven't got much money left,' I said.

'All right. I know I'm going to regret this, but what do you want me to do?'

'Find out when and where Molly Summers was born.'

'What on earth's the point?'

A car came around the sharp bend in the London Road which sheltered the village from most of the noise of the traffic.

I then said, 'It may be that the murdered girl wasn't who we thought she was.'

'What the hell does that mean?'

'Perhaps it wasn't Molly Summers who was killed.'

'Who was it then?'

I read out the baptism entry from the parish register and Emma conceded that it was slightly, but only slightly, odd.

'I had to get a new birth certificate for a second passport,' she said. 'You have to apply to St Catherine's House. I'll go first thing Monday. And, Tom?'

'I owe you one, Emma.'

'Can I suggest you don't share this information with the ... opposition?'

'You can suggest it.'

'Perhaps the' – she dropped her voice – 'perhaps the other side shouldn't know what we're up to.'

'There are no sides on this one, Emma.'

'I don't think Kingsley sees it that way.'

'Kingsley's the least of my problems.'

'What does that mean?' she asked.

'Tell you when I see you.'

'Which will be?'

'Tomorrow night.'

'But Tom, it's Saturday now and the trial starts Monday. Can't you—'

'Tomorrow's my last day with Justine. I'll call you when I get home.'

The rain had eased and I walked back to the cottage wondering what I should tell Justine.

When I entered the lounge, it was early evening. Justine looked particularly alluring, sitting cross-legged in front of the fire, her hair framing her face like a soft yellow mop, sucking her pen as she considered the papers.

'I've tossed a few things together,' she said. 'Some sort of stew. One of old Annie's specials. Daddy used to love it. Loads of carrots, potatoes ... don't worry, Tom. No turnips.'

I stared back at her with crossed arms, my wet shoes suddenly feeling particularly uncomfortable. My ankle again began to throb.

Justine continued writing away. 'Fancy a drink, Tom? Gin's on the sideboard, tonic should be—'

'We need to talk.'

'Oh, God. Not again. What more is there to say? I thought I told you everything. *Everything.*' She paused but my silence provoked her to continue. 'What more can I tell you, Tom? What more do you want of me?'

'It's nothing to do with – those things.'

'Then what?'

'The Sarah Morrow case.'

'Do we have to? I mean, now?'

'Yes, now.' Ever since Emma had accosted me in Johnson's and told me to steer clear of Justine, I had wanted to give Justine a chance. I suppose it was the incorrigible defence advocate in me.

Justine left the brief on the floor and turned towards the fireplace. 'All right,' she said, 'you start.'

I shook a soggy foot. 'Why didn't you tell Sarah Morrow that the judge had offered probation if she—'

'The fire's dying,' Justine said. 'Can you bring over a couple of logs?'

When I had done so, I repeated the question.

'It wasn't that simple, Tom. Sarah didn't want to plead guilty to manslaughter. Not after what that so-called husband did to her. Can you imagine what it's like to be abused?'

She tried to avoid eye contact with me. 'These logs are too big. We'll have to cut them.' With that she handed me a blunt hand-axe covered in rust. 'You do the honours.'

I had never cut a log, a branch, or anything with growth rings in my life and protested, 'Why me?'

Her eye froze. 'You're supposed to be the man.'

The first blow bounced off the bark sending vibrations up my arm.

'You've got to make a small groove first,' she said.

I made a little nick and aimed another blow. 'Did you forget? I mean, that case was a political circus,' I said.

'I didn't forget. Harder.'

Another blow. A few splinters flew towards the embers.

'Then why? She trusted you, Justine and—'

'Come on. Harder.'

I raised the axe as far as I could, and Justine held the log with each hand only inches away from the cut. The blow was accurate but the wood was tough. 'For God's sake, Justine. She could have got away with probation and she ended up—'

'Harder.'

The cut became a gash. A little pink sap sprayed from the wound. 'Well, you know how she ended up.'

Justine moved her fingers closer together and tightened her grip. 'So I screwed up. It happens. It won't bring her back. Come on, much harder.'

I raised the axe up to my face, Justine's fingers looked tiny spread across the bark below. 'Were you thinking of yourself? Your career?' I asked.

'I thought—' She looked at me with a cold determination. 'I thought we could win. Don't you understand winning, Tom? Put your back into it.'

The axe swung, and I thought about my fight with Templeman and how victory had felt. I imagined, for the first time, the jury pronouncing Kingsley not guilty (was *that* winning?) and I became confused. I thought about the funeral entry about Diane Morrow, and when I swung again, I saw that as the blade struck the wood, the log moved, the axe bounced to the left and gashed the side of Justine's hand.

'Oh, God. I'm sorry.' I flung down the axe.

'It's only a graze.' She got up and slowly put the open wound to her mouth.

'Is there anything I can do?' I said rather feebly.

'Haven't you done enough?' Justine replied.

Chapter 40

After washing the wound, Justine wanted to lie down. Consequently, I was left in the lounge by myself. I took out my case papers but could not concentrate. The recent events in Stonebury had troubled me greatly, and I feared that the legal process we were about to embark upon was no more than an artifice. I knew that the trial could be nothing but a shallow caricature of events, an imitation of the truth. For this was not the type of truth to be uncovered in a brightly lit courtroom, but one that was secreted here, in the woods of Stonebury.

It is one of the inviolable taboos of the Bar that you do not look in your opponent's brief. It is a little like being invited to dinner and then rummaging through your host's drawers, or going on a date and snooping in your partner's handbag. But Justine had left some of her papers strewn carelessly on the floor in front of the fire and as the flames began to rise, sparks started to jump mischievously towards her brief.

I moved across the room and gathered up the jumbled mass of documents. I recognised the police report, but did not read it. There were a couple of interview transcripts which both sides had agreed to exclude. They basically consisted of Kingsley boasting about his tawdry novels. Then a copy of the indictment, the plea of guilty to manslaughter – the deal Kingsley reneged on – crossed out in red. A copy of Kingsley's handwritten note, the one found in his cell. I still could not believe his foolishness. Two custody records, more interviews, a bundle of exhibits, letters from the Crown

Prosecution Service. I turned these over rapidly; I didn't want to see a syllable of the correspondence. Statements, further statements. Why couldn't Justine file her papers neatly like a normal barrister?

It was a mess.

When I had sat down at the desk in the opposite corner of the room, as far from her brief as possible, I jotted down a few ideas for the next week.

Accused   –   *Kingsley*
Victim   –   *Molly Summers . . . (?)*
Motive   –   *Lust*

Then I crossed out lust. There was no evidence of sexual abuse. Bloodlust, then? Kingsley was sick but was he bloodthirsty? He had no record for violence.

Motive   –   *Madness? Motiveless? . . . Stonebury?*

Stonebury. Thinking of Kingsley's note and the stones and Blake, I knew Kingsley's motive must still be in Stonebury, somewhere.

Then Mary flowed like a river of many streams.

How distasteful a reference to the shedding of an innocent girl's blood. But Kingsley did not quote it exactly in his notes from the trial. He had changed the beginning. How had he phrased it? Something was that wretched river: the truth? life? death? Before I knew what I was doing, I had found the copy of Kingsley's note in Justine's brief.

The past is a river of many streams.

The past. Why that? I wondered whether the prosecution had formed the link between the note and Blake and Albion and Stonebury. Perhaps they wouldn't. Perhaps . . . what I saw then did not make sense.

I was not holding a copy of Kingsley's handwritten note. I was holding *the* scribbled note itself. Why had Payne given the original exhibit to the prosecution lawyers? How then did my handwriting expert examine it? Had they given him the wrong one? And someone had taken off the court's exhibit label? What was Payne up to?

Justine stirred next door and faintly called my name.

'How are you?' I replied.

'Can you come in here, Tom?'

'Wait there. Just be a second.' I rushed back to the fireplace and flung Justine's papers on to the floor again. They looked too neat. I kicked some of them about with my foot.

'Tom? What are you up to?'

'Just coming.'

The flames were still spitting lively sparks from the fire.

'Tom, I'm waiting.'

The papers didn't look suitably chaotic, so I continued to scuff them around while I said, 'Want some tea?'

'Some *what*?'

'Tea. I'm making camomile tea.' Then I saw on the floor another copy of Kingsley's note. And another. And another. All in his intense spiderish handwriting. How many did he write?

'Can't you just bring me a glass of water?'

I picked up the assorted notes one by one and was sure that our expert, old Mr Dove, had not seen any of them.

'Tom? If you don't come in here, then I'll—'

Payne had not told the court that Kingsley had written so many notes. The question was, why?

The door opened and Justine caught me rifling through her papers. 'I should have stopped them,' she said.

She was not angry. But I was.

For by the time we both sat down, it was absolutely clear to me that someone had been trying to imitate the handwriting of Richard Kingsley.

'You know he's a monster ... and you know he's guilty,' Justine told me. 'I mean, are you going to say he's not?'

The notes fluttered gently in my hand as warm currents floated up from the fire. Justine walked towards me in her nightshirt, saw the astonishment in my eyes and sank back into her armchair. This was not a time for touching.

She gathered her knees under her chin as she began to speak. 'It all happened so fast. You know what the confusion was like what with the judge shouting at you and everything. But I swear – Tom, you've got to believe me – I knew nothing about it till later.'

'Why should I believe anything you tell me?'

'Because you love me.'

'Is that what you think?'

'It's what I believe. I mean, it's what I want to believe ... Oh, God, when we used the note in court to oppose bail, we thought it was genuine. What else could we think, Aubrey and me? It was Richard Kingsley we were prosecuting. You know what the man is capable of.'

Yes, I did know. Glancing down at the note, I remembered how Kingsley had gestured with his finger, like a knife cutting a throat, when I was about to cross-examine the poor girl. Yes, I knew what he was capable of. I knew, too, that he had no respect for youth or innocence or vulnerability – they were all there for him to violate. I knew he had to be stopped. But like this?

'Who did it?' I asked.

'I'm not sure.'

'Who did it?'

'I think ... I think it was Payne's idea. I'm pretty sure of that. I went berserk when he told me later. He was so smug and self-satisfied. But what was I supposed to do?'

'Withdraw from the case.'

'And have them pull even bigger strokes? At least this way I can ... well, exercise some control.'

'Justine, think what you're saying.'

'But I told them there was no way they were going to use this evidence against Kingsley at the retrial.'

That was something. I put the papers down and moved to the window. Small patches of yellow light from the village shone between the trees.

I said, 'And that's why—'

'Why we never got the note tested. We were never going to use it.'

Another piece slotted into position.

'But where did you get a sample of his writing to copy?' I asked.

'Payne said that he seized piles of manuscripts of Kingsley's sleazy novels. I wanted to tell you, Tom. But—'

'But you didn't.'

'But I was scared.'

'Scared? Of what?'

Justine put her head in her hands and once again her soft hair covered her face. 'I was scared of them.'

'Them?'

'All of them. I think . . .'

'What?'

'Oh, I can't tell you.' She sounded terrified.

'You must tell me everything, Justine.'

'I think . . . that heroin was meant for me.'

'For *you*?'

'As a sort of reminder. You know, Remember which side you're on. That sort of thing. Tom, you just don't understand half of what is going on.'

'No, Justine. I don't understand why a young girl should kill herself. I mean, where did she get the heroin?'

'Where do you think?'

'The home? But—'

'Kingsley was a trustee of the home.'

'*What?*'

'We can't use that fact. There's so much that we can't use,' Justine said.

My mind began to race. Just when I thought that things were beginning to make sense, there was something else. There was always something else. 'You've got to pull out of the case,' I said.

'I can't.'

'Don't be crazy. If you don't—'

'I'm frightened, Tom.'

But that was something I already knew. She began sobbing as though a heart would break and I was determined it should not be mine.

'Davenport can get another junior,' I said.

'Aubrey won't let me go.'

'Say you're ill. Say ... anything.'

'Tom, if Kingsley goes down, that will be the end of it.'

'And you believe that?'

'I think so.'

'And you're willing to go along with it?'

'What choice do I have?'

'I don't know. But I do know one thing. If you do go along with it, you're no better than they are. No better than Kingsley. You're just—'

'Oh, please. Don't go all righteous on me, Tom. There's nothing more sickening.' There was suddenly a different tone in her voice; her helpless retreat had turned again into counter-attack. 'You're the one who said we're part of this now. Well, you were right. Congratulations. Go to the top of the class. But for Christ's sake don't get on your damn high horse at the same time.'

'I'm going,' I said.

'That's right. Run away, Tom. Like you ran away from Penny. Like you ran away from your daughter.' She looked at me coldly. 'Like you've run away from everything in your life.'

'You can be a cruel person, Justine.'

'Kingsley has got to be punished, Tom. This thing has got to be done.'

'I'll see you in court,' I said.

I knew I couldn't stay another moment. Justine was clearly set on what she intended to do. The more I thought about what had been going on with the notes, the angrier I became. If I were to be honest, I would have to admit that a large part of that anger was because they were stupid. Stupid enough to give Kingsley an opportunity to make people feel as though he were the victim.

But there was something else. The plotting and scheming seemed to have a certain logic in Stonebury. Like the circles. Something everyone understood, but no one could properly explain. And my head had become so full of lore and legend that I wondered whether I would still recognise the truth if I was unfortunate enough to meet it.

So even though I would be leaving one day early, I sensed that it was the right thing to do. As I looked from the window, a light wind moved silently through the trees. Beyond the woods lay the stones and the village, and beyond that lay the long road from Stonebury to London.

As I drove towards the London Road, it had started to rain again. I passed St Stephen's. The churchyard was made to look even bleaker with the weeds and nettles washed to the ground. I was about to drive past the outer gate when a bedraggled magpie perched upon a gravestone opposite the newly dug grave of Diane Morrow.

It looked at me and I looked back. The bird did not move until I got out of my car and started to walk to the mound of soil that was all that remained of the disappearing witness. Then the magpie flew off.

Rising from behind the gravestone opposite was a girl who shivered and stared and wept and hugged her chattering body with two bony arms, as if the very vibrations would shake her apart.

It was the girl from the fox-hunt.

'What were you thinking of?' I said. 'Scaring my horse like that.'

'I wasn't there,' she said, momentarily arresting the chattering of her teeth.

'Rubbish. I saw you.'

'I wasn't there.'

'Do you know how dangerous it is? Look, I don't agree with fox-hunting either but—'

'I wasn't there,' she insisted.

'So you say. Take a professional's advice: alibi isn't your best defence. Say the horses charged you. Run self-defence.'

She was silent.

'What if I was injured?' I said. 'Would that stop Aubrey Davenport waddling off to pester Charley the Fox? No. All it would do is land you in jail.'

'I don't want to go to no jail, mister. They made me say it.' She grasped the top of the gravestone with two nail-bitten hands.

'So what are you doing here?'

'You know.'

'Do I?'

'Yes,' she said and pointed to the mound of earth above Diane Morrow.

'Your friend?'

'My sister,' she said miserably.

'Why did she kill herself?'

'She didn't.'

'Then who killed her?'

'The heroin.'

'So she didn't want to die?' I asked.

'She didn't want to live neither ... not there.' The girl shivered again and tried to chew at nails that no longer remained. I noticed a tattoo on the back of her hand. 'You wouldn't want to live there,' she said.

'West Albion?'

'No one would. It's like ...'

'Yes?'

'It's like hell, mister. It's like bloody hell and Diane reckoned heroin's the way out.' She looked again at the wet soil above her sister. 'But they can't do her no harm now.'

'They?'

The girl did not respond.

'They?' I repeated. 'Who are *they*?'

The girl waved her frail arm equally in the direction of the village and the circles. And I could not say whether she indicated man or stone. But then I realised something of far greater significance. I *had* seen her before the fox-hunt. I noticed the hair, the nails, the vacant look and at last understood what she meant.

'So you really weren't *there*?' I said.

'No. Not at them stones.'

Another knot was undone. Perhaps the tightest yet.

'Come on,' I said, grabbing her tiny hands. I *had* seen the girl before. At the trial. She was the first witness.

PART IV

RETRIAL

I implored the rapid sword
To secure my liberty,
I asked the poison I abhorred
To succour my timidity.

Alas! the poison and the sword
Only showed contempt for me.
'You deserve not the reward
Of freedom from your slavery.'

The Vampire
Baudelaire

Chapter 41

'And the defendant, members of the jury, is represented by m'learned friend, Mr Thomas Fawley who sits next to me in counsel's row.' Justine waved a delicate hand in my direction but did not look at me. I could see the gash I had made with the axe. 'And Richard Kingsley is also represented by Miss Emma Sharpe who sits behind Mr Fawley.' No gesture. Not her learned friend. Justine never liked Emma.

'Mr Aubrey Davenport who leads me for the Crown will, we hope, join us this afternoon – or, at least, tomorrow. Until then, I'm afraid' – she smiled and tilted her head to one side – 'you are going to have to put up with me.' Justine had already begun her girlish flirtations with the men on the jury. That was to be expected.

Davenport was ill – but not very. Influenza, we were told. I suspected gout.

Justine continued in her gentle way and it was all very pleasant, the professional courtesies at the start of a case, the civilised preludes to battle. We will try to tear each other's eyes out, but we must remain learned friends, bowing respectfully like contestants before the Saturday matinee in Nero's Coliseum.

'So what is this case about?' Justine asked. 'I can answer in one word. Murder.' She didn't stress the word, said it like any other, like you would say, thank you or please. It was a nice touch. I taught her that.

She talked to the jury as if she were reading a story to

a class of children about dungeons and nasty dragons, but where good would triumph, as it must.

'I can tell you that this case will be rather short. Why? Because the most important witness, the one who could tell you blow by blow what happened, is not here. She is dead. Buried in a grave in the village of Stonebury. Her name is Molly Summers.'

Justine glanced at Hilary Hardcastle, who was looking particularly reptilian even by her gruesome standards, and then fixed upon Kingsley.

She continued, 'So what is it to murder someone? Which of us who has not killed can really understand? Who can really say what drives one man to take the life of another? I suppose only one person in this court will ever really know why Molly Summers was murdered.' Justine paused. 'And that person, says the prosecution, is sitting in the dock.'

All eyes moved towards Kingsley, who sat there attentive but unmoved.

'Members of the jury, you might like to remember one thing: the prosecution does not have to prove motive. Or, to put it another way, we don't have to prove *why* Richard Kingsley chose to kill this sixteen-year-old girl in cold blood. We only have to prove that he did murder her. And when we call the evidence' – her voice lowered, she spoke more slowly – 'that is precisely ... precisely what we shall prove.'

I looked round the scene in Court 4 at the Old Bailey. It being a retrial, the court staff had followed the case from Court 8. Leonard sulked at the front of the court. Norman sucked on his biro. And then I remembered what Justine had told me.

Kingsley must be punished. This thing must be done.

I had spent a week in London and a week in Stonebury and was still very far from the truth about the murder of Molly Summers. Every now and then I even thought the unthinkable and imagined that Kingsley might be innocent.

But a look at his face, a minute in his company disabused me of such fantasies immediately.

People had crammed into the rows of the public gallery, squeezing themselves against complete strangers, sketch artists from the tabloids hung over the railings to get a better view. Court 4 was full. Full as it had been during the trials of Victorian poisoners, and when Edwardian arsonists were in the dock.

The gallery was high above the well of the court, like the upper circle of some seedy flea-pit, high above the drama, up amongst the gods.

The defendant just sat in the dock, oblivious to everyone, to everything except the soft tones of Justine Wright, his prosecutor, who was trying to send him to prison for life.

When Justine began to talk about the evidence, Emma and I began to make notes. Justine very fairly admitted that although there was a partially smudged print on the knife, this could not, and should not, be attributed to Kingsley.

It was when Justine began to mention the confession to the police that Emma began to tug furiously at my gown.

'Object, Tom,' she whispered.

'Why?'

'So we can try to get it excluded.'

'By whom?'

'By the judge, of course.'

'Oh, I'm sorry, Emma. For a nightmarish moment I thought we were in Hilary Hardcastle's court.'

'Don't be facetious. Even she has a discretion to exclude it.'

'Yes, but she can never decide which way to rule: in favour of the prosecution or against the defence. Tough choice that. Besides,' I said as Emma sank back into her seat, 'I think we can have some fun with our boys in blue.'

Justine outlined the rest of the evidence with commendable brevity. But she did not mention the notice of alibi. Nor did she mention Philip Templeman. Had she forgotten? Was the omission deliberate? Or perhaps there was another reason?

The jury sat fascinated. Three people stood out immediately. An elderly woman with an intelligent face, her cashmere cardigan thrown over her shoulders. Then there was a big man: tattoos, leather jacket, thick gold bracelet, constantly looking around court. Finally, a woman with good bone structure, mid-thirties like Penny and Justine, Aran jumper, ethnic skirt. She made a very full note.

The grandmother, the taxi-driver and the social worker. Kingsley's fate was in their hands.

'That, members of the jury, is some of the evidence the prosecution will call,' said Justine. She had not mentioned the girl in the graveyard nor, of course, Vera Cavely. 'You will note that the case is largely circumstantial. No doubt Mr Fawley will bring his' – she looked at me and feigned a smile – 'his almost legendary forensic skills to bear upon this point.'

Hardcastle glared at me.

'Don't be taken in,' Justine warned. 'Don't be deceived by Mr Fawley's charms. A circumstantial case is not a weak case.'

Emma and Hilary Hardcastle made a note of this.

'Imagine,' said Justine, 'and I'm sure it would never happen, but imagine Mr Fawley and I had had an argument and he wanted...' She paused and then said, 'And he wanted to hurt me.'

I could feel myself flushing, but could not control it. Everyone looked at me and I felt guilty but for reasons they could not begin to conceive.

Justine continued, 'If Mr Fawley was seen going into a room with a knife and if I was found brutally stabbed to death and the knife was found in his house. And imagine – and this is the diabolical part – imagine he confessed to an honest policeman. Well then, Mr Fawley would say: the case is weak – it is entirely circumstantial.' Again she paused for the jury to catch up. 'And what, ladies and gentlemen, would *you* say to that? These, I think, are the types of issues that you will have to decide in this trial.'

Emma came to my shoulder. 'Lovers' tiff?'

'Something like that,' I said.

'Don't let it get to you. It's not personal. Remember?'

'Emma, it couldn't be more personal.'

The first witness then stormed his way into court.

Chapter 42

The witness arrived in the box with a great deal of fuss and bother. There was the pounding of large boots, the rustling of a starched uniform and short-tempered grunts. Before Norman, the usher, had a chance to raise the card and ask the witness to repeat the oath, the Bible was snatched from his unsuspecting hand and held towards the heavens.

'I swear by Almighty God,' the witness gabbled without taking a breath, the sacred oath becoming one long conundrum ending in, 'and nothing-but-the-truth'. The man looked around, cheeks reddening, buttons popping, and added for good measure, 'So help me ... er, God.'

The judge was far from impressed. 'There is no need,' Hardcastle snarled, 'no need at all to invoke the assistance of the Almighty.'

The policeman was about to argue back when Justine intervened. 'Can we have your name please?'

'PC 732, ma'am.'

There was a swift palpitation of the judicial eyelids. 'You *do* have a name, I suppose? I mean, you haven't changed your name to PC whatsit by deed-poll?'

The officer looked at Hardcastle, the Bible still suspended eight feet nearer its central character than was strictly necessary. 'I do have a name, ma'am.'

'Well, what is it?'

'PC Lynch, ma'am.'

'Well, why ever didn't you say?'

'I dunno, ma'am.'

'Don't call me ma'am. Do use some common sense and let's get on with it,' said Hardcastle.

Justine was perfectly calm. 'Which force are you attached to?'

'Devon and Dorset.'

'And how long have you been there?'

Lynch looked around nervously at the court full of city dwellers. 'All my life, ma'am – er, miss ... er – all my life.'

'Now,' said Justine, 'I'd like to ask you about the murder of Molly Summers.'

I whispered to Justine. 'You can lead PC Plod through this part of his evidence. Do use your common sense.'

Justine's mouth tightened a fraction, but relaxed when she turned towards the jury and the witness. 'Did you assist in the arrest of Richard Kingsley?'

'Yes.'

'Can you tell us where and when he was arrested?'

Lynch looked to the judge. 'Your Honour, I made a note.'

'Well, can't you tell us those simple details without consulting your notes?'

'I'd prefer to use my notebook.'

Hilary forgot for a moment which side she was on and, scenting blood, moved in. 'When was the note made?'

'I can't remember ... exactly. It's written in the notebook – I think.'

That much launched missile, the judicial pencil, fell rapidly to the Bench. 'This is very unsatisfactory.'

I saw the chance to score a few points. 'May I assist the court?' I said. 'I have no objection to the officer using his notebook – if he can't remember.'

'Well, thank you, Mr Fawley.' Hardcastle eyed me suspiciously. 'You've been most helpful.'

A quick bow, then I was behind the curtain again. As I sat down, Emma yanked my gown painfully.

'Just what are you doing?' she said. 'He was squirming there.'

'You ain't seen nothing yet,' I replied.

'We shall see.'

'*You* shan't. You're going to St Catherine's House.'

As Emma got up, she drew very near to my right ear. 'What *has* got into you, Tom?'

Justine eventually managed to navigate her way through Lynch's account. He described the scene at Kingsley's manor, the arrest, how the police wore rubber gloves to avoid leaving fingerprints and momentarily he sounded like a real policeman. He told of how the knife was found and sealed in an exhibit's bag and taken to the forensic science laboratory.

In solemn tones, he said that Kingsley had confessed and then struggled as he was taken away.

It was my turn to cross-examine.

'Is your evidence that after you cautioned Mr Kingsley you asked him if he "did it"?' I smiled as I began.

'Yes, sir.'

'And lo and behold he said, "I was there"?' My gentlest tone.

'Yes.'

'And he said, "My knife was used"?'

'Yes.'

'And he said, "But you'll never prove it"?'

Lynch quickly glanced at his notes.

'Don't worry, Officer,' I reassured him. 'It's not a trick question.'

'Er, yes. That's what he said.' Lynch smiled.

I turned slowly to the jury and shouted, 'This is all *lies*.' The smile vanished. It was time to attack. 'Did you ever show your note of this, this ... *conversation* to Mr Kingsley?'

'No, sir.'

'Why not?'

'I don't know.'

'Ever read it to him?'

'No, sir.'

'Ever let him read it?'

'No, sir.'

'Ever ask him to sign it?'

'No.'

'To witness it?'

'No.'

'Why *not*?'

'I can't remem— I don't know.'

'Ever ask him about it in interview?'

'I didn't interview him.'

'Ever tell the interviewing officers the murder suspect had confessed?'

'No, sir.'

'Why not?'

'I suppose I forgot.'

I looked at him sternly. 'You forgot?' I repeated. Now a change of pace, a scratch of the chin. 'And do you, Mr Lynch, as a *diligent* policeman routinely do those things when someone "confesses"?' I sarcastically stressed the last word.

'This is no place for sarcasm, Mr Fawley,' said Hardcastle.

'Nor for lies, Your Honour.' I turned back to the officer. 'You do usually do those things?'

'Yes, sir.'

'But you didn't here?'

'No, sir.'

'And can you give us a reason why ever not?'

'I don't know ... I mean, no, sir.'

The taxi-driver crossed his arms and stared without sympathy at the cornered policeman.

'Have you finished, Mr Fawley?' asked Hardcastle.

'Not quite,' I said. 'Now your evidence is that Mr Kingsley – let me read my note – "scratched my face as I pushed him to the van and said: 'I've got AIDS, you' –"'

'You bastard.'

'Thank you. "I've got AIDS, you bastard. You're going to die." Is that your evidence?'

'Yes.'

I put my notes down and fixed Lynch for the next round. 'Was Mr Kingsley ever charged with assaulting you?'

'No, sir.' Then Lynch saw an opening. 'It's part of the job. Happens all the time.'

'What? A suspected murderer in a wheelchair scratches your face and tells you you're going to die of AIDS? I imagine that's as common as cow-pat on your rural beat.'

'No, I meant—'

'We all know what you meant, Mr Lynch. It's a tissue of lies as well.'

'No.'

'Really?' I eyed Lynch and tried to decide where to strike next. I looked below his belt. 'I suppose Mr Kingsley didn't have a handbag on him?'

Lynch looked to the judge in confusion, but Hilary was a veteran and could see what was coming.

'Just answer the question,' she said wearily.

'No, he didn't have a handbag.'

'Or a make-up kit?'

'No.'

'Or a nail-file?'

'No.'

'And when he scratched your face, I imagine he broke the skin and it bled?'

Lynch tried to play the martyr. 'A little. Not much.'

I intended to crucify him. 'And he scratched you before he got to the police station?'

'Yes.'

'Well, tell us how it is that he had no human tissue under his fingernails when they were swabbed minutes later?'

He had no answer. Some witnesses babble when they are caught lying, others become quiet. Lynch was a silent perjurer.

'Mr Lynch, was a photograph taken of this *very* serious injury? You know, for compensation or for that other thing – now what's it called? Oh, yes. For evidence?'

Hardcastle didn't bother to interrupt.

'No photograph was taken, sir.'

Then I gushed with enthusiasm. 'Oh, but that's where you are wrong, Mr Lynch.'

In the excitement of bagging a murder suspect he had probably forgotten an arrest photograph, a Polaroid taken by the custody sergeant on arrival at Stonebury police station. There was Kingsley with an arrogant smirk on his face and Lynch standing next to the wheelchair.

'Take a look,' I said. 'Any blood on you?'

'No.'

'Any scratches?'

'No.'

'So much as a nick from shaving?'

'I use an electric razor,' he said.

I noticed that none of the jury had laughed at his attempted riposte. 'Thank you for sharing your depilatory routine with us, Mr Lynch,' I said. 'I mean, that is you in the photograph, Officer?'

'Yes.'

'Well, tell us. Which has been fabricated? The photograph or your evidence? You were trying to get a commendation, weren't you? Did *Sergeant* Lynch sound so attractive?'

'That's enough, Mr Fawley,' Hardcastle said.

'Yes,' I replied. 'I think that's quite enough.'

We rose early and I returned to the robing room with what I knew was a smug grin on my face. But I also knew that it would not and could not last long in that trial. I was Tannoyed to answer the telephone. It was Emma from St Catherine's House.

'So how did the case go?' she asked.

'Oh, so so,' I gloated.

'Oh, God. Are you going to be unbearable?'

'Got to enjoy it while it lasts, Emma. Anyway, how did you get on?'

'Took me ages. Problem is . . .' She paused. 'Well, how can I put this? You see, Tom, there is *no* Molly Summers.'

'What?'

'I'll keep looking – but according to the records, she doesn't exist.'

I looked at my watch and realised I would have just half an hour with Kingsley before they took him back to prison.

Chapter 43

Kingsley sat in the same visiting room where Whitey Innocent gave me his mysterious warning. The defendant had not spoken to me during the course of the first day's proceedings. No notes, no suggestions, no instructions. It was as though everything was going according to plan – his plan. When the jailer let me in, Kingsley put down his copy of the evening paper.

'They've captured my likeness pretty well,' he said. 'But they haven't done you justice, Mr Fawley. They've made you look like a worried cocker spaniel.' He handed me the tabloid sketch.

'It's how I feel,' I said.

'You should get some rest, you know. Too much . . . running about.'

'I assume you're referring to my encounter with your mate Templeman.'

'That's rather a large assumption to make,' Kingsley said.

'He must have told you. Don't even try to pretend—'

'What did you think of him?' Kingsley suddenly interrupted.

'I think he needs to work on his right hook.'

Kingsley smiled. Or at least that part of his face below the eyes smiled. The eyes were unchanged.

I gave the tabloid back to Kingsley and said, 'I do know that you . . . well, that you didn't write the handwritten note.'

'And just how do you know that?'

'The same way that I know Templeman isn't what he seems. Call it—'

'Instinct?' Kingsley asked. 'Or interference in matters that don't concern you, perhaps? I did tell you the handwritten note wasn't mine—'

'No, you just said you wanted a graphologist to examine it. Why couldn't you just have said it wasn't yours?'

'Would you have believed me?'

'Probably not,' I said.

'You see.'

'So what do you want?' I asked. 'An apology?'

'That would be nice. But I'd settle for a teenage girl to—'

'What about the typed note? You haven't said whether...' I paused. I heard a rattle of keys outside as other remand prisoners were being led to the prison van.

'I thought you gave a – satisfactory performance,' Kingsley said.

'Thanks for your undiluted praise.'

'Well, I think you were a bit harsh on that poor policeman.'

'He was trying to set you up for murder.' I realised that was the type of thing I would have said to one of my innocent clients, so I added, 'Whether or not you did it.'

'But the real question, Mr Fawley, is whether they will get their hands on the girl.'

'Which girl?'

'The only one left. I hear young Diane Morrow overdosed on heroin. Such a shame. Young people and drugs, what *can* we do?'

'How did you know her name?'

'Everyone knew. Oh, yes,' Kingsley added, 'apart from you. Are you beginning to get the impression, Mr Fawley, that you haven't been invited to the party?'

'Look, I want to know.'

'To know?'

'Is it true you were a trustee of the home?'

'I don't think the prosecution will introduce that fact,' Kingsley replied.

'That's not what I asked.'

'But that's what I answered.'

'Were you a bloody—'

'Yes, I was a trustee.'

'You never said.'

'You never—'

'I know, I never asked. So who was murdered, Kingsley?'

'Poor innocent Molly Summers. Well, that's what your ... lady friend, Justine Wright told the court.'

'Leave her out of it.'

'No supper at the Savoy tonight?'

'Shut it, Kingsley.'

'Didn't Miss Wright say poor Molly was buried in a little grave in Stonebury?'

'But Molly Summers doesn't exist, does she?'

'You mean she doesn't? I hope we haven't all been chasing the wrong fox.' He smiled, the rows of little round teeth sparkled. 'Can you murder someone who doesn't exist, Mr Fawley? Now there's a question.' He tapped a crooked index finger against his lips. 'Yes, a very interesting philosophical question. Of course, St Matthew said—'

'Just shut up,' I told him. I walked slowly to the door and glanced through the glass panel. The jailer was waiting outside. 'I don't know what's going on, Kingsley. I'm not so sure anyone does any more ... I mean, what's your defence? Is it: A. I wasn't there. B. I was there but did nothing. C. I was there but killed someone else. Or—'

'Or D. I'm just not going to tell you.'

Kingsley made to say something else but I stopped him. 'Just listen, Kingsley. Now I've got a job to do. And I'll do it. I don't like it, but I'll just have to put up with it. But what I won't put up with is your feeble pretence at innocence. It makes me sick.'

Kingsley was silent.

As I closed the door behind me, I heard him say, 'Hope you sent my love to Stonebury. I do so miss the place.'

I spotted Justine walking ahead of me on the south side of Fleet Street on the way back to the Temple. She looked very different from the rest of the rush-hour crowd, somehow above it all, untouched by the grime and the sleaze and the noise. She momentarily gazed into a shop window. As soon as she saw my reflection in the glass, she was off up the hill.

I grabbed Justine's arm and said, 'We've got to talk.'

She stopped, looked at the offending hand in disgust and then pulled away rapidly.

'That piece about circumstantial evidence was a bit below the belt,' I called after her.

She carried on walking.

'Let's not make this worse than it need be. Can't we keep our ... differences out of it, Justine?'

She had reached the arch opposite Fetter Lane which led into the Temple. I again managed to grab her sleeve.

'Justine, why is it no one wants to bring up Kingsley's link to West Albion?' When she did not reply, I added, 'Justine, I'm talking to you.'

'No, Tom. You're talking *at* me.' Her eyes were ablaze. It was more than anger, it was loathing. 'Winning's not good enough for you, is it? You want everything.'

'So?'

'So you can't have me.'

'Gloves off then,' I said.

'What do you want from me?'

'I want us to be civil to each other.'

'You walked out on me, remember?' she said.

'And you know why. Because—'

'Because you wanted to run back to your wife.'

'No. Because what's happening is all wrong, Justine. I had to leave. Can't you see that?'

296

'Oh, I saw it all, Tom.' For a moment, she stopped trying to get her arm free. 'I told you right at the start.'

'What?'

'That you'd leave me.'

'You never said—'

'I told you that all my men abandon me when I need them most. Alex was sent away, my father died, Ignatius ... so why should you be any different?'

'Justine—'

'Let go of me.'

'Just one thing, then. Are you going to call the girl?'

'Get off me, you pig.'

I shook her more vigorously than I intended. 'Are you calling that wretched girl?'

A policeman, seeing the commotion, marched over and removed my hand. He looked a little like that buffoon, Lynch. 'Are you all right, madam?' he asked.

'Just mind your own business,' I said. 'This is private.'

'No, sir. This is public. A public street. Now you just shut it.'

I pulled my hand free of his rough grip. 'How dare you speak to me like that.'

'Is he bothering you, madam?' he asked.

'Just leave me alone,' I said. 'She's my girlfriend.'

'Is *he* your boyfriend, madam?'

Justine looked at the policeman in a helpless way.

I tried to grab her again, to get her attention. 'For God's sake, Justine. *Tell* him.'

'Right,' said the officer when she was again silent. 'On your way or you're nicked.'

'You can't arrest me,' I said. 'I'm ... I'm a barrister.'

'I'll count to five,' he said.

By the time he had reached three, I was on my way to the old bookshop on Chancery Lane, muttering to myself about the prevalence of police brutality. But there was something more important to do. There was a paperback I needed to buy urgently.

*   *   *

I worked late in chambers, waiting for the traffic to die down. By ten o'clock the Temple was again a deserted village with its gas-lights and its cobbles, its fountains and its courtyards, a place stranded at the end of the wrong century.

When I reached Chiswick, I had almost finished the book I had bought, and opened the front door imagining that everything was as it had once been. I imagined that Penny was watching television and Ginny was doing her maths homework at the kitchen table.

But the rooms felt different, the furniture seemed out of place, even the photographs seemed like photographs of strangers. I was visiting my home and realised that I no longer belonged and that, perhaps, I never really did. Stonebury had changed my perspective. It was like putting a different lens on to a camera, a wider one, even if it was not yet properly focused.

I knew that I was on the verge of letting go completely and that my control had gone. I was about to lose everything except – possibly – the one thing I did not want to win. And that was Kingsley's trial.

Chapter 44

He was to be the prosecution's secret weapon. Edward Blythe stood in the witness box on the second day with his silver hair and artificial tan. He had the type of looks that would have made him a matinee idol had he lived forty years earlier. He was the type of man who had very few male friends, who 'simply adored' women but who had never truly loved one.

Even Justine, at least a generation his junior, was taken in. 'Could you please tell us your occupation, Mr Blythe?'

'It's Doctor Blythe actually, young lady. I am Professor of Ancient Religion at the University of Cambridgeshire.'

'And your qualifications and experience?'

'I am a Doctor of Philosophy, visiting lecturer at California University, I have written widely about the ancient world, am President of the British Institute of the Paranormal, and then, of course, I regularly appear on—'

'Your academic qualifications will suffice,' said Justine. 'Do you have a particular specialisation?'

'Yes. Celtic mythology.'

The grandmother gazed at Blythe with unrestrained admiration, the social worker faltered in her note-taking.

However, one woman in court was less than impressed. 'Miss Wright,' said Hardcastle, her eyes as hard as billiard balls, 'what is the relevance of all this?'

'Does Your Honour not have a copy of this expert's report? It was sent to the court last week.'

'No. I haven't seen it. I'm sick and tired of papers going missing. When I find out who's to blame—' Hilary then realised that she hadn't sent the jury out and tried to revert to a friendlier tone. 'I wonder, Miss Wright, do you have a spare copy?'

With some trepidation, Justine began, 'I'm afraid I haven't.'

Anticipating another judicial explosion, I shot to my feet. 'Your Honour can have the defence's copy.'

'Thank you … again, Mr Fawley.'

'Not at all. We got our two copies yesterday. But Miss Sharpe and I can share one.'

Hardcastle began to fume. 'You mean … you mean an expert's report was only served on the defence on the morning of the trial?' The prosecution has a duty to serve such reports well in advance so that the defence can consult its own expert.

I tried to sound a little hurt. 'I'm afraid so, Your Honour.'

Justine attempted to salvage something. 'But we … we served it as soon as—'

'I wasn't addressing you, Miss Wright,' snapped Hardcastle. 'Do you wish the jury to retire, Mr Fawley?' That was the lawyers code for, Do you want to exclude this evidence?

'No, thank you. I wish the jury to hear everything.'

Smiles from the twelve. Jurors hate being sent to their room and missing the action.

Emma tugged my gown. 'She's giving you the green light, Tom.'

'You mean you *don't* object to this evidence?' asked the judge.

'Not at all,' I said. 'I shall be fascinated to hear what the good doctor has to say. I'm a real fan.'

'Fan?'

Edward Blythe's vanity could not be contained. 'Well, I do have my share.'

Hardcastle was dumbfounded. 'Continue, Miss Wright.'

Justine leant slightly towards me. 'Thanks, Tom. Sorry for being such a brat yesterday.'

300

I did not reply.

'Now, Doctor Blythe,' asked Justine, 'have you read the report of the pathologist, Doctor Molesey?'

'I was in court when he gave evidence this morning.'

'You *were*?' Justine was surprised.

'Yes. I asked *that* gentleman if it would be all right.' He pointed to me. 'And he didn't seem to mind.'

I smiled back.

Justine glanced at me suspiciously. 'The pathologist testified that the shallow stab wounds on the victim's back were not fatal. Have you got anything to say about that?'

Blythe had a lot to say. He always had. Like so many people with good looks and intelligence, he was convinced that his every word was golden. In fact, he was a bore.

We were then treated to a potted history of the Celtic peoples of west England, their rites and their rituals. After twenty minutes, Blythe eventually reached the Roman conquest with Hardcastle huffing and puffing about the relevance of it all. I sat there pretending to be captivated.

Blythe said, 'The main social group around Stonebury was a Druid-like sect. The Romans considered them—'

'Did you say *Druid*?' asked Hardcastle.

'Yes, Druid.'

Hardcastle threw down her pencil. 'Now I've heard everything. As trial judge, I have an overriding duty to prevent irrelevant evidence wasting the court's time and—'

I got to my feet. 'Doctor Blythe *is* reaching the relevant evidence. I don't object.'

Emma was incredulous.

'Make it short, Doctor,' Hardcastle said.

'These indigenous peoples were suppressed and persecuted by the Romans because they practised human sacrifice.'

'How?' asked Justine.

'They used to sacrifice enemies or sometimes their own maidens.'

'Maidens?'

301

'Young girls. Maidens. They sacrificed them to the gods. But before death they used to stab them in the back – to release the omens during the death throes.'

Hardcastle was still confused. 'To release the what during the which?'

'They believed that a sacrificial victim would tell prophecies, predict the future, as she was dying. She would pass on messages from the gods.'

'But what, Miss Wright, has all this to do with the murder of Molly Summers?' Hardcastle cracked her dry knuckles. 'I mean, we're talking about two thousand years ago.'

Blythe answered. 'I have inspected the ... should I say, alleged? ... murder weapon. It's an exact replica of a Druid ceremonial knife excavated at the Stonebury Sepulchre by the Victorian archaeologist Aloysius Blythe – no relation. Found very close, I understand, to Mr Kingsley's house.'

Reporters rushed out for the telephones. But I remembered what Emma's friend had said: *Falce aurea*, the golden sickle, the sacrificial knife.

'Anything else?' asked Justine.

'I understand straw was found at the murder scene. The Children of Albion – that's what the cult was called – used to place the dead body in a straw effigy, a Kolosson, but I won't bother you with the details. Then they would burn it. However, I understand it rained heavily on the night of the murder.'

'What about this cult of Albion? Does it still exist in some form?' asked Justine.

This went further than the report and I objected. 'The doctor is an expert on *ancient* religions,' I said. 'Not the outer fringes of the Church of England.'

Hardcastle, leading light of various societies of Christian lawyers, was appalled. 'You may answer.'

He bowed a little towards the judge. 'With the much lamented decline of our main religions, there has been a revival in ancient cults, including, it seems, the Children of

302

Albion. In my opinion, this murder is in all respects consistent with the sacrificial rites of a localised cult.'

'See what you've done,' whispered Emma.

Justine flicked through the report and said she had finished. 'Your Honour, might I have just a moment to speak to m'learned friend?'

Justine and I huddled together, our gowns intertwining.

'What is it, Justine?'

'We've got the girl,' she said.

Chapter 45

As I rose to cross-examine, Blythe stood there with unbearable smugness. Emma warned me to be careful as the jury clearly liked him.

I began, 'You say you are Professor at the University of Cambridgeshire. Has it another name?'

'Cambridgeshire University, I suppose.'

'Until last year, wasn't it known as something else?'

'Yes, but I don't really see—'

'Just answer my question. What was it known as?'

'Peterborough Poly.' He blushed a little.

'And you weren't a professor but a lecturer on a – what is it called?'

'A sandwich course.'

'And did Peterborough Poly have an international reputation for expertise in the ancient world?'

'No. But Peterborough was a glorious Roman town and—'

'And now is a glorified railway junction?'

It was time to see what he really knew. I glanced around the court trying to gauge how far I could push it. 'I imagine, Doctor, that you were at Stonebury on the night of the murder?'

'No.'

'You mean you *weren't*?' I feigned surprise.

'No,' he said in a so-what fashion. 'But my opinion is based upon years of research. And I think—'

'We'll come to what you think, Doctor. Let's investigate what you *know*, shall we? The fact is, from your personal knowledge, you don't know what happened?'

'No.'

'So what you say is speculation?'

'It is an informed reconstruction cross-referenced with scientific data.'

'Does that mean speculation in plain English?'

'Perhaps.'

'Is the answer, Yes?'

'Yes.'

The taxi-driver was unimpressed. He turned to the man next to him and shook his head. No doubt he spent his life tearing around the streets of London speculating about the state of the economy and the England football team, and wanted something more concrete in a court of law.

'You testified about the significance of straw at the scene of the murder?'

'Yes. What I would call the Kolosson dimension.'

'This Kolosson is an effigy – made of straw? To look like a human being?'

'Yes.'

'Like a Stone Age scarecrow?'

'Certainly not.'

'Might there be another explanation for the straw?'

'Such as?' he asked defiantly, pushing out his chin. His ego was bruised and he was not prepared to be reasonable.

'Look at this, please.' I handed Norman a card which he conveyed, grumbling all the time, to the witness. 'What is it?' I asked.

'A postcard which says, "Historic views of Stonebury".'

I had kept it from the village shop and had Tipp-Exed out the messages from Molly. 'Do you see the inner stone circle? Tell us, what else is shown?'

'Well, you can see . . .' He held up the card reluctantly. 'You can see for yourself.'

306

'No. *You* tell us – for the record.'

'Well, it shows some cattle grazing among the stones.'

'Grazing on?'

'Grazing on straw.'

There were tuts from the social worker as she put a line through her note of Blythe's evidence.

To his credit, the professor tried to fight back. 'But this photograph was taken … let me see … yes, three years ago.' He beamed triumphantly. 'We don't know if cattle were allowed to graze there last year.'

'You mean the postcard might be out of date?'

'Precisely.'

'Taken three years ago.'

'Yes.'

'Tell us,' I said. 'How many years ago were the Children of Albion persecuted by Caesar's legions?'

He looked down sheepishly.

'Well?'

'Two thousand years ago.'

Hardcastle had seen enough. She asked whether I had any further questions of 'this man'.

'Just a few,' I said. It was time to move in for the kill. 'You are a bit of a celebrity, aren't you?'

'One doesn't like to boast.'

'Come, come. Don't be shy. You present a television series?'

'Yes. *Myth and Mystery*. Sunday nights.'

'You were asked because you wrote *this* book?' I held up a thick paperback.

'Where did you get that?' whispered Justine.

'Bought it in Chancery Lane yesterday. After you tried to get me arrested.'

That annoyed her. She leapt up. 'Your Honour, I cannot see the relevance of introducing this – literature.'

'I'm entitled to explore the credibility of this … man.' I stressed it in the same dismissive way Hardcastle had. 'I ask for a little latitude.'

The judge licked her lips and said, 'Just this once, Mr Fawley. But, be warned, what's sauce for the goose—'

'I understand. What's your book about, Doctor?'

'Enigmas in England.'

'What's it called?'

'*Enigmatic England.*'

'An ingenious title. Very ... esoteric,' I said, thinking of the woman in the Tate. I then turned towards the public gallery. 'Now, due to your celebrity, members of the public report strange phenomena to you?'

'Yes.'

'And you chronicle them in your book?'

'Yes.'

'And make money from them?'

He was furious. 'I add to the body of literature, if that's what you mean.'

'Ah, yes. I'm sure that's what I mean. And how many people have communicated with you?'

'Literally thousands.'

'I see.' I paused. 'And has a single one witnessed a Druid-like sacrifice?'

'No.'

'Have you ever attended a cult sacrifice? Or a rite of any description?' My questions were now aimed at him rapidly, not giving him much chance to answer. 'Have you even seen a group of wandering Druids? A single Druid? A Child of Albion? A ... baby of Albion?'

He had not.

I opened the book, seemingly at random. 'I notice you received a report last year that made the tabloids?'

'I was informed of an unsolicited but corroborated manifestation of an extra-terrestrial nature.' He gabbled it out as quickly as possible.

'Do you mean ET and his chums dropped in for tea?'

Hardcastle slammed her hand on the desk. 'Mr Fawley, remember my warnings – and those of others.'

I was having too much fun to be worried about the conduct committee. 'Where did this sighting take place?' I asked.

'Walsall.'

'So your testimony comes to this: you have more evidence of little green men landing in Walsall than you have of Druid sacrifices?'

Hardcastle seethed. 'He never said they were *green.*'

'Oh yes. What colour were they?'

'No one said.'

'It's a load of rubbish, isn't it?'

He did not answer.

'Isn't it all nonsense?'

'Possibly.'

'Possibly like the rest of your evidence.' I then asked the judge if I could exhibit the postcard and finally said, 'Thank you, Professor. I need keep you from your adoring public no longer.'

Justine told the court that after lunch she would call the girl.

Chapter 46

Emma and I went to Johnson's wine bar. When I had guided her to an isolated table and ordered two orange juices, she could contain her curiosity no longer.

'What's going on, Tom?'

'It's called a trial. It's what barristers do, Emma.'

She waited for an account executive with his organic wine and pilchard and parsley couscous to pass. 'When are you going to tell me what this trial is about?'

'When I can.'

'Don't you trust me?'

'You're the only person I trust any more. But—'

'But?'

'But I need you to do some more digging. Quite frankly the less you know the better. For—'

'For my own good?'

'For your own safety.' I thought about the heroin planted in my car and my fight with Templeman in the woods.

'Did you say safety? Tom, you're behaving very strangely.' She put her head in her hands and directed a searching look at me. 'I've got to hand it to you. You've really done it. I don't know if you've finally gone mad or have sold your soul to Kingsley.'

'I need you to go to St Catherine's House again. Double-check that there is no Molly Summers on record.'

'Why, Tom? Has Kingsley killed someone who doesn't exist?'

'Possibly.'

'How can you kill someone who ... who doesn't exist?' Emma asked. 'Well, I suppose if anyone can, Kingsley can. But how does it work?'

'I'm not sure. But I'm beginning to have an idea—'

'Which you can't tell me because I'm a weak defenceless girlie.'

'Which I can't tell you because I'm worried about you. Will you go?'

We started to head towards the door when Emma stopped. 'I'm not going until I see the girl testify.'

'You won't be missing much,' I said.

'How do you know? Oh, don't bother. I'll see the girl and then I'll go.'

'Thanks, Emma.'

She paused. 'You never did tell me, Tom. What was the home like?'

'West Albion?' I asked and she nodded. 'Well, imagine the Hammer House of Horror ... with a few turnip fields thrown in.'

'You have a thing about turnips, don't you, Tom?'

The girl's hair was, of course, longer than when she appeared in the first trial. It had become almost prickly. She wore the same wax jacket as when she frightened my horse in Nethersmere Woods. But, to me, she did look different: the look of terror had gone. And I had no intention of writing a note of her evidence.

Of all the barristers I knew, Justine was the perfect advocate to handle such a witness. She talked to her like an older sister.

'I shall have to ask you to speak up,' Justine said. 'You see all these people wish to hear, but just imagine you are chatting to me. OK?'

The girl nodded.

'Now, I would like to ask you about something that happened last year.' Justine's tones were soft, melting in the air, and I remembered such softness and doubted whether it would ever be directed at me again. 'Did something happen last year?'

Again, the girl nodded.

'What?'

'Lots.'

'What about the end of the year?'

I hissed towards Justine. 'Don't lead the witness or I'll object.' Then I started doodling with my black biro.

Justine tried to ignore my barracking. 'Did you meet—'

'Don't *lead*,' I whispered. 'Unless you want to ask about the trustees of the home.'

'Where were you when—'

'Don't *lead*, Justine. Gloves off, remember?'

Justine looked in exasperation at the witness and tried the old advocate's gambit. 'Why are you here?'

'I don't rightly know,' the girl replied.

Hardcastle had been watching with mounting displeasure. 'Get to the point, Miss Wright.'

'I've been told not to lead ... anything,' Justine said.

The judge tried to rescue the situation. 'I want you to think really hard about something happening last year.'

The girl put her nail-bitten hands on the rail of the witness box, screwed up her eyes and looked to all the world as if she thought any harder her head would explode.

There was a terrible tension in court. Jennifer Stone, still on psychiatric duty, rushed up to Justine. Emma whispered to me, 'The girl's going to screw us. I can see it. Miss Muffett's going to screw us.'

Oblivious to the activity around her, the girl just stood there thinking.

Justine finally said, 'Do you know anyone called Molly?'

'I know lots of Mollys.'

'Or Mary?'

She knew lots of those, too.

Hardcastle then asked what the prosecution would never be allowed to do. 'But did any of them *die*?'

'I can't remember,' said the girl.

With that answer, the jury was sent out and Justine applied to treat the girl as a hostile witness.

Hardcastle asked, 'Wasn't this the witness who Mr Justice Manly found in contempt?'

'Yes,' Justine replied.

'What was the contempt?'

'She refused to answer questions.'

I got to my feet. 'But she is answering questions now. She's just not giving us the answers we expected.' I had to try and protect the girl for if Justine were allowed to treat her as hostile, she could be questioned about what she said in the first trial, about Kingsley and the wheelchair and Molly and the woods. That would have been fatal. 'This witness is trying to do her best,' I said. 'She is either forgetful or frightened or both. But she is not hostile.'

Hardcastle disagreed. 'How can she forget what she knew at the last trial?'

I noticed Jennifer Stone urging Justine to her feet.

'Your Honour,' Justine said, 'this is Doctor Stone who dealt with the witness after she collapsed last time.'

'When I cross-examined her,' I added. I knew either Justine or the judge would make the point anyway.

Justine continued, 'Doctor Stone is extremely concerned about the girl's mental state. She might have repressed this traumatic episode.'

'As well as others,' whispered Stone.

Hardcastle folded her hands. 'So I can't hold her in contempt and I can't treat her as hostile? It seems to me that this young lady has had some very sharp advice.'

Emma looked at me with deep suspicion and started to leave court.

'Well, there it is,' said Hardcastle. 'I'll just have to release the girl. Bring back the jury.'

When I looked down at my notepad, I realised that I had been sketching a bird of some kind. Rather like a magpie.

Chapter 47

Justine was very brief with her final witness. It was Allan Greenberg, the fingerprint expert. The prosecution did not rely upon the partial print found on the knife, so Justine quickly called him, asked him if he could identify the print as Kingsley's, got the expected negative answer and sat down.

'I don't know why you wanted him called,' she whispered to me. 'A complete waste of time and money.'

'I presume you have no questions, Mr Fawley?' asked Hardcastle.

'Just a few, Your Honour.' I looked carefully at Greenberg and tried to assess how far I could push him. He had a reputation for being honest, a man who had spent the best years of his life looking fondly at the little oily excretions left by people he would never meet, carelessly daubed on window ledges, toilet seats and bloody murder weapons. He stood with the ill-fitting brown suit which was *de rigueur* for a forensic scientist, unkempt hair spraying all over, and a knitted tie.

'Mr Greenberg,' I began, 'will you tell us how you tried to match the fingerprints in this case?'

'We received the sealed exhibits bag from PC Lynch. We treated the knife with powder and brought out the latent print. We then compared it to the fingerprint form in the name of Richard Kingsley and—'

'Sorry to interrupt. You mean the form upon which the suspect's fingerprints are taken at the police station?'

'The same. On magnification, I could find no similarities between them.'

'Really?' I sounded surprised. 'None at all?'

'None.'

'Do you know this gentleman and his work?' I pointed to another little brown-suited man sitting behind me.

'Yes, I know Geoffrey Snyde. He is editor of *Fingerprint Quarterly*, our journal. He is a respected member of our profession.'

I held up an enlarged photograph of a fingerprint with ten red arrows pointing to certain forks and loops. 'Is this an enlargement of the partial print from the knife?'

'Yes.'

'Now look at this photograph taken from Mr Kingsley's fingerprint form by Mr Snyde. It also has ten arrows.'

Justine objected. 'The defence has served no expert report.'

When Hardcastle eyed me suspiciously, I told her my intentions. 'We only have to serve a report if we intend to rely upon a defence expert. But I intend to rely upon Mr Greenberg, the prosecution expert.'

'You intend to do *what*?' the judge asked.

'I trust the prosecution explicitly,' I said.

As Justine sat down, she mumbled, 'What are you up to?'

'Listen,' I whispered, 'and learn.' I turned back to Greenberg who had been comparing the photographs. 'Do you agree that the ten arrows match up?'

'Yes.'

'So there *are* in fact ten points of similarity?'

'Yes. But I don't know how we missed it.'

'What are the odds that they match?'

'It's a million to one *on* that they belong to the same person.'

'Let's be more precise,' I said. 'It's one million forty-eight thousand to one against there being a mistaken identification.'

'Yes. But I still don't see how we missed it.' Greenberg shook his head, admonishing himself.

I looked at Kingsley who for the first time looked shaken.

Justine whispered to me, 'What the hell are you doing?'

'Your job,' I replied.

'In fairness to the defendant,' said Greenberg, 'our practice is not to rely upon only ten similarities. We need sixteen.'

'But in Canada,' I said, 'ten is enough?'

'Yes.'

'So the Mounties can identify someone with ten but our boys in blue need sixteen?'

'In this country a million to one isn't good enough,' Greenberg said.

'It's good enough for my purposes,' I said and sat down.

All around me there was chaos and mayhem, but I sat in the front row smiling.

As Justine rose to close the prosecution case, I jumped up.

'I wonder,' I said, 'if the officer in the case can be called?'

Very often the supervising officer is called at the end of the case to tie up any administrative loose ends about the investigation. The door opened and Inspector Payne walked reluctantly into court.

Payne took off his beige raincoat and entered the witness box. Justine had him sworn and tendered him to me for questioning.

She asked the judge for a moment. 'Are you going to mention the handwriting, Tom? You know it will ruin me. Is that what you want?'

'You don't know if I'll do it, do you?' I said. She shook her head, biting her bottom lip. 'But you *should* know. You would know if you ever really ... oh, what's the point?'

Justine sat down and was miserable. As I got up, I glanced at Kingsley who was no happier. I smiled at him and he looked away.

'Inspector, you didn't attend Mr Kingsley's home. Your dealings with him were solely at the police station?'

'Yes.'

'So you weren't there during the search? When the exhibits were seized?'

'No. They are placed in a sealed bag at the scene and then placed in a store before transportation to the lab.'

'So you had very little involvement with this case?' I smiled benignly at him.

He half-smiled back. 'Right.'

'*Wrong*,' I shouted.

Justine whispered, 'Please, Tom. Don't.'

'Didn't you fingerprint Mr Kingsley at the station?'

'I can't remember.'

'Well, look at this document.' I handed him the custody record, a document detailing the history of detention. 'Does that jog your memory?'

'It does. Mr Kingsley was rather uncooperative. There was a bit of a struggle before I could fingerprint him. Of course, by then he knew we had the knife. But I eventually got his dabs on the form.'

'Is this the fingerprint form with your signature as the officer taking the prints?' He agreed. 'Anyone else present?'

'No. Just me and Mr Kingsley.'

I folded my arms and looked at Justine as I spoke. 'You see, you were involved – with others – in setting up Richard Kingsley, weren't you?' Justine's eyes began to moisten, but there were no tears.

'Don't be ridiculous.'

'Mr Fawley,' howled the judge. 'This is an allegation of the utmost gravity. I hope you can substantiate it.'

'I can't,' I said.

'You can't? Well, you remember what was said . . . in another place?' A clumsy reference to the disciplinary tribunal.

'I remember.'

'And you can't substantiate this allegation?'

'I can't – but the prosecution can.'

Justine looked down. 'Tom, for God's sake.'

'Miss Wright?' asked Hardcastle incredulously.

'Not the prosecutor,' I said, 'the prosecution – the prosecution evidence.'

'Well, I must have missed something,' said Hardcastle sarcastically.

'Yes, you must,' I said.

'Be very, very careful, Mr Fawley. You're playing with fire.'

I turned back to the inspector. 'The truth is you planted the knife at Mr Kingsley's home.'

'Rubbish.'

'You swear you never touched the knife?'

'Never.'

'Then why is your fingerprint on it?'

'It can't be.'

'Well, it is. You see, Inspector, the print on the knife doesn't match the defendant's.'

Hardcastle threw down her pencil. 'That's enough. You brought out the evidence of a million to one match between the knife and Mr Kingsley's print.'

'No, I didn't. With great respect,' I said, knowing the phrase annoys them. 'There was a match between the knife and a print *on* Mr Kingsley's fingerprint form.' I turned to Payne and held up the incriminating form. 'You see there are Mr Kingsley's ten prints and there is another one on the edge of the form. There was a struggle, wasn't there, Inspector?'

He didn't answer.

'No one else was present, but you got your fingers a bit inky?'

He put his hands in his pocket.

'You weren't at the search? The exhibits were bagged? They were in a store? Then taken to the lab?'

'I must have touched it at the police station,' said Payne.

'Any note of this?'

'No.'

'Any statement?'

'No.'

'Can you bring a single witness to court to verify that?'

'No.'

'No?' I paused to let the truth, if truth it be, sink in. The point was that it seemed like the truth. Then I remembered what Justine had told me at the cottage. 'Wasn't it you who found piles of Kingsley's sleazy manuscripts?'

Payne looked astonished.

'So you were at the manor. And you planted the knife. You know, you should really be more careful,' I said. 'If you *do* insist on setting someone up for murder. The criminal courts may be moral dustbins, Mr Payne. But you really should wear gloves.'

Chapter 48

When I reached Chiswick, the street was deserted and the front of the house was in darkness. The safety light did not come on automatically as I approached the front door.

In the gloom, I rummaged around to find the correct key, but something was wrong. The force of the key against the door was sufficient to open it.

The lounge had been ransacked. Books and records and ornaments were strewn everywhere. Drawers had been opened, paintings removed. Perhaps this was Payne's revenge? Or maybe something to do with Whitey Innocent? Or perhaps Philip Templeman?

There was a sound from the kitchen.

I found a poker from the fire and edged towards the noise. Not so long before, I would have been out of the front door and calling for help. But that was no longer sufficient. I needed to know. I needed to do it myself.

Through the slats of the door, I could see a figure on the floor – with a knife. The electric clock from the cooker caught the serrated metal surface, and for a brilliant second there was a flash. Sweat from my palm moistened the brass of the poker.

I raised it above my head, kicked the door fully open, and let out a primeval scream, lashing out at the darkness.

Sitting on the floor, slicing up pictures of our marriage, was Penny.

'Oh, you're home,' is all she said.

A short while later, after we had eyed each other with a degree of suspicion, Penny explained that she wanted to move out. Permanently. She wanted to take Ginny with her and I could see the sense in that.

'But this is your home,' I said. 'It's not mine, not any more. Hasn't been for a long time. I'll go.'

'It's a little late to be chivalrous, Tom.'

'This is where Ginny grew up. It's all she knows. Stay. For her.'

She looked at me as she sat on the cold tiles. 'Well, I am impressed, I must say.'

'Impressed?'

'You managed to remember your daughter's name.'

I dropped the poker to the floor. 'Of course I remembered her name.'

'Then why didn't you remember her *birthday*?'

Penny's comments scythed me somewhere below the knees and I had to sit down. I slumped on to the breakfast-bar which was covered with cartons of cereal.

'Of course,' Penny continued, 'she got a card from your mistress. I suppose that's the next best thing. Cried herself to sleep. I'm beyond that now. No more left, you see. Got to move on.' She recited the sentences as though repeating an echo, something she had told herself one hundred times.

'Penny, I know you must hate me.'

'That's a quaint word for it. I think I passed hate when you first slept with my best friend. I'm on to pathological loathing now.'

'Can't we—'

'Can't we what? Try again? Pretend it didn't happen? Play happy families and go back to normal?'

'You asked me if it was a passing thing. Well, I think—'

'Don't you *dare* tell me that. Justine might be bored with you, Tom. But that wasn't the point.'

'What was?'

322

'Us. We were killing each other.' She looked with surprise at the knife in her hand and put it down. 'We were destroying each other, and I'm not going to do that to myself. I'm scared, Tom. Scared of what I might do.'

'I've got to ask you something,' I said.

'What?'

'Why did you lie about Justine?'

'And you've only ever told me the truth about her, Tom?'

'This is different. You told me the incident with that teacher happened on the night her father died.'

'It did.'

Why, I wondered, did Penny persist in the deception? I could not let it rest. I was trying to think how to pursue the matter when Penny started speaking again.

'Did Justine ever tell you the other thing?' she said.

'What other thing?'

'About his sister.'

'Whose sister?' I asked. And then I realised. 'You mean the teacher's?'

'No, Tom. The attorney-general's. Of course I mean the teacher's sister. Who do you think we're talking about?'

'Sorry,' I said. 'It's been a long day.'

'Sarah was a couple of years below us, of course. She had a free place. Because her brother taught there, people said.'

'Sarah? Alex Chapple's sister?'

'Sarah Chapple. That's what she was called then. Before she was married. In fact, Tom, you know her. Or rather, you *knew* her is more accurate. It was—'

'Sarah Morrow,' I said, realising at last the connection. 'Why didn't you tell me?'

'Why didn't you ask? None of it was relevant. You knew Sarah Morrow went to the same school as we did. It's all you needed to know to defend her.'

I was still confused about one thing. 'But why,' I asked Penny, 'did Justine represent the sister of someone who did *that* to her?'

'Depends on what you mean by *that*. Anyway, it's something you're going to have to ask Justine,' Penny replied. 'I didn't lie to you, Tom. I've never lied to you. Ever. God, now I'm sounding all sanctimonious. I know I'm not perfect, Tom. I can be cold—'

'You're reserved.'

'And I can be stubborn.'

'You're principled.'

'And I'm a bit bonkers—'

'Did you say, a bit, Pen?'

'All right, I'm nutty as a fruit-cake smothered in almonds. Tom, I know I'm not the easiest person in the world to live with. Living with me is a bit of a bitch. And so am I. I have my faults, Tom. But I don't think that I'm a bad person, either.'

I moved a little closer to her. 'You know the funny thing, Pen? For years I promised you that I'd change—'

'Change?'

'You know, take in less work, spend more time at home.'

'I never believed it.'

'And I never meant it,' I said. 'Not really. Well now . . . now, I feel – somehow different. It's all this . . . this stuff. There's been a lot of stuff going on. I haven't been drinking so much and – well, this sounds stupid, but I don't think it's hopeless.'

'It could never be the same, Tom.'

'Who wants it to be the same?'

'True,' she said.

'So do you still . . . you know, me?'

'You've got a cheek, Tom.'

'Because, I know it sounds absurd, Pen, but I still, well, deep down—'

She held up her hand and I stopped speaking. For a while we looked at each other sitting in the kitchen surrounded by fragments of photographs of our marriage and the odd box of cornflakes.

Finally, Penny said, 'Someone told me that when people lose a limb, they can still feel it. You know, as if it were still there.

That's what it's been like, Tom. You'd gone, but I could still feel you.'

I could see tears in her eyes and was thoroughly ashamed. 'Penny, I'm so very—'

'Then I'd reach out for you, Tom. And...'

'And?'

'And I'd remember again that you weren't really there after all.'

'I'm here now,' I said.

'But for how long?'

'Look,' I said, trying to lighten the situation, 'I know that to you I've just become a lopped-off limb, a leg that's gone walkabout. But to me, you're still my wife. You're still the mother of my daughter. You're the woman I—'

'I'm staying at my parents,' Penny said. 'I can't bring Ginny back here now that I've—' She waved her hand over the carnage. 'I wish, I wish more than anything ... well, you know. But it would be stupid to make any promises.'

'Who's asking for promises?'

'I need time to think. I'm not going to call you, Tom. You've got to make the effort.'

I didn't feel depressed when Penny headed off. There was hope, if only a little. I fell asleep on the sofa. I saw myself heading from the edge of the inner circle towards the dead body, and although there were two people around me, I glided unnoticed.

Emma rang me just before midnight.

'I hear the old battle-axe refused to chuck out the case,' she said.

After Payne's evidence, I made an application to stop the trial. Hardcastle, of course, refused. But everyone knew the case was wafer-thin. We were almost there.

'Good news,' I told Emma. 'Kingsley's agreed not to give evidence.'

'That's fantastic. It's virtually over then?'

'Unless he insists on calling Templeman,' I said. 'But he still hasn't shown up.'

'I imagine he's too afraid you'll bung him in a mud puddle and rifle through his credit cards, Tom.'

'Did you get a statement from the registrar?'

'No point.'

'I thought you said there was no Molly Summers?'

'I did say there was no Molly Summers. And there is no Molly Summers in the birth records, anywhere. But...'

'But what?'

'I've found the murdered girl.' Emma paused as my brain rattled through the permutations, but it was late and I was battle-weary.

'Well, tell me.'

'You really want to know, Tom?'

'I swear, if you don't say within five seconds—'

'There was no Molly Summers. But there was a Molly Blacke. Daughter of Anne-Marie Blacke.'

'I don't get it. The parish register said "A Marie Blacke".'

'Obviously a mistake with the hyphen. Tom, she was illegitimate. I checked the mother's maiden name from that baptism entry you gave me. Old man Summers wasn't her real father.'

'Who was?'

'That I couldn't find out.'

We both stopped talking. The city was unusually quiet that night and all I could hear was the relentless ticking of the carriage clock.

'Emma, how long have you known me?'

'Too long.'

'And do you like me?'

'Have you been drinking? I thought you'd given—'

'No. Do you really like me?'

'Don't be silly.'

'Because when I say what I'm going to say, I don't think you're going to like me any more.'

Emma was the brightest pupil I had ever had and knew what was coming. 'No, Tom,' she said. 'I'm not your dogsbody, you know. Someone else can do your running around.'

'It's got to be you,' I said.

'Come on, Tom. Do you know how far it is to Devon?'

It was a token protest. Emma must have known that I was right. She would have to miss the next part of the trial. There was another piece of the jigsaw to find. In the morning Emma was going to have to drive to Stonebury.

'I want you to find out,' I said.

'Find out what?'

'Who else were trustees of West Albion.'

Chapter 49

When the court assembled on the third morning, I asked the judge to keep the jury out. There was a problem. If Kingsley didn't give evidence, which was the plan, we would move straight into closing speeches. But I wanted to see what Emma would turn up. I needed half a day.

Hardcastle was far from sympathetic. 'You've had a year to prepare for this, Mr Fawley.'

'All I ask is for an adjournment until two o'clock.'

'And waste half a day? Do you know the expense?'

'We have proceeded faster than expected.'

'I'm against you,' she said. 'Bring in the jury.'

'But, Your Honour—'

'Are you going to argue? A man in *your* position?'

Norman trooped off and soon the jury had settled back in their seats and watched Hardcastle invite me to call the evidence for the defence. There was to be none.

As I turned towards the jury box, and was about to say that the defence would call no evidence, I saw two things. First, the taxi-driver and the social worker looked at me expectantly, not wanting the show to end. But I also saw, at the back of the court, the door of the dock ajar.

Richard Kingsley was wheeling himself down the specially made ramp and towards the witness box. He passed Norman a note, which was then handed to me.

Of course, due to his wheelchair, he could not get into the box, so Norman gave him the Holy Bible and before I knew what was happening, Kingsley had sworn to Almighty God that he would tell the truth, the whole truth and nothing but the truth.

It was certain disaster.

'My name is Richard Kingsley and I live at the Manor, Stonebury,' he said without my prompting.

I did not know where to start. We had not discussed or rehearsed this. The plan was that he would *not* testify. I tried to think where I could safely tread, but there were so many areas to avoid.

'Mr Fawley,' said Hardcastle, 'I take it you have *some* questions for your client? You've had questions for everyone else.'

One or two jurors laughed. That was a bad sign. No matter how brilliant your destruction of the prosecution case, the trial inevitably turns on the performance of the accused man. Kingsley had taken his future in his hands.

I looked at him, holding his note and spoke very slowly, 'Did you kill Molly Summers?' I asked, not knowing the answer.

'No. I did not.'

I glanced at the note, digested its contents, was appalled and saw his eyes flash. I said, 'That's all I want to ask you.'

I sat down.

All around me there was furore in court. Hardcastle screamed for silence and Justine was thrown. Everyone had expected me to be hours with Kingsley. But they had not read his note.

Justine began to cross-examine but was clearly off-balance. She was thrown even more when I whispered to her, 'Why did you represent Sarah Chapple?' She did not reply. She continued to cross-examine Richard Kingsley and I did not listen. I did not dare listen, for I glanced again at the note.

I defy all counsel, all redress
But that which ends all counsel,
True redress, Death.

O amiable lovely Death.
I will kiss thy detestable bones,
and be a carrion Monster like thyself.

He included the correct citation from Shakespeare, but I wasn't interested. In my brief, I found a copy of the typed note from the first trial. The typeface on both notes was the same. I knew that, after all, Kingsley had typed the note that drove the girl mad.

'And so do I understand your evidence to come to this?' Justine asked after twenty minutes' sparring, where Kingsley had the upper hand. 'You say you were not in Stonebury on the night of the murder?'

'No.'

'You were with an acquaintance of yours?'

'Yes. In the next village.'

'And he is Philip Templeman?'

'Yes.'

'Is Mr Templeman here today?'

'No.'

'Where is he?'

'I don't know.'

'Have you heard from him?'

'Not recently.'

'Can you say if he is alive?'

'To be honest, no,' said Kingsley.

Of course, I knew that Templeman had tried to attack me in Nethersmere Woods and seemed pretty much alive then.

Justine continued, 'The truth is you've lied to us.'

'Is that the truth?' he replied.

'And you've lied because you know you murdered Molly Summers.'

'So you keep saying.'

'And you *were* at Stonebury that evening.'

'No.'

'Sure?'

'Quite sure.'

Justine turned towards the door and Payne opened it. Yet no one entered. 'You see, Mr Kingsley, you were seen at Stonebury that night.'

I objected. 'Your Honour, *none* of the prosecution witnesses has testified at *this* trial that they saw the defendant at Stonebury. None of them.' Of course, the jury did not know that the girl had changed her story about this.

Justine ignored me. 'Weren't you seen by *this* person?'

The door was still open, but no one came through it. I again objected, wondering whether it was going to be Philip Templeman, who was down as a witness for the defence.

'Why don't you start telling us the truth, Mr Kingsley,' Justine said, 'before it's too late.'

I was still on my feet and was about to object for a third time when, with little mechanical steps and a plastic shopping bag, a woman walked through the court doors.

She said, 'I haven't got long. I must be off.'

It was Vera Cavely.

Chapter 50

I knew that my objections, like the rest of the case, would be hopeless. Vera Cavely was made to leave court again as the jury was ushered out, all trying to stare at the funny little woman muttering to herself.

Hardcastle said, 'This lady is not on the witness list, Miss Wright. And you closed your case last night.'

'All true,' said Justine. 'We didn't know until late last night that she would be prepared to testify.'

'But it's too late. You can't call her now. It's not right to spring witnesses on the defence.'

'I'm sorry, Your Honour. I haven't made myself clear. We *did* disclose her details to the defence.'

'You *did*?' Hardcastle looked at me. 'But the defence would be entitled to have an opportunity to speak to her. They haven't had that.'

'Haven't they?' said Justine, smiling as she sat down.

'What do you say, Mr Fawley?'

There was little point denying the truth. I could not admit that I had spoken to Vera Cavely personally – barristers are not supposed to talk to witnesses. So I merely said, 'The defence has interviewed her. However, I still object to the prosecution re-opening its case.'

Justine got up. 'I don't want to re-open. She is a rebuttal witness.'

I looked at her. 'Rebuttal of what?'

Justine said, 'The alibi notice says the defendant' – she

paused to read it verbatim – '"the defendant was not at the stone circle at the time of the murder." We now hear, for the *first* time, Mr Kingsley was not in Stonebury at all. This evidence rebuts that new contention.'

I still objected but my heart was no longer in it.

'You may proceed, Miss Wright,' the judge ruled. 'Bring back the jury.'

Vera Cavely was made to stand at the back of the court. She was told repeatedly by Norman not to speak but she kept asking him the way to Dover.

Justine continued her cross-examination. 'Do you recognise that lady, Mr Kingsley?'

'Yes, I do.'

Much to Norman's relief, Vera was allowed to leave court.

'Were you in fact in Stonebury on the night of the murder?'

'Yes, I was.'

'So earlier you *lied* on oath?'

'Yes, I did.'

'You don't have much respect for the Bible?'

'Not much.'

'What were you doing that night?'

'I saw Miss Cavely in Stonebury and she told me that there was to be some kind of ... what you might call an initiation ceremony. You know, a local custom, that kind of thing.'

'But there was a murder?'

'So it appears. But I don't know about that. All I wanted to do was to see the ceremony, it was a bit of research. I had an idea to write a novel about a village, its customs, its people. It was completely innocent.'

'Did you see Molly Summers?'

'I saw her being led from the village. That's all. Then I went home.'

'Why?' asked Justine.

'It started to rain. I wasn't very well.'

There was a tut of disbelief from the grandmother. The taxi-driver said something to the next juror.

'All you wanted,' Justine said, 'let me understand this, was to do some research for a novel.'

'Yes.'

'That you never wrote?'

'That I never wrote.'

Justine picked up a book. 'I imagine you are familiar with the work of other authors, and not only those in your field?'

'Of course.'

'For example, do you know the work of Peter Dyson?'

'I don't see the relevance—'

'Just answer the question,' hissed the judge.

'Yes,' said Kingsley. 'I know his work, but can I just say—'

'No,' said Justine. 'You can't just say. You're going to listen while I read. This is the opening of Dyson's earliest novel, *In the Shaddowes*.'

As Justine opened the hardback with its dark shiny cover, I got to my feet. 'Your Honour, this is utterly irrelevant.'

'The relevance may become clear,' Justine replied, 'if m'friend is quiet for a moment.'

'I warned you, Mr Fawley.' Hilary Hardcastle was delighted. 'I told you, what's sauce for the goose – I'll give Miss Wright the same latitude I gave you.'

Justine cleared her throat and once more put on her elder-sister voice. The whole court seemed transported to a lonely village. She read slowly but with purpose.

And so, my Friends, let us beginne. It is the Wisdome of a Corrupte Age that Darknesse is to Light, what Deathe is to that Thing we call Life itself. There is not the One without that you must have the Other. And more: they lend a Forme and a Morality between them.

So as I write this poor Accounte in my final Journal, there is an Eccho in my Mind. For amongst the

Shaddowes of my Past, I see a Face. It is the Face of a young Wretch.

I still see it before me – and perhaps allwaies will? – until I reach my Ende in this Rotten Chamber. For I touched her with Darknesse. And her little Life rose like a Smoak from the Stones and hid the very Sunne.

When Justine had finished, she looked at the defendant who had not seemed to have listened. 'As a novelist yourself, Mr Kingsley, would you say that is Dyson's best work?'

'It's not bad,' he replied haughtily. 'A bit melodramatic. But in my opinion he can do better.'

'Is Mr Dyson outside court today?'

'No.'

'Are you in communication with him?'

'That's a difficult question to answer.'

'Is he going to give evidence in this trial?'

I didn't object. The case had moved beyond objections and I felt exhausted. Kingsley shuffled in his wheelchair miserably.

'Where is Peter Dyson today?' asked Justine.

Kingsley waved his hand.

'Where?' Justine repeated. 'Where?'

'Here,' Kingsley finally said.

'In court?'

'Yes.'

And, of course, it was Richard Kingsley himself. I wondered how I could have been so foolish to have missed it. What had Kingsley said in Battersea Prison when I asked him about Dyson's book?

You don't read this rubbish, do you?

No, I don't really read it.

'The truth is, Mr Kingsley,' Justine continued, moving in for the kill, 'the truth is, you wrote this novel before Molly Summers was murdered, didn't you?'

'Yes.'

'And on the night of her death, you weren't doing some research?'

'No.'

'You were living out your fantasy, weren't you?'

Richard Kingsley did not reply.

Chapter 51

The only evidence that remained was Vera Cavely. There was very little I could do to challenge her, since Kingsley had admitted that he was in Stonebury.

Justine rattled through the woman's testimony, aware, no doubt, that Vera was itching to find the M20. Eventually Justine asked, 'What did Mr Kingsley say to you on the night?'

'He asked me where they's going to take the girl and I says, The stones. Then he asked me, When? And I says, When they's good and ready.'

'Do you have any doubt that you saw Richard Kingsley on the night of the murder?'

'What's I just been saying? I dunno why young folks don't listen any more.' Vera turned to Hilary Hardcastle who nodded with approval at the last sentiment. 'Them youngsters, Judge. Never listens. I must have asked them one hundred times to fetch me carburettor. And do they? Do they heck.'

'Yes, wait there please,' said Justine.

I rose to my feet not knowing what I was going to say. In reality, I didn't want to cross-examine Vera at all, it was too risky. But complete silence would appear as a sign of weakness to the jury.

I took a deep breath and began, 'Miss Cavely, you didn't see Mr Kingsley at the stones that night?'

'No.'

'And you didn't see what happened at the stones?'

'Did I says that?'

'No. But it follows from your evidence.'

'Follows where?'

'Just follows – oh, never mind,' I said. 'You yourself were not at the stones?'

'That's what I've been trying to tell you.'

'What?'

'About them stones.'

'What about them?'

'What I saw *him* do.'

Suddenly I was cornered. Did I press on? Kingsley was sunk anyway, and if I left it, Justine would re-examine.

I had to take a risk. 'Tell us very slowly what you saw.'

'I saw him going to the stones with a knife.'

Hardcastle could not contain her joy and repeated each damaging word aloud. She said, 'Now, Miss Cavely. Let me be clear about what you told Mr Fawley. Was it, I – saw – *him* – going – to – the – stones?'

'Yes.'

'With a knife?' Hilary asked.

'Yes. With a knife. A right sharp one. And I says to him, What is you doing? And he says to me, Be quiet and mind your own affairs.'

'Mind your own what?' the judge asked.

'Affairs. Business. Keep yer snout out, as we says down our way. And I says to him, Well you know, Mr Chapple, that ain't no way to talk.'

Hardcastle's face dropped. 'Pardon? What did you say?'

'Keep yer snout out. It's a saying we has.'

'No. Not that. Did you say Chapple?'

'Yes. That fellow what used to be a teacher.'

'And when did he used to be a teacher?'

'When I still had a carburettor in me car.'

Everyone was confused. The judge threw down her pencil and refused to commit the evidence to paper. In the jury box, the social worker whispered frantically to the grandmother. The taxi-driver clearly could not believe it. Members of the press scribbled away. For her part, Justine sat very still.

Was there, I wondered, any truth in any of this? Or had Vera finally blown her last gasket? It was all too bizarre. I decided not to ask any more questions, having sabotaged the serenity of the court to some effect.

Of course, Vera was supposed to be Justine's witness. Having blown up in her face once, Justine had clearly decided to cut her losses and did not dare to ask any further questions in re-examination.

Vera Cavely was eventually led out of court. All that remained were the speeches. Justine was the first to address the jury. She stood in front of the box and looked at the jurors in pairs, waiting for the bustle and the fidgeting in court to subside.

Finally, there was silence.

'Someone once wrote, members of the jury, that there are monsters in this world. They may look like us, they may talk like us, but deep down they are not like us. You know, you can find the bones of dinosaurs in the museums, and I suppose dragons have virtually disappeared from folklore, but certain creatures still move among us – creatures beyond our understanding. And Richard Kingsley is one of them.'

She looked momentarily at the dock and the shrivelled man in the wheelchair. 'And which of you,' she said, 'can understand, I mean *really* understand why Mr Kingsley took the life of that girl? What unimaginable urge did it satisfy? What sense does it make?'

Justine pulled her black gown around her thin shoulders and spoke very slowly. 'When Richard Kingsley came to Stonebury, he brought a kind of darkness with him. He cast a shadow over the village that took the life of an innocent girl with it before it lifted. And that, members of the jury, was a truly monstrous thing to do.'

I thought of my daughter and how she had cried herself to sleep, and I thought of Emma, who I had sent to Stonebury. And I was worried, because Emma had not rung.

341

Chapter 52

I didn't listen to the rest of Justine's speech, though I sat next to her in court and saw her understated gestures and could feel the vibrations of her words. For I suspected that whatever she said, whatever I would say the next day, the truth was still out there – somewhere. And it seemed to me that the truth was like that fox on the Stonebury hunt, and the more you chased it, the more it ran. But if it wanted to, it would find you, when the time was right.

After the court had risen, I tried to speak to Justine about what Vera had said. But Justine stormed off into the sanctuary of the ladies' robing room. By the time I had disrobed, Justine had disappeared. But Jamie had left a message for me to meet him in Il Paradiso. So, leaving the bar's number with the clerks in case Emma should ring, I set off along the Embankment.

Before long I arrived at Blackfriars Bridge. The mists were beginning to drift on the river towards the Tower of London and anchored barges were rising and falling slowly with the gentle swell. The next day, the jury would go out and either Kingsley would be free of the charge for ever or he would be sent to prison for the rest of his life.

I gazed into the silent waters, not really seeking inspiration, for I didn't know what the night would bring, and I felt that the right words would come when I had to speak. My speech was being written somewhere – but not by me. I finally saw myself at the Sepulchre itself, at the very heart of Stonebury. And it was now me who was on the stone. And I wondered who would wield the knife. But I was confused. And my confusion was provoked by the fact that I saw not two, but three people around me at the stones. I wondered whether old Vera was right and whether one of the faces belonged to Chapple. But even if that was so, who else was there? Who else?

Back Bridge Street and Butter Lane were deserted and no one else was on the door as I entered Il Paradiso. I asked Donald, the barman, whether Jamie had arrived and he merely shrugged and handed me a malt, the best this side of Berwick. I chose a circular table near the door, closed my eyes and waited.

I was unaware of being joined by a man to my right until he spoke. It was Whitey Innocent.

'You look pale, Mr Thomas,' he said.

'Yep, Whitey. I really look like crap. That's what everyone tells me.'

'You been sleeping with the enemy, Mr Thomas?'

'When did you get out, Whitey?'

'Few days back.' His eyes seemed a little wider in the dreary gloom, like a pair of camera shutters opening to gather in more light. 'Hear you had some trouble, Mr Thomas.'

'Nothing I couldn't handle. Anyway, where did you hear that?'

He didn't answer, but said, 'You're too late.'

'Too late?'

He smiled a little, revealing his protruding teeth in all their glory. They were browner than I remembered.

'What am I too late for, Whitey?'

'Not what. Who.'

'Who, then?'

'Your blood-clot detective.'

'You mean Payne?'

'Yes, star.'

'What do you know about a kilo of heroin, Whitey?'

Emmanuel Innocent was silent. He looked greedily at the

glass of malt in front of me, which I pushed towards him. Then he ran a dirty thumbnail over the rim where my lip marks had been left and finished the whisky in one gulp.

When the alcohol bit his throat, he let out a sigh. 'Payne say that bitch screw it up. Screw it up good. And she screw it up 'cos she's screwing ... *you*.' He raised his head slightly, but I couldn't see his pupils. 'You been sleeping with the enemy, Mr Thomas?'

Before I could answer, Donald held up the telephone receiver. Emma had called.

She immediately said, 'Tom, I thought you'd given up drinking. It'll do you no good, you know.'

'Look. Forget about my liver. What have you found out?'

'Can't tell you everything. I'm phoning from a call box outside the village and I'm running out of change.'

'I understand. The main points then.'

'Tom, this is one strange place. It's like walking through a Mary Shelley novel.'

'How do you mean?'

'Well, every house in Stonebury has a thatched roof, a log-fire and a couple of skeletons buried in the garden. I mean, how on earth did you manage to spend all that time—'

'Emma.'

'Sorry. I'm afraid you're not going to believe some of this.' She then started sneezing uncontrollably and it sounded as if she had dropped the receiver.

'Emma. You OK?'

'It just *never* stops raining down here. I'm soaked. The things I do for you. I don't know.' She coughed a couple of times. 'Question: where is old man Summers buried?'

'Nethersmere Woods.'

'Right. And where did he die?'

'Don't know,' I said.

'Nethersmere Woods. I checked the local *Chronicle*. Found the report from his inquest. He died the same year Molly was baptised. *What* a surprise.'

'You've lost me. Why?'

'Guess who represented the Summers family at the inquest?'

'I haven't a clue, Emma.' Then I had a guess. 'Was it Aubrey Davenport?'

'Close. But wrong. It was Ignatius Manly. It must have been before he got silk. I wondered whether the two facts were related—'

'Don't be ludicrous.'

'Oh, really? Well, check this out. The rumour down here is that Ignatius committed suicide. Apparently, they've found a note or—'

'Emma, what are you talking about?'

'Tom, I haven't got time to explain. I've found out something else. Who was the officer in old Summers's case?'

I was beginning to see. 'Inspector Payne?'

'Wrong.' She started coughing again, coughing so roughly it sounded as if her throat-lining had worn through.

'Emma. Are you all right?'

'Am I all right? Do I sound all right? You owe me one, Tom. So help me, I'm not going to let you forget this.'

'Well, if it wasn't Payne, who was it?'

'I didn't say it wasn't Payne.'

'But I thought you—'

'I said it wasn't *Inspector* Payne. It was plain old PC Payne back then. Simply PC Plod. A coincidence?'

'What do you mean?'

'Tom, my money's running out and you can't reverse the charges. Hang on. Someone's outside. I don't like the look of—'

'Get out of there, Emma.'

'No. I've got to tell you this.' She took a big breath and talked very quickly. 'The report said Summers was a poacher and accidentally killed himself in the woods. Shotgun went off or something. Sounds a load of bull, if you ask me. But this is the interesting part.' Her voice became muffled as she put her hand over the receiver. She spoke to someone

346

outside. 'Look. I'm just about finished. You'll have to wait.'

'Just leave, Emma,' I shouted.

'No. You better know this, Tom. About West Albion. The list of trustees, it included—'

Then the line went dead.

When I returned to my table Whitey Innocent had been replaced by Jamie.

'You look ill,' he said, grabbing my arm. 'Not been skimping on the booze again? Better fill your stomach with malt before you start wanting to top yourself like – what is the matter, Tommy?'

I did not reply but thought of that isolated phone box and Emma coughing inside it.

'Had a tiff with your beloved?' Jamie asked, gesturing to Donald with three fingers. 'I just saw her. She looked like shit, too.'

'Penny?'

'No. The Ice Maiden. What is it with those chambers? First, Manly does the death-scene from *Swan Lake* down his stairs at home, then—'

'What do you mean? Manly does the—'

'Haven't you heard? They've found a note. Old Ignatius sent it to the Lord Chancellor's Department, only some dozy clerk just goes and files it away and—'

'Jamie, what did it say? You must tell me.'

'All in good time, Tommy. First let's get another—'

I banged my hand so hard on the table that it hurt. 'Tell me what the bloody note said, will you?'

'Said it was all getting too much. He couldn't keep it all secret any more. Christ only knows what he was on about.'

'Where did you see Justine?' I asked.

'Heading for chambers.'

Donald came over with two full glasses of whisky. Jamie swallowed his immediately, saw that I ignored mine, picked it up, but only managed to drink half of it.

'Don't want your drink, Tommy?'

'I don't want to be a drunk, Jamie.'

'I'm getting a little old for this game, too,' he said, and loosened his tie. 'Tommy, I know I'm *persona non* bloody *grata* in legal circles these days, but have the Ice Maiden's chambers taken to defending down and outs?'

'What are you getting at, Jamie?'

'I saw this strange character walking into their chambers. Looked in a real state.'

I felt a chill. As though someone had walked over a grave, only I did not know to whom it belonged. Almost unaccountably, I feared for Justine's safety. And I saw an image in my mind. It was the Sanctuary Seat in Stonebury. And I kept seeing those curious words from Deuteronomy written on it.

That the slayer might flee hither
And that he might live.

Donald allowed me to make a call. The answerphone was on in Justine's chambers. Her personal line was dead.

Chapter 53

A winter's calm had settled over the Temple. The cobbled alleys were beginning to glisten with the falling temperature. Scattered lights shone from high windows, but no one ventured out into the courtyards.

How must I have appeared? Trying to run, my tie trailing behind me like a leash, jacket slipping off my shoulders and so short of breath that I thought my lungs would explode.

When I reached Justine's chambers, I could see that the curtains were drawn in her room, two storeys above. The light was on and the window was open. Two figures stood opposite each other, like the shadows you make with your hands, silhouetted and barely moving.

I ran through the open reception, past the empty clerks room and started to go upstairs as the central heating throbbed noisily. As I reached the third step, I slipped and twisted my ankle. It was the same ankle I had turned over in the woods at Stonebury. It was excruciating.

I knew I had to get to Justine's room. I crawled up the second flight, each further step was agony. When I reached Justine's door, I could hear voices inside, but they were as calm as the dreamy squares of the Temple.

They were talking about me.

I needed to catch my breath, I needed to rest my ankle. Any normal person would have barged in, but I was restrained for a moment by cowardice and my curiosity.

Justine said, 'You've got Tom all wrong.' It sounded as if she was nearer to me, nearer to the door.

'He's a fool. An ignorant fool.' It was a man's voice, barely audible as it spluttered and wheezed.

'Whatever you have to do – to me,' said Justine, 'don't harm Tom.'

The man said, 'Sarah might be alive if it wasn't for him.'

'Alex, it was my fault.'

'You were both to blame, then. What do you lawyers say? Equally culpable? You see, Justine, there is crime and then there is punishment. That's the way it is.'

'What about forgiveness, Alex?'

'My sister's dead. She can't forgive you – and nor can I.' There was a scraping sound like something hard being picked up from a table. 'Wouldn't it be ironic, Justine. If ... if I used the same knife on you?'

I had to intervene. I didn't know what I would do, but I had to burst in. The swelling on my ankle grew and my head began to pound.

As Chapple continued, Justine was silent. 'You see, Justine, Molly knew too much. Too much pillow-talk, I guess. If you call it pillow-talk when someone's between your thighs. She was a gossipy little girl. We had to stop her blabbing. You know, Molly reminded me a lot of you. Took me back all those years.'

'Did you prefer her to me?' asked Justine. 'Did you, Alex?'

'She was young, she was there and she was available. But you can have too much of a good thing, I suppose. After a while, even abuse becomes boring. That's when the trouble starts. I should never have told her what happened to her father. But I thought it would, you know, add a bit of spice.'

'What do you mean?'

'Oh, don't play the innocent maiden with me, Justine.'

'The maiden?'

'"And the maiden soon forgot her fear." The poem. Of course

you remember our first time. A student-teacher relationship in the finest traditions of the English public school.'

'How do you mean?'

'You came to me for consolation, Justine. You know, on the day your father—'

'Died,' she said plainly. 'He passed away so suddenly.'

'Perhaps,' the man interrupted, 'he couldn't bear to think that other people would begin to ... play with—'

'His daughter?'

'His property,' Chapple said. 'Don't you remember the rest of the poem?'

'No.'

'"To her father white, Came the maiden bright. But his loving look, Like the holy book, All her tender limbs with terror shook."'

There was a slight pause and then Justine spoke. 'He never, you know, went ... the whole way with me.'

'Any way at all is too far for a father to go, Justine.'

'It was how he showed his ... love.'

'But that Sweet Love *was* a crime.'

'Alex, you're hardly in a position to—'

'Come on, I did give you a shoulder to cry on. You can't deny that.'

'It's everything else you gave me, Alex. That was the problem.'

'You really wanted it.'

'I never said I did.'

'You never said you didn't. You see, Justine, when does desire end and when does abuse begin?'

'When you start molesting a vulnerable girl, Alex. That's a pretty good starting-point. Have any of you ever thought of the damage you've caused?' Justine asked.

'Damage? To who?'

'To me. To Molly. To all the other girls.'

I could hear him walking to the far side of the room by the

window, and his voice became muffled and I guessed he had his back to the door.

I wrapped my tie around my ankle to provide a little support and tried the handle. It opened silently. Justine must have had the clerks oil it.

'I tried to warn that boyfriend of yours,' Chapple said. 'Sent him messages in *The Times*. You know, from beyond the grave, that sort of thing. Tried to warn him what he was dealing with. Nethersmere Woods. Summers's death. You remember all that. Payne and I tried to scare him off through that half-blind informer. But Fawley was a fool. I bet he still doesn't know who Molly was. Even now. The idiot ... Justine, would you mind turning off the light?'

'Alex, please don't.' Her voice was barely more than a whisper.

'Don't make it any more difficult,' he shouted. Then with a gentler inflection, he said, 'Come here, Justine.'

'Alex, please.'

'Think about your sins, Justine. Think about your sins and think what must happen to you.'

'Oh God. Alex—'

'I don't remember the knife being this sharp.'

A click of the light switch. This was the time, swollen ankle or not.

I flung open the door and hobbled across the room, pushed Justine to one side, and as the lights from the Great Hall glinted off his knife, I barged him with all my strength. Then I saw him sail through the window.

It was not a dramatic crack but a dull thud that I heard, as his body fell two storeys and hit the concrete outside.

Justine rushed up to me and put her hand to my side. 'My God, Tom. What's happened to you?'

'I know, my ankle. It's agony.'

'No, Tom ... you've been stabbed.'

I could feel nothing except the trickle of blood, like hot water running up your sleeve, not unpleasant if it wasn't for the wetness.

Then the anger built and clouded my mind and I wanted to see his face, this man who had abused Justine and had murdered Molly Summers.

As I peered over the window sill, there was a deep pain, which felt like a handful of needles being driven into my side. It shot up my arm, raced around my head and I cried out. Justine stroked my hair.

Lying in the cobbled yard, his body twisted and quite still, with the colours from the stained-glass windows playing over his contorted face, lying there with his eyes staring towards the ancient round church, was Philip Templeman.

Chapter 54

I looked at my wound. It felt as if a shark had casually swum up the Thames and had taken a bite out of my side. And then, as well as blood, my reasoning flooded out. Hard as I tried, I could not match the scrawny man I had throttled in Nethersmere Woods with the hideously twisted face two storeys below.

'He used many names,' said Justine. 'I've even forgotten some of them.' She had placed me in a chair, the same chair from which, many years previously, she had gazed at Ignatius Manly with wide-eyed naïvety. 'I better call someone,' she said.

'No, let him rot,' I told her.

'But Tom—'

'Let him rot in hell.'

Justine had her hand on my wound and I could feel her fingers, trying not to move, but slipping every now and then with the amount of blood. I felt a part of her inside me and felt very close to her, in the room where we first made love.

'There's a towel in the pantry,' she said.

'Don't go.'

'I'll only be a second, my darling.'

'Was Vera right?'

'Try not to speak, Tom.'

'About Chapple. Was she right?'

'Sort of,' Justine said.

'So she was sort of ... wrong?' Each word seemed to produce more blood.

'Quiet, darling. I'll be back in a minute.'

Justine left me. With the flowing of blood there was also a curious flowing of cares. I couldn't understand Chapple's – or was it Templeman's? – connection with Kingsley. But I didn't care. The man was dead. I had killed him. There is crime and then there is punishment, that's what he had said. And now he was punished. It was like a cheap prophecy in an old movie that had come true and now the prophet himself was dead.

I thought that Justine had been gone for hours but it could only have been a matter of seconds. When she returned with a dripping towel, she tried to smile, but there was fear in her eyes as they reflected my wretched state.

The wet towel burnt into my midriff and I could see the knife lying a few feet away, at the foot of the window. I tried to speak but had to stop. With every breath I felt as though I was sucking the towel deeper into my bowels.

'What is it, darling?' Justine asked.

'The knife. I ... I don't understand how—'

'Alex must have got it from Payne.'

Of course. Whitey Innocent had seen Payne leaving Il Paradiso in a hurry and Payne, of all people, would have access to the exhibits.

'How was Vera ... sort of wrong?' I asked.

I looked at the knife and saw a fine streak of red at its tip and along its serrated edge. There was the instrument of murder no longer with the blood of the murdered girl, but glistening with mine.

'I called an ambulance,' said Justine. 'Won't be long.' She stroked my hair. 'You're so brave.'

But I was not brave. I was stupid. Very stupid. How could I have missed something so obvious? As I looked at the knife, a change must have come over my face, for Justine, I felt sure, sensed it. Suddenly the truth, brilliant, crystalline but ultimately appalling, was revealed.

It was a different knife.

* * *

'You see, you never knew her,' said Justine, walking to the window. 'She was common. Vulgar. No more than a slut. And *she* ...' her voice rose to a crescendo and then fell back to her gentle jury tones. 'And she was going to ruin it all?'

'Were you jealous of Molly? You know, because of her and Alex or something?' Now I felt a worse pain, a hurting so deep, so complete that I could not imagine ever recovering.

'Alex was right. You are a fool, Tom.'

'I worked out the knife.'

'That was easy. No exhibit labels, not coated in fingerprint powder.'

'I still got it,' I said. 'And I detected your feeble lie.'

'Congratulations.'

'So the knife in court—'

'Was planted by Payne at Kingsley's as you said in court.'

But there was something that was puzzling me even more. 'Why did you represent Chapple's sister?' I asked. 'After all that he—'

'Sarah was another victim,' Justine said. 'She's not responsible for what her brother did to me.' But by now, Justine was becoming impatient. It was all so obvious to her. She crouched at my knees and said, 'A lot of bad things have happened, Tom. But we can still have it all. It's not too late.'

'For what?'

'For us.'

'Justine, come on.'

'For you and me.'

'It's too late for Molly Summers. Isn't that the point?'

She put her hands on my knees and used them to lever herself up. The pain was immense and I felt as though I would faint.

Justine looked down at me from what appeared an enormous height. 'You always were weak, Tom. Like Daddy. Couldn't resist a woman. I mean, what chance did poor Daddy have? Living alone. And Annie did this for him and Annie did that for him. What chance did he have? The *slut*.' Justine turned her back on me sharply and gazed down at the body below.

'Annie ... the woman who looked after—'

'She was a slut, just like that daughter of hers.' Justine looked over her shoulder and was virtually smiling. 'Can you believe what the stupid little girl said to me last year? "I be's your half-sister, Miss Wright. That's what Mr Templeman tells me." Can you imagine? That *orphan* and me, related?'

I remembered what I was told in the Tate about Albion: the source, the seed, the father of all things. In some way, was Justine's father the source of all this? And I remembered the strange myth about the King of Syria and his daughters with a taste for castration.

It all started with the daughters. All the trouble started with the daughters.

Justine now stood in front of me. 'When I saw her in the village, Tom, I was ... scared.'

'Scared?' I asked.

Justine did not answer at first. She knelt in front of me and began to weep. Clouds moved slowly across the sky and the room went from darkness to light and then back to darkness.

Without looking up, she finally said, 'I know I'm ill. Always have been. It's just these bad thoughts. I don't know where they come from. But I can't ignore them, I can't pretend they aren't real. You see, they seem to come true.'

'Justine, what are you talking about?'

'That so-called father of hers—'

'You mean Summers?'

'He tried to get money out of us once he knew who sired that bitch. And Daddy said it would ruin his career and I so wanted the man to go away and leave us alone. Then suddenly, it seemed like magic – *pouf*. He was gone.'

'Justine, it was an accident.'

'And I had done it.'

'Look, he was a poacher, wasn't he? His shotgun went off.'

'*Pouf* – he was gone. And I had willed it. Daddy paid Alex

to be a false witness. He got him a job at the school. Then he promised Ignatius the earth if he did nothing at the inquest. And Payne planted the gun on Summers. But that was the easy part. It was her. She was the one I was scared of.'

'But why?' I asked. 'Molly was just a teenager when she died.'

'I used to see her, Tom. All the time. There in the village. I just couldn't stand it.'

'But what did she do?'

'It's not what she did, it's what she was. Every time I came down from London, she seemed to look increasingly like Daddy ... and like me.'

By now, Justine had really worked herself up. Her eyes were clouding over and it was as if she were being filled up with the past. And as I looked at her face, I remembered the first trial. I remembered how Justine had the same grey eyes as the woman juror. I remembered how the juror had the same grey eyes as Molly Summers. Should I have spotted the connection? I didn't know.

But what I did know was that I needed to divert Justine. She was tearing herself up with these thoughts, and I had to challenge them. But at last I knew why it was that when the first time we made love in her chambers I had seen not just her face, but the face of Molly Summers.

'This is all in your mind, Justine,' I said. 'It's just that all you Stonebury girls look alike.'

'Really? Is that all it is? Molly once even cut her hair in my style. Did I imagine that, too?'

'No. Look, you were similar but different. Like apples and pears. Like—'

'Good and bad?' Justine said. 'Well, I was the bad. I don't care what you say, Tom, I felt – I *knew* – it would all come out.'

'But Justine, old man Summers's death was an accident.'

'I willed my father to shoot Summers, Tom. That was no accident.'

'You don't know what you're saying.'

'And what about Molly's death? What was that?'

'I don't know any more,' I said.

Justine again began to weep and this time she was inconsolable. 'I was there,' she cried. 'I wanted her dead. It *was* an accident that I was in Stonebury that night. But I wanted her dead, Tom. I wanted her dead. Doesn't that make me guilty?'

I finally realised who it was I had heard in the worst dream of all. It was the sobbing of a frightened girl, for Justine was in truth no more than that, a girl witnessing her sister being murdered. And Justine was the third person that I had imagined around the stones.

'It was Payne and Chapple,' I told her. 'You're not to blame.' Was that true? It was certainly what I wanted.

'How do you know, Tom? I can't even be sure.'

'Don't you understand, Justine? I was there.'

'There? You?'

'In my dreams, I mean. I've seen it all and you didn't kill her.' Although my dream wasn't as clear to me as my desire, this was the closest to the truth that I could get.

Then I felt as if I were hanging from the edge of a bottomless cliff and one by one my fingers were giving way. Justine very deliberately picked up the knife.

I looked at her and was very sad. 'It's over, Justine.'

She smiled faintly for a moment and then stopped. 'We could have had it all, Tom.' She very slowly moved closer to me.

I imagined another finger sliding off.

'But what am I supposed to do with you?' she said.

I thought I could feel a sea-breeze, could taste salt – was that the blood? – could hear gulls screeching overhead. 'Justine, it's all over,' I said.

Another finger gone. And another.

'My darling, Tom,' she said as she raised the knife.

Then I was gone. Floating. Spinning. Free and unafraid. Blues and whites and greys – and silence.

Chapter 55

There was a high-pitched tone. Loud, piercing, as sharp as the edge of a blade.

'Right. My name is Detective Sergeant John Traynor.'

'And I am Woman Detective Constable Roach.'

Then the first voice continued. 'The time is 0345 hours. We are in the interview room at Chancery Lane police station. In the room with us is – can you identify yourself, please?'

Silence.

'For the tape? Please?'

'My name is . . .'

The room was bleak. White walls and frosted glass. No bright colours, no features, nothing to look at – except them. That was the way it was meant to be. The chair was screwed into the floor at such a precise angle that there was constant eye contact, no way of avoiding them.

'You must give us your name,' he said.

'We can wait all night.' She was smaller but more menacing. 'We can wait all day and all night.'

'My name is . . .'

'Yes?'

'Tom Fawley.' I felt as if I had awoken from a nightmare.

'Right,' said Traynor. 'Now we're getting somewhere.'

But where? Some morbid Frenchman wrote a story about hell. And hell was simply three people locked in a room for ever. The table in front of me did not budge, the hands of the clock did not move, there was no sound except their words and the constant low whir of the tape-machine.

Traynor had been talking but all I heard were the last few words. 'And so, as you of *all* people know, those are your legal rights. Do you understand?'

'What?'

'Your legal rights, sir?'

'Oh, those. Yes, I understand.' My lips moved but it was as if someone else did the talking. Someone a safe distance from my body. Someone whose side had not been bandaged. Someone who cared about what was happening. I didn't like him.

'You understand, Mr Fawley, that you have the right to have a solicitor present and if at any stage – Mr Fawley, are you listening?'

The woman banged the table twice. 'Look at the sergeant when he's talking to you,' she snapped. She had narrow eyes and sharp features. I didn't like her either.

'Do you want a solicitor, sir?' he asked and I shook my head. 'Sorry, the tape doesn't register a nod. Can you confirm that you don't want a solicitor?'

'I don't want a solicitor,' I said.

'Fine. You've been bandaged at the hospital and you've been certified fit to be detained by the police surgeon.' Traynor looked at me with his big, oval eyes. Red-faced, earnest, good old Uncle John to someone, no doubt. 'Can you confirm that you've seen the police surgeon?'

'I – I can't really remember.'

'Are you saying the sergeant is lying?' snapped Roach.

'No. But—'

'So you feel well enough to continue then?' Roach asked.

When I nodded, Traynor said, 'Can you tell us, Mr Fawley, why you are here?'

'I'm being questioned about Alex Chapple.'

'No, sir,' said Traynor a little wearily. 'We've been over that. You're being questioned about Philip Templeman.'

'The attempted murder of Philip Templeman,' interjected Roach.

I tried to protest. 'But aren't they the same—'

'We can come to that, sir.' Traynor looked at the clock. The hands had not moved. 'All in good time.'

'We got plenty of that, you see,' said Roach. 'We got all the time in the world.'

'I have to tell you, Mr Fawley, that you have not been charged' – he dropped his voice – 'at this stage. Are you happy to help us with our enquiries?'

How many cases had I done which were lost the moment the client opened his mouth in the police station? It was always fatal. Never help the police. They can help themselves well enough. Always make no comment. How many clients had we told?

'You haven't got anything to hide, have you?' Roach said without parting her teeth and the words were shredded the moment they reached the air. 'Nothing to be ashamed of?'

'No,' I said. 'How dare you.'

'Oh, I thought you might have been consorting with drug dealers again,' she said. 'That's all.'

Then I remembered her from the Camberwell nightclub when she had arrested Emma's friend, Danny.

'Are you prepared to help us?' repeated Traynor.

Despite all the advice, it is different when you are there. When it is you who is alone in a police station. You just want to go home. Tell us the truth, they say, or at least a part of it, and you can go. Tell us everything, anything, tell us at least something that we want to hear. And then you can go ... perhaps.

'I'm quite content,' I said.

'Content to do what, Mr Fawley?'

'To speak to you.' I could hardly believe what I was saying.

'Good,' said Traynor. 'Well, we are making some progress. I should remind you that you have the right to remain silent. But anything you—'

'I know all that crap,' I said. It's what Danny the pusher had said when Roach arrested him. I thought it sounded rather good.

Traynor seemed genuinely hurt. 'I don't think we've been rude to you, sir.'

'No,' snarled Roach, staring at me.

'I apologise.'

'Very well, apology accepted,' Traynor said. 'Let's recap what you've already told us. Philip Templeman was found in a critical condition—'

'Half dead,' said Roach.

'At 2315 hours last night. He was outside the Great Hall in the Temple. How did he get there, Mr Fawley?'

'He fell,' I said.

'Of course, he fell,' said Roach. 'But how?'

'I suppose I—'

'Look at the sergeant when you're talking,' she said. 'Why are you looking at your fingers?'

'We just want the truth,' said Traynor with half a smile, as if he were asking me for the time.

I knew the technique well. I'd read articles on it, even attended seminars. He is the dominant persuader. The one you can trust. She is the vicious one, constantly picking you up on your behaviour, making you self-conscious, uneasy. She constantly looks for non-verbal signs: a rumbling of the stomach, a slouch, sitting *too* rigidly, nervousness, weakness, fear. She'll interpret them all as signs of guilt.

They sat before me: tough and tender, nasty and nice.

'Now how did he come to fall?' asked Traynor. A smile.

'I pushed him.'

'We know that.'

'You do?'

Roach shredded a few more words. 'You admitted it when you came round in casualty. Why do you think you were arrested? You see, someone called an ambulance to the Temple.'

Justine. What had happened to Justine?

'Then the ambulancemen called the police,' Roach said.

Traynor smiled again. 'And you had met this man, Templeman, how many times before?'

'Once.'

'Where?'

'Stonebury.'

'And you assaulted him then?'

'Well, I grabbed his neck.'

'And you told him you would—'

'Kill him,' I said. 'Well, can I just change that? What I meant was—'

'Sorry to interrupt, sir,' Traynor said. 'Can you just answer yes or no for the moment? We can come to explanations—'

'And excuses,' said Roach.

'A little later.' Traynor appeared genuinely interested. 'So did you tell Philip Templeman that you would kill him? Yes or no?'

I knew that technique, too. It was one I had used in one hundred cross-examinations. Pin them down. Yes or no. Then crucify them.

'Can I just explain something?'

'Yes or no will do, Mr Fawley.'

I felt the tightness of the bandage and wanted to lie down. 'All right. Yes,' I said.

'And did you push him out of a second-storey window the next time you saw him?'

'It didn't happen like that—'

'Yes or no?'

'Yes.' Then I thought of his face against the concrete and felt a strange satisfaction. 'Yes, I pushed him. And he deserved it.'

'And this has something to do with a case you're doing?'

'Don't look surprised,' said Roach. She smiled for the first time, revealing the gaps between her teeth. 'You see, we know *all* about you.'

'All right. It had something to do with the case.'

'And to do with the woman found in the building with you?'

'You mean Justine?'

'Justine Marie Wright, Sergeant,' said Roach.

'Thank you, Leslie. Yes, Justine Marie Wright. Miss Wright has something to do with the case?'

I never knew Justine's middle name before. Funny what you discover when you're being interrogated about a murder. I said, 'Justine is prosecuting.'

'But she knew of some forged documents.'

'Yes.'

'And misled the court?'

'Well, she—'

'They were used in court?'

'Yes.'

'And you found out about it?'

'Yes.'

'And you did *what*?'

What could I say? That was a distortion. Those were the facts, but that wasn't the truth.

'And what did you do about it, Mr Fawley?'

'You won't find the answer on the floor,' said Roach.

I raised my eyes and said, 'I did nothing.'

'Not looking too good, is it?' said the woman.

'Leslie,' hissed Traynor. He didn't want his flow interrupted. He was a professional.

'No, Miss Roach,' I said. 'It's not looking too good.'

Traynor asked, 'Why did you push Mr Templeman out of the window?'

'Because he was trying to hurt Justine.'

'Was she injured in any way?'

'I don't—'

'That you could see?'

'No.'

Traynor looked at the clock. It still hadn't moved. The tape continued to whir and Roach's eyes burnt into my face.

366

'I just want to understand this part,' he said. 'You went to rescue Miss Wright?'

'Yes.'

'And you ended up struggling with her over the knife?'

'I can't remember if we struggled. In fact, I don't think we did.'

But why, then, had Justine stopped? I certainly could not have fought back.

'Mr Fawley?' His voice started to recede and the walls grew darker and darker. I could see Roach's hands moving up and down on the desk but heard no sound. Then Traynor came very close and whispered as if he were telling me a secret. 'I have to tell you, sir, that at this stage it's likely you will be ... well, charged.'

'Charged?'

Roach's lips opened and closed and I could read the 'Yes'.

'Charged with what?'

'With the attempted murder of Philip Templeman. He hasn't died.'

'Not yet,' said Roach.

Traynor looked at me. His eyes, still gentle, moved slowly over my face. What option is there, they seemed to say. You've made all the admissions, what do you expect us to do? Finally, he spoke. 'Is there anything you want to ask us?'

'Just one thing. Who told you Justine's middle name?'

'Well,' said Detective Sergeant John Traynor. He was embarrassed – what could he be hiding? 'Well,' he said, 'it was your wife.'

Chapter 56

I could not say how long I had been in the cell. It seemed like weeks, days at the very least, but I suppose could only have been a matter of a few hours. I slept fitfully. But I saw nothing. It was as though the screen in my head had finally been switched off. Traynor had taken my tie away in case, he said, I was tempted to do 'something silly'.

There were a number of things that did not make sense. My last memory was of Justine standing over me. I remembered the knife with my blood already on it and then I woke up in that dreary little cell. Every time I asked about Justine, I was ignored or told that I was in deep enough trouble as it was.

They hadn't charged me. Was that a good sign? Or were they just waiting for Templeman to die? Then there was a clatter of keys and a dirty yellow shaft of light as the wicket gate was opened.

'We want you,' said the voice. It was WDC Roach. She took me out of the cell and started leading me up countless flights of stairs.

After about five minutes' climbing, she paused on a landing and asked, 'Want a brief, Fawley?'

'What happened to the Mr?'

'It flew out of the window with Philip Templeman. Do you want a solicitor or not . . . Fawley?'

I was too ashamed to tell anyone of my plight and merely asked, 'What time is it?'

'Time to tell us the truth,' she said.

'What time is it?' It was dark outside.

'Six thirty,' she said.

'Morning or night?'

'Morning, of course. We got a long day ahead of us, you and me.'

Roach then led me into the interview room. The desk and chairs were modern. With its whitewashed walls, it looked like a classroom. Traynor sat behind the desk. To his right was a woman in her forties. Her head was down as she scribbled away furiously at the file of papers in front of her. She was vaguely familiar.

But Roach commanded my attention. She looked tired, her translucent skin drawn tightly over her sharp features, and her eyes continued to stare and stare.

'Sorry to drag you back here, Mr Fawley.' Traynor coughed and said, 'Can we have another ... chat?'

I then saw Roach put on the tape-machine.

'Don't worry,' said Traynor. 'It's just for our records. Honestly, no need to worry.'

But I did. I worried terribly. I knew from scores of clients over the years that the instant you're treated well, the moment they show you a little courtesy or concern, that's when you are most vulnerable.

'I've decided,' I said. 'I want a solicitor.'

'You didn't earlier,' said Roach through her teeth.

'Leslie, now if Mr Fawley would like legal representation, then he is entitled to it,' said Traynor.

'Well, he'll have to wait for one,' she snarled. 'This time of day, could take—'

'All right,' I said. 'Let's just get it over with.'

'Well then,' said Traynor. 'Perhaps we can shorten matters.' He looked to his side. 'Can I introduce the lady sitting with us? Doctor?'

'Mr Fawley and I have met before,' she said, still scribbling and not looking up.

Traynor, a stickler for detail, persisted. 'Doctor, can you identify yourself for the tape?'

She looked up for the first time. 'My name is Doctor Jennifer Stone. I am a qualified psychiatrist.'

Then it occurred to me: What was she doing there? A *psychiatrist*? Were they trying to commit me? What if I refused to cooperate? Could they commit me for that? I didn't know. Hadn't Jenny Stone once said that she thought I was neurotic or anally fixated or something?

I stood up.

'Sit *down*,' shouted Roach. 'Don't make it worse for yourself, *Mr* Fawley.'

I refused to answer most of Jennifer Stone's questions, and pretended I was somewhere else, miles away, walking through the woods. But she persisted with one subject until I could bear it no longer.

'It's a simple question,' she said. 'How would you describe your relationship with Justine Wright?'

I was again silent.

'I don't want to get unnecessarily personal,' she said. 'But were you, well, intimate?'

'Want to know if I screwed her?' I shouted.

'Please, there's no need—'

'Want to know the positions? Need some tips, Doctor?'

'Just calm down,' said Traynor.

'Justine Wright is catatonic,' Stone said.

'What the hell does that mean?'

'Stuporose,' she said.

'Are we still speaking English?'

'She's withdrawn from the world,' Traynor explained. 'Like in shock.'

'And we want to know why,' said Roach, but Traynor glared at her and she looked to the clock. It hadn't moved.

'We think ... well, we think we know why,' Stone said.

'When Miss Wright was found by the ambulancemen, she was sitting in a chair next to you. She had the knife. It was as if ... well, almost as if she were frozen or carved in stone. Like she was standing guard over you.'

I thought of the circles at Stonebury, but before I could make any meaningful analogy, I felt a stab of pain in my midriff.

The psychiatrist looked at the bandage at my side, now slightly pink in places with the seeping of blood. 'We just need a little more information. That's all.'

'If you must,' I said.

'Yes, we must,' snapped Roach.

'But how can someone end up like that?' I asked.

'It's a recognised psychiatric condition,' Stone said. 'It's called *flexibilitas cerea*, one aspect of catatonia. Can I ask, did she suffer from delusions?'

'How do you mean?'

'Like a calling, or some sort of mission in life?'

'Well, people had nicknames for her.'

'Like what?'

'The Ice Maiden, the Angel of Vengeance. But you know how people bitch about a successful woman ... don't you, Doctor Stone?'

Roach tutted in disgust.

Jennifer Stone ignored me. 'Did she have any mood changes?'

'Constantly. But surely everybody—'

'Any tactile hallucinations?'

'Any what?'

'Ever complain of insects crawling over her, that sort of thing?'

'No. Of course not.'

Stone continued. 'Did she believe, perhaps, she was being followed?'

'I think we were.' But I wasn't really sure. Not any more.

'Did she have difficulties forming relationships?'

'She did with me.' And then I thought about Penny and Jamie, even, for a moment, about Hilary Hardcastle. 'You see, Doctor, everyone has difficulties forming relationships with me.'

Traynor smiled. Roach raised her eyebrows and tutted once more.

The psychiatrist looked at me carefully, like a butcher, having sharpened a knife and trying to decide where to make the next cut. She asked, 'Was she promiscuous?'

'She was attractive.'

'Did she think she was attractive?'

'She never said.'

'Was she insecure about her childhood?'

'She was the daughter of a judge and owned a horse called Nigel. It's hardly the most normal upbringing,' I said. 'Anyway, who isn't insecure?'

'Are you, Mr Fawley?'

'Look, I'm a lapsed Catholic and a balding barrister. I've every right to be insecure. So what are you getting at?'

'Almost finished,' said Stone. She wrote something down and tapped her chin. 'Did she have any – how can I put this? – any sexual eccentricities?'

'Apart from me?' No one smiled. I thought about what Chapple had said about their first time together on the night of Justine's father's death. But all I said was, 'No. There were no eccentricities.'

'Do you know of any emotionally inappropriate behaviour?'

'What? Like trying to kill me?'

'We're not interested in that,' said Roach.

'Your concern is touching, Constable,' I said.

Stone was keen to press the point. 'What I want to know is, did she do things that were inappropriate? You know, out of context?'

I thought about the first time we made love, on the desk of the judge who had so recently died. I thought about how sex and death always seemed to go together for Justine, for the village of Stonebury. But due to some reason I did not entirely understand, I could not betray Justine.

'No, I don't know of any inappropriate behaviour.'

Jennifer Stone turned to Traynor and said, 'I find that hard to believe.'

'Are you lying?' snapped Roach.

'It doesn't matter,' the psychiatrist said. 'I think we have enough information to confirm our suspicions.'

'What suspicions?'

'Justine Wright has been deteriorating for years.'

'How do you know?' I asked.

'Your wife told us.'

'My *wife?*'

'She's next door,' added Traynor. 'I suppose we can allow you access to her now.'

'If she's willing to speak to you,' said Roach.

'We can normally treat Miss Wright's illness with drugs,' said Stone. 'She refused to take them. She staggered from relapse to relapse as her paranoia became worse. I understand she had to leave the Bar for a couple of years. I'm afraid she has completely withdrawn,' said Stone. 'The prognosis is not good.'

'I don't understand,' I said. 'Why didn't she kill me? I can remember that after Chapple or Templeman had stabbed me and had fallen out of – well, I remember Justine standing over me with the knife. She could have—'

'Her personality began to ... in a sense, dissolve. But there must have been part of her that cared for you. It struggled to save you.'

'To save me from what?' I asked.

'From the part of herself that she did not understand,' Stone said.

We can still have it all. It's not too late for us.

'Saving you from that part of herself,' the psychiatrist continued, 'was probably the last thing she will do.'

As we started to file out of the room, Roach turned off the

tape-machine and Traynor took my arm. He spoke in a low voice so no one else could hear. 'I'm really sorry for all this, Mr Fawley. We're just doing a job, you know. Like you.'

How had I missed all the symptoms of Justine's illness? The sleeplessness, the mood changes, the constant connection between love and death. When I thought about it, some of the evidence was there. Perhaps I was just too close to see? Perhaps I had subconsciously convinced myself not to believe it. Or perhaps it was something that I simply refused to believe. It did frighten me because since the first trial began, Justine had appeared to me to be the saner of the two of us. I had the dreams, I had the doubts. If Justine was lost, then where was I?

Eventually, I asked Stone, 'What will happen to Justine?'

'We'll try therapy, of course,' she replied. 'And if that fails, we'll try drugs again.'

'And if the drugs don't work? What then?'

'Then, Mr Fawley, I'll have to section her. Under the Mental Health Act,' Stone said. 'There's only so much we can do. She's retreated into herself. And if she doesn't want to be found, there's nothing we can do.'

'Is there anything you want?' Traynor asked me.

'Yes,' I said. 'I want to see my wife.'

Chapter 57

Penny sat in the police canteen, sipping a plastic cup of steaming black coffee. She seemed unruffled and hardly bothered to glance up as I joined her.

'You don't look so good,' she said.

'I'll live.'

'I know. I spoke to the police surgeon, such a nice man. He said it was just a superficial wound.'

'It might be superficial to him. He wasn't stabbed with a Neolithic knife.'

'Only a replica one, I understand,' she said, putting down the cup and brushing a few strands of hair from her forehead. 'I've come to a decision.'

'Not in here, Pen.'

'Why not? Aren't you meant to ... come clean in these places?'

They had given me back my tie and I wrapped it round and round my hand. Slowly, my head began to clear. Things began to recover their proper proportions. I missed our house in Chiswick. I longed to see our daughter. But most of all, I hated myself for what I had done to Penny.

'So what have you decided?' I asked. 'Can I come back—'

'Home?' she said.

'You know, I really—'

'Fancy a coffee?'

'No. It looks like tar. I've never understood how you can drink it so ... look, Pen. What I meant to say was—'

Penny grabbed my wrist. 'Never – not for one second in your feeble little mind – imagine that I will forget. I won't. Never. And don't think I forgive you. Because I don't.'

'I see.'

'Do you? Do you really see, Tom? It's always so easy for you Catholics. You think if I say, "OK, Tom, I forgive you," it'll be all right. Well, it won't. It's not like a church confession, Tom. You can't just say three Hail Marys, dip your thumb in some Holy Water and walk out with a clean conscience.'

'I'm beginning to see that.'

'You wanted it all. You wanted me. Then you wanted Justine. Now you want me again.' She put her other hand on mine and stopped me winding the tie. 'Have you ever thought – even for a moment – what I wanted?'

'Of course I—'

'Don't *lie*.' Her nails cut into my skin. 'No more lies. Please, Tom. No more lies.' She sat up straight. 'Well, did you ever think how I felt?' When I couldn't reply, she said, 'I thought not.'

'What do you want then?'

'It's what I don't want. I don't want to be alone. The shame of it. Failure. People talking, you know, warm tea and cold sympathy. We have a daughter and nothing you did with—'

'With Justine?'

'—with that woman, can destroy that fact. You see, Tom, it's no longer about you. It's about me now. I've invested too much to let you ruin it.'

I saw Roach walk into the canteen with a pair of handcuffs and it concentrated my mind wonderfully. 'I'll try, Pen. Really I will. What can I say to make you believe that?'

'For God's sake, don't *say* anything. That's the problem. You're always saying things. You say you'll do this and you say you'll do that. But you never actually *do* anything. Well, the time for talking is over. Just *do* something, if you really ... well, you know.'

Traynor came over with a cup of tea for me. 'I see they

gave you back your...' He indicated towards my tie. 'Just thought I'd tell you. Templeman's not going to die. Well, he will eventually. We all will, I suppose. What I meant was, he's not going to die just yet.' Traynor sensed the tension between Penny and me. 'Well, Mr Fawley, if there's anything you need,' he said as he walked over to Roach.

I turned back to Penny, having remembered something Traynor said. 'How did you end up at the police station, Pen?'

'Emma phoned Chiswick. Reversed the charges.'

'But I thought you were at your parents?'

'Wanted to start cleaning up. You know after I...' She again waved her hand as she had when she was on the kitchen floor with the knife. 'Emma wanted to speak to you again. And we both realised that if you weren't with me ... well, we guessed you'd be with Justine. You're so bloody predictable.'

'I suppose it has its advantages.'

'I phoned that dive bar. Emma gave me the number. Your drinking buddy, Jamie said you'd headed for the Temple.'

'He's not my drinking buddy. Not any more—'

'Don't ruin my story. This is the best bit, Tom. So I phoned the porter's lodge in the Temple. Asked them if they had seen my so-called husband. Oh, yes, they said. Saw him being carted off by the police, Mrs Fawley.'

'I suppose it wasn't difficult to track me down to the local nick after that.'

Penny took another sip of the tarry liquid and winced. 'You know, Chapple once tried to grope me at school.'

'Did it traumatise you, Pen?'

'Not really. I just kneed him in the goolies.'

'So how do we sort ourselves out?' I asked.

'Well, you've got to sort yourself out first. I don't think you want a wife, Tom. What you need is a woman who's a cross between a mistress and your mother.'

'How do you mean?'

379

'You want someone to screw your brains out and then wash the sheets. See if you can work out what you really want, Tom.'

'So you'll have me back?'

'You never *really* left. You just took a sabbatical from your senses for a while. Only—'

'Only what?'

'Only don't do it again, Tom. Or—'

'Yes?'

'Or I'll cut your balls off with that Neolithic knife.'

'Don't you mean, the replica?'

'Yes, Tom,' Penny said, 'I mean the replica.' She smiled for the first time that I could remember for weeks. Then she sipped the dregs from the plastic cup. 'My two vices, I suppose. Strong coffee and weak men.'

'I don't deserve you,' I said.

'No, you deserve a good horsewhipping. But—'

'But?'

'But I still ... well, sort of love you, you adulterous bastard,' Penny said.

'Despite what I've done?'

'Despite what you've done. Look, if men were supposed to be faithful, do you think they would have dicks?'

'So you don't hate me, Pen?'

'Of course I hate you.'

'But I thought you said—'

'You *can* love and hate someone, Tom. It's called being married. I'm your wife and you're my husband. So we'll just have to stop whingeing and get on with each other.' She stood up as the psychiatrist, Jennifer Stone, walked over to Roach on the far side of the canteen. 'You know, Tom,' Penny said, 'I think it's me they should be putting in that loony-bin.'

The clock on the canteen wall, unlike the one in the interview room, worked. It was 8 a.m. The police shifts were swapping over and there was a flurry of uniforms. If I was quick, I could go home, change and perhaps – for once – I would not be late for court.

380

*   *   *

Hilary Hardcastle looked miserable. She sat on the Bench and scowled and moped and frowned, trying to think of some way around it, but knowing there was none. Norman was perched on his chair in the corner of the court, still struggling with the crossword, and the shorthand writer started to record proceedings.

Leonard, the clerk, had begun to speak. 'Will the foreman of the jury please stand?'

The taxi-driver stood up.

'Mr Foreman,' Leonard said, 'do you find the defendant, Richard Kingsley, not guilty of murdering Molly Summers?' There was silence until Leonard added, 'Do you find him not guilty of murder on the direction of Her Honour, the judge?'

Hardcastle nodded.

The taxi-driver took a deep breath and said, 'We find him not guilty.'

'And that is the verdict of you all?'

'I suppose so,' said the foreman.

'Just say yes,' Hardcastle said.

'Er, yes, then,' answered the taxi-driver.

It was my turn. 'Your Honour, may Mr Kingsley be discharged?'

'On *these* matters only, Mr Fawley.' Hilary had not forgotten the sex offences to which Kingsley had pleaded guilty. All she said to the jury was that extraordinary events had overtaken the case and then dismissed them without thanks.

The social worker smiled at me as she left the box. I felt rather light-headed and very tired, but I didn't want to miss the last curtain call for anything.

When the jury finally left, Davenport stumbled to his feet. He was still rather bilious after a bout of food poisoning. It wasn't influenza or gout. He tried to outline the facts of the sex offences, the ages of the girls, and what Kingsley had paid them to do. But he was not on top of the case.

Davenport seemed lost without Justine and I knew how he felt.

'I thought five years' imprisonment was a little vindictive of Hilary,' said Kingsley later in the cells. 'We will appeal, of course.'

I just stared at him. Compared to the dark cubicle in which I had spent the preceding night, the Old Bailey cells seemed palatial.

'What is it? What do you want to know?' he asked.

'The truth.'

'Have you become interested in that? You *have* come a long way. Wasn't it you who told me that too much truth and the lawyers go out of business? Well, you're still wearing the old wig and gown.'

'Let's cut the bull, shall we? You weren't involved in the murder of Molly Summers, were you?'

'I never knew who killed her. But no one would have believed that. I mean, Mr Fawley, you didn't.'

I was silent for a moment. Then I asked, 'Why didn't you tell me you were innocent?'

'Everyone said I was guilty. So I thought – how does the saying go? "In an entirely corrupted age, the safest course is to follow the others."'

'Who said that?'

'The Marquis de Sade,' Kingsley said.

'In *One Hundred and Twenty Days of Sodom*?'

'No, in his book, *Justine*. Are you familiar with the work, Mr Fawley?'

I did not answer.

'Such a shame about Miss Wright,' he said. 'Such a fine ... person.'

'Don't you *dare* talk about—'

'Philip Templeman said he'd give me an alibi. I suppose it was part of the plan to frame me. Templeman never intended to testify.'

'Making up a false alibi could have really damaged your case,' I said. 'I never did understand why you put the first note in my brief.'

'Well, you saw its effect on the girl. I never realised that you would have to make it an exhibit.'

'That was because the poor girl could not read,' I said.

Kingsley tutted. 'The failings of modern education, I don't know. Perhaps if she'd had an attentive teacher like Alex—'

'Don't push your luck, Kingsley.'

'Well, when the *second* note appeared, I realised that I had to take other steps.'

'So that's why—'

'Yes, that's why I asked Miss Cavely to help me out.'

'You could have left it to me.'

'I couldn't afford to take that chance. Accused men are desperate men. And such men, Mr Fawley, sometimes do desperate things.'

'It was a nice touch,' I said. 'Exposing yourself to cross-examination. Forcing the prosecution to call old Vera in rebuttal.'

'No one would have believed her if we called her.'

'That's true, but—'

'Do you still think we're so very different, Mr Fawley?'

As Kingsley licked his lips and I felt his eyes wandering over me, I remembered what he had said about the mind being a receiver. He had said it was all in there, the good, the bad, everything that you wanted, those desires you were too scared to admit.

'Aren't we rather similar?' he asked.

'The difference is, my dial hasn't got stuck,' I said.

As I stood up to go, he slowly rolled his wheelchair towards me. 'Mr Fawley ... Tom, despite everything, I just wanted to say—'

'Don't bother,' I told him as I walked out of the cell.

I never saw Richard Kingsley again.

*   *   *

Emma waited for me in the men's robing room. 'Don't ever do that to me again,' she said, coughing. 'Never keep me in the dark like that.'

'Sorry,' I said. 'But I didn't know where to turn.'

'I hear the teacher, or whoever he was, lived.'

'I could never do anything properly.'

As I put my wig and gown away, I didn't know for how long, she told me about what she had discovered in Stonebury.

'They were all connected with the home,' she said. She tried to scratch some sexist graffiti from one of the lockers. 'Don't men ever grow up?' she said.

'Who was connected—'

'All of them. Kingsley, Payne, your friend the teacher, they had all been trustees of the home. The elders, like Danny said. *Magistri sapentiae.*'

'The most just of men?'

'No, Tom. Just like *most* men. That's why no one would dare mention that Kingsley once was a trustee,' Emma said. 'I guess Ignatius must have known how everyone was linked. Perhaps he knew it would all be uncovered. Maybe he chose his own way out. Though I can't believe he was interested in the girls.'

'Nor can I,' I said.

'So do you think his silence was a meal-ticket to the top?'

'Perhaps. I mean, what could Manly have done?' I said. 'If he had released Kingsley at the first trial, the abuse would just have gone on. Maybe Ignatius couldn't stomach it any more. But to have Kingsley convicted would have risked Kingsley breaking the code of silence on the abuse. In a perverse way, a convicted Richard Kingsley was more dangerous than an acquitted one.'

Emma tried to smile, but instead she sneezed once more. 'I guess that's Kingsley for you. Perverse to the end. I mean, look at his Gothic novel about—'

'A book is just another form of confession, Emma. And like anything else it can be true or false.'

384

'So Kingsley was innocent and Payne and Chapple were guilty?'

'Think it's that simple?'

'What do you mean, Tom?'

'Well, do you think guilt plus innocence equals the truth? This wasn't really about Payne and Chapple. They just wielded the knife.'

'I understand they're going to be charged.'

'That's one type of justice,' I said.

'Is there another?'

'Look what happened to Justine.'

'So what was it all about?'

'It was about Stonebury, Emma. It was about that dial in our minds getting stuck.'

'The *what* getting stuck?' Emma burst into a fit of coughing. 'You're behaving very strangely again, Tom.'

'There was no such thing as innocence in Stonebury. Just degrees of guilt.'

'Still, I do think they were stupid to try to frame Kingsley,' Emma said.

'The glove fitted. Besides, how long do you think a convicted sex offender like that would stay alive in prison? And if he survived, who would have believed him?'

'So why did they kill Molly Summers, Tom?'

'Because she might have talked about old man Summers's death. I think Chapple told her about the cover-up.' And then I remembered what Chapple had said to Justine. 'Or perhaps it was simpler than that. Maybe she was killed just because she was there. Because she was available. Perhaps that's why she never fought back. Because there was no hope. I mean, what do you do when a whole village is corrupt?'

'Hope the knife goes in deeply first time,' Emma said.

As we went to the lifts, we passed groups of bewigged men, and I turned to Emma. I said, 'You know, I still don't really understand the Children of Albion bit. I suppose there was all that Blake stuff about children of a future age, and—'

'They weren't Druids or anything like that, Tom.'

'Then what were they?'

'Complete and utter bastards. They abused young girls, Tom. The oldest ritual in the book. Men abusing women. Except in Stonebury it was not just a ritual, it was a right. I suppose that's why Justine's father leased the old family semi-detached to the local authority,' she said ironically.

'Perhaps it was guilt?' I said. 'To make up for what he did to Justine? For what he didn't do for Molly?'

'No. It was to ensure that the men of Stonebury had a constant supply of vulnerable girls,' Emma said. 'That fits, doesn't it? I mean, look at the name. West Albion. The—'

'The source, the seed, the father of all things,' I said.

'Pardon?'

'Nothing. So why were the girls abused, Emma?'

'Why shouldn't they be?'

'That's hardly a post-feminist explanation.'

'It might just be a true one, Tom. All the men did was to dress up in funny costumes and talk in a strange language so that they could forget what they really were doing.' The barristers by the lift laughed loudly, full of their own importance. 'A little like them,' Emma said.

'A little like us,' I replied.

We passed through the revolving security doors and out into the London air. The streets teemed with people carrying on their lives, oblivious to the Kingsley case, perfectly content to ignore the death of a girl.

As we approached the Temple, Emma stopped outside Johnson's. 'Fancy a swift drink?' she asked.

'Sure,' I said. But as we entered, I again saw the quote from Dr Johnson above the door.

Sir, I have found you an argument,
but I am not obliged to find you an understanding.

The arguments were finally over. But had I really found any understanding at all? I turned to Emma as she approached the bar.

'Look, Emma,' I said. 'Some other time, perhaps.'

'Is something the matter, Tom?'

'No, nothing's wrong. It's just that—'

'What?'

'There's someone I've got to visit.'

Chapter 58

By the time I reached Stonebury, it had started raining. I wandered around the stones as night sank very slowly over the village. I passed the Holestone, the Sepulchre and the others. And when I reached the inner circle, I tried to imagine what a teenage girl would have thought as she was led there for the last time. But the dream would no longer come. So I decided to walk the short distance from the village to the church.

The gate at St Stephen's creaked slightly as I opened it. The graveyard did not frighten me. After all the talk of cults and sects and chants and prayers, it seemed to me that the only real magic in the world is the mind and how it sustains its precarious balance. Some people, like Kingsley, find a balance of their own and live their lives accordingly. But for others, life with its unforgiving demands becomes too much and they fall. And again I thought of Justine.

In the far corner of the churchyard, behind a cherry tree and a few feet from the ramshackle wall, was a relatively fresh mound of earth. Compared to the others, the gravestone was new, and the rain washed it clean of grime.

It said, *Here lies Molly Summers.*

And I wondered, who now weeps for her? Most of the stone was taken up with writing. I moved closer and began to make out the angular letters in the gathering gloom.

We will fall into the hands of the Lord
And not into the hands of men
For as is his majesty
So is his mercy.

Ecclesiasticus

But who had paid for her gravestone? Perhaps it was
Justine? Perhaps it was the only thing Justine had ever really
done for the girl who shared her father's blood. When I had
read the inscription for a second time, I felt as though I would
never stop dreaming about that place. Now it was part of me
and I was part of it. I knew the face above the murdered girl,
and it was the face of someone I had loved and who was now
lost, not only to me, but to the world.

I turned and again felt the wound in my side. It was, then,
rather slowly that I walked past the Sanctuary Seat and the
decaying porch, past the tombstone where a magpie had once
sat, and past all the graves of the faithful. Very soon it was
dark. The images dissolved into one another and I again
imagined a sound. It was the gentle weeping of a woman. A
woman who was witnessing her sister being murdered. The
sighs that I imagined were the sighs of Justine.

When I had closed the gate of St Stephen and the Martyrs,
I paused for just a moment before I walked into the ancient
village of Stonebury. I knew that I would return to London
and to my wife. But as I reached the very centre of the circles,
I wondered whether I would ever *really* leave.